Chamber
of
Horrors

Chamber
of
Horrors

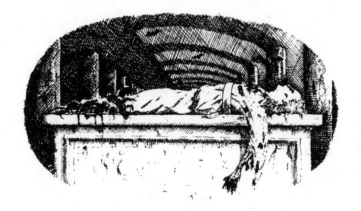

GALLERY BOOKS
An Imprint of W. H. Smith Publishers Inc.
112 Madison Avenue
New York City 10016

First published in Great Britain in 1984 by
Octopus Books Limited

This edition published in 1987 by Gallery Books
An imprint of W.H. Smith Publishers, Inc.
112 Madison Avenue, New York, New York 10016

Illustration by Angela Barrett

ISBN 0-8317-1234-1

Printed in Czechoslovakia

Contents

Wood

ROBERT AICKMAN

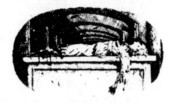

SO MY NIECE, ELINOR, HAS given me one of those weather houses, where the woman comes out when it is likely to be fine, and the man when it is going to rain! I did not think they were made any more. There is something about them that not many people know; at least nowadays. It is this: that just as dowsing can be used to trace many things other than water (which of course makes 'water divining' quite the wrong name for it), so these little weather houses, or some of them, can be attuned to foretell more things than the merely literal state of the heavens.

It is an odd story of which I am reminded by this, and until now I have not cared to make a note of it. There is always a risk of a written record coming into the wrong hands; and so perhaps reaching the eyes or ears of the people described. Moreover, I was always very uncertain how far I could depend upon my own impressions of what happened; and naturally I am even less confident now, nearly twenty years later. Also, one is superstitious about seeming to give a new life, by writing about it, to something which has frightened one. The curious business about Munn and his wife, whatever I thought about the reality of it, even at the time, certainly frightened me – so much that I was the last person to be surprised by what happened to them in the end. But old Pell and his wife are dead now too. So here goes.

I suppose that if anyone at all reads what I am writing, it is more likely than not to be a stranger. A few sentences about myself had, therefore, better come first.

I served my articles as an architect, in the days when that was how one learned a profession, by working at practical and immediate problems from the first, instead of merely listening to lectures and doing exercises; and for several years I worked as an architect's assistant in a good office, doing well and having every prospect of starting in practice on my own. The tone was set in those days by architects such as Ernest George, and there seemed an unlimited number of costly country houses being built, pleasant work for all who had the social knack of getting it – which did not seem very difficult, as I look back on it. But then came the War, the first one, and the real one: the greatest mistake mankind ever made, in my opinion, but, curiously enough, one out of which I myself did quite well, at least in a sense. Before it was over, and to my considerable surprise, I found myself a lieutenant-colonel, though very much of the wartime kind, not the real thing, as I knew perfectly well; but then in the very last month, more or less when Wilfred Owen was killed, if I have it right, I was, not killed, but badly knocked out, since when I have never been quite right in any way, even though I made a good recovery, and a remarkably swift one.

Of course I had always intended to go back into architecture, but I never quite did. There were several factors. One was that I began to receive a pension, which at first seemed fairly good: enough, anyway, to save one from having to rush at things, and to give one time to think. Another, and much more important, was that the profession had completely changed. We were fast on the way to the state of affairs when the word 'art' was seldom mentioned, still less the word 'beauty'. It is odd that the busy, slave-driving old offices, always with several pupils, had much to say about art and beauty – too much, many of the pupils thought; while these new Schools of Architecture lead to nothing but, for example, the buildings you can see beside and around the Festival Hall in London. A third thing was that I never succeeded in marrying and thus taking on a new incentive. The war seemed to do something to me there; or perhaps it was mainly my experiences at the end of the war. But what settled things at first was that I was offered the job of editing a series of architectural lives.

I had always been interested in the actual lives and careers of the architects of history, and the work carried me away completely for a longish time. I was enabled to travel in a modest way (though, there again, I could not have paid for a wife to travel with me), and I was in a position to appoint myself as the author of two or three of the books. I did so, and these books proved to be among the most successful of the series, for what that meant. When I was in my mid-forties, I bought an old cottage outside this Suffolk village; without clearly realizing that East Anglia is pre-eminently the part of England to which unattached and unattachable males with tiny but comparatively secure incomes tend to drift. They settle there on the outskirts of villages, and, I must admit, seem often to live on for ever, though no one quite knows what they do all day. Edward FitzGerald is the archetype and patron of us all; though, speaking for myself, I have so far managed to keep my hands off the local fishing lads. But then FitzGerald was a genius, even though an under-productive one. I, no genius, have managed to have many affairs of the more ordinary kind; mainly, indeed, with married women. It does not seem a thing one should proclaim: but it is no joke being a married woman in East Anglia, if the woman has the smallest imagination. I am, therefore, unabashed.

That odd man, Munn, on the other hand, seemed, during the first years I knew him, to be genuinely uninterested in women. Of course I did not know him really well, then or ever; and one can be utterly mistaken in such assessments. Still, many English males *are* genuinely unconcerned about women; are without the need for them, especially after the age of thirty or so.

Munn struck me in those days as one who instead of embracing a woman, embraced a grievance. Unlike most people with entrenched grievances, he was as reticent about the details as one normally is, or as one should be, about the details of a love relationship. He had been employed in the Inland Revenue, and there had been trouble of some kind, though it was hard to guess what, because he had emerged with a small allowance, upon which, like me, he lived; in his case, in rooms above the village post office. Possibly he unearthed some corruption or other, and had to be sacked, and silenced. If Munn had been still in the employ of the tax people, instead of on bad terms with them, I could never have known him even as an acquaintance; because, say what they will, I cannot accept that any kind of gentleman will, under any circumstances, make a career of prying into the private affairs of others and then mulcting them, commonly to the point of spoiling and destroying their entire lives and those of their families. Munn supplemented his allowance(which, comically enough, was 'tax free') by making funny little figures out of straw and brass wire, which were offered for sale in the post office below under the name of 'daffies'. It was an unusual occupation for a middle-aged man, but I mention it because it had a faint and obscure bearing upon what happened in the future. Meanwhile, the figures, though often quite clumsy, seemed to sell remarkably well; not only to passing motorists, of whom, from other points of view, there were soon far too many, needless to say, but even to the villagers and to rustics apparently from other villages. Sometimes one of our locals, having bought one of Munn's straw figures, would later buy another. Perhaps the first figure had by then worn out, but at least it proved that Munn was meeting a demand, always the great thing in the world, we are told. I have described the figures as 'little' and so most of them were; but always on view were a few larger ones, some, two or three feet high. Naturally, these cost more, and it was the smaller, cheaper figures that most of the motorists went for, and that must have provided most of the turnover – again, as is usual in commerce.

Munn had taken up residence in the village before I arrived, and at first all I knew of him was his tweedy figure toddling about and sometimes bidding me Good-day. His tweeds were very hairy indeed, and more than usually shapeless. One almost felt that he made the suits himself, as well as the straw figures; and perhaps wove the hirsute fabric also. He had profuse white hair under a scarecrow hat; a nose like a reversed peg for that same hat; and a darkly red face, which made one think neither of drink nor of exposure to the elements, neither of sickness nor of shyness. It struck one simply as how he was made, how he was coloured: several shades too red, as some are made too tall, and others too dwarfish.

It was at one of the village inns (I refuse to employ the word 'pub') that

I first exchanged more words with Munn than the time of day. I remember the occasion very well, but I have little recollection of what we said, then or, indeed, at most of our subsequent encounters. Of course he hinted at his troubles, and I at mine. But we were neither of us, perhaps to a fault, involved or much interested in what is called 'the life of the village', so that we undoubtedly ranged over wider fields: the newspapers, the world, and man's future (though, as I have said, seldom woman's). Munn seemed another who did not quite know what next to do in life, or even to aim at doing. He too was, more than anything else, marking time. The main thing we had in common was exile. All the remaining days of our lives seemed to drop upon us like dried-out snowflakes or like daily leaves from the dead calendar of a past forgotten year. Life has become more rigorous than it was then, though it is likely to become
more rigorous still.

And yet –

I think I had been talking in a sketchy way to Munn, on and off, and every now and then, for as long as three or four years, when one morning, as I was on my way to something rather private, and was less than usually open to distraction, he hailed me from across the street and asked if I would look in at his place for a drink that same evening. I can see him as he did it, in my mind's eye, quite clearly: the white shutters across Gabb the butcher's window were behind him in the late autumn sunshine (so that it must presumably have been early closing day or the Sabbath). After all, it was a rather historic moment: I had never before been invited to enter the rooms above the post office. That which at the time I was about to undertake would be completed long before evening, so I accepted for half-past six.

Munn proved to have several rooms, quite a suite, reached by his own stair from the street; and, in general, seemed to be better accommodated than I had supposed, even though the trappings plainly appertained to a 'furnished apartment'. All that looked personal was a mill for making the straw figures. As usual with Munn, the device looked as if he had made it himself; out of rough old planks, long thick nails, and bright steel edges – very sharp, by the look of them. The contraption stood in a corner of the living room, with a bale of straw stuck away behind it, and straw ends all over the carpet beneath and around it. Of course, all was dry, or no doubt there would have been complaints from the sub-postmistress, Mrs Hextable, below. There were also two or three of the figures lying about in various stages of completion.

'My eker-out of income,' said Munn, entering the room behind me and watching my gaze. He crossed to the machine and gave it a hard kick in the midriff, so that the bright cutting wheel spun round like a flying saucer. 'And I wish His Majesty's bloody Commissioners were beneath it,' added Munn.

'But sit yourself down,' he went on, and, without consulting me, mixed a whisky that was far stronger than I normally liked or like, or than he had observed me drink at the inn, supposing that he ever took in such things. 'I propose to ask you a favour.'

He had provided himself with an even stronger whisky than mine. He gave me the impression of a man who so feared to find himself weak that he had both hands on the bull's horns almost before the animal had entered the field, so to speak.

'I am getting married and I want you to be my best man.'

I must admit I had feared that it was going to be something to do with money.

'I expect I can manage that,' I replied, 'though it's something I've never done.'

'At our age, one feels such a fool at having to ask,' said Munn. I saw that his hands were shaking.

I have always felt that the plural possessive is a case that should be used with caution, but all I said was 'Where will it be? And who is she? And congratulations too, of course.'

'It's only in the next county. In fact, just over the border.' Munn expressed it a trifle histrionically, but of course there *is* an enormous difference between Suffolk and Norfolk, and between both and north Essex.

'I shall be hiring a motor,' Munn continued, staring at me, as if the availability of private transport might make all the difference.

'I shall be delighted to do everything I can,' I said, taking a goodish pull on Munn's whisky. 'In fact, I shall be honoured.'

Munn looked a shade doubtful about that, as well he might; but he was wonderfully relieved, and almost gulped as he said, 'Thank you very much. I shall never forget it. I may be able to do the same for you one day.'

'Who knows?' I responded, as the whisky began to rise within me.

'Would Saturday of the week after next suit you?' Munn really seemed to imply that if it would not, the day could be changed.

'Perfectly,' I replied; though almost completely at random.

'I was afraid it might not. Unfortunately it has to be on a Saturday or a Sunday, or my future wife's people couldn't get to it.'

'I quite understand.'

'He's a very busy man, and his wife is closely involved in what they do.'

It seemed that I was meant to take that up, even though, as will be noticed, I had not yet even learned the bride's name. 'And what is that?' I enquired politely.

'It's something I think you ought to know. That's why I raised the matter,' said Munn.

I nodded.

'It's a little hard to talk about,' said Munn, looking at the floor. 'It's the kind of thing that makes people giggle a bit.' Munn drew on himself again and gazed at me. 'I don't really mind if you do giggle. I couldn't possibly blame you.'

'I shall do nothing of the kind,' I rejoined.

But Munn still beat about the bush. 'You know that story of Maurice Baring's? Or is it a play?'

'I am not sure that I do.' Maurice Baring had, after all, written an enormous amount even by the date we had then reached.

'A young man tells a girl he has a secret that he simply must confide in her before she marries him. She swears black and blue that no matter what it may be, she will love him as much as ever. In the end, he discloses that he's the hangman, and she sheers off.'

'No,' I said. 'I can't recall having come upon that.'

'My future father-in-law is an undertaker,' said Munn. 'Not the hangman. Just the undertaker.'

'I shouldn't let that worry you. Indeed, I've always understood it's a most lucrative trade. Whatever happens in the world, the demand's still there. Indeed, as things get worse, it often increases.'

'What a good chap you are!' exclaimed Munn, refilling my glass. 'When I told my brother, he laughed at first, and then began to be very wary. Of course he's been a married man for more than twenty years. Really settled, is Rodney. But it was just the same with three other men I spoke to about it.'

'It doesn't worry me,' I asserted. It was hardly possible to say anything else, though what I had said was not the exact truth.

'It's just the two of them do the whole thing,' Munn continued. 'He was a merchant navy carpenter or something like that to begin with, and then began to specialize. She does the laying-out, as I believe it's called. I'm told she can do the other things too; as well as any professional. Embalming, for example; though of course there's no great demand for that in rural England. All the same, she has an embalmer's full certificate. It's rather comic really. It hangs on their wall. It's one of the first things you see.'

'Someone has to do these things,' I said.

'Yes,' said Munn. 'And it's quite surprising how clean and calm it all is when you get close to it. "Clean" and "calm" are the words that have stayed in my mind all the way through.'

I enquired no further, though I daresay it was obvious enough that Munn wanted to go on talking around the discouraging topic. For my part, I have always been a conventional enough person, and, drink or no drink, I was beginning very clearly to understand why the topic is half tabu. I said I was sorry but that it was time I went, and Munn said he would call for me in the hired motor at 8 a.m. on the following Saturday week. Did I mind it being so early? Munn was once more drawing himself together. But I was past minding almost anything, as long as this absurd ceremony could be decently put into the past, and, as far as I was concerned, buried there. I said I would look for a booklet upon the duties of a best man, but Munn said quite earnestly that it wouldn't be necessary.

In all the circumstances, I never expected to receive one of those smooth cards that announce future weddings; and this was as well because none came. Before the day dawned, I saw Munn, two or three times, stumbling about the village. After all it was not a large village, and an imminent bridegroom could hardly live as a recluse. I thought it best to make no approach, and this was clearly right, because Munn made no approach to me, except that once when we were far enough apart and unmistakably going in different directions, he winked at me. It seemed plain that Munn did not want his future plans to be generally discussed, so I said nothing about the matter to anyone. After a day or two, however, I recollected that a best man is expected to make a presentation of some kind to the bride. The answer to that was simpler than might be expected: I have a rule that when a gift is required, I give a year's membership (or, occasionally longer) of a society which admits one free of charge to a number of buildings of diverse architectural interest. The general public has to pay for admission in every case; and the list of structures includes several important ones to which the general public is not admitted at all. I did reflect that it might not be an absolutely ideal gift for a young girl, but there was no evidence that Munn's intended *was* a young girl. I knew nothing about her. I had not enquired, because I had little doubt that if Munn had wanted me to know at that stage, he would have told me. There was also the question of gifts to the bridesmaids. I dealt with it by assuming that there would be no bridesmaids.

I was right about that, but, for some reason (no doubt, the infrequency of weddings in my life), it had never occurred to me that there might not even be a church.

'I simply couldn't face all that white stuff and slobbering about,' said Munn to me in the car. 'I'm sure you'll agree it's not the thing for chaps of our age.'

So we were making towards a small country town with a convenient registry office. I shall not give the name of the town, because marriage is an institution so delicate that all in any way concerned are very touchy on the subject, and prone to seek legal redress for any possible dubiety or even comment. At the time, I wondered whether Munn was not perhaps a divorced man; or even a potential bigamist. It was the kind of thing that the course of events tended to bring to one's mind; but I have absolutely no reason to think there was any truth in either hypothesis.

In the car, however, Munn did let fall his bride's family name. It was Pell: in East Anglia, a gypsy name, though less eminent in that way than

Mace. I did not remark upon these facts to Munn. He was now referring to the bride herself as 'Vi'. Munn struck me as being less uneasy than I had expected. I observed that he had not bought new clothes for the occasion, but was in his usual shapeless tweeds. I myself was at least wearing a 'dark suit'. I touched my pocket containing the membership card of the society I have mentioned, which I had sealed in an envelope: sealed, I mean, with scarlet sealing wax. I was far from sure what would be the best moment to hand it over. I should have to wait upon events.

The distance was not all that great and we managed to arrive before the registry office was even open. There were, in fact, six or seven minutes to go. I felt that this was the sort of thing that could be counted upon, and concentrated upon the idea that my duties must soon be all over. At least we had the car to wait in; which was fortunate, as it had begun to rain. The car was of moderate size only, and I wondered how many there would be for the return trip. The young driver began to nod to passers-by he knew. Munn had fallen silent. By way of conversation, I enquired how he and his bride had met.

'She came into the post office and liked my straw daffies. She told Mrs Hextable that she would like to meet me. She thought we had interests in common. Mrs Hextable came up and brought me down. And so it proved to be.'

'You mean that you *did* find you had a lot in common?'

'So it seemed. I must admit that I'd been keeping half an eye open for a wife for some time. You may not believe that. I was feeling more and more that I couldn't let my whole life be ruined by the swinish way I was treated.'

'Of course I believe you, and I'm quite sure you're right,' I said firmly; 'and I very sincerely hope you'll be very happy.' I felt quite warm about it.

'Old Pell says he's going to build us a house,' remarked Munn.

I managed to avoid any facetious reference to an abode which would last till Doomsday. Even so, Munn was blushing slightly.

'My God!' I cried. 'What about the ring?' It was the first I had thought of it. I was behaving like the best man in a pantomime, but then, of course, one so often does behave like a character in a pantomime.

'It's all right,' said Munn. 'Here it is.' He handed over a tiny grey box from his jacket pocket.

'Isn't it rather small?'

'She's a small girl.'

At that point, one of the big office doors opened and a clerk emerged.

'Is either of you Mr Munn?'

'I am,' said Munn.

'The Registrar's waiting for you. The bride is inside already with her family.' I cannot recall that I ever learned how they had managed to achieve this: professional influence, no doubt.

We followed the clerk indoors, and, slightly to my surprise, the young driver of the car came after us. As Munn made no objection, it was not for me to speak.

The windows of the room in which the ceremony was to take place were in need of cleaning. Perhaps they were unusually difficult to reach, as they were very high in the walls. The grime on the panes and the increasing rainfall made things very dim, and somewhat obscured my first view of the Pell family.

My main feeling was that they were indeed small: small, smooth, and round was the impression they all left with me. Miss Pell, a little taller than her gnome-like parents, though only a trifle, was a pretty, round-faced, round-eyed girl, arrayed in bright colours, a selection of them. She had very blue eyes and very pink cheeks and very yellow hair, which stuck up sturdily all over her head, rather in the manner of Munn's own white tangle. She was talking as we entered the room, in a noticeably sharp, even metallic voice; there was something stocky and assured in her whole demeanour, which, I must admit, did not attract me; and from pretty well the first instant I was in no doubt at all that it was she who had carried off Munn rather than he who had captured her. Why she should wish to do that was another matter; but no affair of mine, and rather glad I was to be unimplicated. Munn's marriage, hitherto partly comic, partly pathetic because for me, as I entered that registry office, partly disagreeable as well.... I should add that Mr Pell was dressed in a well-fitted black suit, and little Mrs Pell in a tight dress of deepest purple.

'Happy to meet you,' said Mr Pell. One simply could not exclude the sinister overtones of such a greeting from one's mind, absurd though it is to say so.

I simpered.

'I often think the best man is the key to the whole wedding,' continued Mr Pell. Even that implausible compliment added to my uneasiness, lacking as I was in all experience of the tasks required. Moreover, Mr Pell had a grating voice; compulsive antecedent of his daughter's.

'How do you like the bride's clothes?' enquired Mrs Pell. 'Doesn't she look gay? Don't you think Leonard's lucky to get her?' I had forgotten that Munn's name was Leonard (Christian names were not used among men in the present casual way), and had to grope in my mind for what she meant.

'She looks lovely,' I said.

'You'll be able to kiss her in a few minutes, you know. It's the best man's privilege.'

'I shan't forget.'

But the Registrar was awaiting us with some impatience, especially as he had a bad cold. The rubric was minimal, so that only a few minutes had seemingly passed before he was saying 'And I hope you'll be very happy,' and moving back to the fire that was smoking away in his private room. I had passed across the ring at the right moment and, at so spare a solemnization, had little other commitment. We all signed the register, including the driver of the car. There had been no one else present, except the registrar's clerk, who served unobtrusively.

The Pells were cackling away (the verb is unavoidable: though of course voices do run in families, as do handwriting and faiths), and now had come the time for me to kiss Vi. Her cheek (to which I confined myself) struck me hard and chilly, but the bride is in a palpably false position at such moments. All the same, I remembered by contrast other kisses that were coming my way just then. I also noticed that Munn had not kissed Vi at all. He had not touched her in any way except to put the small ring on her stick-like finger. The rain had eased off when we emerged, so I suppose it may all have taken rather longer than I supposed.

To my relief, there was no further celebration. Even drinks all round at the hotel opposite were precluded by the licensing hours, as we all had to agree. Munn, the new Mrs Munn, and I reentered the car and the Pells waved us away. I saw their squat shapes shoulder to shoulder on the pavement: Mr Pell with his right arm raised, Mrs Pell with her left. The rain was now only a light drizzle, to which the Pells seemed impervious. After all, most funerals take place in the wet, I reflected. Could it have been really so difficult for Pell to get away thus briefly and thus early on another day than Saturday? Not that it mattered. I remembered that the Pells had had to travel from somewhere or other. I do not think I then knew where Pell plied his profession: visibly, and, as I had seen for myself, happier than any lark, as are all these men of timber and satin.

Munn was taking his bride back to the rooms over the post office. I had found them, of course, to be more spacious than I had thought before I entered them. I noticed that the word 'honeymoon' was never, in my hearing, mentioned. In the car, however, Vi, from the back seat, did assure me anxiously that, as Munn had said, her father was going to build them a house.

'The first thing we'll do,' she grated on, 'is start looking for a plot. It'll have to be the cheapest we can find, as Daddy doesn't believe in buying things when he can make so much with his own hands.'

There was no reference to Munn making any contribution, nor did he, installed in the back seat beside her, say a word.

'It will only be a teeny house,' Vi explained in her rasping voice, 'but Mummy says you're often best off when you're living small.'

It was necessary to enter into it. 'Have you a builder in mind?' I enquired.

'Of course not, silly. Daddy's going to build it for us.'

I had sensed that this was in the background. 'The whole thing?' I asked. 'The plumbing included? And the electricity?' The latter had just entered our area, but was not yet truthfully in our immediate range.

'We shan't be having silly things like that. Only wood.'

I was constrained to turn in my seat, difficult though it was to do, and look back at her.

'Daddy can make everything needed in this world out of wood.'

There was something almost evangelical in her tone and choice of words. There was also something wild and fantastical: which seemed infectious.

'Even people?' I asked, smiling no doubt, but really asking under some compulsion that remained elusive.

'You're making game of me,' she replied on the instant. Her pink cheeks had darkened, and I noticed that she, for her part, was not smiling at all.

'Lay off, you fool,' said Munn, really quite sharply, and speaking almost for the first time since entering the car. 'Let's change the subject. We haven't even started looking for the land as yet.'

'That's right,' said Vi. 'Though we're going to, aren't we, Leonard?' She left little doubt that they were.

And we did manage to talk of something else. As a matter of fact, we talked of how beautiful the wedding had been: a compulsory theme, needless to say, for all such moments of time, regardless of objectivity.

Munn had been preposterously rude; but I had observed such quick gripings of rage in him before, notably when he thought about the Inland Revenue and how they had treated him.

A few weeks later, the Munns did invite me round one evening, 'after supper'. It was a remarkably formal visit: I must acknowledge that I found it difficult to keep the word 'wooden' out of my mind. Munn's capacity to talk at large about this and that seemed entirely to have shrivelled, as happens so often to a man after marriage, sometimes immediately after; and Vi's sole interest appeared to be her own family and their conversationally equivocal trade.

Inevitably, no doubt, she took the line that there was nothing whatever to be frightened about, and that the details were most interesting when encountered from the inside. The expression 'from the inside' did not appeal to me. And, with Vi, it was difficult even to make a feeble joke about it; or, I thought, about anything.

I learned that the constructions in which her father took so much pride, and she on his behalf, were passed off, at least within the family firm, as 'boxes'. It was not that this usage was specially defined to me. It was simply that the words 'box' and 'boxes', with various other special expressions, were lightly thrown about by Vi, and sometimes by Munn too; so that I quickly realized what was meant, as when one grasps a foreign idiom through contact with those to whom it is habitual.

Thus Vi remarked: 'Daddy's already made our boxes'; as one might lightly describe the planting of two saplings by way of commemoration.

19

It was impossible not to perceive that Munn seemed already to be completely involved; to be seriously and sincerely interested in the gruesome business. Again it is something one commonly notes: that very speedily the husband is all but totally englutinated into the wife's life-pattern.

Perhaps in the present case, a kind of clue was offered – or re-offered.

'As soon as I set eyes on those daffies Leonard made,' observed Vi, her round blue eyes almost alive, 'I *knew.*'

And, this time, suddenly, I knew too. Munn's reference to something of the same kind, when he was asking me to be his best man, had left me groping after some mere folksiness, some rural witchery and magic, which one could only hope was white. Now I realized that, at least for Vi, Munn's journeyman imitations of men (if I may cite Hamlet) were surrogates for those other imitations of men that were put into her father's boxes. (For what, at the end, is man but ravelled straw?)

Munn's cups and plates, or Mrs Hextable's, had all disappeared, and we ate little square sandwiches, with pink stuff inside, off smooth wooden platters, and drank tea out of mugs that had been not thrown but hollowed out. In the end, when Vi was out of the room, Munn offered me a whisky, and whipped out a single glass tumbler from the back of the cupboard.

He drank nothing himself, though before he had customarily exceeded me.

'I've been looking around,' he said in a confidential voice. 'The daffies won't keep two of us, nor will my measly blood money.' It struck me that it was the first time that evening he had referred, even indirectly, to the King Charles's head which previously had floated at almost all times, before his angry gaze.

'And soon there'll be three of us.'

'Indeed?' I replied. I reflected, in a vulgar way, that it seemed quick work. 'I congratulate you both.'

'Vi sets great store by our having a child immediately. And so do her people.'

'I see what you mean,' I said. 'And have you found anything?'

'No damn it, I haven't. It's not easy at our age. But I have something in the back of my mind.'

'And what is that? If you wish to tell me of course.'

'Not just yet, old man.' I could hear Vi approaching from the next room. 'Only if it materializes.'

The door opened. 'If what materializes, Leonard?' enquired Vi, in her unpleasant voice, her head on one side, like the head of a toy bird.

'If Marley's ghost materializes,' said Munn; with more authority than I had observed in him during the whole of the earlier evening.

Vi projected her straight red tongue at him from her round red mouth.

'All things come to him who waits,' said Munn with apparent

vagueness. Married couples quickly learn to fill in with such utterances.

But I never really like drinking alone, so I soon made my excuses, and walked home to my cottage on the outskirts of the community.

I had a strong suspicion of what the something was at the back of Munn's mind.

And soon we walked into one another outside one of the branch banks. Not that either of us ran an account there: if one knows one's onions, one does not bank in one's own gossipy village.

'We're off,' Munn said, 'Vi and I. Next week, in fact: Wednesday, I'm told. The old man's sending one of his wagons. It's the only day he can spare one.'

'Wagons' in the patois of the Pell family had an implication similar to that of 'boxes'; so that the symbolism behind Munn's remarks seemed greatly too oppressive.

But Munn continued the theme. 'I doubt whether we shall meet again, you and I.'

For a moment I could find nothing at all to say, even though words were my trade.

Munn eased matters. 'Not that I shan't send you a change of address,' he said. 'Of course, I shall.'

'In that case,' I observed, smiling, 'I am sure we shall meet. I shall make a point of looking you up.'

'Don't speak too soon. You don't know what I shall be doing.'

'I think I do know.'

'I'm going into the old man's trade.'

'Yes?'

'I'm to serve a quick apprenticeship, to learn from the bottom up, so to speak. And, after that, there's a partnership offered.... So you'll hardly want to know me any more.'

'Nonsense,' I responded, as brightly as I could manage. 'Not see that charming girl you've discovered for yourself! Miss seeing your child! Not likely.' To so many married men, one has to say such things. One feels it is the least one can do; and that it is expected.

'You're a good chap,' said Munn, 'but, for God's sake, don't feel in the least obliged. I know what I'm doing and what the consequences are.'

'All bosh,' I rejoined, in the same spirit as before 'You're taking up one of the safest money-spinners there is, and I look to enjoy some pickings from the rich man's table.'

I received a card bearing Munn's new address (it also bore a faint fringe of acorns), from which for the first time I learned the name of the settlement where the Pells did their work; and, as it happened, I also saw Pell's 'wagon', an outsize model, looking all the blacker for its bulk, as it bore away such of the trappings as were Munn's, and Munn himself on the seat in front, with the sably accoutred driver at the other end, and little Vi wedged between them. It was evening at the time, and rapidly sinking into dusk. I reflected that public use of a 'wagon' for such an uncanonical purpose as this might attract adverse comment if done during the hours of full daylight. As for me, at that moment, I too had a particular reason for sliding about inconspicuously. Indeed, I drew far back into a convenient hedge as the huge 'wagon' sped smoothly by.

I did not go after the 'wagon' that week, or the following week; that month, or the following month; that year, or the following year. The place where the Pells had proved to live was a small industrial town, built, in remote East Anglia, as a single entity during the nineteenth century. Though high ideals lay behind its founding, it had little current reputation for beauty of architecture. Of course, standards change remarkably in such contexts, but, at the time I am talking about, the town was represented as a place more to avoid than visit. Nor did I receive a specific invitation from the Munns. I had not expected one. Indeed, I received no further communication at all from them; not even an undertaker's Christmas card.

Some years later, none the less, I drifted over, and so acquired some idea of what ultimately became of Munn.

By then I had acquired a small, second-hand motor; a two-seater so-called roadster. For some time, I had had a commission to catalogue all the churches in Suffolk. It was no light or brief task, as Suffolk has many churches. Moreover, the prospect of a similar assignment relating to Norfolk was held before me. As far as pleasure went, I should greatly have preferred to travel by train and on foot, which was then perfectly possible; but my employers pressed. I am not sure that by the end, time had been saved; because my second-hand roadster was always breaking down and leaving me helpless, as I have no gift with machines and no love for them.

I acknowledge that for some time I omitted consideration of the town which housed the Pells (and which I had taken to thinking of always in that way). After all, it was agreed that the place had little to offer the connoisseur of *beaux arts;* such as was expected to study my careful lists. I was even ignoring the district around it; which, indeed, was still, in the main, open heath, with few churches, and hardly more houses. (Now it has been utilized in familiar ways: varying from an 'open prison' to a large mineral development.) But, in the end, necessity called, and, picking a rainy day, I set out. I should have preferred to disguise myself.

In the town itself, all went perfectly well, even though the rain inconveniently ceased to fall while I was doing my duty in the church. I recalled that the same had happened during Munn's inauspicious nuptials. The church, paid for entirely from the pocket of the founding industrialist, was splendidly ornate; after the fashion then in the 1920s, deprecated, but now once more respected. The town, as a whole, duly seemed more of sociological than aesthetic interest. But my obligation was exclusively ecclesiastical; and though, as I edged along the streets, I kept half an eye open for the name PELL surmounted by plumes or the staring eyes of black horses, I saw nothing of the kind, and in the end even plucked up courage for a coffee and cake in an anomalous tea-shop, half gentlewoman's chintz and half charge-hand's lincrusta. In those days, it was easier to 'park' one's car; though, on the other hand, one's car could therefore stand out more conspicuously.

It was on a low ridge to the south of the town, as I drove homewards, that I came upon Munn's new abode. Curiously enough, I was deliberately avoiding any kind of main route, and weaving my way through lanes by the use of the map. This was not easy to combine with driving the roadster, but fortunately the lanes carried very little traffic in those days. Possibly there was some finger of fate which pointed my way to the house. I seemed conscious all along of such an element in my relationship with Munn; and what happened next perhaps confirms it.

It was hard to believe that it had been necessary to pay money for the 'plot' on which the house stood. The tiny black structure recalled what one had heard of 'squatters' and their 'rights'. It stood on a sandy, scrubby, nondescript waste, like a thrown-away cabin trunk; or perhaps like a house built by the little people, there one day, gone the next. I am sure I should have known at once that it was the house built by Munn's father-in-law for his chicks with his own hands; but, as it happened, Vi, in her bright colours, was at work in the front garden as my open roadster snorted laboriously up the ridge. At the same time, the rain began to fall once more, this time heavily. I saw Vi go back into the little house; from the other side of which Munn emerged, already clad in heavy oilskins. I suppose it was natural enough for the frail female to withdraw from the inclement weather and for the stouter male to take her place; but there seemed to be something odd and automatic about it, all the same. Moreover, on the instant two flaps opened in the house's single black gable, and a quite life-size wooden cuckoo jumped out, shouting its head off four times. I looked at my watch: it was indeed four o'clock. It seemed odd to have a clock outside a tiny private house, as if it were a town hall; but there could be no doubt about the hour of day being audible over a wide area.

By this time, Munn had looked up and seen me seated there, grinding slowly uphill. To speak plainly, I doubt whether, if I had been travelling faster, I should have stopped; though this may make me sound a cad. With Munn's gaze upon me, I had no alternative. Also, I should have to raise the hood; always a lengthy and injurious undertaking.

I brought the motor to a standstill. Munn just stood there staring at me,

23

silent and motionless. His clothes had never appeared particulary to fit, as I believe I have indicated; but the oilskins seemed to belong to another and much larger man altogether. Munn held a hoe with a very long handle; but it was hard to see what he was doing with it, or what Vi had been doing before him. I have spoken of 'a front garden', but when I stopped the car, I realized that there was nothing: no cultivation of any kind, but only the sparse and stony heath, no different in front of the house from elsewhere.

'Excuse me,' I shouted, 'I must put up my hood.' By now the rain was bucketing down; what people call a 'cloudburst', though no one knows exactly what that is. Raising the hood was always a fearful ploy, but I dashed at it and did better than usual under the continued pressures of the situation. All the same, the job took a minute or two, so that it became rather noticeable that Munn was not offering to help.

When I had adjusted the last screw (car hoods were more elaborately devised in early days), I realized that Munn was no longer there at all. Obviously, instead of coming to my aid, he had returned to the house for shelter.

I think I should almost certainly have proceeded therewith upon my way, though no doubt with qualms. But what happened was that the car refused to start, which was all too customary.

I sat there for some time with the downpour beating on the hood. I daresay I fiddled around a bit with the levers and buttons and so forth, but I had little hope in that direction.

Then I noticed that the glass in the front window of Munn's house was broken. They were narrow French windows; narrow, but a pair of them. And it was not just a matter of the glass being cracked, but of actual black holes. From the whole look of the place, it dawned on me that no one could seriously live there. And yet, without doubt, I had seen both Munn and Mrs Munn. The former had stared, quite unmistakably, at me, for an appreciable period of time.

Hitherto I had spent the day (and long before that) beating around the bush in one way and another precisely in order not to reencounter these Munns and Pells. It now occurred to me that the tribe of them had perhaps so weighed upon my mind that I was seeing members of it where they were not. The little black house was so exactly what I was both looking for and avoiding, that the notion of an hallucination seemed slightly more plausible than it commonly does. I had even heard or read that hallucinations are most likely at just such moments between dark and light as, with the heavily gathering clouds, I had lately passed through.

Perhaps for reasons such as these, perhaps for obscurer, and less resistible reasons, at which I have hinted, I resolved to have a closer look round. I was wearing a motorist's overcoat, substantial even against such weather as this. I climbed down from the car and walked over to the broken windows. There was no hedge, gate, or boundary of any kind.

I looked in, with some caution, through one of the holes in the glass; while the rain from the wide gable above dripped down my neck. Despite the two French doors, there appeared to be only a single room within, stretching from side to side of the house; and with the inside walls painted in the same black as the outside. There were some vague items of litter lying about the floor, but no real furniture that I could see. All the same, I could hear the huge cuckoo clock ticking above my head; and some one, I reflected, had to wind it. ... Or perhaps not. Perhaps Mr Pell could make entirely wooden clocks that required no winding.

I was not yet exactly frightened, but, rather, puzzled. I pushed away at both the French windows, but succeeded only in dislodging further portions of glass, which fell to the black floor inside with astonishingly much noise. I half expected the life-size cuckoo upstairs to croak in protest.

I imagined that there might be a door at the back of the structure; through which, as I could not help thinking, one 'got at the works', in little houses and little artefacts made of wood. I walked round in the rain, and such a door there was. This time, I dragged it open. It stuck and shrieked, but by now I meant business and I pulled hard.

The first thing I saw was a child seated on a shelf with both arms extended. It was presumably clutching something out of sight at each side as its whole posture suggested strain and effort but I realized that it was a figure in wood of remarkable liveliness. I even managed to extend my hand and touch it. It felt like wood too.

The little house was divided into two chambers by a wooden partition which, painted in the usual black, now confronted me, and against which the child's shelf was set on wooden brackets. This rear chamber was six or eight feet deep. The door I had opened, was a large one and admitted a considerable amount of light, except into the further corners; but there was no window, and the carefully painted, elaborately lifelike figure of the child had been sitting there, it was impossible to guess for how long, in complete darkness. All things considered, it was surprisingly well preserved and spruce.

I now saw its two hands were involved with a system of wires and pulleys which went upwards into the dimness, but was rusty, broken and drooping. Here were indeed the customary 'works'. I thought it might be an unusually complex scheme for manipulating the marionette that squatted before me; but it then seemed to me more as though it were the child, with its effortful posture, that was designed to do the manipulation. And the child was so shiny and glossy, where all else was so rotten. *Quis custodiet custodem?* I could not help asking myself.

Beneath the shelf was a low door into the main room of the house, this time ajar. I kicked it open, bent myself double (which was not easy in my very heavy coat), and went through.

The litter on the floor, not merely dusty and dirty but damp and fungoid, proved to be mainly pages from a book or booklet on the collection of taxes. Against the back partition wall, to the right of the door as I looked back at it, was what appeared, after all, to be the ruin of a large, low piece of furniture. It was as dark, as black, as everything else, and I had not made it out when I peered in through the French windows at the front.

I saw that to the inside of the dwarf-sized door a piece of paper had been pasted: the instructions, one could not help thinking, on how to get the best out of the device. I went back and peered. Instructions, after a kind, indeed they were; written out in ink and with no punctuation by a hand to me unknown. I read them; and after a considerable pause brought out my churches notebook from my jacket pocket, and copied them down. Here is what I wrote:

> When the man is sawing wood
> Wait and watch for falling blood
> Blood and sawdust are the same
> In Dame Nature's little game
>
> When the woman's blindly scraping
> Then's the hour for blows and raping
> Within the earth without a sound
> That's what makes the world go round
>
> Whatever else you need to know
> Set the man and woman so
> Let them prophesy for ever
> Curse them once and come back never

Obediently, I gazed around me. I thought that, before departing, I might as well look more closely at the low piece of crumbling furniture set against the partition wall.

There could be no doubt as to what was really there. The 'piece of crumbling furniture' was a pair of old Mr Pell's 'boxes'; set side by side and crumbling indeed. They had no lids – perhaps the lids had crumbled quite away; and inside were the remains, respectively, of the late Mr and Mrs Munn, in no ordinary state of decomposition, but half-merged, in fact much more than half, into the wood from which and to which I was beginning to think we all spring and return. Like a pair of Daphnes, the two of them, I thought; Daphne who was changed by Apollo into a tree. Not that the hideous amalgam in those boxes was imperishable. Far from that: it was already turning into a woody, crawling, wretchedness, damp and primeval-looking, flesh and pulp as one. . . . Daphne? Of what, in that wooden house, did the name remind me? Then of course I remembered. Old Munn's daffies ... I could only wonder.

I made a bolt for it, not looking back, least of all at the little fellow on the shelf, but slamming the door as I ran, so that it jammed fast.

Believe it or not, I had quite forgotten that my car was broken down. I gave one twirl on the starter, leapt in, and had roared on for at least a mile and a half before I recollected that by rights I should not be moving – or escaping – at all. The finger of fate once more I could not but feel.

And perhaps the spell was, in fact, now broken; because, only a few weeks later, I read in the local weekly that there had been a bad fire one night on the heath, with many sheds and shanties burnt out, and several lives lost. In the way of local weeklies, the report concluded by saying that the funerals of the victims would be conducted by Mr Pell.

The Bird

THOMAS BURKE

IT IS A TALE THAT THEY TELL softly in Pennyfields, when the curtains are drawn and the shapes of the night are shut out. . . .

Those who held that Captain Chudder, S.S. *Peacock*, owners, Peter Dubbin & Co., had a devil in him, were justified. But they were nearer the truth who held that his devil was not within him, but at his side, perching at his elbow, dropping sardonic utterance in his ear; moving with him day and night and prompting him – so it was held – to frightful excesses. His devil wore the shape of a white parrot, a bird of lusty wings and the cruellest of beaks. There were those who whispered that the old man had not always been the man that his crew knew him to be: that he had been a normal, kindly fellow until he acquired his strange companion from a native dealer in the malevolent Solomons. Certainly his maniac moods dated from its purchase; and there was truth in the dark hints of his men that there was something wrong with that damned bird . . . a kind of . . . something you sort of felt when it looked at you or answered you back. For one thing, it had a diabolical knack of mimicry, and many a chap would cry: 'Yes, George!' or 'Right, sir!' in answer to a commanding voice which chuckled with glee as he came smartly to order. They invariably referred to it as 'that bloody bird', though actually it had done nothing to merit such opprobrium. When they thought it over calmly, they could think of no harm that it had done to them: nothing to arouse such loathing as every man on the boat felt towards it. It was not spiteful; it was not bad-tempered. Mostly, it was in cheery mood and would chuckle deep in the throat, like the Captain, and echo or answer, quite pleasantly, such remarks, usually rude, as were addressed to it.

And yet . . . Somehow. . . .

There it was. It was always there – everywhere; and in its speech they seemed to find a sinister tone which left them guessing at the meaning of its words. On one occasion, the cook, in the seclusion of the fo'c'sle, had remarked that he would like to wring its neck if he could get hold of it; but old grizzled Snorter had replied that that bird couldn't be killed. There was something about that bird that . . . well, he betted no one wouldn't touch that bird without trouble. And a moment of panic stabbed the crowd as a voice leapt from the sombre shadows of the corner.

'That's the style, me old brown son. Don't try to come it with me – what?' and ceased in a spasmodic flutter of wicked white wings.

That night, as the cook was ascending the companion, he was caught by a huge sea, which swept across the boat from nowhere and dashed him, head-on, below. For a week he was sick with a broken head, and throughout that week the bird would thrust its beak to the berth where he lay, and chortle to him:

'Yep, me old brown son. Wring his bleeding neck – what? Waltz me around again, Willie, round and round and round!'

That is the seamen's story and, as the air of Limehouse is thick with seamen's stories, it is not always good to believe them. But it is a widely known fact that on the last voyage the Captain did have a devil with him, the foulest of all devils that possess mortal men, not the devil of slaughter, but the devil of cruelty. They were from Swatow to London, and it was noted that he was drinking heavily ashore, and he continued the game throughout the voyage. He came aboard from Swatow, drunk, bringing with him a Chinese boy, also drunk. The greaser, being a big man, kicked him below, otherwise, the boat in his charge would have gone there, and so he sat or sprawled in his cabin, with a rum-bottle before him and, on the corner of his chair, the white parrot, which conversed with him and sometimes fluttered on deck to shout orders in the frightful voice of his master and chuckle to see them momentarily obeyed.

'Yes,' repeated old man Snorter, sententiously, 'I'd run a hundred miles 'fore I'd try to monkey with the old man or his bloody bird. There's something about that bird . . . I said so before. I 'eard a story once about a bird. Out in T'ai-ping I 'eard it. It'll make yeh sick if I tell it. . . .'

Now while the Captain remained drunk in his cabin, he kept with him for company the miserable, half-starved Chinky boy whom he had brought aboard. And it would make others sick if the full dark tale were told here of what the master of the *Peacock* did to that boy. You may read of monstrosities in police reports of cruelty cases, you may read old records of the Middle Ages, but the bestialities of Captain Chudder could not be told in words.

His orgy of drink and delicious torture lasted till they were berthed in the Thames, and the details remain sharp and clear in the memories of those who witnessed it. At all the ceremonial horrors which were wrought in that wretched cabin, the parrot was present. It jabbered to the old man, the old man jabbered back, and gave it an occasional sip of rum from his glass, and the parrot would mimic the Chink's entreaties, and wag a grave claw at him as he writhed under the ritual of punishment, and when that day's ceremony was finished it would flutter from bow to stern of the boat, its cadaverous figure stinging the shadows with shapes of fear for all aboard, perching here, perching there, simpering and whining in tune with the Chink's placid moaning.

29

Placid; yes, outwardly. But the old man's wickedness had lighted a flame beneath that yellow skin which nothing could quench, nothing but the floods of vengeance. Had the old man been a little more cute and a little less drunk, he might have remembered that a Chinaman does not forget. He would have read danger in the face that was so submissive under his devilries. Perhaps he did see it, but because of the rum that was in him, felt himself secure from the hate of any outcast Chink; knew that his victim would never once get the chance to repay him, Captain Chudder, master of the *Peacock*, and one of the very smartest. The Chink was alone and weaponless, and dare not come aft without orders. He was master of the boat, he had a crew to help him, and knives and guns, and he had his faithful white bird to warn him. Too, as soon as they docked at Limehouse, he would sling him off or arrange quick transfer to an outward boat, since he had no further use for him.

But it happened that he made no attempt to transfer. He had forgotten that idea. He just sat below, finished his last two bottles, paid off his men, and then, after a sleep, went ashore to report. Having done that, he forgot all trivial affairs, such as business, and set himself seriously to search for amusement. He climbed St. George's, planning a real good booze-up, and the prospect that spread itself before his mind was so compelling that he did not notice a lurking yellow phantom that hung on his shadow. He visited the Baltic on the chance of finding an old pal or so, and, meeting none, he called at a shipping office in Fenchurch Street, where he picked up an acquaintance, and the two returned eastward to Poplar, and the phantom feet *sup-supped* after them. Through the maze and glamour of the London streets and traffic the shadow slid; it dodged and danced about the Captain's little cottage in Gill Street, and when he, and others, came out and strolled to a bar, and, later, to a music-hall, it flitted, moth-like, around them.

Surely since there is no step in the world that has just the obvious stealth of the Chinaman's, he must have heard those whispering feet? Surely his path was darkened by that shadow? But no. After the music-hall he drifted to a water-side wine-shop and then, with a bunch of the others, went wandering.

It was late. Eleven notes straggled across the waters from many grey towers. Sirens were screeching their derisive song, and names of various Scotch whiskies spelt themselves in letters of yellow flame along the night. Far in the darkness a voice was giving the chanty:

'What shall we do with the drunken sailor?'

The Captain braced himself up and promised himself a real glittering night of good-fellowship, and from gin-warmed bar to gin-warmed bar he roved, meeting the lurid girls of the places and taking one of them upstairs.

At the last bar his friends, too, went upstairs with their ladies, and, it being then one o'clock in the morning, he brought a pleasant evening to a close at a certain house in Poplar High Street, where he took an hour's amusement by flinging half-crowns over the fan-tan table.

But always the yellow moth was near, and when, at half past two, he came, with uncertain steps, into the sad street, now darkened and loud only with the drunken, who found unfamiliar turnings in familiar streets, and the old landmarks many yards away from their rightful places, the moth buzzed closer and closer.

The Captain talked as he went. He talked of the night he had had, and the girls his hands had touched. His hard face was cracked to a meaningless smile, and he spat words at obstructive lamp posts and kerbstones, and swears dropped like toads from his lips. But at last he found his haven in Gill Street, and his hefty brother, with whom he lived when ashore, shoved him upstairs to his bedroom. He fell across the bed, and the sleep of the swinish held him fast.

The grey towers were rolling three o'clock, and the thick darkness of the water-side covered the night like a blanket. The lamps were pale and few. The waters sucked miserably at the staples of the wharves. One heard the measured beat of a constable's boot, sometimes the rattle of chains and blocks, mournful hooters, shudders of noise as engines butted lines of trucks at the shunting station.

Captain Chudder slept, breathing stertorously, mouth open, limbs heavy and nerveless. His room was deeply dark, and so little light shone on the back reaches of the Gill Street cottages that the soft raising of the window made no visible aperture. Into this blank space something rose from below, and soon it took the shape of a flat, yellow face which hung motionless, peering into the room. Then a yellow hand came through, the aperture was widened, and swiftly and silently a lithe, yellow body hauled itself up and slipped over the sill.

It glided, with outstretched hand, from the window and, the moment it touched the bed, its feeling fingers went here and there, and it stood still, gazing upon the sleep of drunkenness. Calmly and methodically a yellow hand moved to its waist and withdrew a kris. The same hand raised the kris and held it poised. It was long, keen, and beautifully curved, but not a ray of light was in the room to fall upon it, and the yellow hand had to feel its bright blade to find whether the curve ran from or towards it.

Then, with terrific force and speed, it came down, one – two – three. The last breath rushed from the open lips. Captain Chudder was out.

The strong yellow hand withdraw the kris for the last time, wiped it on the coverlet of the bed, and replaced it in its home. The figure turned, like a wraith, for the window, turned for the window and found, in a moment of panic, that it knew not which way to turn. It hesitated for a moment. It thought it heard a sound at the bed. It touched the coverlet and the boots of the Captain; all was still. Stretching a hand to the wall, Sung Dee began to creep and to feel his way along. Dark as the room was, he had found his way in, without matches or illuminant. Why could he not find his way out? Why was he afraid of something?

Blank wall was all he found at first. Then his hand touched what seemed to be a picture frame. It swung and clicked and the noise seemed to echo through the still house. He moved farther, and a sharp rattle told him that he had struck the loose handle of the door. But that was of little help. He could not use the door, he knew not what perils lay behind it. It was the window he wanted – the window.

Again he heard that sound from the bed. He stepped boldly and judged that he was standing in the middle of the room. Momentarily a sharp shock surged over him. He prayed for matches, and something in his throat was almost crying, 'The window! The window!' He seemed like an island in a sea of darkness, one man surrounded by legions of immortal intangible enemies. His cold Chinese heart went hot with fear.

The middle of the room he judged, and took another step forward, a step which landed his chin sharply against the jutting edge of the mantelshelf over the fireplace. He jumped like a cat and his limbs shook, for now he had lost the door and the bed, as well as the window, and had made terrible noises which might bring disaster. All sense of direction was gone. He knew not whether to go forward or backwards, to right or left. He heard the tinkle of the shunting trains, and he heard a rich voice crying something in his own tongue. But he was lapped around by darkness and terror, and a cruel fancy came to him that he was imprisoned here for ever and for ever, and that he would never escape from this enveloping, suffocating room. He began to think that—

And then a hot iron of agony rushed down his back as, sharp and clear, at his elbow came the Captain's voice:

'Get forrard, you damn lousy Chink – get forrard. Lively there! Get out of my room!'

He sprang madly aside from the voice that had been the terror of his life for so many weeks, and collided with the door; realized that he had made further fearful noises; dashed away from it and crashed into the bed; fell across it and across the warm, wet body that lay there. Every nerve in every limb of him was scared with horror at the contact, and he leapt off, kicking, biting, writhing. He leapt off, and fell against a table, which tottered, and at last fell with a stupendous crash into the fender.

'Lively, you damn Chink!' said the Captain. 'Lively, I tell yeh. Dance, d'yeh hear? I'll have yeh for this. I'll learn you something. I'll give you something with a sharp knife and a bit of hot iron, my cocky. I'll make yer yellow skin crackle, yeh damn lousy chopstick. I'll have yeh in a minute. And when I get yeh, orf with yeh clothes. I'll cut yeh to pieces I will.'

Sung Dee shrieked. He ran round and round, beating the wall with his hands, laughing, crying, jumping, while all manner of shapes arose in his path, lit by the grey light of fear. He realized that it was all up now. He cared not how much noise he made. He hadn't killed the old man; only wounded him. And now all he desired was to find the door and any human creatures who might save him from the Captain. He met the bed again, suddenly, and the tormentor who lay there. He met the upturned table and fell upon it, and he met the fireplace and the blank wall; but never, never the window or the door. They had vanished. There was no way out. He was caught in that dark room, and the Captain would do as he liked with him. . . . He heard footsteps in the passage and sounds of menace and alarm below. But to him they were friendly sounds, and he screamed loudly towards them.

He cried to the Captain, in his pidgin, for mercy.

'Oh, Captain – no burn me today, Captain. Sung Dee be heap good sailor, heap good servant, all same slave. Sung Dee heap plenty solly hurt Captain. Sung Dee be good boy. No do feller bad lings no feller more. O Captain. Let Sung Dee go lis time. Let Sung Dee go. O Captain!'

But 'Oh, my Gawd!' answered the Captain. 'Bless your yellow heart. Wait till I get you trussed up. Wait till I get you below. I'll learn yeh.'

And now those below came upstairs, and they listened in the passage, and for the space of a minute they were hesitant. For they heard all manner of terrible noises, and by the noises there might have been half a dozen fellows in the Captain's room. But very soon the screaming and the pattering feet were still, and they heard nothing but low moans; and at last the bravest of them, the Captain's brother, swung the door open and flashed a large lantern.

And those who were with him fell back in dumb horror, while the brother cried harshly: 'Oh! ... my ... God!' For the lantern shone on a Chinaman seated on the edge of the bed. Across his knees lay the dead body of the Captain, and the Chink was fondling his damp, dead face, talking baby talk to him, dancing him on his knee, and now and then making idiot moans. But what sent the crowd back in horror was that a great death-white Thing was flapping about the yellow face of the Chink, cackling: 'I'll learn yeh! I'll learn yeh!' and dragging strips of flesh away with every movement of the beak.

A Thing About Machines
ROD SERLING

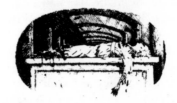

MR BARTLETT FINCHLEY, TALL, tart, and fortyish, looked across his ornate living room to where the television repairman was working behind his set and felt an inner twist of displeasure that the mood of the tastefully decorated room should be so damaged by the T-shirted, dungareed serviceman whose presence was such a foreign element in the room. He looked, gimlet-eyed, at the man's tool box lying on the soft pile of the expensive carpet like a blot on Mr Finchley's escutcheon which emphasized symmetry above all! Mr Finchley, among other things, was both a snob and fastidious. And snobbery and fastidiousness were not simply character traits with him; they were banners that he flaunted with pride. He rose from the chair and walked over to within a few feet of the television set. The repairman looked up at him, smiling, and wiped his forehead.

'How are you today, Mr Finchley?'

Mr Finchley's left eyebrow shot up. 'I'll answer *that* burning question after you tell me what's wrong with that electronic boo-boo, and also acquaint me with how much this current larceny is going to cost me.'

The repairman rose and wiped his hands with a rag. He looked down at the set, then up to Mr Finchley. 'Two hours' labour,' he said, 'a broken set of tubes, new oscillator, new filter.'

Mr Finchley's face froze, his thin lips forming a taut line.

'How very technical,' he announced. 'How very nice! And I presume I'm to be dunned once again for three times the worth of the bloody thing?'

The repairman smiled gently and studied Mr Finchley. 'Last time I was here, Mr Finchley,' he said, 'you'd kicked your foot through the screen. Remember?'

Mr Finchley turned away and put a cigarette in a holder. 'I have a vivid recollection,' he announced. 'It was not working properly.' He shrugged. 'I tried to get it to do so in a normal fashion!'

'By kicking your foot through the screen?' the repairman shook his head. 'Why didn't you just horsewhip it, Mr Finchley? That'd show it who's boss.'

He started to collect his tools and put them into the box. Mr Finchley lit the cigarette in the holder, took a deep drag, and examined his nails.

'What do you say we cease this small talk and get down to some serious larceny? You can read me off the damages ... though I sometimes wonder exactly what is the purpose of the Better Business Bureau when they allow you itinerant extortionists to come back week after week, move wires, around, busily probe with ham-like hands, and accomplish nothing but the financial ruin of every customer on your route!'

The repairman looked up from the tool box, his smile fading. 'We're not a gyp outfit, Mr Finchley. We're legitimate repairmen. But I'll tell you something about *yourself* –'

'Spare me, please,' Mr Finchley interrupted him. 'I'm sure there must be some undernourished analyst with an ageing mother to care for whom I can contact for that purpose.'

The repairman closed the box and stood up. 'Why don't you hear me out. Mr Finchley? That set doesn't work because obviously you got back there and yanked out wires and God knows what else! You had me over here last month to fix your portable radio – because you'd thrown it down the steps.'

'It did not work properly,' Finchley said icily.

'That's the point, Mr Finchley. Why *don't* they work properly? Off-hand I'd say it's because you don't *treat* them properly.'

Mr Finchley let the cigarette holder dangle from his mouth as he surveyed the repairman much as a scientist would look at a bug through a microscope. 'I assume there's no charge for that analysis?' he inquired.

The repairman shook his head. 'What does go wrong with these things, Mr Finchley? Have you any idea?'

Mr Finchley let out a short, frozen chortle. 'Have *I* any idea? Now that's worth a scholarly ten lines in your *Repairman's Journal!* Bilk the customer, but let him do the repairing!'

'The reason I asked that,' the repairman persisted, 'is because whatever it is that really bothers you about that television set *and* the radio ... you're not telling me.'

He waited for a response. Mr Finchley turned his back.

'Well?' the repairman asked.

Finchley drew a deep breath as if the last resisting pocket of his patience had been overrun and was being forced to capitulate. 'Aside from being rather an incompetent clod,' Finchley announced, turning back toward the repairman, 'you're a most insensitive man. I've explained to you already. The television set simply did not work properly. And that rinky-dink original Marconi operating under the guise of a legitimate radio gave me nothing but static.'

The TV repairman flicked the set on, watched the picture, raised and lowered the volume, then shut it off. He turned toward Finchley.

'You're sure that's all that was wrong with it?'

Finchley made a gesture and started out of the room. The repairman, with a smile, followed him.

'I'll send you a bill, Mr Finchley,' he said as they walked toward the front hall.

'Of this I have no doubt,' Finchley responded.

At the front door, the repairman turned to look once again at Finchley who stood on the first step of the long sweeping stairway which led to the second floor.

'Mr Finchley ... what is it with you and machines?'

Finchley's eyes sought the ceiling as if this latest idiocy was more than he could bear. 'I will file *that* idiotic question in my memorabilia to be referred to at some future date when I write my memoirs. You will fill one entire chapter on The Most Forgettable Person I Have Ever Met!'

The repairman shook his head and left. Mr Finchley stood stock-still, his features working. For just one, single fleeting moment, his hauteur, his preemptive mastery of all situations, his snobbery seemed to desert the face, leaving behind a mask of absolute, undiluted terror.

'It just so happens, you boob,' Finchley called out into the empty hall, his voice shaking, 'it just so happens that every machine in my house is —'

He cut himself off abruptly, closed his eyes, shook his head, looked down at his hands that were shaking, grabbed them together, then turned and walked unsteadily into the living room. A clock on the mantelpiece chimed deep, resonant notes that filled the room.

'All right,' Finchley said, holding his voice down, 'that'll be about enough of that! Hear me?'

The clock continued to chime. Finchley walked over toward the mantel and shouted.

'I said that'll be just about enough of that!'

He reached up, grabbed the clock in both hands, ripped the plug out of the wall, and slammed the clock down on the floor, stamping on it with his foot while the chimes continued to blare at him like the death rattle of some dying beast. It took several moments for the chimes to die out and Finchley stood over the wreckage of broken glass and dismembered fly wheels and springs, sweat pouring down his face, his whole body shaking as if with an ague. Then very slowly he recovered composure. The shaking stopped, and he went upstairs to his bedroom.

He closed the door and lay down on the bed, feeling limp, washed out and desperately vulnerable. Soon he fell into an uneasy twisting and turning, dream-filled sleep, full of all the nightmares that he lived with during the day and that were kept hidden underneath the icy façade of superiority which insulated him from the world.

Mr Bartlett Finchley at age forty-two was a practising sophisticate who wrote very special and very precious things for gourmet magazines and the like. He was a bachelor and a recluse. He had few friends — only devotees and adherents to the cause of tart sophistry. He had no interests — save whatever current annoyance he could put his mind to. He had no purpose to his life – except the formulation of day-to-day opportunities to vent his wrath on mechanical contrivances of an age he abhorred.

In short, Mr Bartlett Finchley was a malcontent, born either too late or too early in the century – he was unsure which. The only thing he was certain of as he awoke, drenched with perspiration, from his nap, was that the secret could not be held much longer. The sleepless nights and fear-filled days were telling on him, and this man with no friends and no confidants realized in a hidden portion of his mind that he urgently required both.

Late that afternoon he walked down the sweeping staircase from his sumptuous bedroom, attired in a smoking jacket, and directed himself to the small study off the living room where he could hear the sound of the electric typewriter. His secretary had come in a few hours before and was sitting at the desk typing from Finchley's notes.

Edith Rogers was an attractive thirty-year-old who had been with Finchley for over a year. In a history of some two dozen-odd secretaries, Miss Rogers held the record for tenure. It was rare that anyone stayed with Mr Finchley for over a month. She looked up as the master entered the room, cigarette in holder, holder dangling from mouth. He looked back insouciantly and walked behind her to stare over her shoulder at the page in the typewriter. He then picked up a stack of papers from the desk.

'This is all you've done?' he inquired coldly.

She met his stare, unyielding. 'That's all I've done,' she announced. 'That's forty pages in three and a half hours. That's the best *I* can do, Mr Finchley.'

He waggled a finger at the typewriter. 'It's that ... that idiotic gadget of yours. Thomas Jefferson wrote out the preamble to the Constitution with a feather quill and it took him half a day.'

The secretary turned in her chair and looked directly up into his face. 'Why don't you hire Mr Jefferson?' she said quietly.

Finchley's eyebrow, which was one of the most mobile features in a mobile face, shot up alarmingly. 'Did I ever tell you,' he asked, 'with what degree of distaste I view insubordination?'

Edith Rogers bent over the typewriter. 'Often and endlessly,' she said. Then she straightened up. 'I'll tell you what, Mr Finchley,' she said, rising and reaching for her bag, 'you get yourself another girl, somebody with three arms and with roughly the sensitivity of an alligator. Then you can work together till death do you part. As for me –' she shut her pocketbook '– I've had it!'

'And you are going where?' Finchley asked her as she started into the living room.

'Where?' the girl answered, turning toward him. 'I think I might take in Bermuda for a couple of weeks. Or Mexico City. Or perhaps a quiet sanitarium on the banks of the Hudson. Any place,' she continued, as she walked across the room toward the hall, 'where I can be away from the highly articulate, oh so sophisticated, *bon vivant* of America's winers and diners – Mr Bartlett Finchley.'

She paused for breath in the hall and found him staring at her from the living room.

'You've even got me talking like you,' she said angrily. 'But I'll tell you what you *won't* get me to do. You won't turn me into a female Finchley with a pinched little acorn for a heart and a mean, petty, jaundiced view of everybody else in the world!'

Finchley's instinct conjured up a tart, biting, cutting, and irreproachable reply, but something else deep inside shut it off. He stood for a moment with his mouth open, then he bit his lip and said very quietly in a tone she was quite unfamiliar with, 'Miss Rogers ... please don't leave.'

She noticed something in his face that she had never seen before. It was an unfrocked, naked fear so unlike him as to be unbelievable. 'I beg your pardon?' she asked very softly.

Finchley turned away, embarrassed. 'I do wish you'd ... you'd stay for a little bit.' He wavered an arm in the general direction of the study. 'I don't mean for work. All that can wait. I was just thinking ... well ... we could have dinner or something, or perhaps a cocktail.' He turned to her expectantly.

'I'm not very hungry,' she said after a pause. 'And it's too early for cocktails,' She saw the disappointment cross his face. 'What's your trouble, Mr Finchley?' she asked pointedly but not without sympathy.

Finchley's smile was a ghostly and wan attempt at recovery of aplomb, but his voice quickly took on the sharp, slicing overtones that were so much a part of him. 'Miss Rogers, my dear, you sound like a cave-dwelling orphan whose idea of a gigantic lark is a square dance at the local grange. I was merely suggesting to you that we observe the simple social amenities between an employer and a secretary. I thought we'd go out ... take in a show or something.'

She studied him for a long moment, not really liking the man either at this moment, but vaguely aware of something that was eating at him and forcing this momentary lapse into at least a semblance of courtesy.

'How very sweet, Mr Finchley,' she said. 'Thank you, but no thank you.'

Finchley half snorted as he turned his back to her and once again she felt the snobbery of the man, the insufferable ego, the unbearable superiority that he threw around to hurt and humiliate.

'Tonight,' she said, feeling no more pity or fascination, 'tonight I'm taking a hog-calling lesson. You know what a hog is, don't you, Mr Finchley? He's a terribly bright fathead who writes for gourmet magazines and condescends to let a few other slobs exist in the world for the purpose of taking his rudeness and running back and forth at his beck and call! Good night, Mr Finchley.'

She saw his shoulders slump and he was silent. Again she felt compelled to remain because this was so unlike him, so foreign to him not to top her, not to meet her barb head on, divert it, and send one of his own back at her, stronger, faster, and much more damaging. When he finally turned she saw again that his face had an odd look and there was something supplicating, something frightening and something, inconceivable though it was, lonely.

'Miss Rogers,' he said, his voice gentler than she'd ever heard it, 'before you do ... before you go –' he made a kind of half-hearted gesture, '– have a cup of coffee or something.' He turned away so that she would be unable to see his face. 'I'd like very much,' he continued, 'I'd like very much not to be alone for a while.'

Edith Rogers came back into the living room and stood close to him. 'Are you ill?' she asked.

He shook his head.

'Bad news or something?'

'No.'

There was a silence.

'What's your trouble?' she asked.

He whirled on her, his thin lips twisted. 'Does there have to be trouble just because I –'

He stopped, ran a hand over his face, and half fell into a chair. For the first time she observed the circles under his eyes, the pinched look of the mouth, the strangely haunted look.

'I'm desperately tired,' he said abruptly. 'I haven't slept for four nights and the very thought of being alone now –' He grimaced, obviously hating this, feeling the reluctance of the strong man having to admit a weakness. 'Frankly,' he said, looking away, 'it's intolerable. Things have been happening, Miss Rogers, very odd things.'

'Go on.'

He pointed toward the TV set. 'That ... that thing over there. It goes on late at night and wakes me up. It goes on all by itself.' His eyes swept across the room toward the hall. 'And that portable radio I used to keep in my bedroom. It went on and off, just as I was going to sleep.'

His head went down and when he looked up his eyes darted around paranoically. 'There's a conspiracy in this house, Miss Rogers.' Seeing her expression, he raised his voice in rebuttal. 'That's exactly what it is – a conspiracy! The television set, the radio, lighters, electric clocks, that ... that miserable car I drive.'

He rose from the chair, his face white and intense. 'Last night I drove it into the driveway, mind you. Very slowly. Very carefully.' He took a step toward her, his fingers clenching and unclenching at his sides. 'The wheel turned in my hands. Hear me? *The wheel turned in my hand!* The car deliberately hit the side of the garage. Broke a headlight. – That clock up there on the mantelpiece!'

Edith looked at the mantelpiece. There was no clock there. She turned to him questioningly.

'I ... I threw it away,' Finchley announced lamely. Then, pointedly and forcefully he said, 'What I'm getting at, Miss Rogers, is that for as long as I've lived ... I've never been able to operate *machines*.' He spat out the last word as if it were some kind of epithet.

Edith Rogers stared at him, for the first time seeing a part of the man that had been kept hidden beneath a veneer and a smoking jacket.

'Mr Finchley,' she said very softly, 'I think you ought to see a doctor.'

Finchley's eyes went wide and the face and the voice were the Finchley of old. 'A *doctor*,' he shrieked at her. 'The universal panacea of the dreamless twentieth-century idiot! If you're depressed – see a doctor. If you're happy – see a doctor. If the mortgage is too high and the salary too low – see a doctor. You,' he screamed at her, 'Miss Rogers, *you* see a doctor.' Fury plugged up his voice for a moment and then he screamed at her again. 'I'm a logical, rational, intelligent man. I know what I see. I know what I hear. For the past three months I've been seeing and hearing a collection of wheezy Frankensteins whose whole purpose is to destroy me! Now what do you think about *that*, Miss Rogers?'

The girl studied him for a moment. 'I think you're terribly ill, Mr Finchley. I think you need medical attention.' She shook her head, 'I think you've got a very bad case of nerves from lack of sleep and I think that way down deep you yourself realize that these are nothing more than delusions.'

She looked down at the floor for a moment, then turned and started out of the room.

'Now where are you going?' he shouted at her.

'You don't need company, Mr Finchley,' she said from the hall. 'You need analysis.'

He half ran over to her, grabbed her arm, whirled her around.

'You're no different from a cog-wheeled, electrically generated metal machine yourself. You haven't an iota of compassion or sympathy.'

She struggled to free her arm. 'Mr Finchley, please let me go.'

'I'll let you go,' he yelled, 'when I get good and ready to let you go!'

Edith continued to struggle, hating the scene, desperately wanting to end it, and yet not knowing how.

'Mr Finchley,' she said to him, trying to push him off, 'this is ugly. Now please let me go.' She was growing frightened. *'Let go of me!'*

Suddenly, instinctively, she slapped him across the face. He dropped her arm abruptly and stared at her as if disbelieving that anything of this sort could happen to him. That he, Bartlett Finchley, could be struck by a woman. Again his lips trembled and his features worked. A burning fury took possession of him.

'Get out of here,' he said in a low, menacing voice, 'and don't come back!'

'With distinct pleasure,' Edith said, breathing heavily, 'and with manifest relief.' She whirled around and went to the door.

'Remember,' he shouted at her, 'don't come back. I'll send you a cheque. I will not be intimidated by machines, so it follows that no empty-headed little broad with a mechanical face can do anything to me either.'

She paused at the door, wanting air and freedom and most of all to get out of there. 'Mr Finchley,' she said softly, 'in this conspiracy you're suffering ... this mortal combat between you and the appliances – *I hope you get licked!'*

She went out and slammed the door behind her. He stood there motionless, conjuring up some line of dialogue he could fling at her; some final cutting witticism that could leave him the winner. But no inspiration came and it was in the midst of this that he suddenly heard the electric typewriter keys.

He listened for a horrified moment until the sound stopped. Then he went to his study. There was a paper in the typewriter. Finchley turned the roller so that he could read the words on it. There were three lines of type and each one read 'Get out of here, Finchley.'

That was what the typewriter had written all by itself. 'Get out of here, Finchley.' He ripped the paper from the machine, crumpled it, and flung it on the floor.

'Get out of here, Finchley,' he said aloud. 'Goddamn you. Who are you, to tell me to get out of here?' He shut his eyes tightly and ran a fluttery hand over a perspiring face. 'Why this is ... this is absurd. It's a typewriter. It's a machine. It's a silly, Goddamn machine –'

He froze again as a voice came from the television set in the living room.

'Get out of here, Finchley,' the voice said.

He felt his heart pounding inside him as he turned and raced into the living room. There was a little Mexican girl on the screen doing a dance with a tambourine. He could have sworn that each time she clicked her heels past the camera she stared pointedly at him. But as the music continued and the girl kept on dancing, Finchley reached a point where he was almost certain that the whole thing was a product of his sleeplessness, his imagination, and perhaps just a remnant of the emotional scene he had just gone through with Edith Rogers.

But then the music stopped. The girl bowed to the applause of an unseen audience and, when she had taken her bows, looked directly out of the screen into Finchley's face.

She smiled at him and said very clearly, 'You'd better get out of here, Finchley!'

Finchley screamed, picked up a vase, and threw it across the room. He did not think or aim, but the piece of ceramic smashed into the television set, splintering the glass in front to be followed by a loud noise and a puff of smoke. But clearly – ever so clearly from the smoking shambles of its interior – came the girl's voice again.

'You'd better get out of here, Finchley,' the voice said, and Finchley screamed again as he raced out of the room, into the hall and up the stairs.

On the top landing he turned and shouted down the stairs. 'All right! All right, you machines! You're not going to intimidate *me*! Do you hear me? You are not going to intimidate me! You ... you machines!'

And from down below in the study – dull, methodical, but distinctly audible – came the sound of typewriter keys and Finchley knew what they were writing. He started to cry, the deep, harsh sobs of a man who has gone without sleep, and who has closeted his fears deep inside.

He went blindly into his bedroom and shut the door, tears rolling down his face, making the room into a shimmering, indistinct pattern of satin drapes, pink walls, and fragile Louis XIV furniture, all blurred together in the giant mirror that covered one side of the room.

He flung himself on the bed and buried his face against the pillow. Through the close door he continued to hear the sound of the typewriter keys as they typed out their message over and over again. Finally they stopped and there was silence in the house.

At seven o'clock that evening, Mr Finchley, dressed in a silk bathrobe and a white silk ascot, perched near the pillow of his bed and dialled a number on the ivory-coloured, bejewelled telephone.

'Yes,' he said into the phone. 'Yes. Miss Moore please. Agatha, Bartlett Finchley here. Yes, my dear, it has been a long time.' He smiled, remembering Miss Moore's former attachment to him. 'Which indeed prompts this call,' he explained. 'How about dinner this evening?' His face fell as the words came to him from the other end of the line. 'I see. Well, of course, it *is* short notice. But ... yes ... yes, I see. Yes, I'll call you again, my dear.'

He put the phone down, stared at it for a moment, then picked it up and dialled another number.

'Miss Donley, please,' he said, as if he were announcing a princess entering a state ball. 'Pauline, is this you?' (He was aware that his voice had taken on a false, bantering tone he was unaccustomed to and hated even as he used it.) 'And how's my favourite attractive young widow this evening?' He felt his hand shake. 'Bartlett,' he said. 'Bartlett Finchley. I was wondering if – Oh. I see. I see. Well I'm delighted. I'm simply delighted. I'll send you a wedding gift. Of course. Good night.'

He slammed the telephone down angrily. God, what could be more stupid than a conniving female hell-bent for marriage. He had a dim awareness of the total lack of logic for his anger. But disappointment and the prospect of a lonely evening made him quite unconcerned with logic. He stared at the phone, equating it with his disappointment, choosing to believe at this moment that in the cause and effect of things, this phone had somehow destroyed his plans. He suddenly yanked it out of the wall, flinging it across the room. His voice was tremulous.

'Telephones. Just like all the rest of them. Exactly like all the rest. A whole existence dedicated to embarrassing me or inconveniencing me or making my life miserable.'

He gave the phone a kick and turned his back to it. Bravado crept backwards into his voice.

'Well, who needs you?' he asked rhetorically. 'Who needs any of you? Bartlett Finchley is going out this evening. He's going out to have a wonderful dinner with some good wine and who knows what attractive young lady he may meet during his meanderings. Who knows indeed!'

He went into the bathroom. He studied the thin, aristocratic face that looked back at him from the mirror. Grey, perceptive eyes; thinning but still wavy brown hair; thin expressive lips. If not a strong face, at least an intelligent one. The face of a man who knew what he was about. The face of a thoughtful man of values and awareness.

He opened the medicine cabinet and took out an electric razor. Humming to himself, he plugged it into the wall. adjusted its head, then laid it aside while he put powder on his face. He was dusting off his chin when something made him look down at the electric razor. Its head was staring up at him for all the world like a kind of reptilian beast, gaping at him through a barbed, baleful opening in a grimacing face.

Finchley felt a fear clutch at his insides as he picked up the razor and held it half an arm's length away, studying it thoughtfully and with just a hint of a slowly building tension. This had to stop, he thought. This most definitely and assuredly had to stop.

That idiotic girl was brainless, stupid, and blind – but she had a point. It *was* his imagination. The TV set, the radio, and that damned phone in the other room. It was all part of his imagination. They *were* just machines. They had no entities or purpose or will. He grasped the razor more firmly and started to bring it toward his face. In a brief, fleeting, nightmarish instant the razor seemed to jump out of his hand and attack his face, biting, clawing, ripping at him.

Finchley screamed and flung it away from him, then stumbled backwards against the bathroom door. He scrambled for the ornate gold doorknob, pulled it open and ran stumbling into the bedroom. He tripped over the telephone cord, knocking the receiver off the cradle, and then gasped as a filtered voice came out of the phone.

'Get out of here, Finchley,' it trilled at him. 'Get out of here.'

Down below the typewriter started up again and from the destroyed television set the little Mexican dancer's voice joined the chorus. 'Get out

43

of here, Finchley. Get out of here.'

His hands went to his head, pulling spasmodically at his hair, feeling his heart grow huge inside him as if he were ready to explode and then, joining the rest of the chorus, was the sound of the front-door chimes. They rang several times and after a moment they were the only noises in the house. All the other voices and sounds had stopped.

Finchley tightened his bathrobe strap, went out of the room, and walked slowly down the stairs, letting bravado and aplomb surge back into him until by the time he reached the front door, his face wore the easy smirk of an animal trainer who has just completed placing thousand-pound lions on tiny stools. He adjusted his bathrobe, fluffed out the ascot, raised an eyebrow, then opened the door.

On the porch stood a policeman and, clustered behind him in a semicircle, a group of neighbours. Over their shoulder Finchley could see his car, hanging half over the curb, two deep furrows indicating its passage across the lawn.

'That your car?' the policeman asked him.

Finchley went outside. 'That's correct,' he said coldly. 'It's my car.'

'Rolled down the driveway,' the policeman said accusingly. 'Then across your lawn and almost hit a kid on a bike. You ought to check your emergency brake, mister.'

Finchley looked bored. 'The emergency brake *was* on.'

'I'm afraid it wasn't,' the policeman said, shaking his head. 'Or if it was – it's not working properly. Car rolled right into the street. You're lucky it didn't hit anyone.'

The neighbours made way for Finchley, knowing him to be a man of mercurial moods and an acid, destructive tongue. As he crossed the lawn toward his car, he gazed at a small boy with an all-day sucker in his mouth.

'And how are you this evening, Monstrous?' Mr Finchley said under his breath. He looked his car up and down, back and forth, and felt a cold spasm of fear as the thought came to him that, of all the machines, this was the biggest and the least controllable. Also, wasn't there an odd look about the front end of the thing? The headlights and grill, the bumper. Didn't it resemble a face? Again from deep inside Finchley there blossomed the beginning of hysteria that he had to choke down and hide from the people who were staring at him.

The policeman came up behind him, 'you got the keys?'

'They're in the house,' Finchley said.

'All right then, mister. You'd better pull her back into the garage and then you'd better have those brakes checked first chance you get. Understand?'

There was a pause as Finchley turned his back to him.

'Understand, mister?'

Finchley nodded perfunctorily, then turned and gazed at the circle of faces, his eyes slitted and suspicious. 'All right, dear friends,' he announced, 'you may remain on my property for another three and a half minutes goggling at this amazing sight. I shall then return with my automobile keys. At that time I should like all of you to be off my property or else I shall solicit the aid of this underpaid gendarme to forcibly evict you.' He looked along the line of people, raised an eyebrow and said, 'Understand, clods?'

He very carefully picked his way through the group and headed back toward the house, fastidiously avoiding any contact like a mediaeval baron fresh from a visit to an area of the black plague. Not really frightened of catching it, you understand, but playing it safe, just the same. When he reached his house and left the gaping neighbours behind, his shoulders slumped, the eyebrow went back to normal and his cold, rigidly controlled features suddenly became loose and pliable, the flesh white, the eyes nervous and haunted.

At nine o'clock in the evening, Bartlett Finchley had consumed three quarters of a bottle of excellent bourbon and had forgotten all about going out for the evening. He lay half-dozing on the couch, his well-tailored tuxedo crumpled and unkempt. There was a noise on the stairs and Finchley opened his eyes and turned his head so that he could stare across the room toward the hall. The telephone repairman was just coming down the steps. He paused at the entrance to the living room, looked in.

'She's operating all right now, Mr Finchley,' the repairman said.

'I'm deeply indebted,' Finchley answered acidly. 'Convey my best to Alexander Graham Bell.'

The telephone repairman lingered at the entrance. 'You tripped over the cord – is that what you said?'

'If that's what I said,' Finchley barked at him, 'that's precisely what happened.'

The repairman shrugged. 'Well, you're the boss, Mr Finchley. But those wires sure look as though they've been yanked out.'

Finchley rose to a sitting position on the couch and carefully smoothed back his hair. He took a cigarette from a hand-carved teakwood on the coffee table, careful that the repairman should not see how his fingers shook as he fitted the cigarette in the holder.

'Do they indeed?' Finchley said, concentrating on the cigarette. 'Proving what a vast storehouse of knowledge you've yet to acquire.' Then, looking up with disdain, he said, 'Good night!'

The repairman went out of the front door and Finchley rose from the couch. He hesitated, then went to the television set. Its broken screen was a yawning abyss into the darkness beyond and Finchley hurriedly backed away from it.

At the bar in the corner of the room, he poured himself a large drink, downed half of it in a gulp, then stared almost challengingly at the television set. It stood in silent defeat, this time shattered beyond any repair and Finchley felt satisfaction. He was about to take another drink when the sound of the clock chimes suddenly clanged into the room. Finchley's glass dropped and broke on the bartop. Again the cold, clammy, impossible fear seized him as he looked toward the empty mantel where the clock had been and then down to the floor where he himself had smashed it into nothingness.

And yet there was the sound of the chimes, loud, deep, resonant and enveloping the room. He ran toward the hall and then stopped. From the study came the sound of the electric typewriter, the keys, then the carriage, then the keys again. And still the chimes of the clock joining as an obbligato and Finchley felt a scream building up in his throat.

He ran into the study in time to see the typewriter finishing a final line. He took a stumbling step and ripped the paper out of the carriage. 'Get out of here, Finchley.' It covered the page, line after line after line. And then suddenly came another horror from the living room. The little dancer's voice that he'd heard on the television set that afternoon.

'Get out of here, Finchley,' it called sweetly. 'Get out of here, Finchley.'

The chimes continued to ring and then, inexplicably, another chorus of voices joined the girls.

'Get out of here, Finchley,' it said, like some kind of vast a capella choir. 'Get out of here, Finchley.' Over and over again. 'Get out of here, Finchley. Get out of here, Finchley. *Get out of here, Finchley!*'

Finchley let out one gasping, agonizing sob and thrust his knuckles into his mouth as once again he ran into the living room and stared wildly around. He picked up a chair and threw it at the television set. It missed and shot past to smash against a fragile antique table holding an expensive lamp, both of which went to the floor with a loud clatter of broken wood and glass. And still the voices, the typewriter, the chimes.

And when Finchley, a steady, constant scream coming from his throat like a grotesque human siren, raced back into the hall and started upstairs, another nightmare was heading toward him from the top. There was the electric razor slithering down, step by step, like a snake with an oversized head.

Finchley's scream stopped and he was unable to conjure up another one, though his mouth was open and his eyes popped and he felt pain clawing the inside of his chest. He tripped and landed on his knees as he tried to reach the door. He yanked at it and finally got it open as the electric razor came unerringly after him.

He tore out into the night, the sounds of his house following him, a deafening chorus of, 'Get out of here, Finchley,' orchestrated for typewriter keys, clock chimes, and the hum of an electric razor.

He tripped again and landed in a heap on the sidewalk. He felt the needle of a rose bush through his trousers as he ran toward the garage and was able to scream once again, as the garage doors creaked open and the headlights of the car inside went on and bathed him in hot, white light.

The engine growled like a jungle beast as the car started to roll slowly out toward him. Finchley yelled for help, ran out to the street, tripped and fell, feeling the shock of protesting nerves as the curb tore a bleeding gash down the side of his face to his jaw.

But he had no time for concern because the car was pursuing him. He ran down the street and back and forth across it, and the car, all by itself, followed the contour of the street and refused to allow Finchley out of its sight. When he went on the sidewalk, the car jumped the curb and followed him. When he went back in the street the car did likewise. It was unhurried, calculating, and patient.

When Finchley reached the corner the car seemed to hesitate for a moment, but then it turned and followed him down the next block. Finchley knew his legs were beginning to give out and he could scarcely breathe. Calling on some hidden resource of logic and calculation to overcome his blinding, numbing fear, Finchley jumped over the white picket fence of one of the houses flanking the road and hid behind its front porch.

The car moved slowly past, stopped after a few yards, shifted itself into reverse and backed to a stop directly in front of the house where Finchley was hiding. It idled there at the curb, engine purring, a patient, unhurried stalker menacingly secure in the knowledge of its own superiority.

Finchley ran diagonally across the lawn back toward his own block. The car shifted its gears, made a U-turn in a wide arc, and again bore down on him. Bartlett Finchley made his legs move back and forth, but they grew heavier and heavier and became harder and harder to lift. His heart beat in spasmodic, agonizing thumps and his lungs were torn bellows wheezing hollowly with over-exertion and fast reaching that moment when they would collapse. Pain coursed through Finchley's body with every breath he took.

As he ran through the night it seemed to Finchley that he'd never done anything else all his life. He tried to prod his panicked mind into some kind of thought, rather than to succumb to the enveloping disaster that followed him with such precision and patience, as if never doubting for one moment that this was simply a cat-and-mouse game and that Finchley was the mouse.

He tripped over his feet and again ploughed head first into the street, causing the blood to run afresh down the side of his face. He lay there for a moment, sobbing and moaning.

But again there was the sound of the engine and again the bright lights played on him. He rose to his hands and knees and looked over his shoulder. The car was not a hundred feet away, moving slowly toward him, its headlights two unblinking eyes, the grill a metal mouth that leered at him.

Finchley got up again and ran, up one street and down another, across a lawn and then back onto the sidewalk, down another street, down another, then back to his own block.

How he kept going and moving and breathing, Finchley could not understand. Each breath seemed his last, each movement the final exertion, but he kept running.

Suddenly he realized he was once more in front of his own house. He turned sharply to run into the driveway, past the side of the house to the back yard. Its tyres shrieked as the car followed him up the driveway, picked up speed as it went into the garage, smashed through the opposite wall and into the back yard to meet Finchley just as he came around the corner.

All of the insides of Bartlett Finchley's body constricted at that moment. His throat, his lungs, his heart, the linings of his stomach. He fell once again to his hands and knees and began to crawl across a rock garden, tasting dirt and salty sweat, an hysterical animal, pleading over and over again to be left alone.

His voice was an insane, gurgling chant as he crawled across his patio, topped sideways over a flight of concrete steps, and wound up on the edge of his swimming pool. The lights went on and the pool appeared a blue, shimmering square carved out of a piece of darkness.

Finchley's head slowly rose. The car slowly rolled down the small hill toward him, ploughing up the earth, the garden, pushing aside the patio furniture in its slow, steady, inexorable pursuit. And Finchley, on all fours, his face streaked with mud and torn flesh, his eyes glazed, his hair lying over his forehead in damp masses, his clothes flapping in torn fragments around him, had now reached the pinnacle of his fear. This was the climax of the nightmare. It was the ultimate fear barrier and he smashed through it with one final, piercing, inhuman scream.

He flung up his hands in front of his face, rose to his shaking feet as the car bore down on him. Then he felt himself falling through space. The wet surface of the pool touched him, gathered him in and sucked him down.

In that one brief, fragmentary moment that lay between life and death he saw the headlights of the car blinking down at him through the water and he heard the engine let out a deep roar like some triumphant shout.

Then he could see nothing more because he had reached the bottom of the pool and his eyes had become simply unfunctioning, useless orbs that stared out of a dead face.

A narrow, irregular line of water drops led from the pool to the ambulance where the body of Bartlett Finchley lay on a stretcher. A policeman with a notebook scratched his head and looked from the pool over to an intern who walked around the ambulance past the fascinated faces of neighbours and then closed the two rear doors.

'Heart attack, Doc?' the policeman asked him. 'Is that what you think?'

The intern looked up from his examination papers and nodded. 'That's what it appears.'

The policeman looked over toward the pool again, then up past the crushed garden and overturned patio chairs, to the big, gaping hole in the rear end of the garage where an automobile sat, mute and unrevealing.

'Neighbours said they heard him shouting about something during the night,' the policeman said. 'Sounded scared.' He scratched his head again. 'Whole Goddamn thing doesn't make much sense. The busted garage wall, those tyre tracks leading to the pool.' He shook his head. 'The whole Goddamned thing doesn't make any sense at all.'

The intern leaned against the closed ambulance doors, then looked down at the water drops that led to the pool's edge. 'Funny thing,' the intern said softly.

'What is?' asked the policeman.

'A body will float for a while after a drowning.'

'So?' the policeman inquired.

The intern jerked a thumb in the direction of the ambulance, 'This one wasn't floating. It was down at the bottom of the pool just as if it had been weighted or something. But that's the thing. It hadn't been weighted. It was just lying there down at the bottom. That'll happen, you know, after a couple of weeks when the body gets bloated and water-logged.' The intern pointed toward the pool. 'He hadn't been there but a few hours.'

'It was his face,' the policeman said with a shudder in his voice. 'Did you look closely at his face, Doc? He looked so scared. He looked so God-awful scared. What do you suppose scared him?'

The intern shook his head. 'Whatever it was,' he said, 'it's a little item that he's taken with him!'

He folded the examination papers, went around to the passenger's seat of the ambulance and opened the door, motioning the driver to move out. The policeman folded up his notebook. He was suddenly conscious of all the neighbours.

'All right, everybody,' he said, putting firmness and authority into his voice, 'the show's over. Come on now . . . everybody get out of here and go home!'

The crowd slowly dispersed in soft, whispering groups, voices muted by the fascination of death that all men carry with them in small pockets deep inside them. The policeman followed them toward the front yard, running over in his mind the nature of the report he'd have to write and wondering how in God's name he could submit such an odd-ball story to the powers that be and have it make any sense. A press photographer was the last man on the scene. He took pictures of the pool, the departing ambulance, a few of the neighbours. He asked a few questions of the latter, jotted them down hurriedly and, as an afterthought, took a picture of the car that was sitting in the garage. Then he got in his own car and drove away.

The following afternoon there was a funeral and only about nine people came because Bartlett Finchley had so few friends. It was a sombre but business-like affair with a very brief eulogy and a dry-eyed response. Bartlett Finchley was laid to rest, a lightly lamented minor character, who would be remembered more for his final torment than for his lifelong tartness. The conglomeration of odd and unrelated circumstances surrounding his death – the demolished garage, the destroyed garden, the wrecked patio – were grist for some gossip and conjecture. But they soon palled and were forgotten.

About a year later, the caretaker of the cemetery where Mr Finchley was interred, a taciturn, grim man, did tell an odd story to his wife one night at the dinner table. He had been using a power mower on the cemetery lawn, and two or three times it had shown a disconcerting tendency to veer off to the right and smash against Bartlett Finchley's tombstone.

It had elicited little concern on the part of the caretaker and he brought it up only as an additional support for a rather long standing contention, oft stated to his wife, that those Goddamned power mowers weren't worth their salt and a good old reliable hand mower was really a far better item, albeit slower. And after this briefest of colloquies with his wife, the caretaker had eaten a Brown Betty for dessert, watched television, and gone to bed.

Nothing more was said.

Nothing more needed to be said.

A Woman Seldom Found

WILLIAM SANSOM

ONCE A YOUNG MAN WAS ON A visit to Rome.

It was his first visit; he came from the country – but he was neither on the one hand so young nor on the other hand so simple as to imagine that a great and beautiful capital should hold out finer promises than anywhere else. He already knew that life was largely illusion, that though wonderful things could happen, nevertheless as many disappointments came in compensation: and he knew, too, that life could offer a quality even worse – the probability that nothing would happen at all. This was always more possible in a great city intent on its own business.

Thinking in this way, he stood on the Spanish steps and surveyed the momentous panorama stretched before him. He listened to the swelling hum of the evening traffic and watched as the lights went up against Rome's golden dusk. Shining automobiles slunk past the fountains and turned urgently into the bright Via Condotti, neon-red signs stabbed the shadows with invitations; yellow windows of buses were packed with faces intent on going somewhere – everyone in the city seemed intent on the evening's purpose. He alone had nothing to do.

He felt himself the only person alone of everyone in the city. But searching for adventure never brought it – rather kept it away. Such a mood promised nothing. So the young man turned back up the steps, passed the lovely church and went on up the cobbled hill towards his hotel. Wine-bars and food-shops jostled with growing movement in those narrow streets. But on the broad pavements of the Vittorio Veneto, under the trees mounting to the Borghese Gardens, the high world of Rome would be filling the most elegant cafes in Europe to enjoy with aperitifs the twilight. That would be the loneliest of all! So the young man kept to the quieter, older streets on his solitary errand home.

In one such street, a pavementless alley between old yellow houses, a street that in Rome might suddenly blossom into a secret piazza of fountain and baroque church, a grave secluded treasure-place – he noticed that he was alone but for the single figure of a woman walking down the hill towards him.

As she drew nearer, he saw that she was dressed with taste, that in her carriage was a soft Latin fire, that she walked for respect. Her face was veiled, but it was impossible to imagine that she would not be beautiful. Isolated thus with her, passing so near to her, and she symbolizing the adventure of which the evening was so empty – greater melancholy gripped him. He felt wretched as the gutter, small, sunk, pitiful. So that he rounded his shoulders and lowered his eyes – but not before casting one furtive glance into hers.

He was so shocked at what he saw that he paused, he stared, shocked, into her face. He had made no mistake. She was smiling. Also – she too had hesitated. He thought instantly: 'Whore?' But no – it was not that kind of smile, though as well it was not without affection. And then amazingly she spoke:

'I – I know I shouldn't ask you ... but it is such a beautiful evening – and perhaps you are alone, as alone as I am ...'

She was very beautiful. He could not speak. But a growing elation gave him the power to smile. So that she continued, still hesitant, in no sense soliciting:

'I thought ... perhaps ... we could take a walk, an aperitif. ...'

At last the young man achieved himself:

'Nothing, *nothing* would please me more. And the Veneto is only a minute up there.'

She smiled again.

'My home is just here. ...'

They walked in silence a few paces down the street, to a turning that the young man had already passed. This she indicated. They walked to where the first humble houses ended in a kind of recess. In the recess was set the wall of a garden, and behind it stood a large and elegant mansion. The woman, about whose face shone a curious pale glitter – something fused of the transparent pallor of fine skin, of grey but brilliant eyes, of dark eyebrows and hair of lucent black – inserted her key in the garden gate.

They were greeted by a servant in velvet livery. In a large and exquisite salon, under chandeliers of fine glass and before a moist green courtyard where water played, they were served with a frothy wine. They talked. The wine – iced in the warm Roman night – filled them with an inner warmth of exhilaration. But from time to time the young man looked at her curiously.

With her glances, with many subtle inflections of teeth and eyes she was inducing an intimacy that suggested much. He felt he must be careful. At length he thought the best thing might be to thank her – somehow thus to root out whatever obligation might be in store. But here she interrupted him, first with a smile, then with a look of some sadness. She begged him to spare himself any perturbation: she knew it was strange, that in such a situation he might suspect some second purpose: but the simple truth remained that she was lonely and – this with a certain deference – something perhaps in him, perhaps in that moment of dusk in the street, had proved to her inescapably attractive. She had not been able to help herself.

The possibility of a perfect encounter – a dream that years of disillusion will never quite kill – decided him. His elation rose beyond control. He believed her. And thereafter the perfections compounded. At her invitation they dined. Servants brought food of great delicacy; shell-fish, fat bird-flesh, soft fruits. And afterwards they sat on a sofa near the courtyard, where it was cool. Liqueurs were brought. The servants retired. A hush fell upon the house. They embraced.

A little later, with no word, she took his arm and led him from the room. How deep a silence had fallen between them! The young man's heart beat fearfully – it might be heard, he felt, echoing in the hall whose marble they now crossed, sensed through his arm to hers. But such excitement rose now from certainty. Certainty that at such a moment, on such a charmed evening – nothing could go wrong. There was no need to speak. Together they mounted the great staircase.

In her bedroom, to the picture of her framed by the bed curtains and dimly naked in a silken shift, he poured out his love; a love that was to be eternal, to be always perfect, as fabulous as this their exquisite meeting.

Softly she spoke the return of his love. Nothing would ever go amiss, nothing would ever come between them. And very gently she drew back the bedclothes for him.

But suddenly, at the moment when at last he lay beside her, when his lips were almost upon hers – he hesitated.

Something was wrong. A flaw could be sensed. He listened, felt – and then saw the fault was his. Shaded, soft-shaded lights by the bed – but he had been so careless as to leave on the bright electric chandelier in the centre of the ceiling. He remembered the switch was by the door. For a fraction, then, he hesitated. She raised her eyelids – saw his glance at the chandelier, understood.

Her eyes glittered. She murmured:

'My beloved, don't worry – don't move. . . .'

And she reached out her hand. her hand grew larger, her arm grew longer and longer, it stretched out through the bed-curtains, across the long carpet, huge and overshadowing the whole of the long room, until at last its giant fingers were at the door. With a terminal click, she switched out the light.

The Squaw

BRAM STOKER

NURNBERG AT THE TIME WAS not so much exploited as it has been since then. Irving had not been playing *Faust,* and the very name of the old town was hardly known to the great bulk of the travelling public. My wife and I being in the second week of our honeymoon, naturally wanted someone else to join our party, so that when the cheery stranger, Elias P. Hutcheson, hailing from Isthmain City, Bleeding Gulch, Maple Tree County, Neb., turned up at the station at Frankfurt, and casually remarked that he was going on to see the most all-fired old Methusaleh of a town in Yurrup, and that he guessed that so much travelling alone was enough to send an intelligent, active citizen into the melancholy ward of a daft house, we took the pretty broad hint and suggested that we should join forces. We found, on comparing notes afterwards, that we had each intended to speak with some diffidence or hesitation so as not to appear too eager, such not being a good compliment to the success of our married life; but the effect was entirely marred by our both beginning to speak at the same instant – stopping simultaneously and then going together again. Anyhow, no matter how, it was done; and Elias P. Hutcheson became one of our party. Straightway Amelia and I found the pleasant benefit; instead of quarrelling, as we had been doing, we found that the restraining influence of a third party was such that we took every opportunity of spooning in odd corners. Amelia declares that ever since she has, as the result of that experience, advised all her friends to take a friend on the honeymoon. Well we 'did' Nurnberg together, and much enjoyed the racy remarks of our Transatlantic friend, who, from his quaint speech and his wonderful stock of adventures, might have stepped out of a novel. We kept for the last object of interest in the city to be visited the Burg, and on the day appointed for the visit strolled round the outer wall of the city by the eastern side.

The Burg is seated on a rock dominating the town, and an immensely deep fosse guards it on the northern side. Nurnberg has been happy in that it was never sacked; had it been it would certainly not be so spick and span perfect as it is at present. The ditch has not been used for centuries, and now its base is spread with tea-gardens and orchards, of which some of the trees are of quite respectable growth. As we wandered round the wall, dawdling in the hot July sunshine, we often paused to admire the views spread before us, and in especial the great plain covered with towns and villages and bounded with a blue line of hills, like a landscape of Claude Lorraine. From this we always turned with new delight to the city itself, with its myriad of quaint old gables and acre-wide red roofs dotted with dormer windows, tier upon tier. A little to our right rose the towers of the Burg, and nearer still, standing grim, the Torture Tower, which was, and is, perhaps, the most interesting place in the city. For centuries the tradition of the Iron Virgin of Nurnberg has been handed down as an instance of the horrors of cruelty of which man is capable; we had long looked forward to seeing it; and here at last was its home.

In one of our pauses we leaned over the wall of the moat and looked down. The garden seemed quite fifty or sixty feet below us, and the sun pouring into it with an intense, moveless heat like that of an oven. Beyond rose the grey, grim wall seemingly of endless height, and losing itself right and left in the angles of bastion and counter-scarp. Trees and bushes crowned the wall, and above again towered the lofty houses on whose massive beauty Time has only set the hand of approval. The sun was hot and we were lazy; time was our own, and we lingered, leaning on the wall. Just below us was a pretty sight – a great black cat lying stretched in the sun, whilst round her gambolled prettily a tiny black kitten. The mother would wave her tail for the kitten to play with, or would raise her feet and push away the little one as an encouragement to further play. They were just at the foot of the wall, and Elias P. Hutcheson, in order to help the play, stooped and took from the walk a moderate-sized pebble.

'See!' he said 'I will drop it near the kitten, and they will both wonder where it came from.'

'Oh, be careful,' said my wife; 'you might hit the dear little thing!'

'Not me, ma'am,' said Elias P. 'Why I'm as tender as a Maine cherry-tree. Lor, bless ye, I wouldn't hurt the poor pooty little critter more'n I'd scalp a baby. An' you may bet your variegated socks on that! See, I'll drop it fur away on the outside so's not to go near her!' Thus saying, he leaned over and held his arm out at full length and dropped the stone. It may be that there is some attractive force which draws lesser matters to greater; or more probably that the wall was not plumb but sloped to its base –we not noticing the inclination from above; but the stone fell with a sickening thud that came up to us through the hot air, right on the kitten's head, and shattered out its little brains then and there. The black cat cast a swift upward glance, and we saw her eyes like green fire fixed an instant on Elias P. Hutcheson; and then her attention was given to the kitten, which lay still with just a quiver of her tiny limbs, whilst a thin red stream trickled from a gaping wound. With a muffled cry, such as a human being might give, she bent over the kitten, licking its wound and moaning. Suddenly she seemed to realise that it was dead, and again threw her eyes up at us. I shall never forget the sight, for she looked the perfect incarnation of hate. Her green eyes blazed with lurid fire, and the white, sharp teeth seemed to almost shine through the blood which dabbled her mouth and whiskers. She gnashed her teeth, and her claws stood out stark and at full length on every paw. Then she made a wild rush up the wall as if to reach us, but when the momentum ended fell back, and further added to her horrible appearance for she fell on the kitten, and rose with her back fur smeared with its brains and blood. Amelia turned quite faint, and I had to lift her back from the wall. There was a seat close by in the shade of a spreading plane-tree, and here I placed her whilst she composed herself. Then I went back to Hutcheson, who stood without moving, looking down on the angry cat below.

As I joined him he said:

'Wall, I guess that air the savagest beast I ever see – 'cept once when an Apache squaw had an edge on a half-breed what they nicknamed 'Splinters' 'cos of the way he fixed up her papoose which he stole on a raid just to show that he appreciated the way they had given his mother the fire torture. She got that kinder look so set on her face that it just seemed to grow there. She followed Splinters more'n three years till at last the braves got him and handed him over to her. They did say that no man, white or Injun, had ever been so long a-dying under the tortures of the Apaches. The only time I ever see her smile was when I wiped her out. I kem on the camp just in time to see Splinters pass in his checks, and he wasn't sorry to go either. He was a hard citizen, and though I never could shake with him after that papoose business – for it was bitter bad, and he should have been a white man, for he looked like one – I see he had got paid out in full. Durn me, but I took a piece of his hide from one of his skinnin' posts an' had it made into a pocket-book. It's here now!' and he slapped the breast pocket of his coat.

Whilst he was speaking, the cat was continuing her frantic efforts to get up the wall. She would take a run back and then charge up, sometimes reaching an incredible height. She did not seem to mind the heavy fall which she got each time but started with renewed vigour; and at every tumble her appearance became more horrible. Hutcheson was a kind-hearted man – my wife and I had both noticed little acts of kindness to animals as well as to persons – and he seemed concerned at the state of fury to which the cat had wrought herself.

'Wall now!' he said, 'I du declare that that poor critter seems quite desperate. There! there! poor thing, it was all an accident – though that won't bring back your little one to you. Say! I wouldn't have had such a thing happen for a thousand! Just shows what a clumsy fool of a man can do when he tries to play! Seems I'm darned slipperhanded to even play with a cat. Say Colonel!' – it was a pleasant way he had to bestow titles freely – 'I hope your wife don't hold no grudge against me on account of this unpleasantness? Why, I wouldn't have had it occur on no account.'

He came over to Amelia and apologised profusely, and she with her usual kindness of heart hastened to assure him that she quite understood that it was an accident. Then we all went again to the wall and looked over.

The cat missing Hutcheson's face had drawn back across the moat, and was sitting on her haunches as though ready to spring. Indeed, the very instant she saw him she did spring, and with a blind unreasoning fury, which would have been grotesque, only that it was so frightfully real. She did not try to run up the wall, but simply launched herself at him as though hate and fury could lend her wings to pass straight through the great distance between them. Amelia, womanlike, got quite concerned, and said to Elias P. in a warning voice:

'Oh! You must be careful. That animal would try to kill you if she were here; her eyes look like positive murder.'

He laughed out jovially. 'Excuse me, ma'am,' he said, 'but I can't help laughin'. Fancy a man that has fought grizzlies an' Injuns bein' careful of bein' murdered by a cat!'

When the cat heard him laugh, her whole demeanour seemed to change. She no longer tried to jump or run up the wall, but went quietly over, and sitting again beside the dead kitten began to lick and fondle it as though it were alive.

'See!' said I, 'the effect of a really strong man. Even that animal in the midst of her fury recognises the voice of a master, and bows to him!'

'Like a squaw!' was the only comment of Elias P. Hutcheson, as we moved over the wall and each time saw the cat following us. At first she had kept going back to the dead kitten, and then as the distance grew greater took it in her mouth and so followed. After a while, however, she abandoned this, for we saw her following all alone; she had evidently hidden the body somewhere. Amelia's alarm grew at the cat's persistence, and more than once she repeated her warning; but the American always laughed with amusement, till finally, seeing that she was beginning to be worried he said:

'I say ma'am, you needn't be skeered over that cat. I go heeled, I du!' Here he slapped his pistol pocket at the back of his lumbar region. 'Why sooner'n have you worried, I'll shoot the critter, right here an' risk the police interferin' with a citizen of the United States for carryin' arms contrairy to reg'lations!' As he spoke he looked over the wall, but the cat, on seeing him, retreated, with a growl, into a bed of tall flowers, and was hidden. He went on: 'Blest if that ar critter ain't got more sense of what's good for her than most Christians. I guess we've seen the last of her! You bet, she'll go back now to that busted kitten and have a private funeral of it, all to herself!'

Amelia did not like to say more, lest he might, in mistaken kindness to her, fulfil his threat of shooting the cat: and so went on and crossed the little wooden bridge leading to the gateway whence ran the steep paved roadway between the Burg and the pentagonal Torture Tower. As we crossed the bridge we saw the cat again down below us. When she saw us her fury seemed to return, and she made frantic efforts to get up the steep wall. Hutcheson laughed as he looked down at her, and said:

'Good-bye, old girl. Sorry I injured your feelin's, but you'll get over it in time! So long!' And then we passed through the long, dim archway and came to the gate of the Burg.

When we came out again after our survey of this most beautiful old place which not even the well-intended efforts of the Gothic restorers of forty years ago have been able to spoil – though their restoration was then glaring white – we seemed to have quite forgotten the unpleasant episode of the morning. The old lime tree with its great trunk gnarled with the passing of nearly nine centuries, the deep well cut through the heart of the rock by those captives of old, and the lovely view from the city wall whence we heard, spread over almost a full quarter of an hour, the multitudinous chimes of the city, had all helped to wipe out from our minds the incident of the slain kitten.

We were the only visitors who had entered the Torture Tower that morning – so at least said the old custodian – and as we had the place all to ourselves were able to make a minute and more satisfactory survey than would have otherwise been possible. The custodian, looking to us as the sole source of his gains for the day, was willing to meet our wishes in any way. The Torture Tower is truly a grim place, even now when many thousands of visitors have sent a stream of life, and the joy that follows life, into the place; but at the time I mention it wore its primmest and most gruesome aspect. The dust of ages seemed to have settled on it, and the darkness and the horror of its memories seem to have become sentient in a way that would have satisfied the Pantheistic soul of Philo or Spinoza. The lower chamber where we entered was seemingly, in its normal state, filled with incarnate darkness; even the hot sunlight streaming in through the door seemed to be lost in the vast thickness of the walls, and only showed the masonry rough as when the builder's scaffolding had come down, but coated with dust and marked here and there with patches of dark stain which, if walls could speak, could have given their own dread memories of fear and pain. We were glad to pass up the dusty wooden staircase, the custodian leaving the outer door open to light us somewhat on our way; for to our eyes the one long-wick'd, evil-smelling candle stuck in a sconce on the wall gave an inadequate light. When we came up through the open trap in the corner of the chamber overhead, Amelia held on to me so tightly that I could actually feel her heart beat. I must say for my own part that I was not surprised at her fear, for this room was even more gruesome that that below. Here there was certainly more light, but only just sufficient to realise the horrible surroundings of the place. The builders of the tower had evidently intended that only they who should gain the top should have any of the joys of light and prospect. There, as we had noticed from below, were ranges of windows, albeit of mediaeval smallness, but elsewhere in the tower were only a very few narrow slits such as were habitual in places of mediaeval defence. A few of these only lit the chamber, and these so high up in the wall that from no part could the sky be seen through the thickness of the walls. In racks, and leaning in disorder against the walls, were a number of headsmen's swords, great double-handed weapons with broad blade and keen edge. Hard by were several blocks whereon the necks of the victims had lain, with here and there deep notches where the steel had bitten through the guard of flesh and shored into the wood. Round the chamber, placed in all sorts of irregular ways, were many implements of torture which made one's heart ache to see – chairs full of spikes which give instant and excruciating pain; chairs and couches with dull knobs whose torture was seemingly less, but which, though slower, were equally efficacious; racks, belts, boots, gloves, collars, all made for compressing at will; steel baskets in which the head could be slowly crushed into pulp if necessary; watchmen's hooks with long handle and knife that cut at resistance – this a specialty of the old Nurnberg police system; and many, many other devices for man's injury to man. Amelia grew quite pale with the horror of the things, but fortunately did not faint, for being a little overcome she sat down on a torture chair, but jumped up again with a shriek, all tendency to faint gone. We both pretended that it was the injury done to her dress by the dust of the chair, and the rusty spikes which had upset her, and Mr Hutcheson acquiesced in accepting the explanation with a kind-hearted laugh.

But the central object in the whole of this chamber of horrors was the engine known as the Iron Virgin, which stood near the centre of the room. It was a rudely-shaped figure of a woman, something of the bell order, or, to make a closer comparison, of the figure of Mrs Noah in the children's Ark, but without that slimness of waist and perfect *rondeur* of hip which marks the aesthetic type of the Noah family. One would hardly have recognised it as intended for a human figure at all had not the founder shaped on the forehead a rude semblance of a woman's face. This machine was coated with rust without, and covered with dust; a rope was fastened to a ring in the front of the figure, about where the waist should have been, and was drawn through a pulley, fastened on the wooden pillar which sustained the flooring above. The custodian pulling this rope showed that a section of the front was hinged like a door at one side; we then saw that the engine was of considerable thickness, leaving just room enough inside for a man to be placed. The door was of equal thickness and of great weight, for it took the custodian all his strength, aided though he was by the contrivance of the pulley, to open it. This weight was partly due to the fact that the door was of manifest purpose hung so as to throw its weight downwards, so that it might shut of its own accord when the strain was released. The inside was honeycombed with rust – nay more, the rust alone that comes through time would hardly have eaten so deep into the iron walls; the rust of the cruel stains was deep indeed! It was only, however, when we came to look at the inside of the door that the diabolical intention was manifest to the full. Here were several long spikes, square and massive, broad at the base and sharp at the points, placed in such a position that when the door should close the upper ones would pierce the eyes of the victim, and the lower ones his heart and vitals. The sight was too much for poor Amelia, this time she fainted dead off, and I had to carry her down the stairs, and place her on a bench outside till she recovered. That she felt it to the quick was afterwards shown by the fact that my eldest son bears to this day a rude birthmark on his breast, which has, by family consent, been accepted as representing the Nurnberg Virgin.

When we got back to the chamber we found Hutcheson still opposite the Iron Virgin; he had been evidently philosophising, and now gave us the benefit of his thought in the shape of a sort of exordium.

'Wall I guess I've been learnin' somethin' here while madam has been gettin' over her faint. 'Pears to me that we're a long way behind the times on our side of the big drink. We uster think out on the plains that the Injun could give us points in tryin' to make a man oncomfortable; but I guess you old mediaeval law-and-order party could raise him every time. Splinters was pretty good in his bluff on the squaw, but this here young miss held a straight flush all high on him. The points of them spikes air sharp enough still, though even the edges air eaten out by what uster be on them. It'd be a good thing for our Indian section to get some specimens of this here play-toy to send round to the Reservations jest to knock the stuffin' out of the bucks, and the squaws too, by showing them as how old civilisation lays over them at their best. Guess but I'll get in that box a minute jest to see how it feels!'

'Oh no! no!' said Amelia. 'It is too terrible!'

'Guess, ma'am nothin's too terrible to the explorin' mind. I've been in some queer places in my time. Spent a night inside a dead horse while a prairie fire swept over me in Montana Territory – an' another time slept inside a dead buffler when the Comanches was on the war path an' I didn't keer to leave my kyard on them. I've been two days in a caved-in tunnel in the Billy Broncho gold mine in New Mexico, an' was one of the four shut up for three parts of a day in the caisson what slid over her side when we was settin' the foundations of the Buffalo Bridge. I've not funked an odd experience yet, an' I don't propose to begin now!'

We saw that he was set on the experiment, so I said: 'Well, hurry up, old man, and get through it quick!'

'All right, General,' said he, 'But I calculate we ain't quite ready yet.

The gentlemen, my predecessors, what stood in that thar canister, didn't volunteer for the office – not much! And I guess there was some ornamental tyin' up before the big stroke was made. I want to go into this thing fair and square, so I must get fixed up proper first. I dare say this old galoot can rise some string and tie me up accordin' to sample?'

This was said interrogatively to the old custodian, but the latter, who understood the drift of his speech, though perhaps not appreciating to the full the niceties of dialect and imagery, shook his head. His protest was, however, only formal and made to be overcome. The American thrust a gold piece into his hand saying, 'Take it, pard; it's your pot; and don't be skeer'd. This ain't no necktie party that you're asked to assist in!' He produced some thin frayed rope and proceeded to bind our companion, with sufficient strictness for the purpose. When the upper part of his body was bound, Hutcheson said:

'Hold on a moment, Judge. Guess I'm too heavy for you to tote into the canister. You jest let me walk in, and then you can wash up regardin' my legs!'

Whilst speaking he had backed himself into the opening which was just enough to hold him. It was a close fit and no mistake. Amelia looked on with fear in her eyes, but she evidently did not like to say anything. Then the custodian completed his task by tying the American's feet together so that he was now absolutely helpless and fixed in his voluntary prison. He seemed to really enjoy it, and the incipient smile which was habitual to his face blossomed into actuality as he said:

'Guess this here Eve was made out of the rib of a dwarf! There ain't much room for a full-grown citizen of the United States to hustle. We uster make our coffins more roomier in Idaho territory. Now, Judge, you just begin to let this door down, slow on me. I want to feel the same pleasure as the other jays had when those spikes began to move toward their eyes!'

'Oh no! no! no!' broke in Amelia hysterically, 'It is too terrible! I can't bear to see it! – I can't! I can't!'

But the American was obdurate. 'Say, Colonel,' said he, 'why not take Madame for a little promenade? I wouldn't hurt her feelin's for the world; but now that I am here, havin' kem eight thousand miles, wouldn't it be too hard to give up the very experience I've been pinin' an' pantin' fur? A man can't get to feel like canned goods every time! Me and the Judge here'll fix up this thing in no time an' then you'll come back, an' we'll all laugh together!'

Once more the resolution that is born of curiosity triumphed, and Amelia stayed holding tight to my arm and shivering whilst the custodian began to slacken slowly inch by inch the rope that held back the iron door. Hutcheson's face was positively radiant as his eyes followed the first movements of the spikes.

'Wall!' he said, 'I guess I've not had enjoyment like this since I left Noo

York. Bar a scrap with a French sailor at Wapping – an' that warn't much of a picnic neither – I've not had a show fur real pleasure in this dodrotted Continent, where there ain't no b'ars nor no Injuns, an' wheer nary man goes unheeled. Slow there, Judge! Don't you rush this business! I want a show for my money this game – I du!'

The custodian must have had in him some of the blood of his predecessors in that ghastly tower, for he worked the engine with a deliberate and excruciating slowness which after five minutes, in which the outer edge of the door had not moved half as many inches, began to overcome Amelia. I saw her lips whiten, and felt her hold upon my arm relax. I looked around an instant for a place whereon to lay her, and when I looked at her again found that her eye had become fixed on the side of the Virgin. Following its direction I saw the black cat crouching out of sight. Her green eyes shone like danger lamps in the gloom of the place, and their colour was heightened by the blood which still smeared her coat and reddened her mouth. I cried out:

'The cat! look out for the cat!' for even then she sprang out before the engine. At this moment she looked like a triumphant demon. Her eyes blazed with ferocity, her hair bristled out till she seemed twice her normal size, and her tail lashed about as does a tiger's when the quarry is before it. Elias P. Hutcheson when he saw her was amused, and his eyes positively sparkled with fun as he said:

'Darned if the squaw hain't got on all her war paint! Jest give her a shove off if she comes any of her tricks on me, for I'm so fixed everlastingly by the boss, that durn my skin if I can keep my eyes from her if she wants them! Easy there Judge! Don't you slack that ar rope or I'm euchered!'

At this moment Amelia completed her faint, and I had to clutch hold of her round the waist or she would have fallen to the floor. Whilst attending to her I saw the black cat crouching for a spring, and jumped up to turn the creature out.

But at that instant, with a sort of hellish scream, she hurled herself, not as we expected at Hutcheson, but straight at the face of the custodian. Her claws seemed to be tearing wildly as one sees in the Chinese drawings of the dragon rampant, and as I looked I saw one of them light on the poor man's eye, and actually tear through it and down his cheek, leaving a wide band of red where the blood seemed to spurt from every vein.

With a yell of sheer terror which came quicker than even his sense of pain, the man leaped back, dropping as he did so the rope which held back the iron door. I jumped for it, but was too late, for the cord ran like lightening through the pulley-block, and the heavy mass fell forward from its own weight.

As the door closed I caught a glimpse of our poor companion's face. He seemed frozen with terror. His eyes stared with a horrible anguish as if dazed, and no sound came from his lips.

And then the spikes did their work. Happily the end was quick, for when I wrenched open the door they had pierced so deep that they had locked in the bones of the skull through which they had crushed, and actually tore him – it – out of his iron prison till, bound as he was, he fell at full length with a sickly thud upon the floor, the face turning upward as he fell.

I rushed to my wife, lifted her up and carried her out, for I feared for her very reason if she should wake from her faint to such a scene. I laid her on the bench outside and ran back. Leaning against the wooden column was the custodian moaning in pain whilst he held his reddening handkerchief to his eyes. And sitting on the head of the poor American was the cat, purring loudly as she licked the blood which trickled through the gashed sockets of his eyes.

I think no one will call me cruel because I seized one of the old executioner's swords and shore her in two as she sat.

The Cloth of Madness

SEABURY QUINN

JAMISON ALVARDE, THE NOTED interior decorator, was dying. His family physician knew it; the neat, white-starched nurse – almost waspish in her impersonal devotion to her professional duties – knew it; the eminent graduate of Hopkins and Vienna, called into consultation, whose fee would be more than the annual maintenance of a poor ward in the City Hospital, knew it; Alvarde's next of kin, a niece and nephew, hastily summoned from halfway across the continent, knew it; and – which was most important of all – Jamison Alvarde knew it.

The last rays of the December sun slanted through the casement of the sick man's room, falling directly upon the bed and illuminating his face as though with a rosy spotlight. This was fitting and proper, since he was the principal character in the short tragedy about to be acted.

It was not an ill-looking face the afternoon sun bent its brief valedictory on. Jamison Alvarde's plentiful hair was iron-grey in colour, and swept up from his high, placid forehead in an even-crested pompadour. His eyebrows were heavy and intensely black, and the deep-set eyes beneath them were as grey as frosted glass. While his long illness had etched fine lines about the corners of his eyes and at the ends of his narrow lips, it had not robbed his cheeks of their rich, olive colouring, and even in the ante-chamber of death his mouth retained its firm, almost cruel, set.

In a far corner of the room, the family physician whispered fussily to the next of kin. Waiting for a patient to die is a tiresome business, especially when one is hungry and when one expects to have roast lamb with caper sauce for dinner.

'Yes, yes!' he was saying. 'Mr Alvarde has had a great deal of trouble the last year, a very great deal of trouble. He has never been the same since that terrible affliction fell upon his wife and his friend at his country place in the Highlands. A tragedy, my dear young friends, a very great tragedy; quite enough to break anyone's health. I've no doubt that Mr Alvarde's present illness is directly traceable to that – er – unfortunate occurrence; no doubt whatever.'

Alvarde's wasted, nervous hands paused a minute in their restless fumbling at the bedclothes. His thin, straight lips twisted a moment in an inscrutable smile, and his pale lids slowly lowered till they nearly hid his roving grey eyes. With that unwonted sharpening of the senses which often comes to those weakened in body, he had heard the doctor's whispered conversation.

The mention of that June morning when his wife and friend had been discovered in their rooms, hopelessly imbecile, brought no grimace of horror to the sick man's face. Rather, he smiled whimsically to himself, as if there were something not altogether unpleasing to him in the memory.

The afternoon sun sank behind the line of hills across the river. The great specialist got into his fur-lined overcoat and his imported motor car and drove home. The family physician left instructions to be called immediately there was any change in Mr Alvarde's condition and went home to his lamb and capers. The next of kin tiptoed downstairs to dinner, and Jamison Alvarde was left alone with his thoughts and the white-clad nurse.

'Nurse,' Alvarde raised himself slightly on one elbow, 'open the lower left-hand drawer of the desk and bring me the little black book you'll find there....

'Now give me my fountain pen, please,' he directed, when the sharp-featured girl had brought the book and adjusted the pillows behind his back.

The nurse withdrew to the window, watching the last spots of sunlight on the river, and Alvarde commenced to scribble on the flyleaf of the book before him. As he wrote — difficult, for he was very weak — the same faintly reminiscent smile he had worn in the afternoon settled again on his tight-pressed lips.

Half, three-quarters, of an hour his pen travelled laboriously over the book's blank leaf; then, with a faint sigh of satisfaction, as at a task well done, Jamison Alvarde lay back upon his pillows.

The nurse crossed the room to remove the book and pen, paused a second, looking into her patient's face, then hurried to the telephone to call the family physician.

She might have saved herself the trouble and allowed the good doctor to finish his dinner in peace. Jamison Alvarde had no need of his services, or of any other physician's. Jamison Alvarde was dead.

The customary three days elapsed, and in the morning of the fourth they took Jamison Alvarde from his residence on the Drive to a new home in Shadow Lawns. It was a very stylish and dignified funeral, for Alvarde had left a respectable estate, and the high-priced funeral director who conducted the obsequies understood his business thoroughly.

On the fifth evening Alvarde's attorney — a dapper little man, much addicted to wing collars and neat, double-breasted jackets — called and read his deceased client's last will and testament to the next of kin, who, as was expected, proved also to be his residuary legatees, one-third of the estate having been left the dead man's wife. Then the lawyer took up the business of straightening out Alvarde's affairs.

'It will be necessary,' he informed them, stuffing the will back into his saddle-leather brief-bag, 'to let me have all your uncle's papers which are in the house.'

'The only papers of Uncle Jamison's we found in the house are bound in a little black book,' the niece remarked. 'He'd been writing in it just before he died.'

When the little book was forthcoming and he had tucked it in his overcoat pocket, the lawyer seated himself in his automobile and started on his homeward trip. Before the motor had traversed two blocks he took out the slender volume and opened it. He was no waster of time; his capacity for making every minute count had won him his enviable standing at the bar.

The first words which struck his eye were written in a weak, straggling hand – the words Jamison Alvarde had penned on the night of his death.

'What the devil!' the lawyer exclaimed as he slowly spelt out the sprawling characters of the inscription. 'Did the old fool try to make another will on his death bed?'

I, Jamison Alvarde, being of sound mind and memory (which is more than some I know are), but being weakened in body, and about to die, do declare the following statement to be the true explanation of the mental derangement which occurred to my wife, Edith, and my friend, Hector Fuller, at my country place last summer.

My one regret in publishing this memoir is that I shall not be present to hear the comments of the fools who have sympathized with me in my 'affliction'.

JAMISON ALVARDE.

'Humph,' the lawyer turned the scribbled fly-leaf over. Following the leaf upon which the scrawling introduction was scratched, the book was written in a firm, clear hand, the hand Alvarde had penned in health. The pages were filled with detached paragraphs, like diary entries, but undated. The first sheet was torn diagonally across, so that the first sentence was incomplete.

...somewhat cool for this time of year. Excepting the tower, the house is fully completed, and we shall live here while the carpenters are finishing up.

I have asked Hector Fuller up for the weekend. Edith protested against his coming; for, with every woman's loathing of the unattainable, she has taken his impregnable bachelorhood as a deliberate affront. But Fuller is my friend, and whether Edith is pleased with his visit or not is of no moment to me. This is my house and Edith is my wife; and I mean to be master of both.

Fuller came this afternoon. I watched Edith narrowly when she greeted him, for I had determined to cut her allowance in two if she were discourteous to him. She blushed to the roots of her hair when she gave him her hand, and his face coloured, too. Fuller looked uncomfortably at me out of the corner of his eye, and I caught a sidelong glance from Edith which reminded me of the look Regina, my Irish setter, gives me when she knows I am about to beat her for worrying the poultry. I was sorry for Fuller; having to be polite to a hostess who dislikes you must be an uncomfortable business.

Fuller is a sly old dog! Pretending misogynist that he is, always preaching the joys of an Eveless Eden, I've caught him red-handed in a flirtation with some silly woman – and, I believe, a married one, at that.

This afternoon I came in late from inspecting the decorations of the Grayson mansion drawing-room, and as I was about to mount the stairs I noticed a bit of folded paper lying on the floor. The sight of this trash on my hall carpet angered me; I hate such clutter and disorder.

I was about to pitch the scrap of paper in the fireplace when I noticed that it was house stationery and was written on. I opened it and recognized Fuller's writing.

My darling:
The ordeal was terrible. How I hate to have to pretend; how you hate it; how I hate to see you obliged to do it! If only you-know-who would go away, so that we could cast aside this hideous mask, how happy we could be!

My dear, there are not words enough in all the languages combined to tell you how I love you. I'd rather kiss the print of your little foot in the dust than the lips of any other woman on earth. Oh, if only that brute could be got rid of!

Only a few more days, dear one, and the ghastly comedy we're playing will be finished. Then I will be at liberty to meet you once more at the old accustomed place.

My darling, my darling, I love you!

HECTOR.

'H'm!' I muttered, as I shoved the slushy thing into my jacket pocket. 'That "brute" they're so anxious to be rid of is undoubtedly the lady's husband. Abuse the husband to flatter the wife, every time!'

We husbands are always brutes once we're pledged, with bell, book and candle, to provide a living for some worthless female. We're precious enough before they've put their halter on us, though, I've noticed! I dare say Edith thinks me a brute, though the devil knows it keeps my nose to the grindstone, paying for her fripperies.

I found Fuller in his room, dressing for dinner, and gave him his note.

'Next time, don't be so careless with your *billets d'amour*,' I cautioned. 'Someone might find it and pass it along to her husband, you know.'

The shot went home. Fuller turned as pale as if a ghost had entered the room with me, and faced about with a spring, as though expecting me to attack him.

'I suppose you'll demand that I leave the house immediately?' he asked, when he saw that I had no immediate intention of assaulting him.

I laughed. 'My dear boy,' I told him, 'it's a matter of perfect indifference to me how much you protest your hatred of the sex in public and flirt with them in private. Only you're so ungodly absent-minded with your mash notes! I found that gummy thing of yours lying in plain sight on the hall floor. Is your brain so addled with love of the fair one that you forget to post your letters to her?'

He regarded me a moment as a condemned criminal might the messenger who brings his reprieve, and jammed the note into his waistcoat pocket.

'Thanks, old man,' he gulped. 'Awfully good of you to bring it to me!'

'Oh, that's all right!' I assured him as I started to my own room to dress. 'Don't bother about thanking me.'

Funny, what a doddering fool love can make of a sensible man like Fuller.

I wish Fuller would use more discretion in his choice of a light o' love. She uses lily of the valley.

Lily of the valley is the one thing about which Edith has defied me. Time and again I've ordered her never to bring the pestilent stuff into my house, and every time I've found a phial of it on her dressing-table I've flung it out of the window; yet her hair, her fingertips and her lingerie fairly reek with it, despite my commands.

I came out late from town this evening, and Grigsby, the butler, informed me that Fuller had dropped out during the afternoon and had put up in his usual room. I stopped in his quarters for a little chat before going to bed. He had already turned in, but was still awake. His clothes were sprawled all over the room in the careless way he always throws them when he crawls into bed, and I had no choice but to share the same chair with his dinner jacket.

I'd scarcely gotten seated and lighted a cigar when I began to notice the unpleasant proximity of lily of the valley scent. At first I couldn't make out where the annoying odour came from, but a few sniffs localized its source. Fuller's dinner jacket was redolent with the perfume.

'No doubt you find it very comforting to have your lady love rest her head on your shoulder,' I grumbled, 'but, for heaven's sake, why don't you get her to use some other scent? I loathe this stuff as the devil does holy water.'

He gaped at me like a goldfish viewing the sunlight through the walls of an aquarium.

'What d'ye mean, "some other scent?"' he asked. 'I don't follow you.'

'Why, this infernal lily of the valley.' I tapped the scented shoulder of his jacket in explanation. 'I hate it more than any other smell this side of H. S. Edith uses it until I think, sometimes, I'll have to commit suicide – or murder – to get rid of it.'

Fuller's eyes widened like a cat's in the twilight.

'D-does Edith – Mrs Alvarde – use that perfume?' he stammered.

'You're devilish well right, she does, *ad nauseam!*' I growled as I got up. 'And for the Lord's sake, get your woman to use something else. It's bad enough to have Edith scenting up the place, without your lugging a lot of the stuff in on your clothes.'

I have thought the whole matter over very carefully. I shall kill them both.

The scales fell from my eyes tonight (perhaps I would better say they were snatched from my eyes) and I see what a blind, fatuous, doting cuckold I have been for the fiend only knows how long. The shame of it is maddening.

Spring has broken early this year and summer is upon us; the roses in the lower garden are budding out, and the double row of dogwood trees which flanks the drive is festival-clad in a white surplice of blossoms.

The decorations of the Grayson house were all completed today, but I had to stay late catching up a few loose ends, so that it was well after dark when I reached home.

Fuller was out on one of the visits which have become rather frequent of late, and he and Edith had dined when I arrived. She was in the music room, strumming idly on the piano and singing softly to herself when I passed through the hall. Fuller had gone to his room for some reason or other. I could hear the sickly sentimental refrain of the popular ballad she was thrumming as I went up the stairs:

> There's a kiss that you get from baby,
>   There's a kiss that you get from Dad,
> There's a kiss that you get from Mother,
>   That's the first real kiss you've had.
> There's a kiss with a tender meaning,

> Other kisses you recall;
> But the kisses I get from you, sweetheart,
> Are the sweetest kisses of all.

Something in the spring air, the shower of pearl moonbeams I'd just driven through, or the appealing lilt of the song downstairs – perhaps all three – set my pulses throbbing at an unwonted tempo; I climbed the last ten steps humming the silly words under my breath:

> There's a kiss with a tender meaning,
> Other kisses you recall. . . .

In his room across the hall from mine Fuller was moving about, alternately whistling and humming the same banal refrain. The words came softly through the closed door of his room:

> Other kisses you recall,
> But the kisses I get from you, sweetheart,
> Are the sweetest kisses of all.

Strange how a snatch of song on a spring evening will carry a man's mind back to scenes he has never thought to see reflected on his memory's screen again. As I knotted my tie I remembered my first sweetheart, pretty and blue-eyed and blonde. I used to have a trick of pulling off her glove when I brought her home from some party, and kissing all five of her pink little fingers.

Poor Elsie; when her husband died he left no insurance and God knows how many children. She came to me for help, but she had no business qualifications, couldn't even type; so there was nothing I could do for her.

Then there was another girl – a slender thing with a painted face, a robemaker's mannequin. Her masculine acquaintances had been the sort who wear coloured derby hats and converse in terms of the race-track and poolroom. I was the first man of breeding she had known, and she was as grateful for the common or garden variety of courtesy as a stray dog for a scrap of meat.

She knew only one medium of exchange, and her timid little offers of passion were pitiful to see.

I gave her three hundred dollars: rather a handsome settlement, considering our respective positions. A child more or less doesn't matter to her kind. . . . I've often wondered what became of her . . .

Fuller was still singing to himself when I finished dressing and went down to the dining-room. Edith had left the house and was sitting on a stone bench at the lower end of the terrace, watching the boats go by on the river below. In her white dinner frock, with the moonlight on her arms and shoulders, she was almost as pale as the marble Psyche at the other end of the walk.

A chilly breath of wind swept up from the river, rustling the dogwood blossoms and shaking the scrim curtains at the dining-room windows. Edith felt it as it passed and shivered a little.

'She'll be cold without her wrap,' I speculated as I poured myself a stiff appetizer of Irish whisky and rang for Grigsby to serve dinner.

A bar from the song recurred to me:

> There's a kiss with a tender meaning...
> But the kisses I get from you, sweetheart...

I went into the music-room, picked up Edith's China-silk scarf, and stepped through the French window to the lawn.

Walking quietly across the short-cut grass, I approached her from the rear, softly humming the refrain.

'But the kisses I get from you, sweetheart, are the sweetest kisses of all,' I finished aloud, dropping the shawl over her narrow shoulders, putting my hands over her eyes, and bending forward to kiss her full upon the lips.

Her white, thin hands flew up from her lap and clasped about my neck, drawing my cheek close to hers.

'Oh!' she cried, and the exclamation was about a sob, 'my dear, my dear, I've been thinking you'd never come! I've been so lonesome.'

Then she struck me playfully on the cheek and gave a sniff of disapproval.

'Hector,' she scolded, 'you've been drinking that horrid Irish whiskey, and you know how I hate it. *He* uses it!'

I released her eyes and sprang back, livid with fury. But my mind worked with the agility of a leaping cat. Before Edith had time to recover from the horror the discovery of her error had given her, I had landed fairly on my mental feet.

I threw back my head and laughed; laughed naturally, laughed uproariously.

'By the Lord Harry, old girl,' I cried, pounding my thigh in a perfect paroxysm of counterfeit mirth, 'that's the best joke I've heard you spring in years! Everyone knows you hate Hector Fuller worse than a hen hates a rainstorm, and now you call me by his name and pretend you thought you were kissing him!' Again I rocked forward in a spasm of laughter. 'And I can just about imagine how you'd have written the ten commandments on his face with your nails if it really had been Fuller!'

All the while I was watching her as a snake does a bird, noting the look of blank amazement which slowly replaced the terrified gaze she had first turned to me when she discovered her mistake.

71

'Let's go in the house and have some music; it's too cold for you out here, dear,' I concluded, as soon as I had calmed down my mock amusement.

She rose as obediently as a well-trained dog and accompanied me across the lawn in silence. But she shuddered slightly as I put my arms about her. Women have no control of their emotions.

While I smoked three or four cigarettes, she played and sang for me, and then, pleading a headache – the old, threadbare excuse of all her sex since Eve first left the garden – begged leave to go up to bed.

I let her go and went out to the stable. I harnessed the cob to the village cart and drove furiously along the country lanes for three hours, lashing the horse fiercely whenever he dropped out of a gallop. The poor brute was nearly foundered when I turned him home; but I was as raging wild as ever.

I have thought the whole matter over very carefully. I shall kill them both.

Last night I said I should kill them both. Today I know I *must* kill them. A sentence from Fuller's treacherous note to Edith has been pounding in my head all day with the monody of a funeral dirge:

'. . . if that brute could only be got rid of!'

When faithless wives and false friends conspire to be rid of an inconvenient husband the number of his days is appointed. The dockets of our criminal courts bear eloquent testimony of that.

A weakling would seek divorce as the easy solution of my difficulty; but I am no maudlin fool, ready to efface myself, leaving the way clear for them to flaunt their triumph and my dishonour before the world.

I must be very careful in my execution of these two. Except for them, no one must suspect my vengeance; for it is no part of my plan to die like a felon for having exacted the justice which the law denies me.

I must kill them, but I must be careful – very careful.

If I were a superstitious man I should say that the Fates have decided to aid me in the furtherance of my plans. While I was lunching at the Republique today, Howard Enright dropped into the chair opposite me. I greeted him sourly enough, for I was in no mood for conversation, but he refused to be rebuffed.

He is just back from an extended tour of the East, where he has picked up enough expensive junk for his house to fill three museums and impoverish half a dozen millionaires. Despite my curt answers, he rambled on about the thousand and one *objets de vertu* he'd lugged halfway around the world, until I was ready to believe that he'd brought the whole *Arabian Nights* home with him. Othello's tales of

... anthropophagi,
And men whose heads do grow below their shoulders,

were hackneyed beside the wonders Enright would display at his galleries.

He had a jade Buddha that caught and held the sunlight until the beholder was ready to swear that the image was filled with living fire. He had lachrymatories from Persia -- tall, spindle-necked bottles, coming in pairs, into which the Persian widows wept, that the fullness of the bottles might be an outward and visible sign of the fullness of their grief at their husband's taking-off. He had a great fan from Korea, where there was an ancient custom that no widow might remarry till her husband's grave was dry. The fan, he explained, was to be used by the lady in hastening the aridness of her lord's burial mound. He had bit of porcelain from the dynasties of Han and Ming -- things so fragile that the Chinese called them 'frozen air,' and so precious that they were worth their weight in rubies.

I was thoroughly bored by his graphic cataloguing of the stock of his junkshop, and had given up the attempt to stifle a yawn, when he wound up with:

'And I've something else, Alvarde, that will appeal to you as an interior decorator.'

'Indeed?' I masked the yawn with my hand.

'Yes, sir. Weirdest thing you ever saw; regular old marrow-freezer! They call it "the cloth of madness," and there's a legend to the effect that whoever looks at it loses his reason. Some vengeful old rajah had it woven for the special benefit of some friends he suspected of forgetting that the harem is sacred, inviolate.'

'Well, did it work?' I queried, more for the sake of politeness than anything else.

'They say it did. According to tradition he had an asylumful of crazy friends and acquaintances in less than no time. Anyhow, I couldn't get one of the natives to look at the thing. Rummy lot, these Indians.'

I smiled my appreciation of the wily old maharajah's finesse. 'What does it look like, this "cloth of madness" of yours?'

'Oh,' Enright spread his hands wide in preparation for an eloquent description. 'It's -- it's -- it's -- Oh, hang it all, man, I can't describe the beastly thing to you! All red and full of funny, twisty black lines like snakes and lizards and why, Alvarde, it's like an X-ray of a guilty conscience! Come around to the shop and see for yourself; I'd never be able to make you imagine the thing's damnable fascination.'

'There might be an idea for some bizarre pattern in wallhanging,' I reflected. 'New designs are hard to find nowadays.' So I went with him to the shop.

He undid several yards of cocomatting wrappings and unfurled a small oblong of crimson cloth for my inspection.

At first sight of the thing I was ready to laugh in his face; for, save for a rather unusual combination of involuted and convoluted black lines and stripes on the cloth's red ground, it seemed to differ in no particular from hundreds of other Oriental tapestries.

Enright must have seen the unspoken scepticism in my face, for the corners of his small hazel eyes wrinkled in amusement.

'Go ahead and laugh,' he invited, 'but I'll bet you ten dollars that you'll be ready to cry "nough" by the time you've looked at it steadily for five minutes.'

For answer I drew a bill from my pocket and placed it on a tabouret, without taking my eyes from the bit of weaving.

Enright matched my note with one of his, and drew back, smiling whimsically at me through the smoke of his cigar.

'Hand me your ten when the five minutes are up,' I ordered, keeping my gaze fixed on the cloth.

'Easy now,' he counselled, glancing at his watch; 'you've only been looking forty seconds, so far.'

One who has never tried it has no conception of how time drags while the eyes are focused on an immovable object. In the quiet of the storeroom I could hear the ticking of Enright's watch distinctly, and the ticks seemed a minute apart. An almost uncontrollable desire to rub my eyes, to shut them, to direct them anywhere but at the cloth, came over me. The writhing broad and narrow black bands on the ruby surface seemed to be slowly coming to life. They wound and twisted, one upon another, like the shadows of scores of snakes suspended in the sunlight. They seemed alternately to advance and retreat upon their glaring resting-place, and my eyes ached with the effort to follow their serpentine movements.

I began to be obsessed with the thought that there really were reptiles – dozens of them, scores of them, hundreds of them – behind me; that they would drop upon me any moment, smearing my body with their loathsome slime, tearing my flesh with their fangs, filling my blood with their deadly venom.

'Time up?' I called, my voice sounding hoarse and croaking in my own ears.

'Only two minutes more to go,' Enright answered pleasantly.

'I'll – stick – it – out – if – it – kills – me!' I muttered between my teeth, and, covering my eyes with my hands, fell choking and gasping to my knees.

The infernal cloth had won. Scornful and determined as I had been, it had worn my nerves to shreds and made a whimpering, fear-crazed thing of me in three minutes.

'How much will you take for that thing, Enright?' I asked, when I had recovered my composure to some extent.

'More than you're able to give, son,' he replied. 'I'll get a half-grown fortune from some museum for that bit of fancy work or my name isn't Howard Enright.'

'Well,' I temporized, 'will you rent it to me, then? I'd like to have a modified copy of it made by my paper manufacturer. Some client with a diseased mind might want a chamber of horrors done, and a denatured copy of this cloth would be just the thing.'

'Promise me on your honour as a gentleman not to have a duplicate made, and I'll lend it to you for forty-eight hours for nothing,' Enright offered.

'Done!' I agreed.

I took the tapestry to my papermaker this afternoon. I have ordered two rolls of paper made in exact imitation of it. I shall paper the unfinished tower room with it.

The trap is set. Working at night, and without help, I have hung the walls and ceiling of the tower attic room with the paper. This room is small, hardly more than a large closet, and, being originally intended for a lumber room, is without windows or other communication with the outside except a small fresh-air vent in the roof.

With an idea of obtaining the maximum amount of room for storage purposes, I had dispensed with all wood trim and had the door made flush with the wall. This renders the place ideal for my purpose, for I am able to cover every fractional inch of wall space with the paper; so that, when the door is closed, the maddening design is presented to the gaze from every direction except the floor. This I have painted white, the better to reflect the glare from the cluster of high-power nitrogen-filled electric lights I have placed in the ceiling.

Early this morning, when I had finally completed my work, I switched on the full force of light and looked about me.

From above, the glare of the electric bulbs beat down like the fires that destroyed Sodom and Gomorrah; from the white floor the reflection smote my eyes like splinters of incandescent metal, and from the walls and ceiling the writhing, tortuous design of the demoniacal paper glared like (to use Enright's description) 'an X-ray of a guilty conscience.'

I had been careful to leave the door open when I tried my experiment. Lucky for me I did; for I had scarcely glanced once round the hideous apartment when I began to feel the same panic fear I had experienced when I first looked at the cloth in Enright's store. My eyes seemed bulging from their sockets; my breath came hot and quick, like the breath of a sleeper bound fast in a nightmare, and I all but lost my sense of direction. It was with great effort that I found the open door and staggered through it, with the sweat of mortal terror standing on my forehead.

I have been very good to Edith these last few days. I have endeavoured to anticipate her every wish; have come back from the city loaded with bonbons and flowers like a country bumpkin wooing his sweetheart; I have doubled her allowance of spending money.

Last evening, after dinner, she kissed me, of her own volition. I felt my plan for vengeance weaken a little as her arms went around my neck.... Fool! Her lips are soiled with another man's kisses; her arms are tainted with the embraces of her paramour.

I looked into her eyes, warm and brown and bright, and wondered how often they had shone with love of Fuller. How long, I wondered, had it been since the same arm which rested on my shoulder had clasped the neck of the man who called himself my friend – and stole my honour like a common thief?

I shall invite Fuller to the house to spend the weekend. My trap is set; now to snare the quarry.

It is done.

Last week I mentioned casually to Edith that I had asked Fuller up for the weekend. I saw her eyes brighten at the suggestion, but chose to misinterpret the sign.

'It's no use making a fuss about it,' I told her. 'I know you don't like him; but I want him here, so you might just as well make the best of it.'

She made no reply, simply rose and left the room. As a play-actor Edith is a sad failure. I suppose she feared her joy would be too apparent, even to a doting fool husband if she remained.

When Fuller came I made a great show of urging her to be courteous to him, and greeted him cordially myself.

Fuller's was a charming personality. Quick-witted, loquacious, well read and much travelled, he was an ideal guest, providing his own and his host's entertainment. We passed a pleasant afternoon together.

I never saw Edith more charming than at dinner that night. There was a faint flush in her face, her eyes were very bright. She was wearing a gown of silver over sapphire, and had a jasmine blossom pinned in the smooth coils of her chocolate-coloured hair.

The corners of my mouth flexed grimly at sight of the flower. Once, when I was in South America, I had seen a vicious knife duel between two men, and when I asked the cause of the brawl, I was told that one had offered the other's sister a jasmine bloom. Jasmine, they explained, was the symbol of inconstancy. Strange, that of all the flowers in my grounds and conservatory Edith should have chosen the badge of infidelity to wear that night!

From my seat at the head of the table I could see Fuller worshipping Edith with his eyes. There was that in his adoring gaze which gave one to think of a medieval knight kneeling humbly at his fair lady's feet, while her husband was off to the crusades.

We had coffee in the music room. Edith seemed ill at ease, fumbling with her cup, twirling the stem of her liqueur glass between her fingers, toying nervously with her cigarette. Before Fuller and I had finished, she rose abruptly and went to the piano.

There was no light burning in the room, and the moon laid a path of mother-of-pearl across the polished floor. With the silver radiance of the moonlight on the silver meshes of her gown, Edith was white as a wraith of the night. A snatch from Oscar Wilde's *Salome* flashed through my mind:

> She is like a dead woman; a dead woman who covers herself with a veil and goes seeking for lovers.

I smiled to myself in the darkness. 'She will seek no more after tonight,' I reflected.

> 'Ah, moon of my delight, that know'st no wane,
> The moon of heav'n is rising once again;
> How oft hereafter rising shall she look
> Through this same garden after one – in vain?'

she sang. I rose and began to pace the room.

Gradually, taking great pains to be impersonal about it, I swung the conversation to stories of the vengeance wreaked by outraged husbands on faithless wives and their paramours. Incidentally, I recounted the legend of the cloth of madness; how the Indian prince had demanded his treacherous friends' sanity at the price of their perfidy.

Edith's hands fluttered among the sheets of music on the piano; a leaf of it fell to the floor. Fuller leaped gallantly to his feet to retrieve it for her, and their hands came together in the moonlight. I saw his fingers close round hers and give them a reassuring pressure.

'What would you do, Alvarde, if you caught another man trespassing on your wife's affections?' Fuller suddenly shot at me. 'Kill him?'

Edith gave a short little choking gasp and put her hand to her throat very suddenly. She had always been afraid of me.

'My dear man,' I drawled, 'do I look like such a fool?'

'Fool?'

'Precisely; "fool" is what I said. Why should I hang for another man's sin? I rather think the old rajah's method of revenge would appeal to me.'

'But, you know,' he objected, 'the cloth of madness is only a myth.'

'So is my wife's incontinence,' I answered shortly. 'One is quite as possible as the other.'

And so we let the talk of betrayed friendship and its price drop, and passed to a discussion of interior decorations.

I told them of my more unusual bits of work for a while, then suggested:

'Let's go to the tower rooms. I've evolved a new scheme in wall-hangings for them. One of the rooms especially will interest you two.'

We went through the larger rooms, I pointing out the novelties in colour scheme, pattern and wood trim, they taking only a perfunctory interest in my designs.

At the door of the storeroom I stood aside to let them pass. Edith paused at the threshold, looking questioningly, fearfully, into the velvety darkness of the little chamber. Fuller stepped before her.

'Let me go first,' he said; 'it's dark in there.'

'Yes,' I echoed, all the smouldering resentment I had felt for months flaming up in my voice, 'it is dark in there – we'll lighten it.'

I put out my hand, pushing Edith roughly through the doorway after Fuller, slammed the door, locked it, and pressed the switch which controlled the electric lights. Then I bent listening at the keyhole.

For the space of a long breath all was silent in the little room; then there was a deep-drawn sigh, whether from Edith or Fuller I could not say.

'Well, what's next?' I heard him ask. 'If this is Jamison's idea of a joke, I think he's showing mighty poor taste.'

'Hector,' it was Edith speaking in a still, frightened whisper, 'he *knew*!'

Fuller's steps sounded harshly on the bare, polished floor of the empty room as he strode about it, seeking an exit; his fists pounded the walls in search of the hidden door. I had to stifle the laughter in my throat; for I knew how the rounded walls, the unbroken monotony of the crimson and black paper, and the glaring reflection from the white floor would confound his sense of direction. He was pacing the room like a blind, caged beast, striking the walls again and again in the same place, and meeting with no more success than an imprisoned bumble-bee flying at the transparent walls of a poison-jar.

For several minutes he continued his futile efforts; then I heard him withdraw to the centre of the room.

There was a faint rustle of skirts. She was shrinking up against him.

'She's in his arms, now,' I muttered. 'Let her cling to him; let him hold her. I wish them joy of each other.'

Several minutes more. Then:

'Hector, I'm afraid; I'm terrified. Hold me close, dear.'

I bit my lips. Would that devil's design on the walls never begin to work?

'Hector,' this time the words came quaveringly, as though she were fighting back a chill, 'that paper on the wall – does it seem to you as if the figures on it were moving?'

'Yes, dear.'

'They are like snakes – like horrible twisting snakes. I feel as though they were going to spring at me from the walls.'

'A-a-h!' I murmured to myself. 'They're beginning to notice now.'

Fuller took several quick, decided steps from the room's centre, walking directly toward the door. I drew back and seized a chair, ready to strike him down if he succeeded in breaking through the light wooden frame. I had not counted on his retaining his faculties so long, and had taken no precautions to reinforce the lock, trusting the paper with which it was covered to mask the door effectively.

Within a foot or so of the door he paused irresolutely, waited a moment, and retreated.

'I can't do it!' he almost wailed. 'I can't bear to put my hands against that wall!'

'Hector!' This time there was no mistaking the panic in Edith's voice; every word came with a gasp. 'The paper – the paper on the wall; it – it's – the – cloth – of – madness! It's that awful tapestry he told us about tonight.'

'My God, girl,' his reply came thickly, as though his tongue were swollen in his mouth, 'you're right!'

I could hear them breathing heavily, like spent runners after a race, or those in the presence of mortal danger.

Softly, there came the sound of Edith's sobbing. Very low it was, and very pitiful, like the disconsolate heart-broken sobbing of a little child who has lost its mother, and is afraid.

'Oh!' she whimpered, 'let me hide my face against you, dear. Don't let me look at those ghastly things on the walls. You must shut your eyes, too, dear; you must not look either.'

I waited patiently outside the door. Even closed eyes, I knew, could not withstand the intense glare of those lights and the fascination of those flame-coloured walls.

Her resolution broke even sooner than I had expected.

'I can't bear the darkness,' she wailed. 'I must look, I must see them – the horrible snakes, the hideous snakes that are beckoning to me from the walls. Hold me, Hector, darling; don't let me move – don't let me go to them! Hold me fast in your arms.'

Another pause. Dimly I caught another noise – one that I had not heard before. Sharp and syncopated it was, like the clicking of castanets heard from a distance. It puzzled me at first; then recognition burst upon me, and I had to thrust my tongue against my teeth to keep from laughing aloud. It was a sound I'd heard on very cold nights when I'd passed shivering newsboys filching a little heat from above some engine-room grating. It was the sound of chattering teeth.

It was warm that night; the temperature in that little, poorly ventilated room, with those great lights burning in it, must have been like the entrance to Avernus; yet their teeth were chattering like a monk's clapdish.

I was striding softly across the floor, digging my nails into my palms in an effort to keep from giving audible vent to my feeling of triumph, when my steps were arrested by a titter from the room beyond. Edith was laughing, not mirthfully, but with the shrill cachinnation of hysteria. In a moment her quavering treble was seconded by a deep, masculine baritone. The pair of them were laughing in concert, and from the cracking strain in their voices I knew that they were trying with all their strength to keep silence, yet laughed the harder as they strove.

I turned on my heel and descended to the dining-room. No need to listen further, I knew. A few hours more, at most, and my revenge would be complete. I was shivering a little, myself.

Downstairs, I poured out a stiff peg of Scotch. Raising my glass I looked out into the moonlight, apostrophizing the old rajah who invented the cloth of madness.

'Here's to you, brother!' I said as I turned my glass bottom up.

Shortly after midnight I climbed the stairs to the tower and stopped before the door of the little room where I left them. I listened intently for a minute. There was no more sound from beyond the door than if it had barred the entrance to a tomb.

I pressed the electric switch, reducing the force of the lights within by half, then unlocked the door and opened it a crack, peering through the narrow opening.

Inside, everything was still, still as a nursery at midnight.

Fuller was sitting upright in the middle of the floor, an insane smirk overspreading his face. His collar and tie were undone, his waistcoat was unbuttoned, his shirt-front was partly loosened from its studs, and much wrinkled. His tongue protruded from his mouth, hanging flaccidly over his lower lip, as though he had lost control of it. Altogether, he was a figure of comic tragedy, like that character of Victor Hugo's whose face had been so horribly deformed in childhood, that no matter what his emotion was, he could do nothing but grin.

Nearer the door, just as she had fallen, lay Edith. One arm was extended, the hand resting palm up on the floor, the fingers slightly curled, like a sleeping child's. Her cheek lay pillowed on her arms. Her hair was a little disarranged and the jasmine flower had fallen from it. One of her satin pumps had dropped off and lay gaping emptily beside her, exposing her narrow, silk-cased foot. I could see the veins of her instep showing against the white flesh under her silver-tissue stocking. Her lips were parted very slightly.

The air of the place was heavy with the perfume of lily of the valley.

I gathered her in my arms, and she whimpered a little, like a child that is disturbed in its sleep, as I carried her down to her room.

It was a difficult business disrobing her and getting her into bed, for she seemed to have lost all control of her muscles, even being unable to take the pins from her hair.

Fuller was a heavy man, but somehow I managed to drag him downstairs and tumble him into bed, being careful to scatter his clothes about the room as was his custom when turning in late.

Last of all I returned to the tower and worked like a fiend, obliterating every trace of the wallpaper's design with grey paint I had hidden away for that purpose. Two hours' work, and the little room was as demure in its fresh coating of Quaker drab as a nun's cell. A neat, well-lighted storeroom it was, nothing more. Every lingering sign of the cloth of madness was hidden away forever.

I slept well in the morning next day, rousing only when Grigsby came rushing into my room and shook me roughly by the shoulder.

'Mr Alvarde, sir,' he panted, his eyes bulging from his face like a terrified frog's, 'something terrible has happened, sir!'

'What's the matter?' I growled at him sleepily. 'Cook gone on strike?'

'Oh, no, sir, no!' He wrung his hands together in anguish. 'It's really terrible, sir! Mr Fuller's a-sittin' on the edge of his bed, a-tryin' to put both feet into one leg of his trousers, sir, and he's smilin' something awful.' And Grigsby attempted to twist his heavy features into an imitation of Fuller's demented grin.

I got into my slippers and robe and started across the hall for Fuller's room, running full tilt into Agnes, the waitress. When Edith had failed to come down long after her usual breakfast hour, Agnes had gone upstairs to see what was detaining her, and had come running to me, fear written in every line of her face.

'Oh, sir, something's wrong with Mrs Alvarde! I went in to call her, and she wouldn't answer me, nor look at me, nor nothing; just lies there and laughs and mumbles at herself like she was a baby!'

'You're a pair of fools,' I told her and Grigsby. 'You stay here; I'll go and see for myself.'

It was true. Fuller was as perfect an imbecile as was ever confined in an asylum, and Edith's mental timepiece had been turned back thirty-five years. No babe in arms was ever more helpless in body and mind than she.

The papers and the doctors and the neighbours made a great fuss about it. Everyone sympathized with my unfortunate wife and friend and wondered how I could stand my terrible misfortune with such fortitude. I closed the house and sold it at a loss several months later.

Edith is still at a sanatorium, and the physicians look sorrowfully at me when I go out to visit her, and tell me that she will never be anything but a grown-up infant, though she will probably live to a ripe old age.

Fuller's malady has taken a turn for the worse. Last month they had to restrain him with a strait-jacket. He was raving about some strange kind of cloth – what it was they couldn't make out – and threatening to kill me; me, his best and oldest friend!

'Let me go first, it's dark in there!' Fuller said when he and Edith stood at the entrance of the storeroom. I've often wondered which one of them went into the darkness of insanity first. Edith, I imagine; women have no control of their emotions.

I am a sick man. The physician tells me that there's nothing to worry about, but I read my death sentence in his eyes. If there's such a place as the hell the preachers tell of, I suppose I'll go there. At least, I'll have to die to do it; Edith and Fuller got theirs here, and it will last through all the long years they live like brute beasts in their madhouse cells.

Jamison Alvarde's attorney closed the little black book with a snap and pursed his lips. Anyone looking at him would have said that he was about to whistle.

'Yes,' he said meditatively, tapping his knee with the little book, 'if there's a hell he's undoubtedly there now! It's a pity if he isn't. This scheme of things certainly seems to require a hell – a good hot one, too!'

The Sea Raiders

H. G. WELLS.

UNTIL THE EXTRAORDINARY AFFAIR at Sidmouth, the peculiar species *Haploteuthis ferox* was known to science only generically, on the strength of a half-digested tentacle obtained near the Azores, and a decaying body pecked by birds and nibbled by fish, found early in 1896 by Mr Jennings, near Land's End.

In no department of zoological science, indeed, are we quite so much in the dark as with regard to the deep-sea cephalopods. A mere accident, for instance, it was that led to the Prince of Monaco's discovery of nearly a dozen new forms in the summer of 1895, a discovery in which the before-mentioned tentacle was included. It chanced that a cachalot was killed off Terceira by some sperm whalers, and in its last struggles charged almost to the Prince's yacht, missed it, rolled under, and died within twenty yards of his rudder. And in its agony it threw up a number of large objects, which the Prince, dimly perceiving they were strange and important, was, by a happy expedient, able to secure before they sank. He set his screws in motion, and kept them circling in the vortices thus created until a boat could be lowered. And these specimens were whole cephalopods and fragments of cephalopods, some of gigantic proportions, and almost all of them unknown to science!

It would seem, indeed, that these large and agile creatures, living in the middle depths of the sea, must, to a large extent, for ever remain unknown to us, since under water they are too nimble for nets, and it is only by such rare unlooked-for accidents that specimens can be obtained. In the case of *Haploteuthis ferox*, for instance, we are still altogether ignorant of its habitat, as ignorant as we are of the breeding-ground of the herring or the sea-ways of the salmon. And zoologists are altogether at a loss to account for its sudden appearance on our coast. Possibly it was the stress of a hunger migration that drove it hither out of the deep. But it will be, perhaps, better to avoid necessarily inconclusive discussion, and to proceed at once with our narrative.

The first human being to set eyes upon a living *Haploteuthis* – the first human being to survive, that is, for there can be little doubt now that the wave of bathing fatalities and boating accidents that travelled along the coast of Cornwall and Devon in early May was due to this cause – was a

83

retired tea-dealer of the name of Fison, who was stopping at a Sidmouth boarding-house. It was in the afternoon, and he was walking along the cliff path between Sidmouth and Ladram Bay. The cliffs in this direction are very high, but down the red face of them in one place a kind of ladder staircase has been made. He was near this when his attention was attracted by what at first he thought to be a cluster of birds struggling over a fragment of food that caught the sunlight, and glistened pinkish-white. The tide was right out, and this object was not only far below him, but remote across a broad waste of rock reefs covered with dark seaweed and interspersed with silvery shining tidal pools. And he was, moreover, dazzled by the brightness of the further water.

In a minute, regarding this again, he perceived that his judgment was in fault, for over this struggle circled a number of birds, jackdaws and gulls for the most part, the latter gleaming blindingly when the sunlight smote their wings, and they seemed minute in comparison with it. And his curiosity was, perhaps, aroused all the more strongly because of his first insufficient explanations.

As he had nothing better to do than amuse himself, he decided to make this object, whatever it was, the goal of his afternoon walk, instead of Ladram Bay, conceiving it might perhaps be a great fish of some sort, stranded by some chance, and flapping about in its distress. And so he hurried down the long steep ladder, stopping at intervals of thirty feet or so to take breath and scan the mysterious movement.

At the foot of the cliff he was, of course, nearer his object than he had been; but, on the other hand, it now came up against the incandescent sky, beneath the sun, so as to seem dark and indistinct. Whatever was pinkish of it was now hidden by a skerry of weedy boulders. But he perceived that it was made up of seven rounded bodies, distinct or connected, and that the birds kept up a constant croaking and screaming, but seemed afraid to approach it too closely.

Mr Fison, torn by curiosity, began picking his way across the wave-worn rocks, and, finding the wet seaweed that covered them thickly rendered them extremely slippery, he stopped, removed his shoes and socks, and coiled his trousers above his knees. His object was, of course, merely to avoid stumbling into the rocky pools about him, and perhaps he was rather glad, as all men are, of an excuse to resume, even for a moment, the sensations of his boyhood. At any rate, it is to this, no doubt, that he owes his life.

He approached his mark with all the assurance which the absolute security of this country against all forms of animal life gives its inhabitants. The round bodies moved to and fro, but it was only when he surmounted the skerry of boulders I have mentioned that he realized the horrible nature of the discovery. It came upon him with some suddenness.

The rounded bodies fell apart as he came into sight over the ridge, and displayed the pinkish object to be the partially devoured body of a human being, but whether of a man or woman he was unable to say. And the rounded bodies were new and ghastly-looking creatures, in shape somewhat resembling an octopus, and with huge and very long and flexible tentacles, coiled copiously on the ground. The skin had a glistening texture, unpleasant to see, like shiny leather. The downward bend of the tentacle-surrounded mouth, the curious excrescence at the bend, the tentacles, and the large intelligent eyes, gave the creatures a grotesque suggestion of a face. They were the size of a fair-sized swine about the body, and the tentacles seemed to him to be many feet in length. There were, he thinks, seven or eight at least of the creatures. Twenty yards beyond them, amid the surf of the now returning tide, two others were emerging from the sea.

Their bodies lay flatly on the rocks, and their eyes regarded him with evil interest; but it does not appear that Mr Fison was afraid, or that he realized that he was in any danger. Possibly his confidence is to be ascribed to the limpness of their attitudes. But he was horrified, of course, and intensely excited and indignant at such revolting creatures preying upon human flesh. He thought they had chanced upon a drowned body. He shouted to them, with the idea of driving them off, and, finding they did not budge, cast about him, picked up a big rounded lump of rock, and flung it at one.

And then, slowly uncoiling their tentacles, they all began moving towards him – creeping at first deliberately, and making a soft purring sound to each other.

In a moment Mr Fison realized that he was in danger. He shouted again, threw both his boots and started off, with a leap, forthwith. Twenty yards off he stopped and faced about, judging them slow, and behold! the tentacles of their leader were already pouring over the rocky ridge on which he had just been standing!

At that he shouted again, but this time not threatening, but a cry of dismay, and began jumping, striding, slipping, wading across the uneven expanse between him and the beach. The tall red cliffs seemed suddenly at a vast distance, and he saw, as though they were creatures in another world, two minute workmen engaged in the repair of the ladder-way, and little suspecting the race for life that was beginning below them. At one time he could hear the creatures splashing in the pools not a dozen feet behind him, and once he slipped and almost fell.

They chased him to the very foot of the cliffs, and desisted only when he had been joined by the workmen at the foot of the ladder-way up the cliff. All three of the men pelted them with stones for a time, and then hurried to the cliff top and along the path towards Sidmouth, to secure assistance and a boat, and to rescue the desecrated body from the clutches of these abominable creatures.

And, as if he had not already been in sufficient peril that day, Mr Fison went with the boat to point out the exact spot of his adventure.

As the tide was down, it required a considerable detour to reach the spot, and when at last they came off the ladder-way, the mangled body had disappeared. The water was now running, submerging first one slab of slimy rock and then another, and the four men in the boat – the workmen, that is, the boatman, and Mr Fison – now turned their attention from the bearings off shore to the water beneath the keel.

At first they could see little below them, save a dark jungle of laminaria, with an occasional darting fish. Their minds were set on adventure, and they expressed their disappointment freely. But presently they saw one of the monsters swimming through the water seaward, with a curious rolling motion that suggested to Mr Fison the spinning roll of a captive balloon. Almost immediately after, the waving streamers of laminaria were extraordinarily perturbed, parted for a moment, and three of these beasts became darkly visible, struggling for what was probably some fragment of the drowned man. In a moment the copious olive-green ribbons had poured again over this writhing group.

At that all four men, greatly excited, began beating the water with oars and shouting, and immediately they saw a tumultuous movement among the weeds. They desisted to see more clearly, and as soon as the water was smooth, they saw, as it seemed to them, the whole sea bottom among the weeds set with eyes.

'Ugly swine!' cried one of the men. 'Why, there's dozens!'

And forthwith the things began to rise through the water about them. Mr Fison has since described to the writer this startling eruption out of the waving laminaria meadows. To him it seemed to occupy a considerable time, but it is probable that really it was an affair of a few seconds only. For a time nothing but eyes, and then he speaks of tentacles streaming out and parting the weed fronds this way and that. Then these things, growing larger, until at last the bottom was hidden by their intercoiling forms, and the tips of tentacles rose darkly here and there into the air above the swell of the waters.

One came up boldly to the side of the boat, and, clinging to this with three of its sucker-set tentacles threw four others over the gunwale, as if with an intention either of over-setting the boat or of clambering into it. Mr Fison at once caught up the boathook, and, jabbing furiously at the soft tentacles, forced it to desist. He was struck in the back and almost pitched overboard by the boatman, who was using his oar to resist a similar attack on the other side of the boat. But the tentacles on either side at once relaxed their hold at this, slid out of sight, and splashed into the water.

'We'd better get out of this,' said Mr Fison, who was trembling violently. He went to the tiller, while the boatman and one of the workmen seated themselves, and began rowing. The other workman stood up in the fore part of the boat, with the boathook, ready to strike any more tentacles that might appear. Nothing else seems to have been said. Mr Fison had expressed the common feeling beyond amendment. In a hushed, scared mood, with faces white and drawn, they set about escaping from the position into which they had so recklessly blundered.

But the oars had scarcely dropped into the water before dark, tapering, serpentine ropes had bound them, and were about the rudder; and creeping up the sides of the boat with a looping motion came the suckers again. The men gripped their oars and pulled, but it was like trying to move a boat in a floating raft of weeds. 'Help here!' cried the boatman, and Mr Fison and the second workman rushed to help lug at the oar.

Then the man with the boathook – his name was Ewan, or Ewen – sprang up with a curse, and began striking downward over the side, as far as he could reach, at the bank of tentacles that now clustered along the boat's bottom. And, at the same time, the two rowers stood up to get a better purchase for the recovery of their oars. The boatman handed his to Mr Fison, who lugged desperately, and, meanwhile, the boatman opened a big clasp-knife, and, leaning over the side of the boat, began hacking at the spring arms upon the oar shaft.

Mr Fison, staggering with the quivering rocking of the boat, his teeth set, his breath coming short, and the veins starting on his hands as he pulled at his oar, suddenly cast his eyes seaward. And there, not fifty yards off, across the long rollers of the incoming tide, was a large boat standing in towards them, with three women and a little child in it. A boatman was rowing, and a little man in a pink-ribboned straw hat and whites stood in the stern, hailing them. For a moment, of course, Mr Fison thought of help, and then he thought of the child. He abandoned his oar forthwith, threw up his arms in a frantic gesture, and screamed to the party in the boat to keep away 'for God's sake!' It says much for the modesty and courage of Mr Fison that he does not seem to be aware that there was any quality of heroism in his action at this juncture. The oar he had abandoned was at once drawn under, and presently reappeared floating about twenty yards away.

At the same moment Mr Fison felt the boat under him lurch violently, and a hoarse scream, a prolonged cry of terror from Hill, the boatman, caused him to forget the party of excursionists altogether. He turned, and saw Hill crouching by the forward rowlock, his face convulsed with terror, and his right arm over the side and drawn tightly down. He gave now a succession of short sharp cries, 'Oh! oh! oh! – oh!' Mr Fison believes that he must have been hacking at the tentacles below the water-line, and have been grasped by them, but, of course, it is quite impossible to say now certainly what had happened. The boat was heeling over, so that the gunwale was within ten inches of the water, and both Ewan and the other labourer were striking down into the water, with oar and boathook, on either side of Hill's arm. Mr Fison instinctively placed himself to counterpoise them.

Then Hill, who was a burly, powerful man, made a strenuous effort, and rose almost to a standing position. He lifted his arm, indeed, clean out of the water. Hanging to it was a complicated tangle of brown ropes; and the eyes of one of the brutes that had hold of him, glaring straight and resolute, showed momentarily about the surface. The boat heeled more and more, and the green-brown water came pouring in a cascade over the side. Then Hill slipped and fell with his ribs across the side, and his arm and the mass of tentacles about it splashed back into the water. He rolled over; his boot kicked Mr Fison's knee as that gentleman rushed forward to seize him, and in another moment fresh tentacles had whipped about his waist and neck, and after a brief, convulsive struggle, in which the boat was nearly capsized, Hill was lugged overboard. The boat righted with a violent jerk that all but sent Mr Fison over the other side, and hid the struggle in the water from his eyes.

He stood staggering to recover his balance for a moment, and as he did so, he became aware that the struggle and the inflowing tide had carried them close upon the weedy rocks again. Not four yards off a stable of rock still rose in rhythmic movements above the inwash of the tide. In a moment Mr Fison seized the oar from Ewan, gave one vigorous stroke, then, dropping it, ran to the bows and leapt. He felt his feet slide over the rock, and, by a frantic effort, leapt again towards a further mass. He stumbled over this, came to his knees and rose again.

'Look out!' cried someone, and a large drab body struck him. He was knocked flat into a tidal pool by one of the workmen, and as he went down he heard smothered, choking cries, that he believed at the time came from Hill. Then he found himself marvelling at the shrillness and variety of Hill's voice. Someone jumped over him, and a curving rush of foamy water poured over him, and passed. He scrambled to his feet, dripping, and, without looking seaward, ran as fast as his terror would let him shoreward. Before him, over the flat space of scattered rocks, stumbled the two workmen – one a dozen yards in front of the other.

He looked over his shoulder at last, and, seeing that he was not pursued, faced about. He was astonished. From the moment of the rising of the cephalopods out of the water, he had been acting too swiftly to fully comprehend his actions. Now it seemed to him as if he had suddenly jumped out of an evil dream.

For there were the sky, cloudless and blazing with the afternoon sun, the sea weltering under its pitiless brightness, the soft creamy foam of the breaking water, and the low, long, dark ridges of rock. The righted boat floated, rising and falling gently on the swell about a dozen yards from shore. Hill and the monsters, all the stress and tumult of that fierce fight for life, had vanished as though they had never been.

Mr Fison's heart was beating violently; he was throbbing to the finger-tips, and his breath came deep.

There was something missing. For some seconds he could not think clearly enough what this might be. Sun, sky, sea, rocks — what was it? Then, he remembered the boatload of excursionists. It had vanished. He wondered whether he had imagined it. He turned, and saw the two workmen standing side by side under the projecting masses of the tall pink cliffs. He hesitated whether he should make one last attempt to save the man Hill. His physical excitement seemed to desert him suddenly, and leave him aimless and helpless. He turned shoreward, stumbling and wading towards his two companions.

He looked back again, and there were now two boats floating, and the one farthest out at sea pitched clumsily, bottom upwards.

So it was *Haploteuthis ferox* made its appearance upon the Devonshire coast. So far, this has been its most serious aggression. Mr Fison's account, taken together with the wave of boating and bathing casualties to which I have already alluded, and the absence of fish from the Cornish coasts that year, points clearly to a shoal of these voracious deep-sea monsters prowling slowly along the sub-tidal coastline. Hunger migration has, I know, been suggested as the force that drove them hither; but, for my own part, I prefer to believe the alternative theory of Hemsley. Hemsley holds that a pack or shoal of these creatures may have become enamoured of human flesh by the accident of a foundered ship sinking among them, and have wandered in search of it out of their accustomed zone; first waylaying and following ships, and so coming to our shores in the wake of the Atlantic traffic. But to discuss Hemsley's cogent and admirably-stated arguments would be out of place here.

It would seem that the appetites of the shoal were satisfied by the catch of eleven people – for so far as can be ascertained, there were ten people in the second boat, and certainly these creatures gave no further signs of their presence off Sidmouth that day. The coast between Seaton and Budleigh Salterton was patrolled all that evening and night by four Preventive Service boats, the men in which were armed with harpoons and cutlasses, and as the evening advanced, a number of more or less similarly equipped expeditions, organized by private individuals, joined them. Mr Fison took no part in any of these expeditions.

About midnight excited hails were heard from a boat about a couple of miles out at sea to the south-east of Sidmouth, and a lantern was seen waving in a strange manner to and fro and up and down. The nearer boats at once hurried towards the alarm. The venturesome occupants of the boat, a seaman, a curate, and two schoolboys, had actually seen the monsters passing under their boat. The creatures, it seems, like most deep-sea organisms, were phosphorescent, and they had been floating, five fathoms deep or so, like creatures of moonshine through the blackness of the water, their tentacles retracted and as if asleep, rolling over and over, and moving slowly in a wedge-like formation towards the south-east.

These people told their story in gesticulated fragments, as first one boat drew alongside and then another. At last there was a little fleet of eight or nine boats collected together, and from them a tumult, like the chatter of a marketplace, rose into the stillness of the night. There was little or no disposition to pursue the shoal, the people had neither weapons nor experience for such a dubious chase, and presently – even with a certain relief, it may be – the boats turned shoreward.

And now to tell what is perhaps the most astonishing fact in this whole astonishing raid. We have not the slightest knowledge of the subsequent movements of the shoal, although the whole south-west coast was now alert for it. But it may, perhaps, be significant that a cachalot was stranded off Sark on June 3. Two weeks and three days after this Sidmouth affair, a living *Haploteuthis* came ashore on Calais sands. It was alive, because several witnesses saw its tentacles moving in a convulsive way. But it is probable that it was dying. A gentleman named Pouchet obtained a rifle and shot it.

That was the last appearance of a living *Haploteuthis*. No others were seen on the French coast. On the 15th of June a dead body, almost complete, was washed ashore near Torquay, and a few days later a boat from the Marine Biological station, engaged in dredging off Plymouth, picked up a rotting specimen, slashed deeply with a cutlass wound. How the former specimen had come by its death it is impossible to say. And on the last day of June, Mr Egbert Caine, an artist, bathing near Newlyn, threw up his arms, shrieked, and was drawn under. A friend bathing with him made no attempt to save him, but swam at once for the shore. This is the last fact to tell of this extraordinary raid from the deeper sea. Whether it is really the last of these horrible creatures it is, as yet, premature to say. But it is believed, and certainly it is to be hoped, that they have returned now, and returned for good, to the sunless depths of the middle seas, out of which they have so strangely and so mysteriously arisen.

The Dunwich Horror

H. P. LOVECRAFT

Gorgons and Hydras, the Chimaeras – dire stories of Celaeno and the Harpies – may reproduce themselves in the grain of superstition – but they were there before. They are transcripts, types – the archtypes are in us, the eternal. How else should the recital of that which we know in a waking sense to be false come to affect us all? It is that we naturally conceive terror from such objects, considered in their capacity of being able to inflict upon us bodily injury? O, least of all! These terrors are of older standing. They date beyond body – *or without the body, they would have been the same.... That the kind of fear here treated is purely spiritual – that it is strong in proportion as it is objectless on earth, that it predominates in the period of our sinless infancy – are difficulties the solution of which might afford some probable insight into our ante-mundane condition, and a peep at least into the shadowland of pre-existence.*

– CHARLES LAMB: Witches and Other Night-Fears

WHEN A TRAVELLER IN north central Massachusetts takes the wrong fork at the junction of Aylesbury pike just beyond Dean's Corners he comes upon a lonely and curious country. The ground gets higher, and the brier-bordered stone walls press closer and closer against the ruts of the dusty, curving road. The trees of the frequent forest belts seem too large, and the wild weeds, brambles and grasses attain a luxuriance not often found in settled regions. At the same time the planted fields appear singularly few and barren; while the sparsely scattered houses wear a surprisingly uniform aspect of age, squalor, and dilapidation. Without knowing why, one hesitates to ask directions from the gnarled solitary figures spied now and then on crumbling doorsteps or on the sloping, rock-strewn meadows. Those figures are so silent and furtive that one feels somehow confronted by forbidden things, with which it would be better to have nothing to do. When a rise in the road brings the mountains in view above the deep woods, the feeling of strange uneasiness is increased. The summits are too rounded and symmetrical to give a sense of comfort and naturalness, and sometimes the sky silhouettes with especial clearness the queer circles of tall stone pillars with which most of them are crowned.

Gorges and ravines of problematical depth intersect the way, and the crude wooden bridges always seem of dubious safety. When the road dips again there are stretches of marshland that one instinctively dislikes, and indeed almost fears at evening when unseen whippoorwills chatter and the fireflies come out in abnormal profusion to dance to the raucous, creepily insistent rhythms of stridently piping bull-frogs. The thin, shining line of the Miskatonic's upper reaches has an oddly serpent-like suggestion as it winds close to the feet of the domed hills among which it rises.

As the hills draw nearer, one heeds their wooded sides more than their stone-crowned tops. Those sides loom up so darkly and precipitously that one wishes they would keep their distance, but there is no road by which to escape them. Across a covered bridge one sees a small village huddled between the stream and the vertical slope of Round Mountain, and wonders at the cluster of rotting gambrel roofs bespeaking an earlier architectural period than that of the neighbouring region. It is not reassuring to see, on a closer glance, that most of the houses are deserted and falling to ruin, and that the broken-steepled church now harbours the one slovenly mercantile establishment of the hamlet. One dreads to trust the tenebrous tunnel of the bridge, yet there is no way to avoid it. Once across, it is hard to prevent the impression of a faint, malign odour about the village street, as of the massed mould and decay of centuries. It is always a relief to get clear of the place, and to follow the narrow road around the base of the hills and across the level country beyond till it rejoins the Aylesbury pike. Afterwards one sometimes learns that one has been through Dunwich.

Outsiders visit Dunwich as seldom as possible, and since a certain season of horror all the signboards pointing towards it have been taken down. The scenery, judged by an ordinary aesthetic canon, is more than commonly beautiful; yet there is no influx of artists or summer tourists. Two centuries ago, when talk of witch-blood, Satan-worship, and strange forest presences was not laughed at, it was the custom to give reasons for avoiding the locality. In our sensible age – since the Dunwich horror of 1928 was hushed up by those who had the town's and the world's welfare at heart – people shun it without knowing exactly why. Perhaps one reason – though it cannot apply to uninformed strangers – is that the natives are now repellently decadent, having gone far along that path of retrogression so common in many New England backwaters. They have come to form a race by themselves, with the well-defined mental and physical stigmata of degeneracy and in-breeding. The average of their intelligence is woefully low, whilst their annals reek of overt viciousness and of half-hidden murders, incests, and deeds of almost unnameable violence and perversity. The old gentry, representing the two or three armigerous families which came from Salem in 1692, have kept somewhat above the general level of decay; though many branches are sunk into the sordid populace so deeply that only their names remain as a key to the origin they disgrace. Some of the Whateleys and Bishops still send their eldest sons to Harvard and Miskatonic, though those sons seldom return to the mouldering gambrel roofs under which they and their ancestors were born.

No one, even those who have the facts concerning the recent horror, can say just what is the matter with Dunwich; though old legends speak of unhallowed rites and conclaves of the Indians, amidst which they called forbidden shapes of shadow out of the great rounded hills, and made wild orgiastic prayers that were answered by loud crackings and rumblings from the ground below. In 1747 the Reverend Abijah Hoadley, newly come to the Congregational Church at Dunwich Village, preached a memorable sermon on the close presence of Satan and his imps; in which he said:

It must be allow'd, that these Blasphemies of an infernall Train of Daemons are Matters of too common Knowledge to be deny'd; the cursed Voices of *Azazel* and *Buzrael,* of *Beelzebub* and *Belial,* being heard now from under Ground by above a Score of credible Witnesses now living. I myself did not more than a Fortnight ago catch a very plain Discourse of evill Powers in the Hill behind my House; wherein there were a Rattling and Rolling, Groaning, Screeching, and Hissing, such as no Things of this Earth cou'd raise up, and which must needs have come from those Caves that only black Magick can discover, and only the Divell unlock.

Mr Hoadley disappeared soon after delivering this sermon, but the text, printed in Springfield, is still extant. Noises in the hills continued to be reported from year to year, and still form a puzzle to geologists and physiographers.

Other traditions tell of foul odours near the hill-crowning circles of stone pillars, and of rushing airy presences to be heard faintly at certain hours from stated points at the bottom of the great ravines; while still others try to explain the Devil's Hop Yard -- a bleak, blasted hillside where no tree, shrub, or grass-blade will grow. Then, too, the natives are mortally afraid of the numerous whippoorwills which grow vocal on warm nights. It is vowed that the birds are psychopomps lying in wait for the souls of the dying, and that they time their eerie cries in unison with the sufferer's struggling breath. If they can catch the fleeing soul when it leaves the body, they instantly flutter away chittering in daemoniac laughter; but if they fail, they subside gradually into a disappointed silence.

These tales, of course, are obsolete and ridiculous; because they come down from very old times. Dunwich is indeed ridiculously old – older by far than any of the communities within thirty miles of it. South of the village one may still spy the cellar walls and chimney of the ancient Bishop house, which was built before 1700; whilst the ruins of the mill at the falls, built in 1806, form the most modern piece of architecture to be seen. Industry did not flourish here, and the nineteenth-century factory movement proved short-lived. Oldest of all are the great rings of rough-hewn stone columns on the hilltops, but these are more generally attributed to the Indians than to the settlers. Deposits of skulls and bones, found within these circles and around the sizeable table-like rock on Sentinel Hill, sustain the popular belief that such spots were once the burial-place of the Pocumtucks; even though many ethnologists, disregarding the absurd improbability of such a theory, persist in believing the remains Caucasian.

It was in the township of Dunwich, in a large and partly inhabited farmhouse set against a hillside four miles from the village and a mile and a half from any other dwelling, that Wilbur Whateley was born at 5 a.m. on Sunday, the second of February, 1913. This date was recalled because it was Candlemas, which people in Dunwich curiously observed under another name; and because the noises in the hills had sounded, and all the dogs of the countryside had barked persistently, throughout the night before. Less worthy of notice was the fact that the mother was one of the decadent Whateleys, a somewhat deformed, unattractive albino woman of 35, living with an aged and half-insane father about whom the most frightful tales of wizardry had been whispered in his youth. Lavinia Whateley had no known husband, but according to the custom of the region made no attempt to disavow the child; concerning the other side of whose ancestry the country folk might – and did – speculate as widely as they chose. On the contrary, she seemed strangely proud of the dark, goatish-looking infant who formed such a contrast to her own sickly and pink-eyed albinism, and was heard to mutter many curious prophecies about its unusual powers and tremendous future.

Lavinia was one who would be apt to mutter such things, for she was a lone creature given to wandering amidst thunderstorms in the hills and trying to read the great odorous books which her father had inherited through two centuries of Whateleys, and which were fast falling to pieces with age and wormholes. She had never been to school, but was filled with disjointed scraps of ancient lore that Old Whateley had taught her. The remote farmhouse had always been feared because of Old Whateley's reputation for black magic, and the unexplained death by violence of Mrs Whateley when Lavinia was twelve years old had not helped to make the place popular. Isolated among strange influences, Lavinia was fond of wild and grandiose day-dreams and singular occupations; nor was her leisure much taken up by household cares in a home from which all standards of order and cleanliness had long since disappeared.

There was a hideous screaming which echoed above even the hill noises and the dogs' barking on the night Wilbur was born, but no known doctor or midwife presided at his coming. Neighbours knew nothing of him till a week afterward, when Old Whateley drove his sleigh through the snow into Dunwich Village and discoursed incoherently to the group of loungers at Osborn's general store. There seemed to be a change in the old man – an added element of furtiveness in the clouded brain which subtly transformed him from an object to a subject of fear – though he was not one to be perturbed by any common family event. Amidst it all he showed some trace of the pride later noticed in his daughter, and what he said of the child's paternity was remembered by many of his hearers years afterward.

'I dun't keer what folks think – ef Lavinny's boy looked like his pa, he wouldn't look like nothin' ye expeck. Ye needn't think the only folks is the folks hereabouts. Lavinny's read some, an' has seed some things the most o' ye only tell abaout. I calc'late her man is as good a husban' as ye kin find this side of Aylesbury; an' ef ye knowed as much abaout the hills as I dew, ye wouldn't ast no better church weddin' nor her'n. Let me tell ye suthin – *some day yew folks'll hear a child o' Lavinny's a-callin' its father's name on the top o' Sentinel Hill!*'

The only person who saw Wilbur during the first month of his life were old Zechariah Whateley, of the undecayed Whateleys, and Earl Sawyer's common-law wife, Mamie Bishop. Mamie's visit was frankly one of curiosity, and her subsequent tales did justice to her observations; but Zachariah came to lead a pair of Alderney cows which Old Whateley had bought of his son Curtis. This marked the beginning of a course of cattle-buying on the part of small Wilbur's family which ended only in 1928, when the Dunwich horror came and went; yet at no time did the ramshackle Whateley barn seem overcrowded with livestock. There came a period when people were curious enough to steal up and count the herd that grazed precariously on the steep hillside above the old farmhouse, and they could never find more than ten or twelve anaemic, bloodless-looking specimens. Evidently some blight or distemper, perhaps sprung from the unwholesome pasturage or the diseased fungi and timbers of the filthy barn, caused a heavy mortality amongst the Whateley animals. Odd wounds or sores, having something of the aspect of incisions, seemed to afflict the visible cattle; and once or twice during the earlier months certain callers fancied they could discern similar sores about the throats of the grey, unshaven old man and his slatternly, crinkly-haired albino daughter.

In the spring after Wilbur's birth Lavinia resumed her customary rambles in the hills, bearing in her misproportioned arms the swarthy child. Public interest in the Whateley's subsided after most of the country folk had seen the baby, and no one bothered to comment on the swift development which that newcomer seemed every day to exhibit. Wilbur's growth was indeed phenomenal, for within three months of his birth he had attained a size and muscular power not usually found in infants under a full year of age. His motions and even his vocal sounds showed a restraint and deliberateness highly peculiar in an infant, and no one was really unprepared when, at seven months, he began to walk unassisted, with falterings which another month was sufficient to remove.

It was somewhat after this time – on Hallowe'en – that a great blaze was seen at midnight on the top of Sentinel Hill where the old table-like stone stands amidst its tumulus of ancient bones. Considerable talk was started when Silas Bishop – of the undecayed Bishops – mentioned having seen the boy running sturdily up that hill ahead of his mother about an hour before the blaze was remarked. Silas was rounding up a stray heifer, but he nearly forgot his mission when he fleetingly spied the two figures in the dim light of his lantern. They darted almost noiselessly through the underbrush, and the astonished watcher seemed to think they were entirely unclothed. Afterwards he could not be sure about the boy, who may have had some kind of a fringed belt and a pair of dark trunks or trousers on. Wilbur was never subsequently seen alive and conscious without complete and tightly buttoned attire, the disarrangement or threatened disarrangement of which always seemed to fill him with anger and alarm. His contrast with his squalid mother and grandfather in this respect was thought very notable until the horror of 1928 suggested the most valid of reasons.

The next January gossips were mildly interested in the fact that 'Lavinny's black brat' had commenced to talk, and at the age of only eleven months. His speech was somewhat remarkable both because of its difference from the ordinary accents of the region, and because it displayed a freedom from infantile lisping of which many children of three or four might well be proud. The boy was not talkative, yet when he spoke he seemed to reflect some elusive element wholly unpossessed by Dunwich and its denizens. The strangeness did not reside in what he said, or even in the simple idioms he used; but seemed vaguely linked with his intonation or with the internal organs that produced the spoken sounds. His facial aspect, too, was remarkable for its maturity; for though he shared his mother's and grandfather's chinlessness, his firm and precociously shaped nose united with the expression of his large, dark, almost Latin eyes to give him an air of quasi-adulthood and well-nigh preternatural intelligence. He was, however, exceedingly ugly despite his appearance of brilliancy; there being something almost goatish or animalistic about his thick lips, large-pored, yellowish skin, coarse crinkly hair, and oddly elongated ears. He was soon disliked even more decidedly than his mother and grandsire, and all conjectures about him were spiced with references to the bygone magic of Old Whateley, and how the hills once shook when he shrieked the dreadful name of *Yog-Sothoth* in the midst of a circle of stones with a great book open in his arms before him. Dogs abhorred the boy, and he was always obliged to take various defensive measures against their barking menace.

Meanwhile Old Whateley continued to buy cattle without measurably increasing the size of his herd. He also cut timber and began to repair the unused parts of his house – a spacious, peak-roofed affair whose rear end was buried entirely in the rocky hillside, and whose three least-ruined ground-floor rooms had always been sufficient for himself and his daughter. There must have been prodigious reserves of strength in the old man to enable him to accomplish so much hard labour; and though he still babbled dementedly at times, his carpentry seemed to show the effects of sound calculation. It had already begun as soon as Wilbur was born, when one of the many tool sheds had been put suddenly in order, clapboarded, and fitted with a stout fresh lock. Now, in restoring the abandoned upper storey of the house, he was a no less thorough craftsman. His mania showed itself only in his tight boarding-up of all the windows in the reclaimed section – though many declared that it was a crazy thing to bother with the reclamation at all. Less inexplicable was his fitting up of another downstairs room for his new grandson – a room which several callers saw, though no one was ever admitted to the closely-boarded upper storey. This chamber he lined with tall, firm shelving, along which he began gradually to arrange, in apparently careful order, all the rotting ancient books and parts of books which during his own day had been heaped promiscuously in odd corners of the various rooms.

'I made some use of 'em,' he would say as he tried to mend a torn black-letter page with paste prepared on the rusty kitchen stove, 'but the boy's fitten to make better use of 'em. He'd orter hev 'em as well so as he kin, for they're goin' to be all of his larnin'.'

When Wilbur was a year and seven months old – in September of 1914 – his size and accomplishments were almost alarming. He had grown as large as a child of four, and was a fluent and incredibly intelligent talker. He ran freely about the fields and hills, and accompanied his mother on all her wanderings. At home he would pore diligently over the queer pictures and charts in his grandfather's books, while Old Whateley would instruct and catechise him through long, hushed afternoons. By this time the restoration of the house was finished, and those who watched it wondered why one of the upper windows had been made into a solid plank door. It was a window in the rear of the east gable end, close against the hill; and no one could imagine why a cleated wooden runway was built up to it from the ground. About the period of this work's completion people noted that the old tool-house, tightly locked and windowlessly clapboarded since Wilbur's birth, had been abandoned again. The door swung listlessly open, and when Earl Sawyer once stepped within after a cattle-selling call on Old Whateley he was quite discomposed by the singular odour he encountered – such a stench, he averred, as he had never before smelt in all his life except near the Indian circles on the hills, and which could not come from anything sane or of this earth. But then, the homes and sheds of

Dunwich folk have never been remarkable for olfactory immaculateness.

The following months were void of visible events, save that everyone swore to a slow but steady increase in the mysterious hill noises. On May Eve of 1915 there were tremors which even the Aylesbury .people felt, whilst the following Hallowe'en produced an underground rumbling queerly synchronized with bursts of flame – 'them witch Whateleys' doin's' – from the summit of Sentinel Hill. Wilbur was growing up uncannily, so that he looked like a boy of ten as he entered his fourth year. He read avidly by himself now; but talked much less than formerly. A settled taciturnity was absorbing him, and for the first time people began to speak specifically of the dawning look of evil in his goatish face. He would sometimes mutter an unfamiliar jargon, and chant in bizarre rhythms which chilled the listener with a sense of unexplainable terror. The aversion displayed towards him by dogs had now become a matter of wide remark, and he was obliged to carry a pistol in order to traverse the countryside in safety. His occasional use of the weapon did not enhance his popularity amongst the owners of canine guardians.

The few callers at the house would often find Lavinia alone on the ground floor; while odd cries and footsteps resounded in the boarded-up second storey. She would never tell what her father and the boy were doing up there, though once she turned pale and displayed an abnormal degree of fear as a jocose fish-pedlar tried the locked door leading to the stairway. That pedlar told the store loungers at Dunwich Village that he thought he heard a horse stamping on that floor above. The loungers reflected, thinking of the door and runway, and of the cattle that so swiftly disappeared. Then they shuddered as they recalled tales of Old Whateley's youth, and of the strange things that are called out of the earth when a bullock is sacrificed at the proper time to certain heathen gods. It had for some time been noticed that dogs had begun to hate and fear the whole Whateley place as violently as they hated and feared young Wilbur personally.

In 1917 the war came, and Squire Sawyer Whateley, as chairman of the local draft board, had hard work finding a quota of young Dunwich men fit even to be sent to development camp. The government, alarmed at such signs of wholesale regional decadence, sent several officers and medical experts to investigate; conducting a survey which New England newspaper readers may still recall. It was the publicity attending this investigation which set reporters on the track of the Whateleys, and caused the *Boston Globe* and *Arkham Advertiser* to print flamboyant Sunday stories of young Wilbur's precociousness, Old Whateley's black magic, and the shelves of strange books, the sealed second storey of the ancient farmhouse, and the weirdness of the whole region and its hill noises. Wilbur was four and a half then, and looked like a lad of fifteen. His lips and cheeks were fuzzy with a coarse dark down, and his voice had begun to break.

Earl Sawyer went out to the Whateley place with both sets of reporters and camera men, and called their attention to the queer stench which now seemed to trickle down from the sealed upper spaces. It was, he said, exactly like a smell he had found in the toolshed abandoned when the house was finally repaired; and like the faint odours which he sometimes thought he caught near the stone circle on the mountains. Dunwich folk read the stories when they appeared, and grinned over the obvious mistakes. They wondered, too, why the writers made so much of the fact that Old Whateley always paid for his cattle in gold pieces of extremely ancient date. The Whateleys had received their visitors with ill-concealed distaste, though they did not dare court further publicity by a violent resistance or refusal to talk.

For a decade the annals of the Whateleys sank indistinguishably into the general life of a morbid community used to their queer ways and hardened to their May Eve and All-Hallows orgies. Twice a year they would light fires on the top of Sentinel Hill, at which times the mountain rumblings would recur with greater and greater violence; while at all seasons there were strange and portentous doings at the lonely farmhouse. In the course of time callers professed to hear sounds in the sealed upper storey even when all the family were downstairs, and they wondered how swiftly or how lingeringly a cow or bullock was usually sacrificed. There was talk of a complaint to the Society for the Prevention of Cruelty to Animals but nothing ever came of it, since Dunwich folk are never anxious to call the outside world's attention to themselves.

About 1923, when Wilbur was a boy of ten whose mind, voice, stature, and bearded face gave all the impressions of maturity, a second great siege of carpentry went on at the old house. It was all inside the sealed upper part, and from bits of discarded lumber people concluded that the youth and his grandfather had knocked out all the partitions and even removed the attic floor, leaving only one vast open void between the ground storey and the peaked roof. They had torn down the great central chimney, too, and fitted the rusty range with a flimsy outside tin stovepipe.

In the spring after this event Old Whateley noticed the growing number of whippoorwills that would come out of Cold Spring Glen to chirp under his window at night. He seemed to regard the circumstances as one of great significance, and told the loungers at Osborn's that he thought his time had almost come.

'They whistle jest in tune with my breathin' naow,' he said, 'an' I guess they're gittin' ready to ketch my soul. They know it's a-goin' aout, an' dun't calc'late to miss it. Yew'll know, boys, arter I'm gone, whether they git me er not. Ef they dew, they'll keep up a-singin' an laffin' till break o' day. Ef they dun't they'll kinder quiet daown like. I expeck them an' the souls they hunts fer hev some pretty tough tussles sometimes.'

On Lammas Night, 1924, Dr Houghton of Aylesbury was hastily summoned by Wilbur Whateley, who had lashed his one remaining horse through the darkness and telephoned from Osborn's in the village. He found Old Whateley in a very grave state, with a cardiac action and stertorous breathing that told of an end not far off. The shapeless albino daughter and oddly bearded grandson stood by the bedside, whilst from the vacant abyss overhead there came a disquieting suggestion of rhythmical surging of lapping, as of the waves on some level beach. The doctor, though, was chiefly disturbed by the chattering night birds outside; a seemingly limitless legion of whippoorwills that cried their endless message in repetitions timed diabolically to the wheezing gasps of the dying man. It was uncanny and unnatural – too much, thought Dr Houghton, like the whole of the region he had entered so reluctantly in response to the urgent call.

Towards one o'clock Old Whateley gained consciousness, and interrupted his wheezing to choke out a few words to his grandson.

'More space, Willy, more space soon. Yew grows – an' *that* grows faster. It'll be ready to sarve ye soon, boy. Open up the gates to Yog-Sothoth with the long chant that ye'll find on page 751 *of the complete edition*, and *then* put a match to the prison. Fire from airth can't burn it nohaow.'

He was obviously quite mad. After a pause, during which the flock of whippoorwills outside adjusted their cries to the altered tempo while some indications of the strange hill noises came from afar off, he added another sentence or two.

'Feed it reg'lar, Willy, an' mind the quantity; but dun't let it grow too fast fer the place, fer ef it busts quarters or gits aout afore ye opens to Yog-Sothoth, it's all over an' no use. Only them from beyont kin make it multiply an' work.... Only them, the old uns as wants to come back....'

But speech gave place to gasps again, and Lavinia screamed at the way the whippoorwills followed the change. It was the same for more than an hour, when the final throaty rattle came. Dr Houghton drew shrunken lids over the glazing grey eyes as the tumult of birds faded inperceptibly to silence. Lavinia sobbed, but Wilbur only chuckled whilst the hill noises rumbled faintly.

'They didn't git him,' he muttered in his heavy bass voice.

Wilbur was by this time a scholar of really tremendous erudition in his one-sided way, and was quietly known by correspondence to many librarians in distant places where rare and forbidden books of old days are kept. He was more and more hated and dreaded around Dunwich because of certain youthful disappearances which suspicion laid vaguely at his door; but was always able to silence inquiry through fear or through use of that fund of old-time gold which still, as in his grandfather's time, went forth regularly and increasingly for cattle-buying. He was now tremendously mature of aspect, and his height, having reached the normal adult limit, seemed inclined to wax beyond that figure. In 1925, when a scholarly correspondent from Miskatonic University called upon him one day and departed pale and puzzled, he was fully six and three-quarters feet tall.

Through all the years Wilbur had treated his half-deformed albino mother with a growing contempt, finally forbidding her to go to the hills with him on May Eve and Hallowmass; and in 1926 the poor creature complained to Mamie Bishop of being afraid of him.

'They's more abaout him as I knows than I kin tell ye, Mamie,' she said, 'an' naowadays they's more nor what I know myself. I vaow afur Gawd, I dun't know what he wants nor what he's a-tryin' to dew.'

That Hallowe'en the hill noises sounded louder than ever, and fire burned on Sentinel Hill as usual; but people paid more attention to the rhythmical screaming of vast flocks of unnaturally belated whippoorwills which seemed to be assembled near the unlighted Whateley farmhouse. After midnight their shrill notes burst into a kind of pandemoniac cachinnation which filled all the countryside, and not until dawn did they finally quiet down. Then they vanished, hurrying southward where they were fully a month overdue. What this meant, no one could quite be certain till later. None of the countryfolk seemed to have died -- but poor Lavinia Whateley, the twisted albino, was never seen again.

In the summer of 1927 Wilbur repaired two sheds in the farmyard and began moving his books and effects out to them. Soon afterwards Earl Sawyer told the loungers at Osborn's that more carpentry was going on in the Whateley farmhouse. Wilbur was closing all the doors and windows on the ground floor, and seemed to be taking out partitions as he and his grandfather had done upstairs four years before. He was living in one of the sheds, and Sawyer thought he seemed unusually worried and tremulous. People generally suspected him of knowing something about his mothers disappearance, and very few ever approached his neighbourhood now. His height had increased to more than seven feet, and showed no signs of ceasing its development.

The following winter brought an event no less strange than Wilbur's first trip outside the Dunwich region. Correspondence with the Widener Library at Harvard, the Bibliothèque Nationale in Paris, the British Museum, the University of Buenos Ayres, and the Library of Miskatonic University at Arkham had failed to get him the loan of a book he desperately wanted; so at length he set out in person, shabby, dirty, bearded, and uncouth of dialect, to consult the copy at Miskatonic, which was the nearest to him geographically. Almost eight feet tall, and carrying a cheap new valise from Osborn's general store, this dark and goatish gargoyle appeared one day in Arkham in quest of the dreaded volume kept under lock and key at the college library – the hideous *Necronomicon* and the mad Arab Abdul Alhazred on Olaus Wormius' Latin version, as printed in Spain in the seventeenth century. He had never seen a city before, but had no thought save to find his way to the university grounds; where indeed, he passed heedlessly by the great white-fanged watchdog that barked with unnatural fury and enmity, and tugged frantically at its stout chain.

Wilbur had with him the priceless but imperfect copy of Dr Dee's English version which his grandfather had bequeathed him, and upon receiving access to the Latin copy he at once began to collate the two texts with the aim of discovering a certain passage which would have come on the 751st page of his own defective volume. This much he could not civilly refrain from telling the librarian – the same erudite Henry Armitage (A M Miskatonic, PhD Princeton, LittD Johns Hopkins) who had once called at the farm, and who now politely plied him with questions. He was looking, he had to admit, for a kind of formula or incantation containing the frightful name *Yog-Sothoth*, and it puzzled him to find discrepancies, duplications, and ambiguities which made the matter of determination far from easy. As he copied the formula he finally chose, Dr Armitage looked involuntarily over his shoulder at the open pages; the left-hand one of which, in the Latin version, contained such monstrous threats to the peace and sanity of the world.

Nor is it to be thought [ran the text as Armitage mentally translated it] that man is either the oldest or the last of earth's masters, or that the common bulk of life and substance walks alone. The Old Ones were, the Old Ones are, and the Old Ones shall be. Not in the spaces we know, but *between* them, they walk serene and primal, un-dimensioned and to us unseen. *Yog-Sothoth* knows the gate. *Yog-Sothoth* is the gate. *Yog-Sothoth* is the key and guardian of the gate. Past, present, future, all are one in *Yog-Sothoth*. He knows where the Old Ones broke through of old, and where They shall break through again. He knows where They had trod earth's fields, and where They still tread them, and why no one can behold Them as They tread. By Their smell can men sometimes know Them near, but of Their semblance can no man know, *saving only in the features of those They have begotten on mankind;* and of those are there many sorts, differing in likeness from man's truest eidolon to that shape without sight or substance which is Them. They walk unseen and foul in lonely places where the Words have been spoken and the Rites howled through at their Seasons. The wind gibbers with Their voices, and the earth mutters with Their consciousness. They bend the forest and crush the city, yet may not forest or city behold the hand that smites. Kadath in the cold waste hath known Them, and what man knows Kadath? The ice desert of the South and the sunken isles of Ocean hold stones whereon Their seal is engraven, but who hath seen the deep frozen city or the sealed tower long garlanded with seaweed and barnacles? Great Cthulhu is Their cousin, yet can he spy Them only dimly. *Iä! Shub-Niggurath!* As a foulness shall ye know Them. Their hand is at your throats, yet ye see Them not; and Their habitation is even one with your guarded threshold. *Yog-Sothoth* is the key to the gate, whereby the spheres meet. Man rules now where They ruled once; They shall soon rule where man rules now. After summer is winter, after winter summer. They wait patient and potent, for here shall They reign again.

Dr Armitage, associating what he was reading with what he had heard of Dunwich and its brooding presences, and of Wilbur Whateley and his dim, hideous aura that stretched from a dubious birth to a cloud of probable matricide, felt a wave of fright as tangible as a draught of the tomb's cold clamminess. The bent, goatish giant before him seemed like the spawn of another planet or dimension; like something only partly of mankind, and linked to black gulfs of essence and entity that stretch like titan phantasms beyond all spheres of force and matter, space and time. Presently Wilbur raised his head and began speaking in that strange, resonant fashion which hinted at sound-producing organs unlike the run of mankind's.

'Mr Armitage,' he said, 'I calc'late I've got to take that book home. They's things in it I've got to try under sarten conditions that I can't git here, an' it 'ud be a mortal sin to let a red-tape rule hold me up. Let me take it along, Sir, an' I'll swar they wun't nobody know the difference. I dun't need to tell ye I'll take good keer of it. It wan't me that put this Dee copy in the shape it is....'

He stopped as he saw firm denial on the librarian's face, and his own goatish features grew crafty. Armitage, half-ready to tell him he might make a copy of what parts he needed, thought suddenly of the possible consequences and checked himself. There was too much responsibility in giving such a being the key to such blasphemous outer spheres. Whateley saw how things stood, and tried to answer lightly.

'Wal, all right, ef ye feel that way abaout it. Maybe Harvard wun't be so fussy as yew be.' And without saying more he rose and strode out of the building, stooping at each doorway.

Armitage heard the savage yelping of the great watchdog, and studied Whateley's gorilla-like lope as he crossed the bit of campus visible from the window. He thought of the wild tales he had heard, and recalled the old Sunday stories in the *Advertiser*; these things, and the lore he had picked up from Dunwich rustics and villagers during his one visit there. Unseen things not of earth or at least not of tri-dimensional earth – rushed foetid and horrible through New England's glens, and brooded obscenely on the mountain tops. Of this he had long felt certain. Now he seemed to sense the close presence of some terrible part of the intruding horror, and to glimpse a hellish advance in the black dominion of the ancient and once passive nightmare. He locked away the *Necronomicon* with a shudder of disgust, but the room still reeked with an unholy and unidentifiable stench. 'As a foulness shall ye know them,' he quoted. Yes – the odour was the same as that which had sickened him at the Whateley farmhouse less than three years before. He thought of Wilbur, goatish and ominous, once again, and laughed mockingly at the village rumours of his parentage.

'Inbreeding?' Armitage muttered half-aloud to himself. 'Great God, what simpletons! Show them Arthur Machen's Great God Pan and they'll think it a common Dunwich scandal! But what thing – what cursed shapeless influence on or off this three-dimensional earth – was Wilbur Whateley's father? Born on Candlemas – nine months after May Eve of 1912, when the talk about the queer earth noises reached clear to Arkham – what walked on the mountains that May night? What Roodmas horror fastened itself on the world in half-human flesh and blood?'

During the ensuing weeks Dr Armitage set about to collect all possible data on Wilbur Whateley and the formless presences around Dunwich. He got in communication with Dr Houghton of Aylesbury, who had attended Old Whateley in his last illness, and found much to ponder over in the grandfather's last words as quoted by the physician. A visit to Dunwich Village failed to bring out much that was new; but a close survey of the *Necronomicon*, in those parts which Wilbur had sought so avidly, seemed to supply new and terrible clues to the nature, methods, and desires of the strange evil so vaguely threatening this planet. Talks with several students of archaic lore in Boston, and letters to many others elsewhere, gave him a growing amazement which passed slowly through varied degrees of alarm to a state of really acute spiritual fear. As the summer drew on he felt dimly that something ought to be done about the lurking terrors of the upper Miskatonic valley, and about the monstrous being known to the human world as Wilbur Whateley.

The Dunwich horror itself came between Lammas and the equinox in 1928, and Dr Armitage was among those who witnessed its monstrous prologue. He had heard, meanwhile, of Whateley's grotesque trip to Cambridge, and of his frantic efforts to borrow or copy from the *Necronomicon* at the Widener Library. Those efforts had been in vain, since Armitage had issued warnings of the keenest intensity to all librarians having charge of the dreaded volume. Wilbur had been shockingly nervous at Cambridge; anxious for the book, yet almost equally anxious to get home again, as if he feared the results of being away long.

Early in August the half-expected outcome developed, and in the small hours of the third Dr Armitage was awakened suddenly by the wild, fierce cries of the savage watchdog on the college campus. Deep and terrible, the snarling, half-mad growls and barks continued; always in mounting volume, but with hideously significant pauses. Then there rang out a scream from a wholly different throat – such a scream as roused half the sleepers of Arkham and haunted their dreams ever afterwards – such a scream as could come from no being born of earth, or wholly of earth.

Armitage, hastening into some clothing and rushing across the street and lawn to the college buildings, saw that others were ahead of him; and heard the echoes of a burglar-alarm still shrilling from the library. An open window showed black and gaping in the moonlight. What had come had indeed completed its entrance; for the barking and the screaming, now fast fading into a mixed low growling and moaning, proceeded unmistakably from within. Some instinct warned Armitage that what was taking place was not a thing for unfortified eyes to see, so he brushed back the crowd with authority as he unlocked the vestibule door. Among the others he saw Professor Warren Rice and Dr Francis Morgan, men to whom he had told some of his conjectures and misgivings; and these two he motioned to accompany him inside. The inward sounds, except for a watchful, droning whine from the dog, had by this time quite subsided; but Armitage now perceived with a sudden start that a loud chorus of whippoorwills among the shrubbery had commenced a damnably rhythmical piping, as if in unison with the last breaths of a dying man.

The building was full of a frightful stench which Dr Armitage knew too well, and the three men rushed across the hall to the small genealogical reading-room whence the low whining came. For a second nobody dared to turn on the light, then Armitage summoned up his courage and snapped the switch. One of the three – it is not certain which – shrieked aloud at what sprawled before them among disordered tables and overturned chairs. Professor Rice declares that he wholly lost consciousness for an instant, though he did not stumble or fall.

The thing that lay half-bent on its side in a foetid pool of greenish-yellow ichor and tarry stickiness was almost nine feet tall, and the dog had torn off all the clothing and some of the skin. It was not quite dead, but twitched slightly and spasmodically while its chest heaved in monstrous unison with the mad piping of the expectant whippoorwills outside. Bits of shoe-leather and fragments of apparel were scattered about the room, and just inside the window an empty canvas sack lay where it had evidently been thrown. Near the central desk a revolver had fallen, a dented but undischarged cartridge later explaining why it had not been fired. The thing itself, however, crowded out all other images at the time. It would be trite and not wholly accurate to say that no human pen could describe it, but one may properly say that it could not be vividly visualized by anyone whose ideas of aspect and contour are too closely bound up with the common life-forms of this planet and of the three known dimensions. It was partly human, beyond a doubt, with very manlike hands and head, and the goatish, chinless face had the stamp of the Whateleys upon it. But the torso and lower parts of the body were teratologically fabulous, so that only generous clothing could ever have enabled it to walk on earth unchallenged or uneradicated.

Above the waist it was semi-anthropomorphic; though its chest, where the dog's rending paws still rested watchfully, had the leathery, reticulated hide of a crocodile or alligator. The back was piebald with yellow and black, and dimly suggested the squamous covering of certain snakes. Below the waist, though, it was the worst; for here all human resemblance left off and sheer phantasy began. The skin was thickly covered with coarse black fur, and from the abdomen a score of long greenish-grey tentacles with red sucking mouths protruded limply. Their arrangement was odd, and seemed to follow the symmetries of some cosmic geometry unknown to earth or the solar system. On each of the hips, deep set in a kind of pinkish, ciliated orbit, was what seemed to be a rudimentary eye; whilst in lieu of a tail there depended a kind of trunk or feeler with purple annular markings, and with many evidences of being an undeveloped mouth or throat. The limbs, save for their black fur, roughly resembled the hind legs of prehistoric earth's giant saurians, and terminated in ridgy-veined pads that were neither hooves nor claws. When the thing breathed, its tail and tentacles rhythmically changed colour, as if from some circulatory cause normal to the non-human greenish tinge, whilst in the tail it was manifest as a yellowish appearance which alternated with a sickly greenish-white in the spaces between the purple rings. Of genuine blood there was none; only the foetid greenish-yellow ichor which trickled along the painted floor beyond the radius of the stickiness, and left a curious discoloration behind it.

As the presence of the three men seemed to rouse the dying thing, it began to mumble without turning or raising its head. Dr Armitage made no written record of its mouthings, but asserts confidently that nothing in English was uttered. At first the syllables defied all correlation with any speech of earth, but towards the last there came some disjointed fragments evidently taken from the *Necronomicon*, that monstrous blasphemy in quest of which the thing had perished. These fragments, as Armitage recalls them, ran something like '*N'gai, n'gha'ghaa, bugg-shoggog, y'hah: Yog-Sothoth, Yog-Sothoth....*' They trailed off into nothingness as the whippoorwills shrieked in rhythmical crescendos of unholy anticipation.

Then came a halt in the gasping, and the dog raised its head in a long, lugubrious howl. A change came over the yellow, goatish face of the prostrate thing, and the great black eyes fell in appallingly. Outside the window the shrilling of the whippoorwills had suddenly ceased, and above the murmurs of the gathering crowd there came the sound of a panic-struck whirring and fluttering. Against the moon vast clouds of feathery watchers rose and raced from sight, frantic at that which they had sought for prey.

All at once the dog started up abruptly, gave a frightened bark, and leaped nervously out of the window by which it had entered. A cry rose from the crowd, and Dr Armitage shouted to the men outside that no one must be admitted till the police or medical examiner came. He was thankful that the windows were just too high to permit of peering in, and drew the dark curtains carefully down over each one. By this time two policemen had arrived; and Dr Morgan, meeting them in the vestibule, was urging them for their own sakes to postpone entrance to the stench-filled reading-room till the examiner came and the prostrate thing could be covered up.

Meanwhile frightful changes were taking place on the floor. One need not describe the *kind* and *rate* of shrinkage and disintegration that occurred before the eyes of Dr Armitage and Professor Rice; but it is permissible to say that, aside from the external appearance of face and hands, the really human element in Wilbur Whateley must have been very small. When the medical examiner came, there was only a sticky whitish mass on the painted boards, and the monstrous odour had nearly disappeared. Apparently Whateley had had no skull or body skeleton; at least, in any true or stable sense. He had taken somewhat after his unknown father.

Yet all this was only the prologue of the actual Dunwich horror. Formalities were gone through by bewildered officials, abnormal details were duly kept from press and public, and men were sent to Dunwich and Aylesbury to look up property and notify any who might be heirs of the late Wilbur Whateley. They found the countryside in great agitation, both because of the growing rumblings beneath the domed hills, and because of the unwonted stench and the surging, lapping sounds which came increasingly from the great empty shell formed by Whateley's boarded-up farmhouse. Earl Sawyer, who tended the horse and cattle during Wilbur's absence, had developed a woefully acute case of nerves. The officials devised excuses not to enter the noisome boarded place; and were glad to confine their survey of the deceased's living quarters, the newly mended sheds, to a single visit. They filed a ponderous report at the courthouse in Aylesbury, and litigations concerning heirship are said to be still in progress amongst the innumerable Whateleys, decayed and undecayed, of the upper Miskatonic valley.

An almost interminable manuscript in strange characters, written in a huge ledger and adjudged a sort of diary because of the spacing and the variations in ink and penmanship, presented a baffling puzzle to those who found it on the old bureau which served as its owner's desk. After a week of debate it was sent to Miskatonic University, together with the deceased's collection of strange books, for study and possible translation; but even the best linguists soon saw that it was not likely to be unriddled with ease. No trace of the ancient gold with which Wilbur and Old Whateley had always paid their debts had yet been discovered.

It was in the dark of September ninth that the horror broke loose. The hill noises had been very pronounced during the evening, and dogs barked frantically all night. Early risers on the tenth noticed a peculiar stench in the air. About seven o'clock Luther Brown, the hired boy at George Corey's, between Cold Spring Glen and the village, rushed frenziedly back from his morning trip to Ten-Acre Meadow with the cows. He was almost convulsed with fright as he stumbled into the kitchen; and in the yard outside the no less frightened herd were pawing and lowing pitifully, having followed the boy back in the panic they shared with him. Between gasps Luther tried to stammer out his tale to Mrs Corey.

'Up thar in the rud beyont the glen, Mis' Corey – they's suthin' ben thar! It smells like thunder, an' all the bushes an' little trees is pushed back from the rud like they'd a haouse ben moved along of it. An' that ain't the wust, nuther. They's *prints* in the rud, Mis' Corey – great raound prints as big as barrel-heads, all sunk dawon deep like a elephant had ben along, *only they's a sight more nor four feet could make*! I looked at one or two afore I run, an' I see every one was covered with lines spreadin' aout from one place, like as if big palm-leaf fans – twict or three times as big as any they is – hed of ben paounded dawon into the rud. An' the smell was awful, like what it is around Wizard Whateley's ol' haouse. . . .'

Here he faltered, and seemed to shiver afresh with the fright that had sent him flying home. Mrs Corey, unable to extract more information, began telephoning the neighbours; thus starting on its rounds the overture of panic that heralded the major terrors. When she got Sally Sawyer, housekeeper at Seth Bishop's, the nearest place to Whateley's, it became her turn to listen instead of transmit; for Sally's boy Chauncey, who slept poorly, had been up on the hill towards Whateley's, and had dashed back in terror after one look at the place, and at the pasturage where Mr Bishop's cows had been left out all night.

'Yes, Mis' Corey,' came Sally's tremulous voice over the party wire, 'Cha'ncey he just come back a-postin', and couldn't haff talk fer bein' scairt! He says Ol' Whateley's house is all bowed up, with timbers scattered raound like they'd ben dynamite inside; only the bottom floor ain't through, but is all covered with a kind o' tar-like stuff that smells awful an' drips daown offen the aidges onto the graoun' whar the side timbers is blowed away. An' they's awful kinder marks in the yard, tew – great raound marks bigger raound than a hogshead, an' all sticky with stuff like is on the blowed-up haouse. Cha'ncey he says they leads off into the medders, whar a great swath wider'n a barn is matted daown, an' all the stun walls tumbled every whichway wherever it goes.

'An' he says, says he, Mis' Corey, as haow he sot to look fer Seth's caows, frightened ez he was an' faound 'em in the upper pasture nigh the Devil's Hop Yard in an awful shape. Haff on 'em's clean gone, an' nigh haff o' them that's left is sucked most dry o' blood, with sores on 'em like they's ben on Whateleys cattle ever senct Lavinny's black brat was born. Seth hes gone aout naow to look at 'em, though I'll vaow he wun't keer ter git very nigh Wizard Whateley's! Cha'ncey didn't look keerful ter see what the big matted-daown swath led arter it lef the pasturage, but he says he thinks it p'inted towards the glen rud to the village.

'I tell ye, Mis' Corey, they's suthin' abroad as hadn't orter be abroad, an' I for one think that black Wilbur Whateley, as come to the bad end he desarved, is at the bottom of the breedin' of it. He wa'n't all human hisself, I allus says to everybody; an' I think he an' Ol' Whateley must a raised suthin' in that there nailed-up haouse as ain't even so human as he was. They's allus ben unseen things araound Dunwich – livin' things – as ain't human an' ain't good fer human folks.

'The graoun' was a-talkin' las' night, an' towards mornin' Cha'ncey he heered the whippoorwills so laoud in Col' Spring Glen he couldn't sleep. nun. Then he thought he heered another faint-like saound over towards Wizard Whateley's – a kinder rippin' or tearin' o' wood, like some big box er crate was bin' opened fur off. What with this an' that, he didn't git to sleep at all till sunup, an' no sooner was he up this mornin', but he's got to go over to Whateley's an' see what's the matter. He see enough I tell ye, Mis' Corey! This dun't mean no good, an' I think as all the men-folks ought to git up a party an' do suthin'. I know suthin' awful's abaout, an' feel my time is nigh, though only Gawd knows jest what it is.

'Did your Luther take accaount o' whar them git tracks led tew? No? Wal, Mis' Corey, ef they was on the glen rud this side o' the glen, an' ain't got to your haouse yet, I calc'late they must go into the glen itself. They would do that. I allus says Col' Spring Glen ain't no healthy nor decent place. The whippoorwills an' fireflies there never did act like they was creaters o' Gawd, an' they's them as says ye kin hear strange things a-rushin' an' a-talkin' in the air dawon thar ef ye stand in the right place, atween the rock falls an' Bear's Den.'

By that noon fully three-quarters of the men and boys of Dunwich were trooping over the roads and meadows between the newmade Whateley ruins and Cold Spring Glen, examining in horror the vast monstrous prints, the maimed Bishop cattle, the strange, noisome wreck of the farmhouse, and the bruised, matted vegetation of the fields and roadside. Whatever had burst loose upon the world had assuredly gone down into the great sinister ravine; for all the trees on the banks were bent and broken, and a great avenue had been gouged in the precipice-hanging underbrush. It was as though a house, launched by an avalanche, had slid down through the tangled growths of the almost vertical slope. From below no sound came, but only a distant, undefinable foetor; and it is not to be wondered at that the men preferred to stay on the edge and argue, rather than descend and beard the unknown Cyclopean horror in its lair. Three dogs that were with the party had barked furiously at first, but seemed cowed and reluctant when near the glen. Someone telephoned the news to the *Aylesbury Transcript*; but the editor, accustomed to wild tales from Dunwich, did no more than concoct a humorous paragraph about it; an item soon afterwards reproduced by the Associated Press.

That night everyone went home, and every house and barn was barricaded as stoutly as possible. Needless to say, no cattle were allowed to remain in open pasturage. About two in the morning a frightful stench and the savage barking of the dogs awakened the household at Elmer Frye's, on the eastern edge of Cold Spring Glen, and all agreed that they could hear a sort of muffled swishing or lapping sound from somewhere outside. Mrs Frye proposed telephoning the neighbours, and Elmer was about to agree when the noise of splintering wood burst in upon their deliberations. It came, apparently, from the barn; and was quickly followed by a hideous screaming and stamping amongst the cattle. The dogs slavered and crouched close to the feet of the fear-numbed family. Frye lit a lantern through force of habit, but knew it would be death to go out into that black farmyard. The children and the women-folk whimpered, kept from screaming by some obscure, vestigial instinct of defence which told them their lives depended on silence. At last the noise of the cattle subsided to a pitiful moaning, and a great snapping, crashing, and crackling ensued. The Fryes, huddled together in the sitting-room, did not dare to move until the last echoes died away far down in Cold Spring Glen. Then, amidst the dismal moans from the stable and the daemoniac piping of the late whippoorwills in the glen, Selina Frye tottered to the telephone and spread what news she could of the second phase of the horror.

The next day all the countryside was in a panic; and cowed, uncommunicative groups came and went where the fiendish thing had occurred. Two titan swaths of destruction stretched from the glen to the Frye farmyard, monstrous prints covered the bare patches of ground, and one side of the old red barn had completely caved in. Of the cattle, only a quarter could be found and identified. Some of these were in curious fragments, and all that survived had to be shot. Earl Sawyer suggested that help be asked from Aylesbury or Arkham, but others maintained it would be of no use. Old Zebulon Whateley, of a branch that hovered about halfway between soundness and decadence, made darkly wild suggestions about rites that ought to be practised on the hill-tops. He came of a line where tradition ran strong, and his memories of chantings in the great stone circles were not altogether connected with Wilbur and his grandfather.

Darkness fell upon a stricken countryside too passive to organize for real defence. In a few cases closely related families would band together and watch in the gloom under one roof; but in general there was only a repetition of the barricading of the night before, and a futile, ineffective gesture of loading muskets and setting pitchforks handily about. Nothing, however, occurred except some hill noises; and when the day came there were many who hoped that the new horror had gone as swiftly as it had come. There were even bold souls who proposed an offensive expedition down in the glen, though they did not venture to set an actual example to the still reluctant majority.

When night came again the barricading was repeated, though there was less huddling together of families. In the morning both the Frye and the Seth Bishop households reported excitement among the dogs and vague sounds and stenches from afar, while early explorers noted with horror a fresh set of the monstrous tracks in the road skirting Sentinel Hill. As before, the sides of the road showed a bruising indicative of the blasphemously stupendous bulk of the horror; whilst the conformation of the tracks seemed to argue a passage in two directions, as if the moving mountain had come from Cold Spring Glen and returned to it along the same path. At the base of the hill a thirty-foot swath of crushed shrubbery saplings led steeply upwards, and the seekers gasped when they saw that even the most perpendicular places did not deflect the inexorable trail. Whatever the horror was, it could scale a sheer stony cliff of almost complete verticality; and as the investigators climbed round the hill's summit by safer routes they saw that the trail ended – or rather, reversed – there.

It was here that the Whateleys used to build their hellish fires and chant their hellish rituals by the table-like stone on May Eve and Hallowmass. Now that very stone formed the centre of a vast space thrashed around by the mountainous horror, whilst upon its slightly concave surface was a thick and foetid deposit of the same tarry stickiness observed on the floor of the ruined Whateley farmhouse when the horror escaped. Men looked at one another and muttered. Then they looked down the hill. Apparently the horror had descended by a route much the same as that of its ascent. To speculate was futile. Reason, logic, and normal ideas of motivation stood confounded. Only old Zebulon, who was not with the group, could have done justice to the situation or suggested a plausible explanation.

Thursday night began much like the others, but it ended less happily. The whippoorwills in the glen had screamed with such unusual persistence that many could not sleep, and about 3 a.m. all the party telephones rang tremulously. Those who took down their receivers heard a fright-mad voice shriek out, 'Help, oh, my Gawd!...' and some thought a crashing sound followed the breaking off of the exclamation. There was nothing more. No one dared do anything, and no one knew till morning whence the call came. Then those who had heard it called everyone on the line, and found that only the Fryes did not reply. The truth appeared an hour later, when a hastily assembled group of armed men trudged out to the Frye place at the head of the glen. It was horrible, yet hardly a surprise. There were more swaths and monstrous prints, but there was no longer any house. It had caved in like an eggshell, and amongst the ruins nothing living or dead could be discovered. Only a stench and a tarry stickiness. The Elmer Fryes had been erased from Dunwich.

In the meantime a quieter yet even more spiritually poignant phase of the horror had been blackly unwinding itself behind the closed door of a shelf-lined room in Arkham. The curious manuscript record or diary of Wilbur Whateley, delivered to Miskatonic University for translation, had caused much worry and bafflement among the experts in language both ancient and modern; its very alphabet, notwithstanding a general resemblance to the heavily-shaded Arabic used in Mesopotamia, being absolutely unknown to any available authority. The final conclusion of the linguists was that the text represented an artificial alphabet, giving the effect of a cipher; though none of the usual methods of cryptographic solution seemed to furnish any clue, even when applied on the basis of every tongue the writer might conceivably have used. The ancient books taken from Whateley's quarters, while absorbingly interesting and in several cases promising to open up new and terrible lines of research among philosophers and men of science, were of no assistance whatever in this matter. One of them, a heavy tome with an iron clasp, was in another unknown alphabet – this one of a very different cast, and resembling Sanskrit more than anything else. The old ledger was at length given wholly into the charge of Dr Armitage, both because of his peculiar interest in the Whateley matter, and because of his wide linguistic learning and skill in the mystical formulae of antiquity and the middle ages.

Armitage had an idea that the alphabet might be something esoterically used by certain forbidden cults which have come down from old times, and which have inherited many forms and traditions from the wizards of the Saracenic world. That question, however, he did not deem vital; since it would be unnecessary to know the origin of the symbols if, as he suspected, they were used as a cipher in a modern language. It was his belief that, considering the great amount of text involved, the writer would scarcely have wished the trouble of using another speech than his own, save perhaps in certain special formulae and incantations. Accordingly he attacked the manuscript with the preliminary assumption that the bulk of it was in English.

Dr Armitage knew, from the repeated failures of his colleagues, that the riddle was a deep and complex one; and that no simple mode of solution could merit even a trial. All through late August he fortified himself with the mass lore of cryptography; drawing upon the fullest resources of his own library, and wading night after night amidst the arcana of Trithemius' *Poligraphia*, Giambattista Porta's *De Furtivis Literarum Notis*, De Vigenere's *Traite des Chiffres*, Falconer's *Cryptomenysis Patefacta*, Davys' and Thicknesses' eighteenth-century treatises, and such fairly modern authorities as Blair, von Marten and Klüber's script itself, and in time became convinced that he had to deal with one of those subtlest and most ingenious of cryptograms, in which many separate lists of corresponding letters are arranged like the multiplication table, and the message built up with arbitrary key-words known only to the initiated. The older authorities seemed rather more helpful than the newer ones, and Armitage concluded that the code of the manuscript was one of great antiquity, no doubt handed down through a long line of mystical experiments. Several times he seemed near daylight, only to be set back by some unforeseen obstacle. Then, as September approached, the clouds began to clear. Certain letters, as used in certain parts of the manuscript, emerged definitely and unmistakably; and it became obvious that the text was indeed in English.

On the evening of September second the last major barrier gave way, and Dr Armitage read for the first time a continuous passage of Wilbur Whateley's annals. It was in truth a diary, as all had thought; and it was couched in a style clearly showing the mixed occult erudition and general illiteracy of the strange being who wrote it. Almost the first long passage that Armitage deciphered, an entry dated November 26, 1916, proved highly startling and disquieting. It was written, he remembered, by a child of three and a half who looked like a lad of twelve or thirteen.

Today learned the Aklo for the Sabaoth (it ran), which did not like, it being answerable from the hill and not from the air. That upstairs more ahead of me than I had thought it would be, and is not like to have much earth brain. Shot Elam Hutchins's collie Jack when he went to bite me, and Elam says he would kill me if he dast. I guess he won't. Grandfather kept me saying the Dho formula last night, and I think I saw the inner city at the 2 magnetic poles. I shall go to those poles when the earth is cleared off, if I can't break through with the Dho-Hna formula when I commit it. They from the air told me at Sabbat that it will be years before I can clear off the earth, and I guess grandfather will be dead then, so I shall have to learn all the angles of the planes and all the formulas between the Yr and the Nhhngr. They from outside will help, but they cannot take body without human blood. That upstairs looks it will have the right cast. I can see it a little when I make the Voorish sign or blow the powder of Ibn Ghazi at it, and it is near like them at May Eve on the Hill. The other face may wear off some. I wonder how I shall look when the earth is cleared and there are no earth beings on it. He that came with the Aklo Sabaoth said I may be transfigured there being much of outside to work on.

Morning found Dr Armitage in a cold sweat of terror and a frenzy of wakeful concentration. He had not left the manuscript all night, but sat at his table under the electric light turning page after page with shaking hands as fast as he could decipher the cryptic text. He had nervously telephoned his wife he would not be home, and when she brought him a breakfast from the house he could scarcely dispose of a mouthful. All that day he read on, now and then halted maddeningly as a reapplication of the complex key became necessary. Lunch and dinner were brought him, but he ate only the smallest fraction of either. Toward the middle of the next night he drowsed off in his chair, but soon woke out of a tangle of nightmares almost as hideous as the truth and menaces to man's existence that he had uncovered.

On the morning of September fourth Professor Rice and Dr Morgan insisted on seeing him for a while, and departed trembling and ashen-grey. That evening he went to bed, but slept only fitfully. Wednesday – the next day – he was back at the manuscript, and began to take copious notes both from the current sections and from those he had already deciphered. In the small hours of that night he slept a little in an easy chair in his office, but was at the manuscript again before dawn. Some time before noon his physician, Dr Hartwell, called to see him and insisted that he cease work. He refused; intimating that it was of the most vital importance for him to complete the reading of the diary and promising an explanation in due course of time. That evening, just as twilight fell, he finished his terrible perusal and sank back exhausted. His wife, bringing his dinner, found him in a half-comatose state; but he was conscious enough to warn her off with a sharp cry when he saw her eyes wander toward the notes he had taken. Weakly rising, he gathered up the scribbled papers and sealed them all in a great envelope, which he immediately placed in his inside coat pocket. He had sufficient strength to get home, but was so clearly in need of medical aid that Dr Hartwell was summoned at once. As the doctor put him to bed he could only mutter over and over again, '*But what, in God's name, can we do?*'

Dr Armitage slept, but was partly delirious the next day. He made no explanations to Hartwell, but in his calmer moments spoke of the imperative need of a long conference with Rice and Morgan. His wilder wanderings were very startling indeed, including frantic appeals that something in a boarded-up farmhouse be destroyed, and fantastic references to some plan for the extirpation of the entire human race and all animal and vegetable life from the earth by some terrible elder race of beings from another dimension. He would shout that the world was in danger, since the Elder Things wished to strip it and drag it away from the solar system and cosmos of matter into some other plane or phase of entity from which it had once fallen, vigintillions of aeons ago. At other times he would call for the dreaded *Necronomicon* and the *Daemonolatreia* of Remigius, in which he seemed hopeful of finding some formula to check the peril he conjured up.

'Stop them, stop them!' he would shout. 'Those Whateleys meant to let them in, and the worst of all is left! Tell Rice and Morgan we must do something – it's a blind business, but I know how to make the powder.... It hasn't been fed since the second of August, when Wilbur came here to his death, and at that rate....'

But Armitage had a sound physique despite his seventy-three years, and slept off his disorder that night without developing any real fever. He woke late Friday, clear of head, though sober with a gnawing fear and tremendous sense of responsibility. Saturday afternoon he felt able to go over to the library and summon Rice and Morgan for a conference, and the rest of that day and evening the three men tortured their brains in the wildest speculation and the most desperate debate. Strange and terrible books were drawn voluminously from the stack shelves and from secure places of storage; and diagrams and formulae were copied with feverish haste and in bewildering abundance. Of scepticism there was none. All three had seen the body of Wilbur Whateley as it lay on the floor in a room of that very building, and after that not one of them could feel even slightly inclined to treat the diary as a madman's raving.

Opinions were divided as to notifying the Massachusetts State Police, and the negative finally won. There were things involved which simply could not be believed by those who had not seen a sample, as indeed was made clear during certain subsequent investigations. Late at night the conference disbanded without having developed a definite plan, but all day Sunday Armitage was busy comparing formulae and mixing chemicals obtained from the college laboratory. The more he reflected on the hellish diary, the more he was inclined to doubt the efficacy of any material agent in stamping out the entity which Wilbur Whateley had left behind him – the earth threatening entity which, unknown to him, was to burst forth in a few hours and become the memorable Dunwich horror.

Monday was a repetition of Sunday with Dr Armitage, for the task in hand required an infinity of research and experiment. Further consultations of the monstrous diary brought about various changes of plan, and he knew that even in the end a large amount of uncertainty must remain. By Tuesday he had a definite line of action mapped out, and believed he would try a trip to Dunwich within a week. Then, on Wednesday, the great shock came. Tucked obscurely away in a corner of the *Arkham Advertiser* was a facetious little item from the Associated Press, telling what a record-breaking monster the bootleg whisky of Dunwich had raised up.

Armitage, half stunned, could only telephone for Rice and Morgan. Far into the night they discussed, and the next day was a whirlwind of preparation on the part of them all. Armitage knew he would be meddling with terrible powers, yet saw that there was no other way to annul the deeper and more malign meddling which others had done before him.

Friday morning Armitage, Rice, and Morgan set out by motor for Dunwich, arriving at the village about one in the afternoon. The day was pleasant, but even in the brightest sunlight a kind of quiet dread and portent seemed to hover about the strangely domed hills and the deep, shadowy ravines of the stricken region. Now and then on some mountain top a gaunt circle of stones could be glimpsed against the sky. From the air of hushed fright at Osborn's store they knew something hideous had happened, and soon learned of the annihilation of the Elmer Frye house and family. Throughout that afternoon they rode around Dunwich, questioning the natives concerning all that had occurred, and seeing for themselves with rising pangs of horror the drear Frye ruins with their lingering traces of the tarry stickiness, and blasphemous tracks in the Frye yard, the wounded Seth Bishop cattle, and the enormous swaths of disturbed vegetation in various places. The trail up and down Sentinel Hill seemed to Armitage of almost cataclysmic significance, and he looked long at the sinister altar-like stone on the summit.

At length the visitors, appraised of a party of State Police which had come from Aylesbury that morning in response to the first telephone reports of the Frye tragedy, decided to seek out the officers and compare notes as far as practicable. This, however, they found more easily planned than performed; since no sign of the party could be found in any direction. There had been five of them in a car, but now the car stood empty near the ruins in the Frye yard. The natives, all of whom had talked with the policemen, seemed at first as perplexed as Armitage and his companions. Then old Sam Hutchins thought of something and turned pale, nudging Fred Farr and pointing to the dank, deep hollow that yawned close by.

'Gawd,' he gasped, 'I tell 'em not ter go daown into the glen, an' I never thought nobody'd dew it with them tracks an' that smell an' the whippoorwills a-screechin' daown thar in the dark o' noonday....'

A cold shudder ran through natives and visions alike, and every ear seemed strained in a kind of instinctive, unconscious listening. Armitage, now that he had actually come upon the horror and its monstrous work, trembled with the responsibility he felt to be his. Night would soon fall, and it was then that the mountainous blasphemy lumbered upon its eldritch course. *Negotium perambulans in tenebris....* The old librarian rehearsed the formulae he had memorized, and clutched the paper containing the alternative one he had not memorized. He saw that his electric flashlight was in working order. Rice, beside him, took from a valise a metal sprayer of the sort used in combating insects; whilst Morgan uncased the big-game rifle on which he relied despite his colleague's warnings that no material weapon would be of help.

Armitage, having read the hideous diary, knew painfully well what kind of a manifestation to expect; but he did not add to the fright of the Dunwich people by giving any hints or clues. He hoped that it might be conquered without any revelation to the world of the monstrous thing it had escaped. As the shadows gathered, the natives commenced to disperse homeward, anxious to bar themselves indoors despite the present evidence that all human locks and bolts were useless before a force that could bend trees and crush houses when it chose. They shook their heads at the visitors' plan to stand guard at the Frye ruins near the glen; and, as they left, had little expectancy of ever seeing the watchers again.

There were rumblings under the hills that night, and the whippoorwills piped threateningly. Once in a while a wind, sweeping up out of Cold Spring Glen, would bring a touch of ineffable foetor to the heavy night air; such a foetor as all three of the watchers had smelled once before, when they stood above a dying thing that had passed for fifteen years and a half as a human being. But the looked-for terror did not appear. Whatever was down there in the glen was biding its time, and Armitage told his colleagues it would be suicidal to try to attack it in the dark.

Morning came wanly, and the night-sounds ceased. It was a grey, bleak day, with now and then a drizzle of rain; and heavier and heavier clouds seemed to be piling themselves up beyond the hills to the north-west. The men from Arkham were undecided what to do. Seeking shelter from the increasing rainfall beneath one of the few undestroyed Frye outbuildings, they debated the wisdom of waiting, or of taking the aggressive and going down into the glen in quest of their nameless, monstrous quarry. The downpour waxed in heaviness, and distant peals of thunder sounded from far horizons. Sheet lightning shimmered, and then a forky bolt flashed near at hand, as if descending into the accursed glen itself. The sky grew very dark, and the watchers hoped that the storm would prove a short, sharp one followed by clear weather.

It was still gruesomely dark when, not much over an hour later, a confused babel of voices sounded down the road. Another moment brought to view a frightened group of more than a dozen men, running, shouting, and even whimpering hysterically. Someone in the lead began sobbing out words, and the Arkham men started violently when those words developed a coherent form.

'Oh, my Gawd, my Gawd,' the voice choked out. 'It's a-goin' agin, *an' this time by day!* It's aout – it's aout an' a-movin' this very minute, an' only the Lord knows when it'll be on us all!'

The speaker panted into silence, but another took up his message.

'Nigh on a haour ago Zeb Whateley here heered the 'phone a-ringin', an' it was Mis' Corey, George's wife, that lives daown by the junction. She says the hired boy Luther was aout drivin' in the caows from the storm arter the big bolt, when he see all the trees a-bendin' at the maouth o' the glen – opposite side ter this – an' smelt the same awful smell like he smelt when he faound the big tracks las' Monday mornin'. An' she says he says they was a swishin' lappin' saound, more nor what the bendin' trees an' bushes could make, an' all on a suddent the trees along the rud begun ter git pushed one side, an' they was a awful stompin' an' splashin' in the mud. But mind ye, Luther he didn't see nothin' at all, only just the bendin' trees an' underbrush.

'Then fur ahead where Bishop's Brook goes under the rud he heerd a awful creakin' an' strainin' on the bridge, an' says he could tell the saound o' wood a-startin' to crack an' split. An' all the whiles he never see a thing, only them trees an' bushes a-bendin'. An' when the swishin' saound got very fur off – on the rud towards Wizard Whateley's an' Sentinel Hill – Luther he had the guts ter step up whar he'd heerd it fust an' look at the graound. It was all mud an' water, an' the sky was dark, an' the rain was wipin' aout all tracks abaout as fast as could be; but beginnin' at the glen maouth, what the trees hed moved, they was still some o' them awful prints big as bar'ls like he seen Monday.'

At this point the first excited speaker interrupted.

'But *that* ain't the trouble naow – that was only the start. Zeb here was callin' folks up an' everybody was a-listenin' in when a call from Seth Bishop's cut in. His haousekeeper Sally was carryin' on fit to kill – she'd jest seed the trees a-bendin' beside the rud, an' says they was a kind o' mushy saound, like a elephant puffin' an' treading', a-headin' fer the haouse. Then she up an' spoke suddent of a fearful smell, an' says her boy Cha'ncey was a-screamin' as haow it was jest like what he smelt up to the Whateley rewins Monday mornin'. An' the dog was all barkin' an' whinin' awful.

'An 'then she let aout a turrible yell, an' says the shed daown the rud had jest caved in like the storm hed blowed it over, only the wind w'an't strong enough to dew that. Everybody was a-listenin', an' we could hear lots o'folks on the wire a-gaspin'. All to once Sally she yelled again, an' says the front yard picket fence hed just crumbled up, though they wa'n't no sign o' what done it. Then everybody on the line could hear Cha'ncey an' old Seth Bishop a-yellin' tew, an' Sally was shriekin' aout that suthin' heavy hed struck the haouse – not lightnin' nor nothin', but suthin' heavy again the front, that kep' a-launchin' itself again an' agin, though ye couldn't see nothin' aout the front winders. An' then ... an' then....'

Lines of fright deepened on every face; and Armitage, shaken as he was, had barely poise enough to prompt the speaker.

'An' then ... Sally she yelled aout, "Oh help, the haouse is a-cavin' in" ... an' on the wire we could hear a turrible crashin' an' a hull flock o' screamin' . . . jes like when Elmer Frye's place was took, only wuss. . . .'

The man paused, and another of the crowd spoke.

'That's all – not a saound nor speak over the 'phone arter that. Jest still-like. We that heerd it got aout Fords an' wagons an' rounded up as many able-bodied men-folks as we could git, at Corey's place, an' come up here ter see what yew thought best ter dew. Not but what I think it's the Lord's jedgment fer our iniquities, that no mortal kin ever set aside.'

Armitage saw that the time for positive action had come, and spoke decisively to the faltering group of frightened rustics.

'We must follow it, boys.' He made his voice as reassuring as possible. 'I believe there's a chance of putting it out of business. You men know that those Whateleys were wizards – well, this thing is a thing of wizardry, and must be put down by the same means. I've seen Wilbur Whateley's diary and read some of the strange old books he used to read; and I think I know the right kind of spell to recite to make the thing fade away. Of course, one can't be sure, but we can always take a chance. It's invisible – I knew it would be – but there's powder in this long-distance sprayer that might make it show up for a second. Later on we'll try it. It's a frightful thing to have alive, but it isn't as bad as what Wilbur would have let in if he'd lived longer. You'll never know what the world escaped. Now we've only this one thing to fight, and it can't multiply. It can, though, do a lot of harm; so we mustn't hesitate to rid the community of it.

'We must follow it – and the way to begin is to go to the place that has just been wrecked. Let somebody lead the way – I don't know your roads very well, but I've an idea there might be a shorter cut across lots. How about it?'

The men shuffled about a moment, and then Earl Sawyer spoke softly, pointing with a grimy finger through the steadily lessening rain.

'I guess ye kin git to Seth Bishop's quickest by cuttin' across the lower medder here, wadin' the brook at the low place, an' climbin' through Carrier's mowin' an' the timber-lot beyont. That comes aout on the upper rud mighty nigh Seth's – a leetle t'other side.'

Armitage, with Rice and Morgan, started to walk in the direction indicated; and most of the natives followed slowly. The sky was growing lighter, and there were signs that the storm had worn itself away. When Armitage inadvertently took a wrong direction, Joe Osborn warned him and walked ahead to show the right one. Courage and confidence were mounting, though the twilight of the almost perpendicular wooded hill which lay towards the end of their short cut, and among whose fantastic ancient trees they had to scramble as if up a ladder, put these qualities to a severe test.

At length they emerged on a muddy road to find the sun coming out. They were a little beyond the Seth Bishop place, but bent trees and hideously unmistakable tracks showed what had passed by. Only a few moments were consumed in surveying the ruins just round the bend. It was the Frye incident all over again, and nothing dead or living was found in either of the collapsed shells which had been the Bishop house and barn. No one cared to remain there amidst the stench and tarry sickness, but all turned instinctively to the line of horrible prints leading on towards the wrecked Whateley farmhouse and the altar-crowned slopes of Sentinel Hill.

As the men passed the site of Wilbur Whateley's abode they shuddered visibly, and seemed again to mix hesitancy with their zeal. It was no joke tracing down something as big as a house that one could not see, but that had all the vicious malevolence of a daemon. Opposite the base of Sentinel Hill the tracks left the road, and there was a fresh bending and matting visible along the broad swarth marking the monster's former route to and from the summit.

Armitage produced a pocket telescope of considerable power and scanned the steep green side of the hill. Then he handed the instrument to Morgan, whose sight was keener. After a moment of gazing Morgan cried out sharply, passing the glass to Earl Sawyer and indicating a certain spot on the slope with his finger. Sawyer, as clumsy as most non-users of optical devices are, fumbled a while; but eventually focused the lenses with Armitage's aid. When he did so his cry was less restrained than Morgan's had been.

'Gawd almighty, the grass an' bushes is a'movin'! It's a-goin' up – slow-like – creepin' – up ter the top this minute, heaven only knows what fur!'

Then the germ of panic seemed to spread among the seekers. It was one thing to chase the nameless entity, but quite another to find it. Spells might be all right – but suppose they weren't? Voices began questioning Armitage about what he knew of the thing, and no reply seemed quite to satisfy. Everyone seemed to feel himself in close proximity to phases of Nature and of being utterly forbidden and wholly outside the sane experience of mankind.

In the end the three men from Arkham – old, white-bearded Dr Armitage, stocky, iron-grey Professor Rice, and lean, youngish Dr Morgan, ascended the mountain alone. After much patient instruction regarding its focusing and use, they left the telescope with the frightened group that remained in the road; and as they climbed they were watched closely by those among whom the glass was passed round. It was hard going, and Armitage had to be helped more than once. High above the toiling group the great swath trembled as its hellish maker repassed with snail-like deliberateness. Then it was obvious that the pursuers were gaining.

Curtis Whateley – of the undecayed branch – was holding the telescope when the Arkham party detoured radically from the swath. He told the crowd that the men were evidently trying to get to a subordinate peak which overlooked the swath at a point considerably ahead of where the shrubbery was now bending. This, indeed, proved to be true; and the party were seen to gain the minor elevation only a short time after the invisible blasphemy had passed it.

Then Wesley Corey, who had taken the glass, cried out that Armitage was adjusting the sprayer which Rice held, and that something must be about to happen. The crowd stirred uneasily, recalling that his sprayer was expected to give the unseen horror a moment of visibility. Two or three men shut their eyes, but Curtis Whateley snatched back the telescope and strained his vision to the utmost. He saw that Rice, from the party's point of advantage above and behind the entity, had an excellent chance of spreading the potent powder with marvellous effect.

Those without the telescope saw only an instant's flash of grey cloud – a cloud about the size of a moderately large building – near the top of the mountain. Curtis, who held the instrument, dropped it with a piercing shriek into the ankle-deep mud of the road. He reeled, and would have crumbled to the ground had not two or three others seized and steadied him. All he could do was moan half-inaudibly.

'Oh, oh, great Gawd ... *that*....'

There was a pandemonium of questioning, and only Henry Wheeler thought to rescue the fallen telescope and wipe it clean of mud. Curtis was past all coherence, and even isolated replies were almost too much for him.

'Bigger'n a barn ... all made o' squirmin' ropes ... hull thing sort o' shaped like a hen's egg bigger'n anything with dozens o' legs like hogs-heads that haff shut up when they step ... nothin' solid abaout it – all like jelly, an' made o' sep'rit wrigglin' ropes pushed clost together ... great bulgin' eyes all over it ... ten or twenty maouths or trunks a-stickin' aout all along the sides, big as stove-pipes an all a-tossin' an openin' an' shuttin' ... all grey, with kinder blue or purple rings ... *an Gawd in Heaven – that haff face on top* ...'

This final memory, whatever it was, proved too much for poor Curtis; and he collapsed completely before he could say more. Fred Farr and Will Hutchins carried him to the roadside and laid him on the damp grass. Henry Wheeler, trembling, turned the rescued telescope on the mountain to see what he might. Through the lenses were discernible three tiny figures, apparently running towards the summit as fast as the steep incline allowed. Only these – nothing more. Then everyone noticed a strangely unseasonable noise in the deep valley behind, and even in the underbrush of Sentinel Hill itself. It was a piping of unnumbered whippoorwills, and in their shrill chorus there seemed to lurk a note of tense and evil expectancy.

Earl Sawyer now took the telescope and reported the three figures as standing on the topmost ridge, virtually level with the altar-stone but at a considerable distance from it. One figure, he said, seemed to be raising its hands above its head at rhythmic intervals; and as Sawyer mentioned the circumstance the crowd seemed to hear a faint, half-musical sound from the distance, as if a loud chant were accompanying the gestures. The weird silhouette on that remote peak must have been a spectacle of infinite grotesqueness and impressiveness, but no observer was in a mood for aesthetic appreciation. 'I guess he's sayin' the spell,' whispered Wheeler as he snatched back the telescope. The whippoorwills were piping wildly, and in a singularly curious irregular rhythm quite unlike that of the visible ritual.

Suddenly the sunshine seemed to lessen without the intervention of any discernible cloud. It was a very peculiar phenomenon, and was plainly marked by all. A rumbling sound seemed brewing beneath the hills, mixed strangely with a concordant rumbling which clearly came from the sky. Lightning flashed aloft, and the wondering crowd looked in vain for the portents of storm. The chanting of the men from Arkham now became unmistakable, and Wheeler saw through the glass that they were all raising their arms in the rhythmic incantation. From some farmhouse far away came the frantic barking of dogs.

The change in the quality of the daylight increased, and the crowd gazed about the horizon in wonder. A purplish darkness, born of nothing more than a spectral deepening of the sky's blue, pressed down upon the rumbling hills. Then the lightning flashed again, somewhat brighter than before, and the crowd fancied that it had showed a certain mistiness around the altar-stone on the distant height. No one, however, had been using the telescope at that instant. The whippoorwills continued their irregular pulsation, and the men of Dunwich braced themselves tensely against some imponderable menace with which the atmosphere seemed surcharged.

Without warning came those deep, cracked, raucous vocal sounds which will never leave the memory of the stricken group who heard them. Not from any human throat were they born, for the organs of man can yield no such acoustic perversions. Rather would one have said they came from the pit itself, had not their source been so unmistakably the altar-stone on the peak. It is almost erroneous to call them *sounds* at all, since so much of their ghastly, infra-bass timbre spoke to dim seats of consciousness and terror far subtler than the ear; yet one must do so, since their form was indisputably though vaguely that of half-articulate *words*. They were loud – loud as the rumblings and the thunder above which they echoed – yet did they come from no visible being. And because imagination might suggest a conjectural source in the world of non-viable beings, the huddled crowd at the mountain's base huddled still closer, and winced as if in expectation of a blow.

'*Ygnaiih ... ygnaiih ... thflthkh'ngha ... Yog-Sothoth ..*' rang the hideous croaking out of space. '*Y'bthnk ... h'ehye – n'grkdl'lh. ...*'

122

The speaking impulse seemed to falter here, as if some frightful psychic struggle were going on. Henry Wheeler strained his eye at the telescope, but saw only the three grotesquely silhouetted human figures on the peak, all moving their arms furiously in strange gestures as their incantation drew near its culmination. From what black wells of Acherontic fear or feeling, from what unplumbed gulfs of extra-cosmic consciousness or obscure, long-latent heredity, were those half-articulate thunder-croakings drawn? Presently they began to gather renewed force and coherence as they grew in stark, utter, ultimate frenzy

'Eh-y-ya-ya-yahaah – e'yayayaaaa . . . ngh'aaaaa . . . nhy'aaa . . . h'yuh . . . h'yuh . . . HELP! HELP! . . . *ff – ff – ff* – FATHER! FATHER! YOG-SOTHOTH! . . .'

But that was all. The pallid group in the road, still reeling at the *indisputably English* syllables that had poured thickly and thunderously down from the frantic vacancy beside that shocking altar-stone, were never to hear such syllables again. Instead, they jumped violently at the terrific report which seemed to rend the hills; the deafening, cataclysmic peal whose source, be it inner earth or sky, no hearer was ever able to place. A single lightning bolt shot from the purple zenith to the altar-stone, and a great tidal wave of viewless force and indescribable stench swept down from the hill to all the countryside. Trees, grass, and underbrush were whipped into a fury; and the frightened crowd at the mountain's base, weakened by the lethal foetor that seemed about to asphyxiate them, were almost hurled off their feet. Dogs howled from the distance, green grass and foliage wilted to a curious, sickly yellow-grey, and over field and forest were scattered the bodies of dead whippoorwills.

The stench left quickly, but the vegetation never came right again. To this day there is something queer and unholy about the growths on and around that fearsome hill. Curtis Whateley was only just regaining consciousness when the Arkham men came slowly down the mountain in the beams of a sunlight once more brilliant and untainted. They were grave and quiet, and seemed shaken by memories and reflections even more terrible than those which had reduced the group of natives to a state of cowed quivering. In reply to a jumble of questions they only shook their heads and reaffirmed one vital fact.

'The thing has gone for ever,' Armitage said. 'It has been split up into what it was originally made of, and can never exist again. It was an impossibility in a normal world. Only the least fraction was really matter in any sense we know. It was like its father – and most of it has gone back to him in some vague realm or dimension outside our material universe; some vague abyss out of which only the most accursed rites of human blasphemy could ever have called him for a moment on the hills.'

There was a brief silence, and in that pause the scattered senses of poor Curtis Whateley began to knit back into a sort of continuity; so that he put his hands to his head with a moan. Memory seemed to pick itself up where it had left off, and the horror of the sight that had prostrated him burst in upon him again.

'*Oh, oh, my Gawd, that haff face – that face on top of it . . . that face with the red eyes an' crinkly albino hair, an' no chin, like the Whateleys. . . . It was a octopus, centipede, spider kind o' thing, but they was a haff-shaped man's face on top of it, an' it looked like Wizard Whateley's, only it was yards an' yards acrost. . . .*'

He paused exhausted, as the whole group of natives stared in a bewilderment not quite crystallized into fresh terror. Only old Zebulon Whateley, who wanderingly remembered ancient things but who had been silent heretofore, spoke aloud.

'Fifteen year' gone,' he rambled, 'I heered Ol' Whateley say as haow some day we'd hear a child o' Lavinny's a-callin its father's name on the top o' Sentinel Hill. . . .'

But Joe Osborn interrupted him to question the Arkham men anew.

'*What was it, anyhaow,* an' haowever did young Wizard Whateley call it aout o' the air it come from?'

Armitage chose his words very carefully.

'It was – well, it was mostly a kind of force that doesn't belong in our part of space; a kind of force that acts and grows and shapes itself by other laws than those of our sort of Nature. We have no business calling in such things from outside, and only very wicked people and very wicked cults ever try to. There was some of it in Wilbur Whateley himself – enough to make a devil and a precocious monster of him, and to make his passing out a pretty terrible sight. I'm going to burn his accursed diary, and if you men are wise you'll dynamite that altar-stone up there, and pull down all the rings of standing stones on the other hills. Things like that brought down the beings those Whateleys were so fond of – the beings they were going to let in tangibly to wipe out the human race and drag the earth off to some nameless place for some nameless purpose.

'But as to this thing we've just sent back – the Whateleys raised it for a terrible part in the doings that were to come. It grew fast and big from the same reason that Wilbur grew fast and big – but it beat him because it had a greater share of the *outsideness* in it. You needn't ask how Wilbur called it out of the air. He didn't call it out. *It was his twin brother, but it looked more like the father than he did.*'

124

Dad

JOHN BLACKBURN

I TRIED TO BE FOND OF DAD and he tried to be fond of me, though our relationship was a strange one. I admired his strength and he was proud of my fortitude. But I despised his brain and he despised my body, and you can't blame either of us for that. He was a fool and I was a weakling. I hadn't got a leg.

No, that's not quite true. I'd got one leg, but the other hadn't developed when Mum was carrying me and it's just a stump which ends a few inches below the hip. Maybe that's why Mum killed herself after I was born, but I'm not sure and Dad rarely talked about her. Dad talked about sport and the glory and comradeship it had brought him. He boasted about his own huge, powerful legs.

A notable sportsman was Dad. He'd played centre forward for a couple of First Division football clubs and was also a bit of a long distance runner. When he became too old to run or kick a ball about, he took up road walking and used to march to Brighton and back. Many's the time I've seen him setting off with that swinging, strutting stride which made him look as bent as myself. A stupid pastime in my opinion, but he was a stupid man, and so proud of his body and the honours it had earned him. Our sitting-room gleamed like Aladdin's cave with his cups and shields and medallions, and I had to polish them and hear him talk about his triumphs.

'Shine 'em up, lad, because they'll be yours to treasure when I'm in my grave. That plaque you're busy with is a right beauty and I got it for winning the '58 Cheshire Marathon. My legs left the rest of the field standing and the Duchess presented it to me with her own two hands.'

Two hands – two legs. He glanced at my one leg and its steel partner and I made myself a promise. After Dad died his trophies would cease to gleam.

Not that I disliked Dad. As I've said I admired his strength and he was always kind to me in his rough way. It was just that he made me feel inadequate, and when he retired and I started work at the disabled persons' centre, the feeling of inadequacy increased. I remember coming home one day and finding him perched halfway up the old pear tree in the garden. Swinging from the boughs like an ape and stuffing the fruit into a

125

haversack. Throwing them down for me to catch and whooping congratulations when I managed to grab one, which only happened twice. I can't move very quickly and Dad hurled those pears at me like cricket balls. They were as hard as cricket balls too, and quite uneatable unless you kept them in a drawer for weeks. But Dad didn't want to eat his crop and he gave it away to neighbours. He just wanted to prove that he was as tough as ever. To show me that an old man had the courage and agility to climb a tree.

I paid a chap to cut down that tree after Dad's funeral, and I can still hear the whirr of the band saw biting through the trunk and the crash of branches splintering on the ground. That recollection is clear and distinct, but my memory's hazy about some things and I'm not quite sure exactly why Dad died. The coroner suggested that alcohol was mainly to blame, but Dad could take his booze and he'd only had his usual quota of five pints at the local.

We always went to the local on Fridays, but that evening I hadn't wanted to go with him. I was tired and my stump had been troubling me all day and I said that I'd rather stay at home and read or watch the telly. The last thing I wanted was to lean against a crowded bar counter with Dad but he insisted, and we joined his cronies, who were all ex-sportsmen with a single common interest.

'Remember how I knocked out Abdul the Turk at the end of the tenth round?' 'Remember how I breasted the tape a split second before Joe Palmer?' 'Remember how I took the ball from Harry Dodd and booted her in?'

Remember! I didn't have to remember, because I'd heard every story a score of times and maybe boredom caused my blackout. Boredom and frustration and pain. Standing for long periods always hurts me, but Dad considers it unsociable to sit down in a pub and he tries to pretend I'm not a cripple. I counted the minutes till he finished his last drink and I was staggering when we went out into the street and he gripped my arm to steady me.

A kindly act, but a final reminder that I was a deformed weakling and he was an all-powerful hero. A hero who screamed when I pulled my arm away and he lost his balance and fell in front of the bus, but I'm not certain why he fell. Did he slip, or was he pushed?

Poor Dad. The wheel crushed his thighs and he would have been a worse cripple than me if he hadn't died during the amputations, though I didn't know that at the time. I was so dazed and shattered that the ambulance crew had to give me sedatives and I was barely conscious when I heard the news.

Yes, poor old Dad. No legs, no life and no more boasting. No more trees to climb or treasures gleaming in the sitting-room to gloat over. As I said, the tree was cut down and Dad's trophies are in the attic now; dull, tarnished and covered with cobwebs. How I laughed when I bolted the trap door behind them. How happy I was for a while.

But I didn't remain happy for long. The aches and pains started about a month later and the dreams followed them. Though I'm not superstitious and I'd seen Dad's coffin lowered into the grave with a pair of his football boots on top of it, I began to suspect that animal strength might conquer death. That Dad was digging his way up from the earth. That my Dad hadn't died.

And I was right. After they took me to hospital for treatment – I couldn't even understand what they called my condition – Dad came and visited me. I didn't see him at first, but I heard him. I heard him at night and I heard him during the day. He spoke to me through the lips of the doctors and the nurses and the WVS lady who came round with the library books. Not his actual voice, and I couldn't make out what he was actually saying, but I knew he was pleading with me. Dad wanted me to give him something, but I didn't know what the thing was.

No, until recently I hadn't a clue what Dad was after. I thought he might be hoping for forgiveness on account of all the boredom and humiliation he'd caused me. Or perhaps he was offering me encouragement and advice. 'Be a good boy and work hard at the centre, Tommy. Forget you're a cripple and follow my example. Remember how I strode along the embankment on my way to Brighton ... Remember how I romped home at the White City ... Remember how I scored a hat trick for Tynecastle United.'

Or maybe he wanted me to plant another pear tree or release his trophies from the attic. Those were my last thoughts before the voices of the doctors and the nurses and the health visitors stopped and Dad spoke through the lips of the chief surgeon whose name I can't quite remember. Mr Macadam or Mackenzie or Macalpine; some such Scottish name.

Yes, I'm sure it was Macadam, and when he bent over my bed his Scottish accent became more pronounced and he clicked his tongue sadly.

'Aye,' he said. 'I'm sorra to say that the lump above yer knee is a bit worryin' and I'd best have another squint at it.'

He had his squint and then they made me sign some papers, as I was alone in the world with no close relatives. Mum dead because she gave me birth; Dad under the soil because I killed him.

'Not to worry though, lad. It's just a wee lump and I'll patch yer up and make yer as good as new,' Macadam had promised and I believed him because I've faith in the medical profession and he had no reason to dislike me or wish to hurt me. I was sure I'd come through the operation with flying colours and I was quite happy before Matron jabbed a needle into my arm and they wheeled me to the theatre.

But when I got to the theatre and saw Macadam put on his green mask I knew the truth and I was too weak and drowsy to resist or ask the nurses to help me. I saw Dad watching me from behind Macadam's eyes. I knew that Dad had possessed Macadam's soul. I knew what Dad wanted, and Dad got his wish.

Dad told Mr Macadam to cut off my one good leg.

The Cold Embrace

MISS BRADDON

HE WAS AN ARTIST – SUCH THINGS as happened to him happen sometimes to artists.

He was a German – such things as happened to him happen sometimes to Germans.

He was young, handsome, studious; enthusiastic, metaphysical, reckless, unbelieving, heartless.

And being young, handsome, and eloquent, he was beloved.

He was an orphan, under the guardianship of his dead father's brother, his uncle Wilhelm, in whose house he had been brought up from a little child; and she who loved him was his cousin – his cousin Gertrude, whom he swore he loved in return.

Did he love her? Yes, when he first swore it. It soon wore out, this passionate love; how threadbare and wretched a sentiment it became at last in the selfish heart of the student! But in its first golden dawn, when he was only nineteen, and had just returned from his apprenticeship to a great painter at Antwerp, and they wandered together in the most romantic outskirts of the city at rosy sunset, by holy moonlight, or bright and joyous morning, how beautiful a dream!

They keep it a secret from Wilhelm, as he has the father's ambition of a wealthy suitor for his only child – a cold and dreary vision beside the lover's dream.

So they are betrothed; and standing side by side, when the dying sun and the pale rising moon divide the heavens, he puts the betrothal ring upon her finger, the white and tapered finger whose slender shape he knows so well. This ring is a peculiar one, a massive golden serpent, its tail in its mouth, the symbol of eternity; it had been his mother's, and he would know it amongst a thousand. If he were to become blind tomorrow, he could select it from amongst a thousand by the touch alone.

He places it on her finger, and they swear to be true to each other for ever and ever – through trouble and danger – in sorrow and change – in wealth and poverty. Her father must needs be won to consent to their union by and by, for they were now betrothed, and death alone could part them.

But the young student, the scoffer at revelation, yet the enthusiastic adorer of the mystical asks:

'Can death part us? I would return to you from the grave, Gertrude. My soul would come back to be near my love. And you – you, if you died before me – the cold earth would not hold you from me; if you loved me you would return, and again these fair arms would be clasped round my neck as they are now.'

But she told him, with a holier light in her deep-blue eyes than had ever shone in his – she told him that the dead who die at peace with God are happy in heaven, and cannot return to the troubled earth; and that it is only the suicide – the lost wretch on whom sorrowful angels shut the door of Paradise – whose unholy spirit haunts the footsteps of the living.

The first year of their betrothal is passed, and she is alone, for he has gone to Italy, on a commission for some rich man, to copy Raphaels, Titians, Guidos, in a gallery at Florence. He has gone to win fame, perhaps; but it is not the less bitter – he is gone!

Of course her father misses his young nephew, who has been as a son to him; and he thinks his daughter's sadness no more than a cousin should feel for a cousin's absence.

In the meantime, the weeks and months pass. The lover writes – often at first, then seldom – at last, not at all.

How many excuses she invents for him! How many times she goes to the distant little post-office, to which he is to address his letters! How many times she hopes, only to be disappointed! How many times she despairs only to hope again!

But real despair comes at last, and will not be put off any more. The rich suitor appears on the scene, and her father is determined. She is to marry at once. The wedding-day is fixed – the fifteenth of June.

The date seems burnt into her brain.

The date, written in fire, dances for ever before her eyes.

The date, shrieked by the Furies, sounds continually in her ears.

But there is time yet – it is the middle of May – there is time for a letter to reach him at Florence; there is time for him to come to Brunswick, to take her away and marry her, in spite of her father – in spite of the whole world.

But the days and weeks fly by, and he does not write – he does not come. This is indeed despair which usurps her heart, and will not be put away.

It is the fourteenth of June. For the last time she goes to the little post-office; for the last time she asks the old question, and they give her for the last time the dreary answer, 'No; no letter.'

For the last time – for tomorrow is the day appointed for her bridal. Her father will hear no entreaties; her rich suitor will not listen to her prayers. They will not be put off a day – an hour; tonight alone is hers – this night, which she may employ as she will.

She takes another path than that which leads home; she hurries through some by-streets of the city, out on to a lonely bridge, where he and she had stood so often in the sunset, watching the rose-coloured light glow, fade, and die upon the river.

He returns from Florence. He had received her letter. That letter, blotted with tears, entreating, despairing – he had received it, but he loved her no longer. A young Florentine, who had sat to him for a model, had bewitched his fancy – that fancy which with him stood in place of a heart – and Gertrude had been half-forgotten. If she had a richer suitor, good; let her marry him; better for her, better far for himself. He had no wish to fetter himself with a wife. Had he not his art always? – his eternal bride, his unchanging mistress.

Thus he though it wiser to delay his journey to Brunswick, so that he should arrive when the wedding was over – arrive in time to salute the bride.

And the vows – the mystical fancies – the belief in his return, even after death, to the embrace of his beloved? O, gone out of his life; melted away for ever, those foolish dreams of his boyhood.

So on the fifteenth of June he enters Brunswick, by that very bridge on which she stood, the stars looking down on her, the night before. He strolls across the bridge and down by the water's edge, a great rough dog at his heels, and the smoke from his short meerschaum-pipe curling in blue wreaths fantastically in the pure morning air. He has his sketch-book under his arm, and attracted now and then by some object that catches his artist's eye, stops to draw; a few weeds and pebbles on the river's brink – a crag on the opposite shore – a group of pollard willows in the distance. When he has done, he admires his drawing, shuts his sketch-book, empties the ashes from his pipe, refills from his tobacco-pouch, sings the refrain of a gay drinking-song, calls to his dog, smokes again, and walks on. Suddenly he opens his sketch-book again; this time that which attracts him is a group of figures: but what is it?

It is not a funeral, for there are no mourners.

It is not a funeral, but it is a corpse lying on a rude bier, covered with an old sail, carried between two bearers.

It is not a funeral, for the bearers are fishermen – fishermen in their everyday garb.

About a hundred yards from him they rest their burden on a bank – one stands at the head of the bier, the other throws himself down at the foot of it.

And thus they form a perfect group; he walks back two or three paces, selects his point of sight, and begins to sketch a hurried outline. He has finished it before they move; he hears their voices, though he cannot hear their words, and wonders what they can be talking of. Presently he walks on and joins them.

'You have a corpse there, my friends?' he says.

'Yes; a corpse washed ashore an hour ago.'

'Drowned?'

'Yes, drowned. A young girl, very handsome.'

'Suicides are always handsome,' says the painter; and then he stands for a little while idly smoking and meditating, looking at the sharp outline of the corpse and the stiff folds of the rough canvas covering.

Life is such a golden holiday for him – young, ambitious, clever – that it seems as though sorrow and death could have no part in his destiny.

At last he says that, as this poor suicide is so handsome, he should like to make a sketch of her.

He gives the fishermen some money, and they offer to remove the sailcloth that covers her features.

No; he will do it himself. He lifts the rough, coarse, wet canvas from her face. What face?

The face that shone on the dreams of his foolish boyhood; the face which once was the light of his uncle's home. His cousin Gertrude – his betrothed!

He sees, as in one glance, while he draws one breath, the rigid features – the marble arms – the hands crossed on the cold bosom; and, on the third finger of the left hand, the ring which had been his mother's – the golden serpent; the ring which, if he were to become blind, he could select from a thousand others by the touch alone.

But he is a genius and a metaphysician – grief, true grief, is not for such as he. His first thought is flight – flight anywhere out of that accursed city – anywhere far from the brink of that hideous river – anywhere away from memory, away from remorse – anywhere to forget.

He is miles on the road that leads away from Brunswick before he knows that he has walked a step.

It is only when his dog lies down panting at his feet that he feels how exhausted he is himself, and sits down upon a bank to rest. How the landscape spins round and round before his dazzled eyes, while his morning's sketch of the two fishermen and the canvas-covered bier glares redly at him out of the twilight!

At last, after sitting a long time by the roadside, idly playing with his dog, idly smoking, idly lounging, looking as any idle, light-hearted travelling student might look, yet all the while acting over that morning's scene in his burning brain a hundred times a minute; at last he grows a little more composed, and tries presently to think of himself as he is, apart from his cousin's suicide. Apart from that, he was no worse off than he was yesterday. His genius was not gone; the money he had earned at Florence still lined his pocket-book; he was his own master, free to go whither he would.

And while he sits on the roadside, trying to separate himself from the scene of that morning – trying to put away the image of the corpse covered with the damp canvas sail – trying to think of what he should do next, where he should go, to be farthest away from Brunswick and remorse, the old diligence comes rumbling and jingling along. He remembers it; it goes from Brunswick to Aix-la-Chapelle.

He whistles to his dog, shouts to the postillion to stop, and springs into the *coupé*.

During the whole evening, through the long night, though he does not once close his eyes, he never speaks a word; but when morning dawns, and the other passengers awake and begin to talk to each other, he joins in the conversation. He tells them that he is an artist, that he is going to Cologne and to Antwerp to copy the Rubenses, and the great picture by Quentin Matsys, in the museum. He remembered afterwards that he talked and laughed boisterously, and that when he was talking and laughing loudest, a passenger, older and graver than the rest, opened the window near him, and told him to put his head out. He remembered the fresh air blowing in his face, the singing of the birds in his ears, and the flat fields and roadside reeling before his eyes. He remembered this, and then falling in a lifeless heap on the floor of the diligence.

It is a fever that keeps him for six long weeks laid on a bed at a hotel in Aix-la-Chapelle.

He gets well, and, accompanied by his dog, starts on foot for Cologne. By this time he is his former self once more. Again the blue smoke from his short meerschaum curls upwards in the morning air – again he sings some old university drinking-song – again stops here and there, meditating and sketching.

He is happy, and has forgotten his cousin – and so on to Cologne.

It is by the great cathedral he is standing, with his dog at his side. It is night, the bells have just chimed the hour, and the clocks are striking eleven; the moonlight shines full upon the magnificent pile, over which the artist's eye wanders, absorbed in the beauty of form.

He is not thinking of his drowned cousin, for he has forgotten her and is happy.

Suddenly someone, something from behind him, puts two cold arms round his neck, and clasps its hands on his breast.

And yet there is no one behind him, for on the flags bathed in the broad moonlight there are only two shadows, his own and his dog's. He turns quickly round – there is no one – nothing to be seen in the broad square but himself and his dog; and though he feels, he cannot see the cold arms clasped round his neck.

It is not ghostly, this embrace, for it is palpable to the touch – it cannot be real, for it is invisible.

He tries to throw off the cold caress. He clasps the hands in his own to tear them asunder, and to cast them off his neck. He can feel the long delicate fingers cold and wet beneath his touch, and on the third finger of the left hand he can feel the ring which was his mother's – the golden serpent – the ring which he has always said he would know among a thousand by the touch alone. He knows it now!

His dead cousin's cold arms are round his neck – his dead cousin's wet hands are clasped upon his breast. He asks himself if he is mad. 'Up, Leo!' he shouts. 'Up, up, boy!' and the Newfoundland leaps to his shoulders – the dog's paws are on the dead hands, and the animal utters a terrific howl, and springs away from his master.

The student stands in the moonlight, the dead arms around his neck, and the dog at a little distance moaning piteously.

Presently a watchman, alarmed by the howling of the dog, comes into the square to see what is wrong.

In a breath the cold arms are gone.

He takes the watchman home to the hotel with him and gives him money; in his gratitude he could have given that man half his little fortune.

Will it ever come to him again, this embrace of the dead?

He tries never to be alone; he makes a hundred acquaintances, and shares the chamber of another student. He starts up if he is left by himself in the public room at the inn where he is staying, and runs into the street. People notice his strange actions, and begin to think that he is mad.

But, in spite of all, he is alone once more; for one night the public room being empty for a moment, when on some idle pretence he strolls into the street, the street is empty too, and for the second time he feels the cold arms round his neck, and for the second time, when he calls his dog, the animal slinks away from him with a piteous howl.

After this he leaves Cologne, still travelling on foot – of necessity now, for his money is getting low. He joins travelling hawkers, he walks side by side with labourers, he talks to every foot-passenger he falls in with, and tries from morning till night to get company on the road.

At night he sleeps by the fire in the kitchen of the inn at which he stops; but do what he will, he is often alone, and it is now a common thing for him to feel the cold arms around his neck.

Many months have passed since his cousin's death – autumn, winter, early spring. His money is nearly gone, his health is utterly broken, he is the shadow of his former self, and he is getting near Paris. He will reach the city at the time of the Carnival. To this he looks forward. In Paris, in Carnival time, he need never, surely,, be alone, never feel that deadly caress; he may even recover his lost gaiety, his lost health, once more resume his profession, once more earn fame and money by his art.

How hard he tries to get over the distance that divides him from Paris, while day by day he grows weaker, and his step slower and more heavy!

But there is an end at last; the long dreary roads are passed. This is Paris, which he enters for the first time – Paris, of which he has dreamed so much

– Paris, whose million voices are to exorcise his phantom.

To him tonight Paris seems one vast chaos of lights, music, and confusion – lights which dance before his eyes and will not be still – music that rings in his ears and deafens him – confusion which makes his head whirl round and round.

But, in spite of all, he finds the opera-house, where there is a masked ball. He has enough money left to buy a ticket of admission, and to hire a domino to throw over his shabby dress. It seems only a moment after his entering the gates of Paris that he is in the very midst of all the wild gaiety of the opera-house ball.

No more darkness, no more loneliness, but a mad crowd, shouting and dancing, and a lovely Débardeuse hanging on his arm.

The boisterous gaiety he feels surely is his old light-heartedness come back. He hears the people round him talking of the outrageous conduct of some drunken student, and it is to him they point when they say this – to him, who has not moistened his lips since yesterday at noon, for even now he will not drink; though his lips are parched, and his throat burning, he cannot drink. His voice is thick and hoarse, and his utterance indistinct; but still this must be his old light-heartedness come back that makes him so wildly gay.

The little Débardeuse is wearied out – her arm rests on his shoulder heavier than lead – the other dancers one by one drop off.

The lights in the chandeliers one by one die out.

The decorations look pale and shadowy in that dim light which is neither night nor day.

A faint glimmer from the dying lamps, a pale streak of cold grey light from the new-born day, creeping in through half-opened shutters.

And by this light the bright-eyed Débardeuse fades sadly. He looks her in the face. How the brightness of her eyes dies out! Again he looks her in the face. How white that face has grown! Again – and now it is the shadow of a face alone that looks in his.

Again – and they are gone – the bright eyes, the face, the shadow of the face. He is alone; alone in that vast saloon.

Alone, and, in the terrible silence, he hears the echoes of his own footsteps in that dismal dance which has no music.

No music but the beating of his heart against his breast. For the cold arms are round his neck – they whirl him round, they will not be flung off, or cast away; he can no more escape from their icy grasp than he can escape from death. He looks behind him – there is nothing but himself in the great empty *salle;* but he can feel – cold, deathlike, but oh, how palpable! – the long slender fingers, and the ring which was his mother's. He tries to shout, but he has no power in his burning throat. The silence of the place is only broken by the echoes of his own footsteps in the dance from which he cannot extricate himself. Who says he has no partner? The cold hands are clasped on his breast, and now he does not shun their caress. No! One more polka, if he drops down dead.

The lights are all out, and, half an hour after, the *gendarmes* come in with a lantern to see that the house is empty; they are followed by a great dog that they have found seated howling on the steps of the theatre. Near the principal entrance they stumble over –

The body of a student, who has died from want of food, exhaustion, and the breaking of a blood-vessel.

Royal Jelly

ROALD DAHL

'IT WORRIES ME TO DEATH, Albert, it really does,' Mrs Taylor said.

She kept her eyes fixed on the baby who was lying absolutely motionless in the crook of her left arm.

'I just know there's something wrong.'

The skin on the baby's face had a pearly translucent quality, and was stretched very tightly over the bones.

'Try again,' Albert Taylor said.

'It won't do any good.'

'You have to keep trying, Mabel,' he said.

She lifted the bottle out of the saucepan of hot water and shook a few drops of milk onto the inside of her wrist, testing for temperature.

'Come on,' she whispered. 'Come on, my baby. Wake up and take a bit more of this.'

There was a small lamp on the table close by that made a soft yellow glow all around her.

'Please,' she said. 'Take just a weeny bit more.'

The husband watched her over the top of his magazine. She was half dead with exhaustion, he could see that, and the pale oval face, usually so grave and serene, had taken on a kind of pinched and desperate look. But even so, the drop of her head as she gazed down at the child was curiously beautiful.

'You see,' she murmured. 'It's no good. She won't have it.'

She held the bottle up to the light, squinting at the calibrations.

'One ounce again. That's all she's taken. No – it isn't even that. It's only three quarters. It's not enough to keep body and soul together, Albert, it really isn't. It worries me to death.'

'I know,' he said.

'If only they could *find out* what was wrong.'

'There's nothing wrong, Mabel. It's just a matter of time.'

'Of course there's something wrong.'

'Dr Robinson says no.'

'Look,' she said, standing up. 'You can't tell me it's natural for a six-weeks-old child to weigh less, less by more than *two whole pounds* than she did when she was born! Just look at those legs! They're nothing but skin and bone!'

The tiny baby lay limply on her arm, not moving.

Dr Robinson said you was to stop worrying, Mabel. So did that other one.'

'Ha!' she said. 'Isn't that wonderful! I'm to stop worrying!'

'Now, Mabel.'

'What does he want me to do? Treat it as some sort of a joke?'

'He didn't say that.'

'I hate doctors! I hate them all!' she cried, and swung away from him and walked quickly out of the room toward the stairs, carrying the baby with her.

Albert Taylor stayed where he was and let her go.

In a little while he heard her moving about in the bedroom directly over his head, quick nervous footsteps going tap tap tap on the linoleum above. Soon the footsteps would stop, and then he would have to get up and follow her, and when he went into the bedroom he would find her sitting beside the cot as usual, staring at the child and crying softly to herself and refusing to move.

'She's starving, Albert,' she would say.

'Of course she's not starving.'

'She *is* starving. I know she is. And Albert?'

'Yes?'

'I believe you know it too, but you won't admit it. Isn't that right?'

Every night now it was like this.

Last week they had taken the child back to the hospital, and the doctor had examined it carefully and told them that there was nothing the matter.

'It took us nine years to get this baby, Doctor,' Mabel had said. 'I think it would kill me if anything should happen to her.'

That was six days ago and since then it had lost another five ounces.

But worrying about it wasn't going to help anybody, Albert Taylor told himself. One simply had to trust the doctor on a thing like this. He picked up the magazine that was still lying on his lap and glanced idly down the list of contents to see what it had to offer this week:

AMONG THE BEES IN MAY

HONEY COOKERY

THE BEE FARMER AND THE B. PHARM.

EXPERIENCES IN THE CONTROL OF NOSEMA

THE LATEST ON ROYAL JELLY

THIS WEEK IN THE APIARY

REGURGITATIONS

BRITISH BEEKEEPERS ANNUAL DINNER

ASSOCIATION NEWS

All his life Albert Taylor had been fascinated by anything that had to do with bees. As a small boy he used often to catch them in his bare hands and go running with them into the house to show to his mother, and sometimes he would put them on his face and let them crawl about over his cheeks and neck, and the astonishing thing about it all was that he never got stung. On the contrary, the bees seemed to enjoy being with him. They never tried to fly away, and to get rid of them he would brush them off gently with his fingers. Even then they would frequently return and settle again on his arm or hand or knee, any place where the skin was bare.

His father, who was a bricklayer, said there must be some witch's stench about the boy, something noxious that came oozing out through the pores of the skin, and that no good would ever come of it, hypnotizing insects like that. But the mother said it was a gift given him by God, and even went so far as to compare him with St. Francis and the birds.

As he grew older, Albert Taylor's fascination with bees developed into an obsession, and by the time he was twelve he had built his first hive. The following summer he had captured his first swarm. Two years later, at the age of fourteen, he had no less than five hives standing neatly in a row against the fence in his father's small back yard, and already – apart from the normal task of producing honey – he was practising the delicate and complicated business of rearing his own queens, grafting larvae into artificial cell cups, and all the rest of it.

He never had to use smoke when there was work to do inside a hive, and he never wore gloves on his hands or a net over his head. Clearly there was some strange sympathy between this boy and the bees, and down in the village, in the shops and pubs, they began to speak about him with a certain kind of respect, and people started coming up to the house to buy his honey.

When he was eighteen, he had rented one acre of rough pasture alongside a cherry orchard down the valley about a mile from the village, and there he had set out to establish his own business. Now, eleven years later, he was still in the same spot, but he had six acres of ground instead of one, two hundred and forty well-stocked hives, and a small house that he'd built mainly with his own hands. He had married at the age of twenty and that, apart from the fact that it had taken them nine years to get a child, had also been a success. In fact, everything had gone pretty well for Albert until this strange little baby girl came along and started frightening them out of their wits by refusing to eat properly and losing weight every day.

He looked up from the magazine and began thinking about his daughter.

This evening, for instance, when she had opened her eyes at the beginning of the feed, he had gazed into them and seen something that frightened him to death – a kind of misty vacant stare, as though the eyes themselves were not connected to the brain at all but were just lying loose in their sockets like a couple of small grey marbles.

Did those doctors really know what they were talking about?

He reached for an ashtray and started slowly picking the ashes out from the bowl of his pipe with a matchstick.

One could always take her along to another hospital, somewhere in Oxford perhaps. He might suggest that to Mabel when he went upstairs.

He could still hear her moving around in the bedroom, but she must have taken off her shoes now and put on slippers because the noise was very faint.

He switched his attention back to the magazine and went on with his reading. He finished an article called 'Experiences in the Control of Nosema.' then turned over the page and began reading the next one, 'The Latest on Royal Jelly.' He doubted very much whether there would be anything in this that he didn't know already:

What is this wonderful substance called royal jelly?

He reached for the tin of tobacco on the table beside him and began filling his pipe, still reading.

Royal jelly is a glandular secretion produced by the nurse bees to feed the larvae immediately they have hatched from the egg. The pharingeal glands of bees produce this substance in much the same way as the mammary glands of vertebrates produce milk. The fact is of great biological interest because no other insects in the world are known to have evolved such a process.

All old stuff, he told himself, but for want of anything better to do, he continued to read.

Royal jelly is fed in concentrated form to all bee larvae for the first three days after hatching from the egg; but beyond that point, for all those who are destined to become drones or workers, this precious food is greatly diluted with honey and pollen. On the other hand, the larvae which are destined to become queens are fed throughout the whole of their larval period on a concentrated diet of pure royal jelly. Hence the name.

Above him, up in the bedroom, the noise of the footsteps had stopped altogether. The house was quiet. He struck a match and put it to his pipe.

Royal jelly must be a substance of tremendous nourishing power, for on this diet alone, the honey-bee larva increases in weight fifteen hundred times in five days.

That was probably about right, he thought, although for some reason it had never occurred to him to consider larval growth in terms of weight before.

This is as if a seven-and-a-half-pound baby should increase in that time to five tons.

Albert Taylor stopped and read that sentence again.

He read it a third time.

This is as if a seven-and-a-half-pound baby ...

'Mabel!' he cried, jumping up from his chair. 'Mabel! Come here!'

He went out into the hall and stood at the foot of the stairs calling for her to come down.

There was no answer.

He ran up the stairs and switched on the light on the landing. The bedroom door was closed. He crossed the landing and opened it and stood in the doorway looking into the dark room. 'Mabel,' he said. 'Come downstairs a moment will you please? I've just had a bit of an idea. It's about the baby.'

The light from the landing behind him cast a faint glow over the bed and he could see her dimly now, lying on her stomach with her face buried in the pillow and her arms up over her head. She was crying again.

'Mabel,' he said, going over to her, touching her shoulder. 'Please come down a moment. This may be important.'

'Go away,' she said. 'Leave me alone.'

'Don't you want to hear about my idea?'

'Oh, Albert, I'm *tired*,' she sobbed. 'I'm so tired I don't know what I'm doing any more. I don't think I can go on. I don't think I can stand it.' There was a pause. Albert Taylor turned away from her and walked slowly over to the cradle where the baby was lying, and peered in. It was too dark for him to see the child's face, but when he bent down close he could hear the sound of breathing, very faint and quick. 'What time is the next feed?' he asked.

'Two o'clock, I suppose.'

'And the one after that?'

'Six in the morning.'

'I'll do them both,' he said 'You go to sleep.'

She didn't answer.

'You get properly into bed, Mabel, and go straight to sleep, you understand? And stop worrying. I'm taking over completely for the next twelve hours. You'll give yourself a nervous breakdown going on like this.'

'Yes,' she said. 'I know.'

'I'm taking the nipper and myself *and* the alarm clock into the spare room this very moment, so you just lie down and relax and forget all about us. Right?' Already he was pushing the cradle out through the door.

'Oh Albert,' she sobbed.

'Don't you worry about a thing. Leave it to me.'

'Albert . . .'

'Yes?'

'I love you, Albert.'

'I love you too, Mabel. Now go to sleep.'

Albert Taylor didn't see his wife again until nearly eleven o'clock the next morning.

'Good *gracious* me!' she cried, rushing down the stairs in dressing-gown and slippers. 'Albert! Just look at the time! I must have slept twelve hours at least! Is everything all right? What happened?'

He was sitting quietly in his armchair, smoking a pipe and reading the morning paper. The baby was in a sort of carrier cot on the floor at his feet, sleeping.

'Hullo, dear,' he said, smiling.

She ran over to the cot and looked in. 'Did she take anything, Albert? How many times have you fed her? She was due for another one at ten o'clock, did you know that?'

Albert Taylor folded the newspaper neatly into a square and put it away on the side table. 'I fed her at two in the morning,' he said, 'and she took about half an ounce, no more. I fed her again at six and she did a bit better that time, two ounces . . .'

'*Two ounces!* Oh, Albert, that's marvellous!'

'And we just finished the last feed ten minutes ago. There's the bottle on the mantelpiece. Only one ounce left. She drank three. How's that?' He was grinning proudly, delighted with his achievement.

The woman quickly got down on her knees and peered at the baby.

'Don't she look better?' he asked eagerly. 'Don't she look fatter in the face?'

'It may sound silly,' the wife said, 'but I actually think she does. Oh, Albert, you're a marvel! How did you do it?'

'She's turning the corner,' he said. 'That's all it is. Just like the doctor prophesied, she's turning the corner.'

'I pray to God you're right, Albert.'

'Of course I'm right. From now on, you watch her go.'

The woman was gazing lovingly at the baby.

'You look a lot better youself too, Mabel.'

'I feel wonderful. I'm sorry about last night.'

'Let's keep it this way,' he said. I'll do all the night feeds in future. You do the day ones.'

She looked up at him across the cot, frowning. 'No,' she said. 'Oh no, I wouldn't allow you to do that.'

'I don't want you to have a breakdown, Mabel.'

'I won't not now I've had some sleep.'

'Much better we share it.'

'No, Albert. This is my job and I intend to do it. Last night won't happen again.

There was a pause. Albert Taylor took the pipe out of his mouth and examined the grain on the bowl. 'All right,' he said. 'In that case I'll just relieve you of the donkey work, I'll do all the sterilizing and the mixing of the food and getting everything ready. That'll help you a bit, anyway.'

She looked at him carefully, wondering what could have come over him all of a sudden.

'You see, Mabel, I've been thinking . . .'

'Yes, dear,'

'I've been thinking that up until last night I've never even raised a finger to help you with this baby.'

'That isn't true.'

'Oh yes it is. So I've decided that from now on I'm going to do *my* share of the work. I'm going to be the feed-mixer and the bottle-sterilizer. Right?'

'It's very sweet of you, dear, but I really don't think it's necessary ...'

'Come on!' he cried. 'Don't change the luck! I done it the last three times and just *look* what happened! When's the next one? Two o'clock, isn't it?'

'Yes.'

'It's all mixed,' he said. 'Everything's all mixed and ready and all you've got to do when the time comes is to go out there to the larder and take it off the shelf and warm it up. That's *some* help, isn't it?'

The woman got up off her knees and went over to him and kissed him on the cheek. 'You're such a nice man,' she said. 'I love you more and more every day I know you.'

Later, in the middle of the afternoon, when Albert was outside in the sunshine working among the hives, he heard her calling to him from the house.

'Albert!' she shouted. 'Albert, come here!' She was running through the buttercups toward him.

He started forward to meet her, wondering what was wrong.

'Oh, Albert! Guess what!'

'What?'

'I've just finished giving her the two-o'clock feed and she's taken the whole lot!'

'No!'

'Every drop of it! Oh, Albert, I'm so happy! She's going to be all right! She's turned the corner just like you said!' She came up to him and threw her arms around his neck and hugged him, and he clapped her on the back and laughed and said what a marvellous little mother she was.

'Will you come in and watch the next one and see if she does it again, Albert?'

He told her he wouldn't miss it for anything, and she hugged him again, then turned and ran back to the house, skipping over the grass and singing all the way.

Naturally, there was a certain amount of suspense in the air as the time approached for the six-o'clock feed. By five thirty both parents were already seated in the living room waiting for the moment to arrive. The bottle with the milk formula in it was standing in a saucepan of warm water on the mantelpiece. The baby was asleep in its carrier cot on the sofa.

At twenty minutes to six it woke up and started screaming its head off.

'There you are!' Mrs Taylor cried. 'She's asking for the bottle. Pick her up quick, Albert, and hand her to me here. Give me the bottle first.'

He gave her the bottle, then placed the baby on the woman's lap.

143

Cautiously, she touched the baby's lips with the end of the nipple. The baby seized the nipple between its gums and began to suck ravenously with a rapid powerful action.

'Oh, Albert, isn't it wonderful?' she said, laughing.

'It's terrific, Mabel.'

In seven or eight minutes, the entire contents of the bottle had disappeared down the baby's throat.

'You clever girl,' Mrs Taylor said. 'Four ounces again.'

Albert Taylor was leaning forward in his chair, peering intently into the baby's face. 'You know what?' he said. 'She even seems as though she's put on a touch of weight already. What do you think?'

The mother looked down at the child.

'Don't she seem bigger and fatter to you, Mabel, than she was yesterday?'

'Maybe she does, Albert. I'm not sure. Although actually there couldn't be any *real* gain in such a short time as this. The important thing is that she's eating normally.'

'She's turned the corner,' Albert said. 'I don't think you need worry about her any more.'

'I certainly won't.'

'You want me to go up and fetch the cradle back into our own bedroom, Mabel?'

'Yes, please,' she said.

Albert went upstairs and moved the cradle. The woman followed with the baby, and after changing its nappy, she laid it gently down on its bed. Then she covered it with sheet and blanket.

'Doesn't she look lovely, Albert?' she whispered. 'Isn't that the most beautiful baby you've ever seen in your *entire* life?'

'Leave her be now, Mabel,' he said. 'Come on downstairs and cook us a bit of supper. We both deserve it.'

After they had finished eating, the parents settled themselves in armchairs in the living room, Albert with his magazine and his pipe, Mrs Taylor with her knitting. But this was a very different scene from the one of the night before. Suddenly, all tensions had vanished. Mrs Taylor's handsome oval face was glowing with pleasure, her cheeks were pink, her eyes were sparkling bright, and her mouth was fixed in a little dreamy smile of pure content. Every now and again she would glance up from her knitting and gaze affectionately at her husband. Occasionally, she would stop the clicking of her needles altogether for a few seconds and sit quite still, looking at the ceiling, listening for a cry or a whimper from upstairs. But all was quiet.

'Albert,' she said after a while.

'Yes, dear?'

'What was it you were going to tell me last night when you came rushing up to the bedroom? You said you had an idea for the baby.'

Albert Taylor lowered the magazine onto his lap and gave her a long sly look.

'Did I?' he said.

'Yes.' She waited for him to go on, but he didn't.

'What's the big joke?' she asked. 'Why are you grinning like that?'

'It's a joke all right,' he said.

'Tell it to me, dear.'

'I'm not sure I ought to,' he said. 'You might call me a liar.'

She had seldom seen him looking so pleased with himself as he was now, and she smiled back at him, egging him on.

'I'd just like to see your face when you hear it, Mabel, that's all.'

'Albert, what *is* all this?'

He paused, refusing to be hurried.

'You do think the baby's better, don't you?' he asked.

'Of course I do.'

'You agree with me that all of a sudden she's feeding marvellously and looking one-hundred-per-cent different?'

'I do, Albert, yes.'

'That's good,' he said, the grin widening. 'You see, it's me that did it.'

'Did what?'

'I cured the baby.'

'Yes, dear, I'm sure you did.' Mrs Taylor went right on with her knitting.

'You don't believe me, do you?'

'Of course I believe you, Albert. I give you all the credit, every bit of it.'

'Then how did I do it?'

'Well,' she said, pausing a moment to think. 'I suppose it's simply that you're a brilliant feed-mixer. Ever since you started mixing the feeds she's got better and better.'

'You mean there's some sort of an art in mixing the feeds?'

'Apparently there is.' She was knitting away and smiling quietly to herself, thinking how funny men were.

'I'll tell you a secret,' he said. 'You're absolutely right. Although, mind you, it isn't so much *how* you mix it that counts. It's what you put in. You realize that, don't you, Mabel?'

'Mrs Taylor stopped knitting and looked up sharply at her husband.

'Albert,' she said, 'don't tell me you've been putting things into that child's milk?'

He sat there grinning.

'Well, have you or haven't you?'

'It's possible,' he said.

'I don't believe it.'

He had a strange fierce way of grinning that showed his teeth.

'Albert,' she said. 'Stop playing with me like this.'

'Yes, dear, all right.'

'You haven't *really* put anything into her milk, have you? Answer me properly, Albert. This could be serious with such a tiny baby.'

'The answer is yes, Mabel.'

'*Albert Taylor!* How could you?'

'Now don't get excited,' he said. 'I'll tell you all about it if you really want me to, but for heaven's sake keep your hair on.'

'It was beer!' she cried. 'I just know it was beer!'

'Don't be so daft, Mabel, please.'

'Then what was it?'

Albert laid his pipe down carefully on the table beside him and leaned back in his chair. 'Tell me,' he said, 'did you ever by any chance happen to hear me mentioning something called royal jelly?'

'I did not.'

'It's magic,' he said. 'Pure magic. And last night I suddenly got the idea that if I was to put some of this into the baby's milk ...'

'How *dare* you!'

'Now, Mabel, you don't even know what it is yet.'

'I don't care what it is,' she said. 'You can't go putting foreign bodies like that into a tiny baby's milk. You must be mad.'

'It's perfectly harmless, Mabel, otherwise I wouldn't have done it. It comes from bees.'

'I might have guessed that.'

'And it's so precious that practically no one can afford to take it. When they do, it's only one little drop at a time.'

'And how much did you give to our baby, might I ask?'

'Ah,' he said, 'that's the whole point. That's where the difference lies. I reckon that our baby, just in the last four feeds, has already swallowed about fifty times as much royal jelly as anyone else in the world has ever swallowed before. How about that?'

'Albert, stop pulling my leg.'

'I swear it,' he said proudly.

She sat there staring at him, her brow wrinkled, her mouth slightly open.

'You know what this stuff actually costs, Mabel, if you want to buy it? There's a place in America advertising it for sale this very moment for something like five hundred dollars a pound jar! *Five hundred dollars!* That's more than gold, you know!'

She hadn't the faintest idea what he was talking about.

'I'll prove it,' he said, and he jumped up and went across to the large bookcase where he kept all his literature about bees. On the top shelf, the back numbers of *The American Bee Journal* were neatly stacked alongside those of *The British Bee Journal*, *Beecraft*, and other magazines. He took

146

down the last issue of *The American Bee Journal* and turned to a page of small classified advertisements at the back.

'Here you are,' he said. 'Exactly as I told you. 'We sell royal jelly – $480 per lb. jar wholesale.'

He handed her the magazine so she could read it herself.

'Now do you believe me? This is an actual shop in New York, Mabel. It says so.'

'It doesn't say you can go stirring it into the milk of a practically new-born baby,' she said. 'I don't know what's come over you, Albert, I really don't.'

'It's curing her, isn't it?'

'I'm not so sure about that now.'

'Don't be so damn silly, Mabel. You know it is.'

'Then why haven't other people done it with *their* babies?'

'I keep telling you,' he said. 'It's too expensive. Practically nobody in the world can afford to buy royal jelly just for *eating* except maybe one or two multimillionaires. The people who buy it are the big companies that make woman's face creams and things like that. They're using it as a stunt. They mix a tiny pinch of it into a big jar of face cream and it's selling like hot cakes for absolutely enormous prices. They claim it takes out the wrinkles.'

'And does it?'

'Now how on earth would I know that, Mabel? Anyway,' he said, returning to his chair, 'that's not the point. The point is this. It's done so much good to our little baby just in the last few hours that I think we ought to go right on giving it to her. Now don't interrupt, Mabel. Let me finish. I've got two hundred and forty hives out there and if I turn over maybe a hundred of them to making royal jelly, we ought to be able to supply her with all she wants.'

'Albert Taylor,' the woman said, stretching her eyes wide and staring at him. 'Have you gone out of your mind?'

'Just hear me through, will you please?'

'I forbid it,' she said, 'absolutely. You're not to give my baby another drop of that horrid jelly, you understand?'

'Now, Mabel . . .'

'And quite apart from that, we had a shocking honey crop last year, and if you go fooling around with those hives now, there's no telling what might not happen.'

'There's nothing wrong with my hives, Mabel.'

'You know very well we had only half the normal crop last year.'

'Do me a favour, will you?' he said. 'Let me explain some of the marvellous things this stuff does.'

'You haven't even told me what it is yet.'

'All right, Mabel. I'll do that too. Will you listen? Will you give me a chance to explain it?'

She sighed and picked up her knitting once more. 'I suppose you might as well get it off your chest, Albert. Go on and tell me.'

He paused, a bit uncertain now how to begin. It wasn't going to be easy to explain something like this to a person with no detailed knowledge of apiculture at all.

'You know, don't you,' he said, 'that each colony has only one queen?'

'Yes.'

'And that this queen lays all the eggs?'

'Yes, dear. That much I know.'

'All right. Now the queen can actually lay two different kinds of eggs. You didn't know that, but she can. It's what we call one of the miracles of the hive. She can lay eggs that produce drones, and she can lay eggs that produce workers. Now if that isn't a miracle, Mabel, I don't know what is.'

'Yes, Albert, all right.'

'The drones are the males. We don't have to worry about them. The workers are all females. So is the queen, of course. But the workers are unsexed females, if you see what I mean. Their organs are completely undeveloped, whereas the queen is tremendously sexy. She can actually lay her own weight in eggs in a single day.'

He hesitated, marshalling his thoughts.

'Now what happens is this. The queen crawls around on the comb and lays her eggs in what we call cells. You know all those hundreds of little holes you see in a honeycomb? Well, a brood comb is just about the same except the cells don't have honey in them, they have eggs. She lays one egg to each cell, and in three days each of these eggs hatches out into a tiny grub. We call it a larva.

'Now, as soon as this larva appears, the nurse bees – they're young workers – all crowd round and start feeding it like mad. And you know what they feed it on?'

'Royal jelly,' Mabel answered patiently.

'Right!' he cried. 'That's exactly what they do feed it on. They get this stuff out of a gland in their heads and they start pumping it into the cell to feed the larva. And what happens then?'

He paused dramatically, blinking at her with his small watery-gray eyes. Then he turned slowly in his chair and reached for the magazine that he had been reading the night before.

'You want to know what happens then?' he asked, wetting his lips.

'I can hardly wait.'

' "Royal jelly," ' he read aloud, ' "must be a substance of tremendous nourishing power, for on this diet alone, the honey-bee larva increases in weight *fifteen hundred times* in five days!" '

'How much?'

'*Fifteen hundred times*, Mabel. And you know what that means if you put it

148

in terms of a human being? It means,' he said, lowering his voice, leaning forward, fixing her with those small pale eyes, 'it means that in five days a baby weighing seven and a half pounds to start off with would increase in weight to *five tons!*'

For the second time, Mrs Taylor stopped knitting.

'Now you mustn't take that too literally, Mabel.'

'Who says I mustn't?'

'It's just a scientific way of putting it, that's all.'

'Very well, Albert. Go on.'

'But that's only half the story,' he said. 'There's more to come. The really amazing thing about royal jelly, I haven't told you yet. I'm going to show you now how it can transform a plain dull-looking little worker bee with practically no sex organs at all into a great big beautiful fertile queen.'

'Are you saying our baby is dull-looking and plain?' she asked sharply.

'Now don't go putting words into my mouth, Mabel, please. Just listen to this. Did you know that the queen bee and the worker bee, although they are completely different when they grow up, are both hatched out of exactly the same kind of egg?'

'I don't believe that,' she said.

'It's true as I'm sitting here, Mabel, honest it is. Any time the bees want a queen to hatch out of the egg instead of a worker, they can do it.'

'How?'

'Ah,' he said, shaking a thick forefinger in her direction. 'That's just what I'm coming to. That's the secret of the whole thing. Now – what do *you* think it is, Mabel, that makes this miracle happen?'

'Royal jelly,' she answered. 'You already told me.'

'Royal jelly it is!' he cried, clapping his hands and bouncing up on his seat. His big round face was glowing with excitement now, and two vivid patches of scarlet had appeared high up on each cheek.

'Here's how it works. I'll put it very simply for you. The bees want a new queen. So they build an extra-large cell, a queen cell we call it, and they get the old queen to lay one of her eggs in there. The other one thousand nine hundred and ninety nine eggs she lays in ordinary worker cells. Now. As soon as these eggs hatch out into larvae, the nurse bees rally round and start pumping in the royal jelly. All of them get it, workers as well as queen. But here's the vital thing, Mabel, so listen carefully. Here's where the difference comes. The worker larvae only receive this special marvellous food for the *first three days* of their larval life. After that they have a complete change of diet. What really happens is they get weaned, except that it's not like an ordinary weaning because it's so sudden. After the third day they're put straight away onto more or less routine bees' food – a mixture of honey and pollen – and then about two weeks later they emerge from the cells as workers.

'But not so the larva in the queen cell! This one gets royal jelly *all the way through its larval life.* The nurse bees simply pour it into the cell, so much so in fact that the little larva is literally floating in it. And that's what makes it into a queen!'

'You can't prove it,' she said.

'Don't talk so damn silly, Mabel, please. Thousands of people have proved it time and time again, famous scientists in every country in the world. All you have to do is take a larva out of a worker cell and put it in a queen cell – that's what we call grafting – and just so long as the nurse bees keep it well supplied with royal jelly, then presto! – it'll grow up into a queen! And what makes it more marvellous still is the absolutely enormous difference between a queen and a worker when they grow up. The abdomen is a different shape. The sting is different. The legs are different. The ...'

'In what way are the legs different?' she asked, testing him.

'The legs? Well, the workers have little pollen baskets on their legs for carrying the pollen. The queen has none. Now here's another thing. The queen has fully developed sex organs. The workers don't. And most amazing of all, Mabel, the queen lives for an average of four to six years. The worker hardly lives that many months. And all this difference simply because one of them got royal jelly and the other didn't!'

'It's pretty hard to believe,' she said, 'that a food can do all that.'

'Of course it's hard to believe. It's another of the miracles of the hive. In fact it's the biggest ruddy miracle of them all. It's such a hell of a big miracle that it's baffled the greatest men of science for hundreds of years. Wait a moment. Stay there. Don't move.'

Again he jumped up and went over to the bookcase and started rummaging among the books and magazines.

'I'm going to find you a few of the reports. Here we are. Here's one of them. Listen to this.' He started reading aloud from a copy of the *American Bee Journal:*

' "Living in Toronto at the head of a fine research laboratory given to him by the people of Canada in recognition of his truly great contribution to humanity in the discovery of insulin, Dr Frederick A. Banting became curious about royal jelly. He requested his staff to do a basic fractional analysis. ..." '

He paused.

'Well, there's no need to read it all, but here's what happened. Dr Banting and his people took some royal jelly from queen cells that contained two-day-old larvae, and then they started analyzing it. And what d'you think they found?

'They found,' he said 'that royal jelly contained phenols, sterols, glycerils, dextrose, *and* – now here it comes – and eighty to eighty-five per cent *unidentified* acids!'

He stood beside the bookcase with the magazine in his hand, smiling a funny little furtive smile of triumph, and his wife watched him, bewildered.

He was not a tall man; he had a thick plump pulpy-looking body that was built close to the ground on abbreviated legs. The legs were slightly bowed. The head was huge and round, covered with bristly short-cut hair, and the greater part of the face – now that he had given up shaving altogether – was hidden by a brownish yellow fuzz about an inch long. In one way or another, he was rather grotesque to look at, there was no denying that.

'Eighty to eighty-five per cent,' he said, 'unidentified acids. Isn't that fantastic?' He turned back to the bookshelf and began hunting through the other magazines.

'What does it mean, unidentified acids?'

'That's the whole point! No one knows! Not even Banting could find out. You've heard of Banting?'

'No.'

'He just happens to be about the most famous living doctor in the world today, that's all.'

Looking at him now as he buzzed around in front of the bookcase with his bristly head and his hairy face and his plump pulpy body, she couldn't help thinking that somehow, in some curious way, there was a touch of the bee about this man. She had often seen women grow to look like the horses that they rode, and she had noticed that people who bred birds or bull terriers or pomeranians frequently resembled in some small but startling manner the creature of their choice. But up until now it had never occurred to her that her husband might look like a bee. It shocked her a bit.

'And did Banting ever try to eat it,' she asked, 'This royal jelly?'

'Of course he didn't eat it, Mabel. He didn't have enough for that. It's too precious.'

'You know something?' she said, staring at him but smiling a little all the same. 'You're getting to look just a teeny bit like a bee yourself, did you know that?'

He turned and looked at her.

'I suppose it's the beard mostly,' she said. 'I do wish you'd stop wearing it. Even the color is sort of bee-ish, don't you think?'

'What the hell are you talking about, Mabel?'

'Albert,' she said. 'Your language.'

'Do you want to hear any more of this or don't you?'

'Yes, dear, I'm sorry. I was only joking. Do go on.'

He turned away again and pulled another magazine out of the bookcase and began leafing through the pages. 'Now just listen to this, Mabel. 'In 1939, Heyl experimented with twenty-one-day-old rats, injecting them with royal jelly in varying amounts. As a result, he found a precocious follicular development of the ovaries directly in proportion to the quantity of royal jelly injected." '

'There!' she cried. 'I knew it!'

'Knew what?'

'I knew something terrible would happen.'

'Nonsense. There's nothing wrong with that. Now here's another, Mabel. ' "Still and Burdett found that a male rat which hitherto had been unable to breed, upon receiving a minute daily dose of royal jelly, became a father many times over." '

'Albert,' she cried, 'this stuff is *much* too strong to give a baby! I don't like it at all.'

'Nonsense, Mabel.'

'Then why do they only try it out on rats, tell me that? Why don't some of these famous scientists take it themselves? They're too clever, that's why. Do you think Dr Banting is going to risk finishing up with precious ovaries? Not him.'

'But they *have* given it to people, Mabel. Here's a whole article about it. Listen.' He turned the page and again began reading from the magazine. ' "In Mexico, in 1953, a group of enlightened physicians began prescribing minute doses of royal jelly for such things as cerebral neuritis, arthritis, diabetes, antointoxication from tobacco, impotence in men, asthma, croup, and gout.... There are stacks of signed testimonials ... A celebrated stockbroker in Mexico City contracted a particularly stubborn case of psoriasis. He became physically unattractive. His clients began to forsake him. His business began to suffer. In desperation he turned to royal jelly – one drop with every meal – and presto! – he was cured in a fortnight. A waiter in the Café Jena, also in Mexico City, reported that his father, after taking minute doses of this wonder substance in capsule form, sired a healthy boy child at the age of ninety. A bullfight promoter in Acapulco, finding himself landed with a rather lethargic-looking bull, injected it with one gram of royal jelly (an excessive dose) just before it entered the arena. Thereupon, the beast became so swift and savage that it promptly dispatched two picadors, three horses, and a matador, and finally ..." '

'Listen!' Mrs Taylor said, interrupting him. 'I think the baby's crying.'

Albert glanced up from his reading. Sure enough, a lusty yelling noise was coming from the bedroom above.

'She must be hungry,' he said.

His wife looked at the clock. 'Good gracious me!' she cried, jumping up. 'It's past her time again already! You mix the feed, Albert, quickly, while I bring her down! But hurry! I don't want to keep her waiting.'

In half a minute, Mrs Taylor was back, carrying the screaming infant in her arms. She was flustered now, still quite unaccustomed to the ghastly nonstop racket that a healthy baby makes when it wants its food. 'Do be quick, Albert!' she called, settling herself in the armchair and arranging the child on her lap. 'Please hurry!'

Albert entered from the kitchen and handed her the bottle of warm milk. 'It's just right,' he said. 'You don't have to test it.'

She hitched the baby's head a little higher in the crook of her arm, then pushed the rubber teat straight into the wide-open yelling mouth. The baby grabbed the teat and began to suck. The yelling stopped. Mrs Taylor relaxed.

'Oh, Albert, isn't she lovely?'

'She's terrific, Mabel – thanks to royal jelly.'

'Now, dear, I don't want to hear another word about that nasty stuff. It frightens me to death.'

'You're making a big mistake,' he said.

'We'll see about that.'

The baby went on sucking the bottle.

'I do believe she's going to finish the whole lot again, Albert.'

'I'm sure she is,' he said.

And a few minutes later, the milk was all gone.

'Oh, what a good girl you are!' Mrs Taylor cried, as very gently she started to withdraw the nipple. The baby sensed what she was doing and sucked harder, trying to hold on. The woman gave a quick little tug, and *plop*, out it came.

'Waa! Waa! Waa! Waa! Waa!' the baby yelled.

'Nasty old wind,' Mrs Taylor said, hoisting the child onto her shoulder and patting its back.

It belched twice in quick succession.

'There you are, my darling, you'll be all right now.'

For a few seconds, the yelling stopped. Then it started again.

'Keep belching her,' Albert said. 'She's drunk it too quick.'

His wife lifted the baby back onto her shoulder. She rubbed its spine. She changed it from one shoulder to the other. She lay it on its stomach on her lap. She sat it on her knee. But it didn't belch again, and the yelling became louder and more insistent every minute.

'Good for the lungs,' Albert Taylor said, grinning. 'That's the way they exercise their lungs, Mabel, did you know that?'

'There, there, there,' the wife said, kissing it all over the face. 'There, there, there.'

They waited another five minutes, but not for one moment did the screaming stop.

'Change the nappy,' Albert said. 'It's got a wet nappy, that's all it is.' He fetched a clean one from the kitchen, and Mrs Taylor took the old one off and put the new one on.

This made no difference at all.

'Waa! Waa! Waa! Waa! Waa!' the baby yelled.

'You didn't stick the safety pin through the skin, did you, Mabel?'

'Of course I didn't,' she said, feeling under the nappy with her fingers to

153

make sure.

The parents sat opposite one another in their armchairs, smiling nervously, watching the baby on the mother's lap, waiting for it to tire and stop screaming.

'You know what?' Albert Taylor said at last.

'What?'

'I'll bet she's still hungry. I'll bet all she wants is another swig at that bottle. How about me fetching her an extra lot?'

'I don't think we ought to do that, Albert.'

'It'll do her good,' he said, getting up from his chair. 'I'm going to warm her up a second helping.'

He went into the kitchen, and was away several minutes. When he returned he was holding a bottle brimful of milk.

'I made her a double,' he announced. 'Eight ounces. Just in case.'

'Albert! Are you mad! Don't you know it's just as bad to overfeed as it is to underfeed?'

'You don't have to give her the lot, Mabel. You can stop any time you like. Go on,' he said, standing over her. 'Give her a drink.'

Mrs Taylor began to tease the baby's upper lip with the end of the nipple. The tiny mouth closed like a trap over the rubber teat and suddenly there was silence in the room. The baby's whole body relaxed and a look of absolute bliss came over its face as it started to drink.

'There you are Mabel! What did I tell you?'

The woman didn't answer.

'She's ravenous, that's what she is. Just look at her suck.'

Mrs Taylor was watching the level of the milk in the bottle. It was dropping fast, and before long three or four ounces out of the eight had disappeared.

'There,' she said. 'That'll do.'

'You can't pull it away now, Mabel.'

'Yes, dear. I must.'

'Go on, woman. Give her the rest and stop fussing.'

'But *Albert* . . .'

'She's famished, can't you see that? Go on, my beauty,' he said. 'You finish that bottle.'

'I don't like it, Albert,' the wife said, but she didn't pull the bottle away.

'She's making up for lost time, Mabel, that's all she's doing.'

Five minutes later the bottle was empty. Slowly, Mrs Taylor withdrew the nipple, and this time there was no protest from the baby, no sound at all. It lay peacefully on the mother's lap, the eyes glazed with contentment, the mouth half open, the lips smeared with milk.

'Twelve whole ounces, Mabel!' Albert Taylor said. 'Three times the normal amount! Isn't that amazing!'

The woman was staring down at the baby. And now the old anxious tight-lipped look of the frightened mother was slowly returning to her face.

'What's the matter with _you_?' Albert asked. 'You're not worried by that, are you? You can't expect her to get back to normal on a lousy four ounces, don't be ridiculous.'

'Come here, Albert,' she said.

'What?'

'I said come here.'

He went over and stood beside her.

'Take a good look and tell me if you see anything different.'

He peered closely at the baby. 'She seems bigger, Mabel, if that's what you mean. Bigger and fatter.'

'Hold her,' she ordered. 'Go on, pick her up.'

He reached out and lifted the baby up off the mother's lap. 'Good God!' he cried. 'She weighs a ton!'

'Exactly.'

'Now isn't that marvellous!' he cried, beaming. 'I'll bet she must almost be back to normal already!'

'It frightens me, Albert. It's too quick.'

'Nonsense, woman.'

'It's that disgusting jelly that's done it,' she said. 'I hate the stuff.'

'There's nothing disgusting about royal jelly,' he answered, indignant.

'Don't be a fool, Albert! You think it's _normal_ for a child to start putting on weight at this speed?'

'You're never satisfied!' he cried. 'You're scared stiff when she's losing and now you're absolutely terrified because she's gaining! What's the matter with you, Mabel?'

The woman got up from her chair with the baby in her arms and started toward the door. 'All I can say is,' she said, 'it's lucky I'm here to see you don't give her any more of it, that's all I can say.' She went out, and Albert watched her through the open door as she crossed the hall to the foot of the stairs and started to ascend and when she reached the third or fourth step she suddenly stopped and stood quite still for several seconds as though remembering something. Then she turned and came down again rather quickly and re-entered the room.

'Albert,' she said.

'Yes?'

'I assume there wasn't any royal jelly in this last feed we've just given her?'

'I don't see why you should assume that, Mabel.'

'Albert!'

'What's wrong?' he asked, soft and innocent.

'How _dare_ you!' she cried.

Albert Taylor's great bearded face took on a pained and puzzled look. 'I think you ought to be very glad she's got another big dose of it inside her,'

155

he said. 'Honest I do. And this *is* a big dose, Mabel, believe you me.'

The woman was standing just inside the doorway clasping the sleeping baby in her arms and staring at her husband with huge eyes. She stood very erect, her body absolutely stiff with fury, her face paler, more tight-lipped than ever.

'You mark my words,' Albert was saying, 'you're going to have a nipper there soon that'll win first prize in any baby show in the *entire* country. Hey, why don't you weigh her now and see what she is? You want me to get the scales, Mabel, so you can weigh her?'

The woman walked straight over to the large table in the centre of the room and laid the baby down and quickly started taking off its clothes. 'Yes!' she snapped. 'Get the scales!' Off came the little nightgown, then the undervest.

Then she unpinned the nappy and she drew it away and the baby lay naked on the table.

'But Mabel!' Albert cried. 'It's a miracle! She's fat as a puppy!'

Indeed, the amount of flesh the child had put on since the day before was astounding. The small sunken chest with the rib-bones showing all over it was now plump and round as a barrel, and the belly was bulging high in the air. Curiously, though, the arms and legs did not seem to have grown in proportion. Still short and skinny, they looked like little sticks protruding from a ball of fat.

'Look !' Albert said. 'She's even beginning to get a bit of fuzz on the tummy to keep her warm!' He put out a hand and was about to run the tips of his fingers over the powdering of silky yellowy-brown hairs that had suddenly appeared on the baby's stomach.

'*Don't you touch her!*' the woman cried. She turned and faced him, her eyes blazing, and she looked suddenly like some kind of a little fighting bird with her neck arched over toward him as though she were about to fly at his face and peck his eyes out.

'Now wait a minute,' he said, retreating.

'You must be mad!' she cried.

'Now wait just one minute, Mabel, will you please, because if you're still thinking this stuff is dangerous ... That *is* what you're thinking isn't it? All right, then. Listen carefully. I shall now proceed to *prove* to you once and for all, Mabel, that royal jelly is absolutely harmless to human beings, even in enormous doses. For example -- why do you think we had only half the usual honey crop last summer? Tell me that.'

His retreat, walking backwards, had taken him three or four yards away from her, where he seemed to feel more comfortable.

'The reason we had only half the usual crop last summer,' he said slowly, lowering his voice, 'was because I turned one hundred of my hives over to the production of royal jelly.'

'You *what?*'

'Ah,' he whispered. 'I thought that might surprise you a bit. And I've been making it ever since right under your very nose.' His small eyes were glinting at her, and a slow sly smile was creeping around the corners of his mouth.

'You'll never guess the reason, either,' he said. 'I've been afraid to mention it up to now because I thought it might ... well ... sort of embarrass you.'

There was a slight pause. He had his hands clasped high in front of him, level with his chest, and he was rubbing one palm against the other, making a soft scraping noise.

'You remember that bit I read you out of the magazine? That bit about the rat? Let me see now, how does it go? ' "Still and Burdett found that a male rat which hitherto had been unable to breed ..."' He hesitated, the grin widening, showing his teeth.

'You get the message, Mabel?'

She stood quite still, facing him.

'The very first time I ever read that sentence, Mabel, I jumped straight out of my chair and I said to myself if it'll work with a lousy rat, I said, then there's no reason on earth why it shouldn't work with Albert Taylor.'

He paused again, craning his head forward and turning one ear slightly in his wife's direction, waiting for her to say something. But she didn't.

'And here's another thing,' he went on. 'It made me feel so absolutely marvellous, Mabel, and so sort of completely different to what I was before that I went right on taking it even after you'd announced the joyful tidings. *Buckets* of it I must have swallowed during the last twelve months.'

The big heavy haunted-looking eyes of the woman were moving intently over the man's face and neck. There was no skin showing at all on the neck, not even at the sides below the ears. The whole of it, to a point where it disappeared into the collar of the shirt, was covered all the way around with those shortish silky hairs, yellowy black.

'Mind you,' he said, turning away from her, gazing lovingly now at the baby, 'it's going to work far better on a tiny infant than on a fully developed man like me. You've only got to look at her to see that, don't you agree?'

The woman's eyes travelled slowly downward and settled on the baby. The baby was lying naked on the table, fat and white and comatose, like some gigantic grub that was approaching the end of its larval life and would soon emerge into the world complete with mandibles and wings.

'Why don't you cover her up, Mabel?' he said. 'We don't want our little queen to catch a cold.'

157

The Boarded Window

AMBROSE BIERCE

IN 1830, ONLY A FEW MILES away from what is now the great city of Cincinnati, lay an immense and almost unbroken forest. The whole region was sparsely settled by people of the frontier – restless souls who no sooner had hewn fairly habitable homes out of the wilderness and attained to that degree of prosperity which to-day we should call indigence than, impelled by some mysterious impulse of their nature, they abandoned all and pushed farther westward, to encounter new perils and privations in the effort to regain the meagre comforts which they had voluntarily renounced. Many of them had already forsaken that region for the remoter settlements, but among those remaining was one who had been of those first arriving. He lived alone in a house of logs surrounded on all sides by the great forest, of whose gloom and silence he seemed a part, for no one had even known him to smile nor speak a needless word. His simple wants were supplied by the sale or barter of skins of wild animals in the river town, for not a thing did he grow upon the land which, if needful, he might have claimed by right of undisturbed possession. There were evidences of 'improvement' – a few acres of ground immediately about the house had once been cleared of its trees, the decayed stumps of which were half concealed by the new growth that had been suffered to repair the ravage wrought by the axe. Apparently the man's zeal for agriculture had burned with a failing flame, expiring in penitential ashes.

The little log house, with its chimney of sticks, its roof of warping clapboards weighted with traversing poles and its 'chinking' of clay, had a single door and, directly opposite, a window. The latter, however, was boarded up – nobody could remember a time when it was not. And none knew why it was so closed; certainly not because of the occupant's dislike of light and air, for on those rare occasions when a hunter had passed that lonely spot the recluse had commonly been seen sunning himself on his doorstep if heaven had provided sunshine for his need. I fancy there are few persons living to-day who ever knew the secret of that window, but I am one, as you shall see.

The man's name was said to be Murlock. He was apparently seventy years old, actually about fifty. Something besides years had had a hand in his aging. His hair and long, full beard were white, his grey, lustreless eyes sunken, his face singularly seamed with wrinkles which appeared to belong to two intersecting systems. In figure he was tall and spare, with a stoop of the shoulders – a burden bearer. I never saw him; these particulars I learned from my grandfather, from whom also I got the man's story when I was a lad. He had known him when living nearby in that early day.

One day Murlock was found in his cabin, dead. It was not a time and place for coroners and newspapers, and I suppose it was agreed that he had died from natural causes or I should have been told, and should remember. I know only that with what was probably a sense of the fitness of things the body was buried near the cabin, alongside the grave of his wife, who had preceded him by so many years that local tradition had retained hardly a hint of her existence. That closes the final chapter of this true story – excepting, indeed, the circumstance that many years afterwards, in company with an equally intrepid spirit, I penetrated to the place and ventured near enough to the ruined cabin to throw a stone against it, and ran away to avoid the ghost which every well-informed boy thereabout knew haunted the spot. But there is an earlier chapter – that supplied by my grandfather.

When Murlock built his cabin and began laying sturdily about with his axe to hew out a farm – the rifle, meanwhile, his means of support – he was young, strong and full of hope. In that eastern country whence he came he had married, as was the fashion, a young woman in all ways worthy of his honest devotion, who shared the dangers and privations of his lot with a willing spirit and light heart. There is no known record of her name; of her charms of mind and person tradition is silent and the doubter is at liberty to entertain his doubt; but God forbid that I should share it! Of their affection and happiness there is abundant assurance in every added day of the man's widowed life; for what but the magnetism of a blessed memory could have chained that venturesome spirit to a lot like that?

One day Murlock returned from gunning in a distant part of the forest to find his wife prostrate with fever, and delirious. There was no physician within miles, no neighbour; nor was she in a condition to be left, to summon help. So he set about the task of nursing her back to health, but at the end of the third day she fell into unconsciousness and so passed away, apparently, with never a gleam of returning reason.

From what we know of a nature like his we may venture to sketch in some of the details of the outline picture drawn by my grandfather. When convinced that she was dead, Murlock had sense enough to remember that the dead must be prepared for burial. In performance of this sacred duty he blundered now and again, did certain things incorrectly, and others which he did correctly were done over and over. His occasional failures to accomplish some simple and ordinary act filled him with astonishment, like that of a drunken man who wonders at the suspension of familiar natural laws. He was surprised, too, that he did not weep – surprised and a little ashamed; surely it is unkind not to weep for the dead. 'To-morrow,' he said aloud, 'I shall have to make the coffin and dig the grave; and then I shall miss her, when she is no longer in sight; but now – she is dead, of course, but it is all right – it *must* be all right, somehow. Things cannot be so bad as they seem.'

He stood over the body in the fading light, adjusting the hair and putting the finishing touches to the simple toilet, doing all mechanically, with soulless care. And still through his consciousness ran an undersense of conviction that all was right – that he should have her again as before, and everything explained. He had had no experience in grief; his capacity had not been enlarged by use. His heart could not contain it all, nor his imagination rightly conceive it. He did not know he was so hard struck; *that* knowledge would come later, and never go. Grief is an artist of powers as various as the instruments upon which he plays his dirges for the dead, evoking from some the sharpest, shrillest notes, from others the low, grave chords that throb recurrent like the slow beating of a distant drum. Some natures it startles; some it stupefies. To one it comes like the stroke of an arrow, stinging all the sensibilities to a keener life; to another as the blow of a bludgeon which, in crushing, benumbs. We may conceive Murlock to have been that way affected, for (and here we are upon surer ground than that of conjecture) no sooner had he finished his pious work than, sinking into a chair by the side of the table upon which the body lay, and noting how white the profile showed in the deepening gloom, he laid his arms upon the table's edge, and dropped his face into them, tearless yet and unutterably weary. At that moment came in through the open window a long, wailing sound like the cry of a lost child in the far deeps of the darkening wood! But the man did not move. Again, and nearer than before, sounded that unearthly cry upon his failing sense. Perhaps it was a wild beast; perhaps it was a dream. For Murlock was asleep.

Some hours later, as it afterwards appeared, this unfaithful watcher awoke, and lifting his head from his arms intently listened – he knew not why. There in the black darkness by the side of the dead, recalling all without a shock, he strained his eyes to see – he knew not what. His senses were all alert, his breath was suspended, his blood had stilled its tides as if to assist the silence. Who – what had waked him, and where was it?

Suddenly the table shook beneath his arms, and at the same moment he heard, or fancied that he heard, a light, soft step – another – sounds as of bare feet upon the floor!

He was terrified beyond the power to cry out or move. Perforce he waited – waited there in the darkness through seeming centuries of such dread as one may know, yet live to tell. He tried vainly to speak the dead woman's name, vainly to stretch forth his hand across the table to learn if she were there. His throat was powerless, his arms and hands were like lead. Then occurred something most frightful. Some heavy body seemed hurled against the table with an impetus that pushed it against his breast so sharply as nearly to overthrow him, and at the same instant he heard and felt the fall of something upon the floor with so violent a thump that the whole house was shaken by the impact. A scuffling ensued, and a confusion of sounds impossible to describe. Murlock had risen to his feet. Fear had by excess forfeited control of his faculties. He flung his hands upon the table. Nothing was there!

There is a point at which terror may turn to madness; and madness incites to action. With no definite intent, from no motive but the wayward impulse of a madman, Murlock sprang to the wall, with a little groping seized his loaded rifle, and without aim discharged it. By the flash which lit up the room with a vivid illumination, he saw an enormous panther dragging the dead woman towards the window, its teeth fixed in her throat! Then there were darkness blacker than before, and silence; and when he returned to consciousness the sun was high and the wood vocal with songs of birds.

The body lay near the window, where the beast had left it when frightened away by the flash and report of the rifle. The clothing was deranged, the long hair in disorder, the limbs lay anyhow. From the throat, dreadfully lacerated, had issued a pool of blood not yet entirely coagulated. The ribbon with which he had bound the wrists was broken; the hands were tightly clenched. Between the teeth was a fragment of the animal's ear.

Earth to Earth

ROBERT GRAVES

YES, YES AND YES! DON'T get me wrong, for goodness' sake. I am heart and soul with you. I agree that Man is wickedly defrauding the Earth-Mother of her ancient dues by not putting back into the soil as much nourishment as he takes out. And that modern plumbing is, if you like, a running sore in the body politic. And that municipal incinerators are genocidal rather than germicidal ... And that cremation should be made a capital crime. And that dust bowls created by the greedy plough ...

... Yes, yes and yes again. *But!*

Elsie and Roland Hedge – she a book-illustrator, he an architect with suspect lungs – had been warned against Dr Eugen Steinpilz. 'He'll bring you no luck,' I told them. 'My little finger says so decisively.'

'You too?' asked Elsie indignantly. (This was at Brixham, South Devon, in March 1940.) 'I suppose you think that because of his foreign accent and his beard he must be a spy?'

'No,' I said coldly, 'that point hadn't occurred to me. But I won't contradict you.'

The very next day Elsie deliberately picked a friendship – I don't like the phrase, but that's what she did – with the Doctor, an Alsatian with an American passport, who described himself as a *Naturphilosoph*; and both she and Roland were soon immersed in Steinpilzerei up to the nostrils. It began when he invited them to lunch and gave them cold meat and two rival sets of vegetable dishes – potatoes (baked), carrots (creamed), bought from the local fruiterer; and potatoes (baked) and carrots (creamed), grown on compost in his own garden.

The superiority of the latter over the former in appearance, size and especially flavour came as an eye-opener to Elsie and Roland. Yes, and yes, I know just how they felt. Why shouldn't I? When I visit the market here in Palma, I always refuse La Torre potatoes, because they are raised for the early English market and therefore reek of imported chemical fertilizer. Instead I buy Son Sardina potatoes, which taste as good as the ones we used to get in England fifty years ago. The reason is that the Son Sardina farmers manure their fields with Palma kitchen-refuse, still available by the cartload – this being too backward a city to afford effective modern methods of destroying it.

Thus Dr Steinpilz converted the childless and devoted couple to the Steinpilz method of composting. It did not, as a matter of fact, vary greatly from the methods you read about in the *Gardening Notes* of your favourite national newspaper, except that it was far more violent. Dr Steinpilz had invented a formula for producing extremely fierce bacteria, capable (Roland claimed) of breaking down an old boot or the family Bible or a torn woollen vest into beautiful black humus almost as you watched. The formula could not be bought, however, and might be communicated under oath of secrecy only to members of the Eugen Steinpilz Fellowship – which I refused to join. I won't pretend therefore to know the formula myself, but one night I overheard Elsie and Roland arguing in their garden as to whether the planetary influences were favourable; and they also mentioned a ram's horn in which, it seems, a complicated mixture of triturated animal and vegetable products – technically called 'the Mother' – was to be cooked up. I gather also that a bull's foot and a goat's pancreas were part of the works, because Mr Pook the butcher afterwards told me that he had been puzzled by Roland's request for these unusual cuts. Milkwort and penny-royal and bee-orchid and vetch certainly figured among the Mother's herbal ingredients; I recognized these one day in a gardening basket Elsie had left at the post office.

The Hedges soon had their first compost heap cooking away in the garden, which was about the size of a tennis court and consisted mostly of well-kept lawn. Dr Steinpilz, who supervised, now began to haunt the cottage like the smell of drains; I had to give up calling on them. Then, after the Fall of France, Brixham became a war-zone whence everyone but we British and our Free French or Free Belgians allies were extruded. Consequently Dr Steinpilz had to leave; which he did with very bad grace, and was killed in a Liverpool air-raid the day before he should have sailed back to New York. But that was far from closing the ledger. I think Elsie must have been in love with the Doctor, and certainly Roland had a hero-worship for him. They treasured a signed collection of all his esoteric books, each called after a different semi-precious stone, and used to read them out aloud to each other at meals, in turns. Then to show that this was a practical philosophy, not just a random assemblage of beautiful thoughts about Nature, they began composting in a deeper and even more religious way than before. The lawn had come up, of course; but they used the sods to sandwich layers of kitchen waste, which they mixed with the scrapings from an abandoned pigsty, two barrowfuls of sodden poplar leaves from the recreation ground, and a sack of rotten turnips. Looking over the hedge, I caught the fanatic gleam in Elsie's eye as she turned the hungry bacteria loose on the heap, and could not repress a premonitory shudder.

So far, not too bad, perhaps. But when serious bombing started and food became so scarce that housewives were fined for not making over their swill to the national pigs, Elsie and Roland grew worried. Having already abandoned their ordinary sanitary system and built an earth-closet in the garden, they now tried to convince neighbours of their duty to do the same, even at the risk of catching cold and getting spiders down the neck. Elsie also sent Roland after the slow-moving Red Devon cows as they lurched home along the lane at dusk, to rescue the precious droppings with a kitchen shovel; while she visited the local ash-dump with a packing case mounted on wheels, and collected whatever she found there of an organic nature – dead cats, old rags, withered flowers, cabbage stalks and such household waste as even a national wartime pig would have coughed at. She also saved every drop of their bath-water for sprinkling the heaps; because it contained she said, valuable animal salts.

The test of a good compost heap, as every illuminate knows, is whether a certain revolting-looking, if beneficial, fungus sprouts from it. Elsie's heaps were grey with this crop, and so hot inside that they could be used for haybox cookery; which must have saved her a deal of fuel. I call them 'Elsie's heaps', because she now considered herself Dr Steinpilz's earthly delegate; and loyal Roland did not dispute this claim.

A critical stage in the story came during the Blitz. It will be remembered that trainloads of Londoners, who had been evacuated to South Devon when war broke out, thereafter de-evacuated and re-evacuated and re-de-evacuated themselves, from time to time, in a most disorganized fashion. Elsie and Roland, as it happened, escaped having evacuees billeted on them, because they had no spare bedroom; but one night an old naval pensioner came knocking at their door and demanded lodging for the night. Having been burned out of Plymouth, where everything was chaos, he had found himself walking away and blundering along in a daze until he fetched up here, hungry and dead-beat. They gave him a meal and bedded him on the sofa; but when Elsie came down in the morning to fork over the heaps, she found him dead of heart-failure.

Roland broke a long silence by coming, in some embarrassment, to ask my advice. Elsie, he said, had decided that it would be wrong to trouble the police about the case; because the police were so busy these days, and the poor old fellow had claimed to possess neither kith nor kin. So they'd read the burial service over him and, after removing his belt-buckle, trouser buttons, metal spectacle-case and a bunch of keys, which were irreducible, had laid him reverently in the new compost heap. Its other contents, he added, were a cartload of waste from the cider-factory, salvaged cow-dung, and several basketfuls of hedge clippings. Had they done wrong?

'If you mean "will I report you to the Civil Authorities?" the answer is no,' I assured him. 'I wasn't looking over the hedge at the relevant hour, and what you tell me is only hearsay.' Roland shambled off satisfied.

The War went on. Not only did the Hedges convert the whole garden into serried rows of Eugen Steinpilz memorial heaps, leaving no room for planting the potatoes or carrots to which the compost had been prospectively devoted, but they scavenged the offal from the Brixham fish-market and salvaged the contents of the bin outside the surgical ward at the Cottage Hospital. Every spring, I remember, Elsie used to pick big bunches of primroses and put them straight on the compost, without even a last wistful sniff; virgin primroses were supposed to be particularly relished by the fierce bacteria.

Here the story becomes a little painful for members, say, of a family reading circle; I will soften it as much as possible. One morning a policeman called on the Hedges with a summons, and I happened to see Roland peep anxiously out of the bedroom window, but quickly pull his head in again. The policeman rang and knocked and waited, then tried the back door; and presently went away. The summons was for a blackout offence, but apparently the Hedges did not know this. Next morning he called again, and when nobody answered, forced the lock of the back door. They were found dead in bed together, having taken an overdose of sleeping tablets. A note on the coverlet ran simply:

> Please lay our bodies on the heap nearest the pigsty. Flowers by request. Strew some on the bodies, mixed with a little kitchen waste, and then fork the earth lightly over.
>
> E.H.; R.H.

George Irks, the new tenant, proposed to grow potatoes and dig for victory. He hired a cart and began throwing the compost into the River Dart, 'not liking the look of them toadstools', as he subsequently explained. The five beautifully clean human skeletons which George unearthed in the process were still awaiting identification when the War ended.

A Warning to the Curious

M. R. JAMES

THE PLACE ON THE EAST COAST which the reader is asked to consider is Seaburgh. It is not very different now from what I remember it to have been when I was a child. Marshes intersected by dykes to the south, recalling the early chapters of *Great Expectations*; flat fields to the north, merging into heath; heath, fir woods, and, above all, gorse, inland. A long sea-front and a street: behind that a spacious church of flint, with a broad, solid western tower and a peal of six bells. How well I remember their sound on a hot Sunday in August, as our party went slowly up the white, dusty slope of road towards them, for the church stands at the top of a short, steep incline. They rang with a flat clacking sort of sound on those hot days, but when the air was softer they were mellower too. The railway ran down to its little terminus farther along the same road. There was a gay white windmill just before you came to the station, and another down near the shingle at the south end of the town, and yet others on higher ground to the north. There were cottages of bright red brick with slate roofs ... but why do I encumber you with these commonplace details? The fact is that they come crowding to the point of the pencil when it begins to write of Seaburgh. I should like to be sure that I had allowed the right ones to get on to the paper. But I forgot. I have not quite done with the word-painting business yet.

Walk away from the sea and the town, pass the station, and turn up the road on the right. It is a sandy road, parallel with the railway, and if you follow it, it climbs to somewhat higher ground. On your left (you are now going northward) is heath, on your right (the side towards the sea) is a belt of old firs, wind-beaten, thick at the top, with the slope that old seaside trees have; seen on the skyline from the train they would tell you in an instant, if you did not know it, that you were approaching a windy coast. Well, at the top of my little hill, a line of these firs strikes out and runs towards the sea, for there is a ridge that goes that way; and the ridge ends in a rather well-defined mound commanding the level fields of rough grass, and a little knot of fir trees crowns it. And here you may sit on a hot spring day, very well content to look at blue sea, white windmills, red cottages, bright green grass, church tower, and distant martello tower on the south.

As I have said, I began to know Seaburgh as a child; but a gap of a good many years separates my early knowledge from that which is more recent. Still it keeps its place in my affections, and any tales of it that I pick up have an interest for me. One such tale is this: it came to me in a place very remote from Seaburgh, and quite accidentally, from a man whom I had been able to oblige – enough in his opinion to justify his making me his confidant to this extent.

I know all that country more or less (he said). I used to go to Seaburgh pretty regularly for golf in the spring. I generally put up at the 'Bear,' with a friend – Henry Long it was, you knew him perhaps – ('Slightly,' I said) and we used to take a sitting-room and be very happy there. Since he died I haven't cared to go there. And I don't know that I should anyhow after the particular thing that happened on our last visit.

It was in April, 19— we were there, and by some chance we were almost the only people in the hotel. So the ordinary public rooms were practically empty, and we were the more surprised when, after dinner, our sitting-room door opened and a young man put his head in. We were aware of this young man. He was rather a rabbity anaemic subject – light hair and light eyes – but not unpleasing. So when he said: 'I beg your pardon, is this a private room?' we did not growl and say: 'Yes, it is,' but Long said, or I did – no matter which: 'Please come in.' 'Oh, may I?' he said, and seemed relieved. Of course it was obvious that he wanted company; and as he was a reasonable kind of person – not the sort to bestow his whole family history on you – we urged him to make himself at home. 'I dare say you find the other rooms rather bleak,' I said. Yes, he did: but it was really too good of us, and so on. That being got over, he made some pretence of reading a book. Long was playing Patience, I was writing. It became plain to me after a few minutes that this visitor of ours was in rather a state of fidgets or nerves, which communicated itself to me, and so I put away my writing and turned to at engaging him in talk.

After some remarks, which I forget, he became rather confidential. 'You'll think it very odd of me' (this was the sort of way he began), 'but the fact is I've had something of a shock.' Well, I recommended a drink of some cheering kind, and we had it. The waiter coming in made an interruption (and I thought our young man seemed very jumpy when the door opened), but after a while he got back to his woes again. There was nobody he knew in the place, and he did happen to know who we both were (it turned out there was some common acquaintance in town), and really he did want a word of advice, if we didn't mind. Of course we both said: 'By all means,' or 'Not at all,' and Long put away his cards. And we settled down to hear what his difficulty was.

'It began,' he said, 'more than a week ago, when I bicycled over to Froston, only about five or six miles, to see the church; I'm very much interested in architecture, and it's got one of those pretty porches with

167

niches and shields. I took a photograph of it, and then an old man who was tidying up in the churchyard came and asked if I'd care to look into the church. I said yes, and he produced a key and let me in. There wasn't much inside, but I told him it was a nice little church, and he kept it very clean, "but," I said, "the porch is the best part of it." We were just outside the porch then, and he said, "Ah, yes, that is a nice porch; and do you know, sir, what's the meanin' of that coat of arms there?"

'It was the one with the three crowns, and though I'm not much of a herald, I was able to say yes, I thought it was the old arms of the kingdom of East Anglia.

' "That's right, sir," he said, "and do you know the meanin' of them three crowns that's on it?"

'I said I'd no doubt it was known, but I couldn't recollect to have heard it myself.

' "Well, then," he said, "for all you're a scholard, I can tell you something you don't know. Them's the three 'oly crowns what was buried in the ground near by the coast to keep the Germans from landing – ah, I can see you don't believe that. But I tell you, if it hadn't have been for one of them 'oly crowns bein' there still, them Germans would a landed here time and again, they would. Landed with their ships, and killed man, woman and child in their beds. Now then, that's the truth what I'm telling you, that is; and if you don't believe me, you ast the rector. There he comes: you ast him, I says."

'I looked round, and there was the rector, a nice-looking old man, coming up the path; and before I could begin assuring my old man, who was getting quite excited, that I didn't disbelieve him, the rector struck in, and said: "What's all this about, John? Good day to you, sir. Have you been looking at our little church?"

'So then there was a little talk which allowed the old man to calm down, and then the rector asked him again what was the matter.

' "Oh," he said, "it warn't nothink, only I was telling this gentleman he'd ought to ast you about them 'oly crowns."

' "Ah, yes, to be sure," said the rector, "that's a very curious matter, isn't it? But I don't know whether the gentleman is interested in our old stories, eh?"

' "Oh, he'll be interested fast enough," says the old man, "he'll put his confidence in what you tells him, sir; why, you known William Ager yourself, father and son too."

'Then I put in a word to say how much I should like to hear all about it, and before many minutes I was walking up the village street with the rector, who had one or two words to say to parishioners, and then to the rectory, where he took me into his study. He had made out, on the way, that I really was capable of taking an intelligent interest in a piece of folk-lore, and not quite the ordinary tripper. So he was very willing to talk, and it is rather surprising to me that the particular legend he told me has not made its way into print before. His account of it was this: "There has always been a belief in these parts in the three holy crowns. The old people say they were buried in different places near the coast to keep off the Danes or the French or the Germans. And they say that one of the three was dug up a long time ago, and another has disappeared by the encroaching of the sea, and one's still left doing its work, keeping off invaders. Well, now, if you have read the ordinary guides and histories of this county, you will remember perhaps that in 1687 a crown, which was said to be the crown of Redwald, King of the East Angles, was dug up at Rendlesham, and alas! alas! melted down before it was even properly described or drawn. Well, Rendlesham isn't on the coast, but it isn't so very far inland, and it's on a very important line of access. And I believe that is the crown which the people mean when they say that one has been dug up. Then on the south you don't want me to tell you where there was a Saxon royal place which is now under the sea, eh? Well, there was the second crown, I take it. And up beyond these two, they say, lies the third."

'"Do they say where it is?" of course I asked.

'He said, "Yes, indeed, they do, but they don't tell," and his manner did not encourage me to put the obvious question. Instead of that I waited a moment, and said: "What did the old man mean when he said you knew William Ager, as if that had something to do with the crowns?"

'"To be sure," he said, "now that's another curious story. These Agers – it's a very old name in these parts, but I can't find that they were ever people of quality or big owners – these Agers say, or said, that their branch of the family were the guardians of the last crown. A certain old Nathaniel Ager was the first one I knew – I was born and brought up quite near here – and he, I believe, camped out at the place during the whole of the war of 1870. William, his son, did the same, I know, during the South African War. And young William, *his* son, who has only died fairly recently, took lodgings at the cottage nearest the spot, and I've no doubt hastened his end, for he was a consumptive, by exposure and night watching. And he was the last of that branch. It was a dreadful grief to him to think that he was the last, but he could do nothing, the only relations at all near to him were in the colonies. I wrote letters for him to them imploring them to come over on business very important to the family, but there has been no answer. So the last of the holy crowns, if it's there, has no guardian now."

'That was what the rector told me, and you can fancy how interesting I found it. The only thing I could think of when I left him was how to hit upon the spot where the crown was supposed to be. I wish I'd left it alone.

'But there was a sort of fate in it, for as I bicycled back past the churchyard wall my eye caught a fairly new gravestone, and on it was the name of William Ager. Of course I got off and read it. It said "of this parish, died at Seaburgh, 19—, aged 28." There it was, you see. A little judicious questioning in the right place, and I should at least find the cottage nearest the spot. Only I didn't quite know what was the right place to begin my questioning at. Again there was fate: it took me to the curiosity-shop down that way – you know – and I turned over some old books, and, if you please, one was a prayer-book of 1740 odd, in a rather handsome binding – I'll just go and get it, it's in my room.'

He left us in a state of some surprise, but we had hardly time to exchange any remarks when he was back, panting, and handed us the book opened at the fly-leaf, on which was, in a straggly hand:

'Nathaniel Ager is my name and England is my nation,
Seaburgh is my dwelling-place and Christ is my Salvation,
When I am dead and in my Grave, and all my bones are rotton,
I hope the Lord will think on me when I am quite forgotton.'

This poem was dated 1754, and there were many more entries of Agers, Nathaniel, Frederick, William, and so on, ending with William, 19—.

'You see,' he said, 'anybody would call it the greatest bit of luck. *I* did, but I don't now. Of course I asked the shopman about William Ager, and of course he happened to remember that he lodged in a cottage in the North Field and died there. This was just chalking the road for me. I knew which the cottage must be: there is only one sizable one about there. The next thing was to scrape some sort of acquaintance with the people, and I took a walk that way at once. A dog did the business for me: he made at me so fiercely that they had to run out and beat him off, and then naturally begged my pardon, and we got into talk. I had only to bring up Ager's name, and pretend I knew, or thought I knew something of him, and then the woman said how sad it was him dying so young, and she was sure it came of him spending the night out of doors in the cold weather. Then I had to say: "Did he go out on the sea at night?" and she said: "Oh, no, it was on the hillock yonder with the trees on it." And there I was.

'I know something about digging in these barrows: I've opened many of them in the down country. But that was with owner's leave, and in broad daylight and with men to help. I had to prospect very carefully here before I put a spade in: I couldn't trench across the mound, and with those old firs growing there I knew there would be awkward tree roots. Still the soil was very light and sandy and easy, and there was a rabbit hole or so that might be developed into a sort of tunnel. The going out and coming back at odd hours to the hotel was going to be the awkward part. When I made up my mind about the way to excavate I told the people that I was called away for a night, and I spent it out there. I made my tunnel: I won't bore you with the details of how I supported it and filled it in when I'd done, but the main thing is that I got the crown.'

Naturally we both broke out into exclamations of surprise and interest. I for one had long known about the finding of the crown at Rendlesham and had often lamented its fate. No one has ever seen an Anglo-Saxon crown – at least no one had. But our man gazed at us with a rueful eye. 'Yes,' he said, 'and the worst of it is I don't know how to put it back.'

'Put it back?' we cried out. 'Why, my dear sir, you've made one of the most exciting finds ever heard of in this country. Of course it ought to go to the Jewel House at the Tower. What's your difficulty? If you're thinking about the owner of the land, and treasure-trove, and all that, we can certainly help you through. Nobody's going to make a fuss about technicalities in a case of this kind.'

Probably more was said, but all he did was to put his face in his hands, and mutter: 'I don't know how to put it back.'

At last Long said: 'You'll forgive me, I hope, if I seem impertinent, but are you *quite* sure you've got it?' I was wanting to ask much the same question myself, for of course the story did seem a lunatic's dream when one thought over it. But I hadn't quite dared to say what might hurt the poor young man's feelings. However, he took it quite calmly – really, with the calm of despair, you might say. He sat up and said: 'Oh, yes, there's no doubt of that: I have it here, in my room, locked up in my bag. You can come and look at if it you like: I won't offer to bring it here.'

We were not likely to let the chance slip. We went with him; his room was only a few doors off. The boots was just collecting shoes in the passage: or so we thought: afterwards we were not sure. Our visitor – his name was Paxton – was in a worse state of shivers than before, and went hurriedly into the room, and beckoned us after him, turned on the light, and shut the door carefully. Then he unlocked his kit-bag, and produced a bundle of clean pocket-handkerchiefs in which something was wrapped, laid it on the bed, and undid it. I can now say I *have* seen an actual Anglo-Saxon crown. It was of silver – as the Rendlesham one is always said to have been – it was set with some gems, mostly antique intaglios and cameos, and was of rather plain, almost rough workmanship. In fact, it was like those you see on the coins and in the manuscripts. I found no reason to think it was later than the ninth century. I was intensely interested, of course, and I wanted to turn it over in my hands, but Paxton prevented me. 'Don't *you* touch it,' he said, 'I'll do that.' And with a sigh that was, I declare to you, dreadful to hear, he took it up and turned it about so that we could see every part of it. 'Seen enough?' he said at last, and we nodded. He wrapped it up and locked it in his bag, and stood looking at us dumbly. 'Come back to our room,' Long said, 'and tell us what the trouble is.' He thanked us, and said: 'Will you go first and see if – if the coast is clear?' That wasn't very intelligible, for our proceedings hadn't been, after all, very suspicious, and the hotel, as I said, was practically empty. However, we were beginning to have inklings of – we didn't know what, and anyhow nerves are infectious. So we did go, first peering out as we opened the door, and fancying (I found we both had the fancy) that a shadow, or more than a shadow – but it made no sound – passed from before us to one side as we came out into the passage. 'It's all right,' we whispered to Paxton – whispering seemed the proper tone – and we went, with him between us, back to our sitting-room. I was preparing, when we got there, to be ecstatic about the unique interest of what we had seen, but when I looked at Paxton I saw that would be terribly out of place, and I left it to him to begin.

'What *is* to be done?' was his opening. Long thought it right (as he explained to me afterwards) to be obtuse, and said: 'Why not find out who the owner of the land is, and inform——' 'Oh, no, no!' Paxton broke in impatiently, 'I beg your pardon: you've been very kind, but don't you see it's *got* to go back, and I daren't be there at night, and daytime's impossible. Perhaps, though, you don't see: well, then, the truth is that I've never been alone since I touched it.' I was beginning some fairly stupid comment, but Long caught my eye, and I stopped. Long said: 'I think I do see, perhaps: but wouldn't it be – a relief – to tell us a little more clearly what the situation is?'

Then it all came out: Paxton looked over his shoulder and beckoned to us to come nearer to him, and began speaking in a low voice: we listened most intently, of course, and compared notes afterwards, and I wrote down our version, so I am confident I have what he told us almost word for word. He said: 'It began when I was first prospecting, and put me off again and again. There was always somebody – a man – standing by one of the firs. This was in daylight, you know. He was never in front of me. I always saw him with the tail of my eye on the left or the right, and he was never there when I looked straight for him. I would lie down for quite a long time and take careful observations, and make sure there was no one, and then when I got up and began prospecting again, there he was. And he began to give me hints, besides; for wherever I put that prayer-book – short of locking it up, which I did at last – when I came back to my room it was always out on my table open at the fly-leaf where the names are, and one of my razors across it to keep it open. I'm sure he just can't open my bag, or something more would have happened. You see, he's light and weak, but all the same I daren't face him. Well, then, when I was making the tunnel, of course it was worse, and if I hadn't been so keen I should have dropped the whole thing and run. It was like someone scraping at my back all the time: I thought for a long time it was only soil dropping on me, but as I got nearer the – the crown, it was unmistakable. And when I actually laid it bare and got my fingers into the ring of it and pulled it out, there came a sort of cry behind me – oh, I can't tell you how desolate it was! And horribly threatening too. It spoilt all my pleasure in my find – cut it off that moment. And if I hadn't been the wretched fool I am, I should have put the thing back and left it. But I didn't. The rest of the time was just awful. I had hours to get through before I could decently come back in the hotel. First I spent time filling up my tunnel and covering my tracks, and all the while he was there trying to thwart me. Sometimes, you know, you see him, and sometimes you don't, just as he pleases, I think: he's there, but he has some power over your eyes. Well, I wasn't off the spot very long before sunrise, and then I had to get to the junction for Seaburgh, and take a train back. And though it was daylight fairly soon, I don't know if that made it much better. There were always hedges, or gorsebushes, or park fences along the road – some sort of cover, I mean – and I was never easy for a second. And then when I began to meet people going to work, they always looked behind me very strangely: it might have been that they were surprised at seeing anyone so early; but I didn't think it was only that, and I don't now: they didn't look exactly at *me*. And the porter at the train was like that too. And the guard held open the door after I'd got into the carriage – just as he would if there was somebody else coming, you know. Oh, you may be very sure it isn't my fancy,' he said with a dull sort of laugh. Then he went on: 'And even if I do get it put back, he won't forgive me: I can tell that. And I was so happy a fortnight ago.' He dropped into a chair, and I believe he began to cry.

We didn't know what to say, but we felt we must come to the rescue somehow, and so – it really seemed the only thing – we said if he was so set on putting the crown back in its place, we would help him. And I must say that after what we had heard it did seem the right thing. If these horrid consequences had come on this poor man, might there not really be something in the original idea of the crown having some curious power bound up with it, to guard the coast? At least, that was my feeling, and I think it was Long's too. Our offer was very welcome to Paxton, anyhow. When could we do it? It was nearing half-past ten. Could we contrive to make a late walk plausible to the hotel people that very night? We looked out of the window: there was a brilliant full moon – the Paschal moon. Long undertook to tackle the boots and propitiate him. He was to say that we should not be much over the hour, and if we did find it so pleasant that we stopped out a bit longer we would see that he didn't lose by sitting up. Well, we were pretty regular customers of the hotel, and did not give much trouble, and were considered by the servants to be not under the mark in the way of tips; and so the boots *was* propitiated, and let us out on to the sea-front, and remained, as we heard later, looking after us. Paxton had a large coat over his arm, under which was the wrapped-up crown.

So we were off on this strange errand before we had time to think how very much out of the way it was. I have told this part quite shortly on purpose, for it really does represent the haste with which we settled our plan and took action. 'The shortest way is up the hill and through the churchyard,' Paxton said, as we stood a moment before the hotel looking up and down the front. There was nobody about – nobody at all.

Seaburgh out of the season is an early, quiet place. 'We can't go along the dyke by the cottage, because of the dog,' Paxton also said, when I pointed to what I thought a shorter way along the front and across two fields. The reason he gave was good enough. We went up the road to the church, and turned in at the churchyard gate. I confess to having thought that there might be some lying there who might be conscious of our business: but if it was so, they were also conscious that one who was on their side, so to say, had us under surveillance, and we saw no sign of them. But under observation we felt we were, as I have never felt it at another time. Specially was it so when we passed out of the churchyard into a narrow path with close high hedges, through which we hurried as Christian did through that Valley; and so got out into open fields. Then along hedges, though I would sooner have been in the open, where I could see if anyone was visible behind me; over a gate or two, and then a swerve to the left, taking us up on to the ridge which ended in that mound.

As we neared it, Henry Long felt, and I felt too, that there were what I can only call dim presences waiting for us, as well as a far more actual one attending us. Of Paxton's agitation all this time I can give you no adequate picture: he breathed like a hunted beast, and we could not either of us look at his face. How he would manage when we got to the very place we had not troubled to think: he had seemed so sure that that would not be difficult. Nor was it. I never saw anything like the dash with which he flung himself at a particular spot in the side of the mound, and tore at it, so that in a very few minutes the greater part of his body was out of sight. We stood holding the coat and that bundle of handkerchiefs, and looking, very fearfully, I must admit, about us. There was nothing to be seen: a line of dark firs behind us made one skyline, more trees and the church tower half a mile off on the right, cottages and a windmill on the horizon on the left, calm sea dead in front, faint barking of a dog at a cottage on a gleaming dyke between us and it: full moon making that path we know across the sea: the eternal whisper of the Scotch firs just above us, and of the sea in front. Yet, in all this quiet, an acute, an acrid consciousness of a restrained hostility very near us, like a dog on a leash that might be let go at any moment.

Paxton pulled himself out of the hole, and stretched a hand back to us. 'Give it to me,' he whispered, 'unwrapped.' We pulled off the handkerchiefs, and he took the crown. The moonlight just fell on it as he snatched it. We had not ourselves touched that bit of metal, and I have thought since that it was just as well. In another moment Paxton was out of the hole again and busy shovelling back the soil with hands that were already bleeding. He would have none of our help, though. It was much the longest part of the job to get the place to look undisturbed: yet – I don't know how – he made a wonderful success of it. At last he was satisfied, and we turned back.

We were a couple of hundred yards from the hill when Long suddenly said to him: 'I say, you've left your coat there. That won't do. See?' And I certainly did see it – the long dark overcoat lying where the tunnel had been. Paxton had not stopped, however: he only shook his head, and held up the coat on his arm. And when we joined him, he said, without any excitement, but as if nothing mattered any more: 'That wasn't my coat.' And, indeed, when we looked back again, that dark thing was not to be seen.

Well, we got out on to the road, and came rapidly back that way. It was well before twelve when we got in, trying to put a good face on it, and saying – Long and I – what a lovely night it was for a walk. The boots was on the look-out for us, and we made remarks like that for his edification as we entered the hotel. He gave another look up and down the sea-front before he locked the front door, and said: 'You didn't meet many people about, I s'pose, sir?' 'No, indeed, not a soul,' I said; at which I remember Paxton looked oddly at me. 'Only I thought I see someone turn up the station road after you gentlemen,' said the boots. 'Still, you was three together, and I don't suppose he meant mischief.' I didn't know what to say; Long merely said 'Good night,' and we went off upstairs, promising to turn out all lights, and to go to bed in a few minutes.

Back in our room, we did our very best to make Paxton take a cheerful view. 'There's the crown safe back,' we said; 'very likely you'd have done better not to touch it' (and he heavily assented to that), 'but no real harm has been done, and we shall never give this away to anyone who would be so mad as to go near it. Besides, don't you feel better yourself? I don't mind confessing,' I said, 'that on the way there I was very much inclined to take your view about – well, about being followed; but going back, it wasn't at all the same thing, was it?' No, it wouldn't do: '*You've* nothing to trouble yourselves about,' he said, 'but I'm not forgiven. I've got to pay for that miserable sacrilege still. I know what you are going to say. The Church might help. Yes, but it's the body that has to suffer. It's true I'm not feeling that he's waiting outside for me just now. But——' Then he stopped. Then he turned to thanking us, and we put him off as soon as we could. And naturally we pressed him to use our sitting-room next day, and said we should be glad to go out with him. Or did he play golf, perhaps? Yes, he did, but he didn't think he should care about that to-morrow. Well, we recommended him to get up late and sit in our room in the morning while we were playing, and we would have a walk later in the day. He was very submissive and *piano* about it all: ready to do just what we thought best, but clearly quite certain in his own mind that what was coming could not be averted or palliated. You'll wonder why we didn't insist on accompanying him to his home and seeing him safe into the care of brothers or someone. The fact was he had nobody. He had had a flat in town, but lately he had made up his mind to settle for a time in Sweden, and he had dismantled his flat and shipped off his belongings, and was whiling away a fortnight or three weeks before he made a start. Anyhow, we didn't see what we could do better than sleep on it – or not sleep very much, as was my case – and see what we felt like tomorrow morning.

We felt very different, Long and I, on as beautiful an April morning as you could desire; and Paxton also looked very different when we saw him at breakfast. 'The first approach to a decent night I seem ever to have had,' was what he said. But he was going to do as we had settled: stay in probably all the morning, and come out with us later. We went to the links; we met some other men and played with them in the morning, and had lunch there rather early, so as not to be late back. All the same, the snares of death overtook him.

Whether it could have been prevented, I don't know. I think he would have been got at somehow, do what we might. Anyhow, this is what happened.

We went straight up to our room. Paxton was there, reading quite peaceably. 'Ready to come out shortly?' said Long, 'say in half an hour's time?' 'Certainly,' he said: and I said we would change first, and perhaps have baths, and call for him in half an hour. I had my bath first, and went and lay down on my bed, and slept for about ten minutes. We came out of our rooms at the same time, and went together to the sitting-room. Paxton wasn't there – only his book. Nor was he in his room, nor in the downstairs rooms. We shouted for him. A servant came out and said: 'Why, I thought you gentlemen was gone out already, and so did the other gentleman. He heard you a-calling from the path there, and run out in a hurry, and I looked out of the coffee-room window, but I didn't see you. 'Owever, he run off down the beach that way.'

Without a word we ran that way too – it was the opposite direction to that of last night's expedition. It wasn't quite four o'clock, and the day was fair, though not so fair as it had been, so there was really no reason, you'd say, for anxiety: with people about, surely a man couldn't come to much harm.

But something in our look as we ran out must have struck the servant, for she came out on the steps, and pointed, and said, 'Yes, that's the way he went.' We ran on as far as the top of the shingle bank, and there pulled up. There was a choice of ways: past the houses on the sea-front, or along the sand at the bottom of the beach, which, the tide being now out, was fairly broad. Or of course we might keep along the shingle between these two tracks and have some view of both of them; only that was heavy going. We chose the sand, for that was the loneliest, and someone *might* come to harm there without being seen from the public path.

Long said he saw Paxton some distance ahead, running and waving his stick, as if he wanted to signal to people who were on ahead of him. I couldn't be sure: one of these sea-mists was coming up very quickly from the south. There was someone, that's all I could say. And there were tracks on the sand as of someone running who wore shoes; and there were other tracks made before those – for the shoes sometimes trod in them and interfered with them – of someone not in shoes. Oh, of course, it's only my word you've got to take for all this: Long's dead, we'd no time or means to make sketches or take casts, and the next tide washed everything away. All we could do was to notice these marks as we hurried on. But there they were over and over again, and we had no doubt whatever that what we saw was the track of a bare foot, and one that showed more bones than flesh.

The notion of Paxton running after – after anything like this, and supposing it to be the friends he was looking for, was very dreadful to us. You can guess what we fancied: how the thing he was following might stop suddenly and turn round on him, and what sort of face it would show, half-seen at first in the mist – which all the while was getting thicker and thicker. And as I ran on wondering how the poor wretch could have been lured into mistaking that other thing for us, I remembered his saying, 'He has some power over your eyes.' And then I wondered what the end would be, for I had no hope now that the end could be averted, and – well, there is no need to tell all the dismal and horrid thoughts that flitted through my head as we ran on into the mist. It was uncanny, too, that the sun should still be bright in the sky and we could see nothing. We could only tell that we were now past the houses and had reached that gap there is between them and the old martello tower. When you are past the tower, you know, there is nothing but shingle for a long way – not a house, not a human creature, just that spit of land, or rather shingle, with the river on your right and the sea on your left.

But just before that, just by the martello tower, you remember there is the old battery, close to the sea. I believe there are only a few blocks of concrete left now: the rest has all been washed away, but at this time there was a lot more, though the place was a ruin. Well, when we got there, we clambered to the top as quick as we could to take breath and look over the shingle in front if by chance the mist would let us see anything. But a moment's rest we must have. We had run a mile at least. Nothing whatever was visible ahead of us, and we were just turning by common consent to get down and run hopelessly on, when we heard what I can only call a laugh: and if you can understand what I mean by a breathless, a lungless laugh, you have it: but I don't suppose you can. It came from below, and swerved away into the mist. That was enough. We bent over the wall. Paxton was there at the bottom.

You don't need to be told that he was dead. His tracks showed that he had run along the side of the battery, had turned sharp round the corner of it, and, small doubt of it, must have dashed straight into the open arms of someone who was waiting there. His mouth was full of sand and stones, and his teeth and jaws were broken to bits. I only glanced once at his face.

At the same moment, just as we were scrambling down from the battery to get to the body, we heard a shout, and saw a man running down the bank of the martello tower. He was the caretaker stationed there, and his keen old eyes had managed to descry through the mist that something was wrong. He had seen Paxton fall, and had seen us a moment after, running up – fortunate this, for otherwise we could hardly have escaped suspicion of being concerned in the dreadful business. Had he, we asked, caught sight of anybody attacking our friend? He could not be sure.

We sent him off for help, and stayed by the dead man till they came with the stretcher. It was then that we traced out how he had come, on the narrow fringe of sand under the battery wall. The rest was shingle, and it was hopelessly impossible to tell whither the other had gone.

What were we to say at the inquest? It was a duty, we felt, not to give up, there and then, the secret of the crown, to be published in every paper. I don't know how much you would have told; but what we did agree upon was this: to say that we had only made acquaintance with Paxton the day before, and that he had told us he was under some apprehension of danger at the hands of a man called William Ager. Also that we had seen some other tracks besides Paxton's when we followed him along the beach. But of course by that time everything was gone from the sands.

No one had any knowledge, fortunately, of any William Ager living in the district. The evidence of the man at the martello tower freed us from all suspicion. All that could be done was to return a verdict of wilful murder by some person or persons unknown.

Paxton was so totally without connections that all the inquiries that were subsequently made ended in a No Thoroughfare. And I have never been at Seaburgh, or even near it, since.

The Night of the Tiger

STEPHEN KING

I FIRST SAW MR LEGERE when the circus swung through Steubenville, but I'd only been with the show for two weeks; he might have been making his irregular visits indefinitely. No one much wanted to talk about Mr Legere, not even the last night when it seemed that the world was coming to an end – the night that Mr Indrasil disappeared.

But if I'm going to tell it to you from the beginning, I should start by saying that I'm Eddie Johnston, and I was born and raised in Sauk City. Went to school there, had my first girl there, and worked in Mr Lillie's five-and-dime there for a while after I graduated from high school. That was a few years back ... more than I like to count, sometimes. Not that Sauk City's such a bad place; hot, lazy summer nights sitting on the front porch is all right for some folks, but it just seemed to *itch* me, like sitting in the same chair too long. So I quit the five-and-dime and joined Farnum & Williams' All-American 3-Ring Circus and Side Show. I did it in a moment of giddiness when the calliope music kind of fogged my judgment, I guess.

So I became a roustabout, helping put up tents and take them down, spreading sawdust, cleaning cages, and sometimes selling cotton candy when the regular salesman had to go away and bark for Chips Baily, who had malaria and sometimes had to go someplace far away and holler. Mostly things that kids do for free passes – things I used to do when I was a kid. But times change. They don't seem to come around like they used to.

We swung through Illinois and Indiana that hot summer, and the crowds were good and everyone was happy. Everyone except Mr Indrasil. Mr Indrasil was never happy. He was the lion-tamer, and he looked like old pictures I've seen of Rudolph Valentino. He was tall, with handsome, arrogant features and a shock of wild black hair. And strange, mad eyes – the maddest eyes I've ever seen. He was silent most of the time; two syllables from Mr Indrasil was a sermon. All the circus people kept a mental as well as a physical distance, because his rages were legend. There was a whispered story about coffee spilled on his hands after a particularly difficult performance and a murder that was almost done to a young roustabout before Mr Indrasil could be hauled off him. I don't know about that. I do know that I grew to fear him worse than I had cold-eyed Mr

179

Edmont, my high school principal, Mr Lillie, or even my father, who was capable of cold dressing-downs that would leave the recipient quivering with a shame and dismay.

When I cleaned the big cats' cages, they were always spotless. The memory of the few times I had the vituperative wrath of Mr Indrasil called down on me still have the power to turn my knees watery in retrospect. Mostly it was his eyes – large and dark and totally blank. The eyes, and the feeling that a man capable of controlling seven watchful cats in a small cage must be part savage himself. And the only two things he was afraid of were Mr Legere and the circus's one tiger, a huge beast called Green Terror.

As I said, I first saw Mr Legere in Steubenville, and he was staring into Green Terror's cage as if the tiger knew all the secrets of life and death.

He was lean, dark, quiet. His deep, recessed eyes held an expression of pain and brooding violence in their green-flecked depths, and his hands were always crossed behind his back as he stared moodily in at the tiger.

Green Terror was a beast to be stared at. He was a huge, beautiful specimen with a flawless striped coat, emerald eyes, and heavy fangs like ivory spikes. His roars usually filled the circus grounds – fierce, angry, and utterly savage. He seemed to scream defiance and frustration at the whole world.

Chips Baily, who had been with Farnum & Williams since Lord knew when, told me that Mr Indrasil used to use Green Terror in his act, until one night when the tiger leaped suddenly from its perch and almost ripped his head from his shoulders before he could get out of the cage. I noticed that Mr Indrasil always wore his hair long down the back of his neck.

I can still remember the tableau that day in Steubenville. It was hot, sweatingly hot, and we had a shirt-sleeve crowd. That was why Mr Legere and Mr Indrasil stood out. Mr Legere, standing silently by the tiger cage, was fully dressed in a suit and vest, his face unmarked by perspiration. And Mr Indrasil, clad in one of his beautiful silk shirts and white whipcord breeches, was staring at them both, his face dead-white, his eyes bulging in lunatic anger, hate, and fear. He was carrying a currycomb and brush, and his hands were trembling as they clenched on them spasmodically.

Suddenly he saw me, and his anger found vent. 'You!' He shouted. 'Johnston!'

'Yes, sir?' I felt a crawling in the pit of my stomach. I knew I was about to have the Wrath of Indrasil vented on me, and the thought turned me weak with fear. I like to think I'm as brave as the next, and if it had been anyone else, I think I would have been fully determined to stand up for myself. But it wasn't anyone else. It was Mr Indrasil, and his eyes were mad.

'These cages, Johnston. Are they supposed to be clean?' He pointed a finger, and I followed it. I saw four errant wisps of straw and an incriminating puddle of hose water in the far corner of one.

'Y-yes, sir,' I said, and what was intended to be firmness became palsied bravado.

Silence, like the electric pause before a downpour. People were beginning to look, and I was dimly aware that Mr Legere was staring at us with his bottomless eyes.

'Yes, sir?' Mr Indrasil thundered suddenly. 'Yes, sir? Yes, sir? Don't insult my intelligence, boy! Don't you think I can see? *Smell?* Did you use the disinfectant?'

'I used disinfectant yest –'

'Don't answer me back!' He screeched, and then the sudden drop in his voice made my skin crawl. 'Don't you *dare* answer me back.' Everyone was staring now. I wanted to retch, to die. 'Now you get the hell into that tool shed, and you get that disinfectant and swab out those cages', he whispered, measuring every word. One hand suddenly shot out, grasping my shoulder. 'And don't you ever, ever speak back to me again.'

I don't know where the words came from, but they were suddenly there, spilling off my lips. 'I didn't speak back to you, Mr Indrasil, and I don't like you saying I did. I – I resent it. Now let me go.'

His face went suddenly red, then white, then almost saffron with rage. His eyes were blazing doorways to hell. Right then I thought I was going to die.

He made an inarticulate gagging sound, and the grip on my shoulder became excruciating. His right hand went up ... up ... up, and then descended with unbelievable speed. If that hand had connected with my face, it would have knocked me senseless at best. At worst, it would have broken my neck.

It did not connect. Another hand materialized magically out of space, right in front of me. The two straining limbs came together with a flat smacking sound. It was Mr Legere.

'Leave the boy alone', he said emotionlessly.

Mr Indrasil stared at him for a long second, and I think there was nothing so unpleasant in the whole business as watching the fear of Mr Legere and the mad lust to hurt (or to kill!) mix in those terrible eyes.

Then he turned and stalked away.

I turned to look at Mr Legere. 'Thank you', I said.

'Don't thank me.' And it wasn't a 'don't thank *me*', but a '*don't* thank me'. Not a gesture of modesty, but a literal command. In a sudden flash of intuition – empathy, if you will – I understood exactly what he meant by that comment. I was a pawn in what must have been a long combat between the two of them. I had been captured by Mr Legere rather than Mr Indrasil. He had stopped the lion-tamer not because he felt for me, but because it gained him an advantage, however slight, in their private war.

'What's your name?' I asked, not at all offended by what I had inferred.

He had, after all, been honest with me.

'Legere', he said briefly. He turned to go.

'Are you with a circus?' I asked, not wanting to let him go so easily. 'You seemed to know – him.'

A faint smile touched his thin lips, and warmth kindled in his eyes for a moment. 'No. You might call me a policeman'. And before I could reply, he had disappeared into the surging throng passing by.

The next day we picked up stakes and moved on.

I saw Mr Legere again in Danville and, two weeks later, in Chicago. In the time between I tried to avoid Mr Indrasil as much as possible and kept the cat cages spotlessly clean. On the day before we pulled out for St Louis, I asked Chips Baily and Sally O'Hara, the red-headed wire walker, if Mr Legere and Mr Indrasil knew each other. I was pretty sure they did, because Mr Legere was hardly following the circus to eat our fabulous lime ice.

Sally and Chips looked at each other over their coffee cups. 'No one knows much about what's between those two', she said. 'But it's been going on for a long time – maybe twenty years. Every since Mr Indrasil came over from Ringling Brothers, and maybe before that'.

Chips nodded. 'This Legere guy picks up the circus almost every year when we swing through the Midwest and stays with us until we catch the train for Florida in Little Rock. Makes old Leopard Man touchy as one of his cats'.

'He told me he was a policeman', I said. 'What do you suppose he looks for around here? You don't suppose Mr Indrasil – ?'

Chips and Sally looked at each other strangely, and both just about broke their backs getting up. 'Got to see those weights and counter-weights get stored right', Sally said, and Chips muttered something not too convincing about checking on the rear axle of his U-Haul. And that's about the way any conversation concerning Mr Indrasil or Mr Legere usually broke up – hurriedly, with many hardforced excuses.

We said farewell to Illinois and comfort at the same time. A killing hot spell came on, seemingly at the very instant we crossed the border, and it stayed with us for the next month and a half, as we moved slowly across Missouri and into Kansas. Everyone grew short of temper, including the animals. And that, of course, included the cats, which were Mr Indrasil's responsibility. He rode the roustabouts unmercifully, and myself in particular. I grinned and tried to bear it, even though I had my own case of prickly heat. You just don't argue with a crazy man, and I'd pretty well decided that was what Mr Indrasil was.

No one was getting any sleep, and that is the curse of all circus performers. Loss of sleep slows up reflexes, and slow reflexes make for danger. In Independence, Sally O'Hara fell seventy-five feet into the nylon netting and fractured her shoulder. Andrea Solienni, our bareback rider, fell off one of her horses during rehearsal and was knocked unconscious by a flying hoof. Chips Baily suffered silently with the fever that was always with him, his face a waxen mask, with cold perspiration clustered at each temple.

And in many ways, Mr Indrasil had the roughest row to hoe of all. The cats were nervous and short-tempered, and every time he stepped into the Demon Cat Cage, as it was billed, he took his life in his hands. He was feeding the lions inordinate amounts of raw meat right before he went on, something that lion-tamers rarely do, contrary to popular belief. His face grew drawn and haggard, and his eyes were wild.

Mr Legere was almost always there, by Green Terror's cage, watching him. And that, of course, added to Mr Indrasil's load. The circus began eyeing the silk-shirted figure nervously as he passed, and I knew they were all thinking the same thing I was: *He's going to crack wide open, and when he does –*.

When he did, God alone knew what would happen.

The hot spell went on, and temperatures were climbing well into the nineties every day. It seemed as if the rain gods were mocking us. Every town we left would receive the showers of blessing. Every town we entered was hot, parched, sizzling. And one night, on the road between Kansas City and Green Bluff, I saw something that upset me more than anything else.

It was hot – abominably hot. It was no good even trying to sleep. I rolled about on my cot like a man in a fever-delirium, chasing the sandman but never quite catching him. Finally I got up, pulled on my pants, and went outside.

We had pulled off into a small field and drawn into a circle. Myself and two other roustabouts had unloaded the cats so they could catch whatever breeze there might be. The cages were there now, painted dull silver by the swollen Kansas moon, and a tall figure in white whipcord breeches was standing by the biggest of them. Mr Indrasil. He was baiting Green Terror with a long, pointed pike. The big cat was padding silently around the cage, trying to avoid the sharp tip. And the frightening thing was, when the staff did punch into the tiger's flesh, it did not roar in pain and anger as it should have. It maintained an ominous silence, more terrifying to the person who knows cats than the loudest of roars.

It had gotten to Mr Indrasil, too. 'Quiet bastard, aren't you?' He grunted. Powerful arms flexed, and the iron shaft slid forward. Green Terror flinched, and his eyes rolled horribly. But he did not make a sound. 'Yowl!' Mr Indrasil hissed. 'Go ahead and yowl, you monster! *Yowl!*' And he drove his spear deep into the tiger's flank.

Then I saw something odd. It seemed that a shadow moved in the darkness under one of the far wagons, and the moonlight seemed to glint on staring eyes – green eyes. A cool wind passed silently through the clearing, lifting dust and rumpling my hair. Mr Indrasil looked up, and there was a queer listening expression on his face. Suddenly he dropped the bar, turned, and strode back to his trailer.

I stared again at the far wagon, but the shadow was gone. Green Terror stood motionlessly at the bars of his cage, staring at Mr Indrasil's trailer. And the thought came to me that it hated Mr Indrasil not because he was cruel or vicious, for the tiger respects these qualities in its own animalistic way, but rather because he was a deviate from even the tiger's savage norm. He was a rogue. That's the only way I can put it. Mr Indrasil was not only a human tiger, but a rogue tiger as well. The thought jelled inside me, disquieting and a little scary. I went back inside, but still I could not sleep.

The heat went on. Every day we fried, every night we tossed and turned, sweating and sleepless. Everyone was painted red with sunburn, and there were fist-fights over trifling affairs. Everyone was reaching the point of explosion.

Mr Legere remained with us, a silent watcher, emotionless on the surface, but, I sensed, with deep-running currents of – what? Hate? Fear? Vengeance? I could not place it. But he was potentially dangerous, I was sure of that. Perhaps more so than Mr Indrasil was, if anyone ever lit his particular fuse.

He was at the circus at every performance, always dressed in his nattily creased brown suit, despite the killing temperatures. He stood silently by Green Terror's cage, seeming to commune deeply with the tiger, who was always quiet when he was around.

From Kansas to Oklahoma, with no let-up in the temperature. A day without a heat prostration case was a rare day indeed. Crowds were beginning to drop off; who wanted to sit under a stifling canvas tent when there was an air-conditioned movie just around the block?

We were all as jumpy as cats, to coin a particularly applicable phrase. And as we set down stakes in Wildwood Green, Oklahoma, I think we all knew a climax of some sort was close at hand. And most of us knew it would involve Mr Indrasil. A bizarre occurrence had taken place just prior to our first Wildwood performance. Mr Indrasil had been in the Demon Cat Cage, putting the ill-tempered lions through their paces. One of them missed its balance on its pedestal, tottered and almost regained it. Then, at that precise moment, Green Terror let out a terrible, ear-splitting roar.

The lion fell, landed heavily, and suddenly launched itself with rifle-bullet accuracy at Mr Indrasil. With a frightened curse, he heaved his chair at the cat's feet, tangling up the driving legs. He darted out just as the lion smashed against the bars. As he shakily collected himself preparatory to re-entering the cage, Green Terror let out another roar – but this one monstrously like a huge, disdainful chuckle. Mr Indrasil stared at the beast, white-faced, then turned and walked away. He did not come out of his trailer all afternoon.

That afternoon wore on interminably. But as the temperature climbed, we all began looking hopefully toward the west, where huge banks of thunderclouds were forming.

'Rain, maybe,' I told Chips, stopping by his barking platform in front of the sideshow.

But he didn't respond to my hopeful grin. 'Don't like it,' he said. 'No wind. Too hot. Hail or tornadoes.' His face grew grim. 'It ain't no picnic, ridin' out a tornado with a pack of crazy-wild animals all over the place, Eddie. I've thanked God more'n once when we've gone through the tornado belt that we don't have no elephants.'

'Yeah', he added gloomily, 'you better hope them clouds stay right on the horizon.'

But they didn't. They moved slowly towards us, cyclopean pillars in the sky, purple at the bases and awesome blue-black through the cumulonimbus. All air movement ceased, and the heat lay on us like a woollen winding-shroud. Every now and again, thunder would clear its throat further west.

About four, Mr Farnum himself, ringmaster and half-owner of the circus, appeared and told us there would be no evening performance; just batten down and find a convenient hole to crawl into in case of trouble. There had been corkscrew funnels spotted in several places between Wildwood and Oklahoma City, some within forty miles of us.

There was only a small crowd when the announcement came, apathetically wandering through the sideshow exhibits or ogling the animals. But Mr Legere had not been present all day; the only person at Green Terror's cage was a sweaty high-school boy with a clutch of books. When Mr Farnum announced the US Weather Bureau tornado warning that had been issued, he hurried quickly away.

I and the other two roustabouts spent the rest of the afternoon working our tails off, securing tents, loading animals back into their wagons, and making generally sure that everything was nailed down.

Finally only the cat cages were left, and there was a special arrangement for those. Each cage had a special mesh 'breezeway' accordioned up against it, which, when extended completely, connected with the Demon Cat Cage. When the smaller cages had to be moved, the felines could be herded into the big cage while they were loaded up. The big cage itself rolled on gigantic casters and could be muscled around to a position where each cat could be let back into its original cage. It sounds complicated, and it was, but it was just the only way.

We did the lions first, then Ebony Velvet, the docile black panther that had set the circus back almost one season's receipts. It was a tricky business coaxing them up and then back through the breezeways, but all of us preferred it to calling Mr Indrasil to help.

By the time we were ready for Green Terror, twilight had come – a queer, yellow twilight that hung humidly around us. The sky above had taken on a flat, shiny aspect that I had never seen and which I didn't like in the least.

'Better hurry', Mr Farnum said, as we laboriously trundled the Demon Cat Cage back to where we could hook it to the back of Green Terror's show cage. 'Barometer's falling off fast'. He shook his head worriedly. 'Looks bad, boys. Bad'. He hurried on, still shaking his head.

We got Green Terror's breezeway hooked up and opened the back of his cage. 'In you go', I said encouragingly.

Green Terror looked at me menacingly and didn't move.

Thunder rumbled again, louder, closer, sharper. The sky had gone jaundice, the ugliest colour I have ever seen. Wind-devils began to pick jerkily at our clothes and whirl away the flattened candy wrappers and cotton-candy cones that littered the area.

'Come on, come on', I urged and poked him easily with the blunt-tipped rods we were given to herd them with.

Green Terror roared ear-splittingly, and one paw lashed out with blinding speed. The hardwood pole was jerked from my hands and splintered as if it had been a greenwood twig. The tiger was on his feet now, and there was murder in his eyes.

'Look', I said shakily. 'One of you will have to go get Mr Indrasil, that's all. We can't wait around'. As if to punctuate my words, thunder cracked louder, the clapping of mammoth hands.

Kelly Nixon and Mike McGregor flipped for it; I was excluded because of my previous run-in with Mr Indrasil. Kelly drew the task, threw us a wordless glance that said he would prefer facing the storm, and then started off.

He was gone almost ten minutes. The wind was picking up velocity now, and twilight was darkening into a weird six o'clock night. I was scared, and am not afraid to admit it. That rushing, featureless sky, the deserted circus grounds, the sharp, tugging wind-vortices – all that makes a memory that will stay with me always, undimmed.

And Green Terror would not budge into his breezeway.

Kelly Nixon came rushing back, his eyes wide. 'I pounded on his door for 'most five minutes!' He gasped. 'Couldn't raise him!'

We looked at each other, at a loss. Green Terror was a big investment for the circus. He couldn't just be left in the open. I turned bewilderedly, looking for Chips, Mr Farnum, or anybody who could tell me what to do. But everyone was gone. The tiger was our responsibility. I considered trying to load the cage bodily into the trailer, but *I* wasn't going to get my fingers in that cage.

'Well, we've just got to go and get him', I said. 'The three of us. Come on.' And we ran toward Mr Indrasil's trailer through the gloom of coming night.

We pounded on his door until he must have thought all the demons of hell were after him. Thankfully, it finally jerked open. Mr Indrasil swayed and stared down at us, his mad eyes rimmed and oversheened with drink. He smelled like a distillery.

'Damn you, leave me alone,' he snarled.

'Mr Indrasil –' I had to shout over the rising whine of the wind. It was like no storm I had ever heard of or read about, out there. It was like the end of the world.

'You,' he gritted softly. He reached down and gathered my shirt up in a knot. 'I'm going to teach you a lesson you'll never forget.' He glared at Kelly and Mike, cowering back in the moving storm shadows. 'Get out!'

They ran. I didn't blame them; I've told you – Mr Indrasil was crazy. And not just ordinary crazy – he was like a crazy animal, like one of his own cats gone bad.

'All right,' he muttered, staring down at me, his eyes like hurricane lamps. 'No juju to protect you now. No grisgris.' His lips twitched in a wild, horrible smile. 'He isn't here now, is he? We're two of a kind, him and me. Maybe the only two left. My nemesis – and I'm his'. He was rambling, and I didn't try to stop him. At least his mind was off me.

'Turned the cat against me, back in '58. Always had the power more'n me. Fool could make a million – the two of us could make a million if he wasn't so damned high and mighty – what's that?'

It was Green Terror, and he had begun to roar earsplittingly.

'Haven't you got that damned tiger in?' He screamed, almost falsetto. He shook me like a rag doll.

'He won't go!' I found myself yelling back. 'You've got to –'

But he flung me away. I stumbled over the fold-up steps in front of his trailer and crashed into a bone-shaking heap at the bottom. With something between a sob and a curse Mr Indrasil strode past me, face mottled with anger and fear. I got up, drawn after him as if hypnotized. Some intuitive part of me realized I was about to see the last act played out.

Once clear of the shelter of Mr Indrasil's trailer, the power of the wind was appalling. It screamed like a runaway freight train. I was an ant, a speck, an unprotected molecule before that thundering, cosmic force.

And Mr Legere was standing by Green Terror's cage.

It was like a tableau from Dante. The near-empty cage-clearing inside the circle of trailers; the two men, facing each other silently, their clothes and hair rippled by the shrieking gale; the boiling sky above; the twisting wheatfields in the background, like damned souls bending to the whip of Lucifer.

'It's time, Jason', Mr Legere said, his words flayed across the clearing by the wind.

Mr Indrasil's wildly whipping hair lifted around the livid scar across the back of his neck. His fists clenched, but he said nothing. I could almost feel him gathering his will, his life force, his *id*. It gathered around him like an unholy nimbus.

And, then, I saw with sudden horror that Mr Legere was unhooking Green Terror's breezeway – and the back of the cage was open! I cried out, but the wind ripped my words away.

The great tiger leaped out and almost flowed past Mr Legere. Mr Indrasil swayed, but did not run. He bent his head and stared down at the tiger.

And Green Terror stopped.

He swung his huge head back to Mr Legere, almost turned, and then slowly turned back to Mr Indrasil again. There was a terrifyingly palpable sensation of directed force in the air, a mesh of conflicting wills centred around the tiger. And the wills were evenly matched.

I think, in the end, it was Green Terror's own will – his hate of Mr Indrasil – that tipped the scales. The cat began to advance, his eyes hellish, flaring beacons. And something strange began to happen to Mr Indrasil. He seemed to be folding in on himself, shrivelling, accordioning. The silk shirt lost shape, the dark, whipping hair became a hideous toadstool around his collar. Mr Legere called something across to him, and, simultaneously, Green Terror leaped.

I never saw the outcome. The next moment I was slammed flat on my back, and the breath seemed to be sucked from my body. I caught one crazily tilted glimpse of a huge, towering cyclone funnel, and then the darkness descended.

When I awoke, I was in my cot just aft of the grainery bins in the all-purpose storage trailer we carried. My body felt as if it had been beaten with padded Indian clubs.

Chips Baily appeared, his face lined and pale. He saw my eyes were open and grinned relievedly. 'Didn't know as you were ever gonna wake up. How you feel?'

'Dislocated,' I said. 'What happened? How'd I get here?'

'We found you piled up against Mr Indrasil's trailer. The tornado almost carried you away for a souvenir, m'boy.'

At the mention of Mr Indrasil, all the ghastly memories came flooding back. 'Where is Mr Indrasil? And Mr Legere?'

His eyes went murky, and he started to make some kind of an evasive answer.

'Straight talk,' I said, struggling up on one elbow. 'I have to know Chips. I *have* to.'

Something in my face must have decided him. 'Okay. But this isn't exactly what we told the cops – in fact we hardly told the cops any of it. No sense havin' people think we're crazy. Anyhow, Indrasil's gone. I didn't even know that Legere guy was around.'

'And Green Terror?'

Chips' eyes were unreadable again. 'He and the other tiger fought to death.'

'*Other* tiger? There's no other –'

'Yeah, but they found two of 'em, lying in each other's blood. Hell of a mess. Ripped each other's throats out.'

'What – Where –'.

'Who knows? We just told the cops we had two tigers. Simpler that way.' And before I could say another word, he was gone.

And that's the end of my story – except for two little items. The words Mr Legere shouted just before the tornado hit: '*When a man and an animal live in the same shell, Indrasil, the instincts determine the mould!*'

The other thing is what keeps me awake nights. Chips told me later, offering it only for what it might be worth. What he told me was that the strange tiger had a long scar on the back of its neck.

The Interruption
W. W. JACOBS

THE LAST OF THE FUNERAL guests had gone and Spencer Goddard, in decent black, sat alone in his small, well-furnished study. There was a queer sense of freedom in the house since the coffin had left it; the coffin which was now hidden in its solitary grave beneath the yellow earth. The air, which for the last three days had seemed stale and contaminated, now smelt fresh and clean. He went to the open window and, looking into the fading light of the autumn day, took a deep breath.

He closed the window, and, stooping down, put a match to the fire, and, dropping into his easy chair, sat listening to the cheery crackle of the wood. At the age of thirty-eight he had turned over a fresh page. Life, free and unencumbered, was before him. His dead wife's money was at last his, to spend as he pleased instead of being doled out in reluctant driblets.

He turned at a step at the door and his face assumed the appearance of gravity and sadness it had worn for the last four days. The cook, with the same air of decorous grief, entered the room quietly and, crossing to the mantelpiece, placed upon it a photograph.

'I thought you'd like to have it, sir,' she said, in a low voice, 'to remind you.'

Goddard thanked her, and, rising, took it in his hand and stood regarding it. He noticed with satisfaction that his hand was absolutely steady.

'It is a very good likeness – till she was taken ill,' continued the woman. 'I never saw anybody change so sudden.'

'The nature of her disease, Hannah,' said her master.

The woman nodded, and, dabbing at her eyes with her handkerchief, stood regarding him.

'Is there anything you want?' he inquired, after a time.

She shook her head. 'I can't believe she's gone,' she said, in a low voice. 'Every now and then I have a queer feeling that she's still here——'

'It's your nerves,' said her master sharply.

'– and wanting to tell me something.'

By a great effort Goddard refrained from looking at her.

'Nerves,' he said again. 'Perhaps you ought to have a little holiday. It has been a great strain upon you.'

190

'You, too, sir,' said the woman respectfully. 'Waiting on her hand and foot as you have done, I can't think how you stood it. If you'd only had a nurse——'

'I preferred to do it myself, Hannah,' said her master. 'If I had had a nurse it would have alarmed her.'

The woman assented. 'And they are always peeking and prying into what doesn't concern them,' she added. 'Always think they know more than the doctors do.'

Goddard turned a slow look upon her. The tall, angular figure was standing in an attitude of respectful attention; the cold slatey-brown eyes were cast down, the sullen face expressionless.

'She couldn't have had a better doctor,' he said, looking at the fire again. 'No man could have done more for her.'

'And nobody could have done more for her than you did, sir,' was the reply. 'There's few husbands that would have done what you did.'

Goddard stiffened in his chair. 'That will do, Hannah,' he said curtly.

'Or done it so well,' said the woman, with measured slowness.

With a strange, sinking sensation, her master paused to regain his control. Then he turned and eyed her steadily. 'Thank you,' he said slowly; 'you mean well, but at present I cannot discuss it.'

For some time after the door had closed behind her he sat in deep thought. The feeling of well-being of a few minutes before had vanished, leaving in its place an apprehension which he refused to consider, but which would not be allayed. He thought over his actions of the last few weeks, carefully, and could remember no flaw. His wife's illness, the doctor's diagnosis, his own solicitous care, were all in keeping with the ordinary. He tried to remember the woman's exact words – her manner. Something had shown him Fear. What?

He could have laughed at his fears next morning. The dining-room was full of sunshine and the fragrance of coffee and bacon was in the air. Better still, a worried and commonplace Hannah. Worried over two eggs with false birth-certificates, over the vendor of which she became almost lyrical.

'The bacon is excellent,' said her smiling master, 'so is the coffee; but your coffee always is.'

Hannah smiled in return, and, taking fresh eggs from a rosy-cheeked maid, put them before him.

A pipe, followed by a brisk walk, cheered him still further. He came home glowing with exercise and again possessed with that sense of freedom and freshness. He went into the garden – now his own – and planned alterations.

After lunch he went over the house. The windows of his wife's bedroom were open and the room neat and airy. His glance wandered from the made-up bed to the brightly polished furniture. Then he went to the dressing-table and opened the drawers, searching each in turn. With the exception of a few odds and ends they were empty. He went out on to the landing and called for Hannah.

'Do you know whether your mistress locked up any of her things?' he inquired.

'What things?' said the woman.

'Well, her jewellery mostly.'

'Oh!' Hannah smiled. 'She gave it all to me,' she said, quietly.

Goddard checked an exclamation. His heart was beating nervously, but he spoke sternly.

'When?'

'Just before she died – of gastro-enteritis,' said the woman.

There was a long silence. He turned and with great care mechanically closed the drawers of the dressing-table. The tilted glass showed him the pallor of his face, and he spoke without turning round.

'That is all right, then,' he said, huskily. 'I only wanted to know what had become of it. I thought, perhaps Milly——'

Hannah shook her head. 'Milly's all right,' she said, with a strange smile. 'She's as honest as we are. Is there anything more you want, sir?'

She closed the door behind her with the quietness of the well-trained servant; Goddard, steadying himself with his hand on the rail of the bed, stood looking into the future.

The days passed monotonously, as they pass with a man in prison. Gone was the sense of freedom and the idea of a wider life. Instead of a cell, a house with ten rooms – but Hannah, the jailer, guarding each one. Respectful and attentive, the model servant, he saw in every word a threat against his liberty – his life. In the sullen face and cold eyes he saw her knowledge of power; in her solicitude for his comfort and approval, a sardonic jest. It was the master playing at being the servant. The years of unwilling servitude were over, but she felt her way carefully with infinite zest in the game. Warped and bitter, with a cleverness which had never before had scope, she had entered into her kingdom. She took it little by little, savouring every morsel.

'I hope I've done right, sir,' she said one morning. 'I have given Milly notice.'

Goddard looked up from his paper. 'Isn't she satisfactory?' he inquired.

'Not to my thinking, sir,' said the woman. 'And she says she is coming to see you about it. I told her that would be no good.'

'I had better see her and hear what she has to say,' said her master.

'Of course, if you wish to,' said Hannah; 'only, after giving her notice, if she doesn't go, I shall. I should be sorry to go – I've been very comfortable here – but it's either her or me.'

'I should be sorry to lose you,' said Goddard in a hopeless voice.

'Thank you, sir,' said Hannah. 'I'm sure I've tried to do my best. I've been with you some time now – and I know all your little ways. I expect I understand you better than anybody else would. I do all I can to make you comfortable.'

'Very well, I will leave it to you,' said Goddard in a voice which strove to be brisk and commanding. 'You have my permission to dismiss her.'

'There's another thing I want to see you about,' said Hannah: 'my wages. I was going to ask for a rise, seeing that I'm really housekeeper here now.'

'Certainly,' said her master, considering, 'that only seems fair. Let me see – what are you getting?'

'Thirty-six.'

Goddard reflected for a moment and then turned with a benevolent smile. 'Very well,' he said cordially, 'I'll make it forty-two. That's ten shillings a month more.'

'I was thinking of a hundred,' said Hannah dryly.

The significance of the demand appalled him. 'Rather a big jump,' he said at last. 'I really don't know that I——'

'It doesn't matter,' said Hannah. 'I thought I was worth it – to you – that's all. You know best. Some people might think I was worth *two* hundred. That's a bigger jump, but after all a big jump is better than——'

She broke off and tittered. Goddard eyed her.

' – than a big drop,' she concluded.

Her master's face set. The lips almost disappeared and something came into the pale eyes that was revolting. Still eyeing her, he rose and approached her. She stood her ground and met him eye to eye.

'You are jocular,' he said at last.

'Short life and a merry one,' said the woman.

'Mine or yours?'

'Both, perhaps,' was the reply.

'If – if I give you a hundred,' said Goddard, moistening his lips, 'that ought to make your life merrier, at any rate.'

Hannah nodded. 'Merry and long, perhaps,' she said slowly. 'I'm careful, you know – very careful.'

'I'm sure you are,' said Goddard, his face relaxing.

'Careful what I eat and drink, I mean,' said the woman, eyeing him steadily.

'That is wise,' he said slowly. 'I am myself – that is why I am paying a good cook a large salary. But don't overdo things, Hannah; don't kill the goose that lays the golden eggs.'

'I am not likely to do that,' she said coldly. 'Live and let live; that is my motto. Some people have different ones. But I'm careful; nobody won't catch me napping. I've left a letter with my sister, in case.'

Goddard turned slowly and in a casual fashion put the flowers straight in a bowl on the table, and, wandering to the window, looked out. His face was white again and his hands trembled.

'To be opened after my death,' continued Hannah. 'I don't believe in doctors – not after what I've seen of them – I don't think they know enough; so if I die I shall be examined. I've given good reasons.'

'And suppose,' said Goddard, coming from the window, 'suppose she is curious, and opens it before you die?'

'We must chance that,' said Hannah, shrugging her shoulders; 'but I don't think she will. I sealed it up with sealing-wax, with a mark on it.'

'She might open it and say nothing about it,' persisted her master.

An unwholesome grin spread slowly over Hannah's features. 'I should know it soon enough,' she declared boisterously, 'and so would other people. Lord, there would be an upset! Chidham would have something to talk about for once. We should be in the papers – both of us.'

Goddard forced a smile. 'Dear me!' he said gently. 'Your pen seems to be a dangerous weapon, Hannah, but I hope that the need to open it will not happen for another fifty years. You look well and strong.'

The woman nodded. 'I don't take up my troubles before they come,' she said, with a satisfied air; 'but there's no harm in trying to prevent them coming. Prevention is better than cure.'

'Exactly,' said her master; 'and, by the way, there's no need for this little financial arrangement to be known by anybody else. I might become unpopular with my neighbours for setting a bad example. Of course, I am giving you this sum because I really think you are worth it.'

'I'm sure you do,' said Hannah. 'I'm not sure I ain't worth more, but this'll do to go on with. I shall get a girl for less than we are paying Milly, and that'll be another little bit extra for me.'

'Certainly,' said Goddard, and smiled again.

'Come to think of it,' said Hannah, pausing at the door, 'I ain't sure I shall get anybody else; then there'll be more than ever for me. If I do the work I might as well have the money.'

Her master nodded, and, left to himself, sat down to think out a position which was as intolerable as it was dangerous. At a great risk he had escaped from the dominion of one woman only to fall, bound and helpless, into the hands of another. However, vague and unconvincing the suspicions of Hannah might be, they would be sufficient. Evidence could be unearthed. Cold with fear one moment, and hot with fury the next, he sought in vain for some avenue of escape. It was his brain against that of a cunning, illiterate fool; a fool whose malicious stupidity only added to his danger. And she drank. With largely increased wages she would drink more and his very life might depend upon a hiccuped boast. It was clear that she was enjoying her supremacy; later on her vanity would urge her to display it before others. He might have to obey the crack of her whip before witnesses, and that would cut off all possibility of escape.

He sat with his head in his hands. There must be a way out and he must find it. Soon. He must find it before gossip began; before the changed position of master and servant lent colour to her story when that story became known. Shaking with fury, he thought of her lean, ugly throat and the joy of choking her life out with his fingers. He started suddenly, and took a quick breath. No, not fingers – a rope.

Bright and cheerful outside and with his friends, in the house he was quiet and submissive. Milly had gone, and, if the service was poorer and the rooms neglected, he gave no sign. If a bell remained unanswered he made no complaint, and to studied insolence turned the other cheek of politeness. When at this tribute to her power the woman smiled, he smiled in return. A smile which, for all its disarming softness, left her vaguely uneasy.

'I'm not afraid of you,' she said once, with a menacing air.

'I hope not,' said Goddard in a slightly surprised voice.

'Some people might be, but I'm not,' she declared. 'If anything happened to me——'

'Nothing could happen to such a careful woman as you are,' he said, smiling again. 'You ought to live to ninety – with luck.'

It was clear to him that the situation was getting on his nerves. Unremembered but terrible dreams haunted his sleep. Dreams in which some great, inevitable disaster was always pressing upon him, although he could never discover what it was. Each morning he awoke unrefreshed to face another day of torment. He could not meet the woman's eyes for fear of revealing the threat that was in his own.

Delay was dangerous and foolish. He had thought out every move in that contest of wits which was to remove the shadow of the rope from his own neck and place it about that of the woman. There was a little risk, but the stake was a big one. He had but to see the ball rolling and others would keep it on its course. It was time to act.

He came in a little jaded from his afternoon walk, and left his tea untouched. He ate but little dinner, and, sitting hunched up over the fire, told the woman that he had taken a slight chill. Her concern, he felt grimly, might have been greater if she had known the cause.

He was no better next day, and after lunch called in to consult his doctor. He left with a clean bill of health except for a slight digestive derangement, the remedy for which he took away with him in a bottle. For two days he swallowed one tablespoonful three times a day in water, without result, then he took to his bed.

'A day or two in bed won't hurt you,' said the doctor. 'Show me that tongue of yours again.'

'But what is the matter with me, Roberts?' inquired the patient.

The doctor pondered. 'Nothing to trouble about – nerves a bit wrong – digestion a little bit impaired. You'll be all right in a day or two.'

Goddard nodded. So far, so good; Roberts had not outlived his usefulness. He smiled grimly after the doctor had left at the surprise he was preparing for him. A little rough on Roberts and his professional reputation, perhaps, but these things could not be avoided.

He lay back and visualized the programme. A day or two longer, getting gradually worse, then a little sickness. After that a nervous, somewhat shamefaced patient hinting at things. His food had a queer taste – he felt worse after taking it; he knew it was ridiculous, still – there was some of his beef-tea he had put aside, perhaps the doctor would like to examine it? and the medicine? Secretions, too; perhaps he would like to see those?

Propped on his elbow, he stared fixedly at the wall. There would be a trace – a faint trace – of arsenic in the secretions. There would be more than a trace in the other things. An attempt to poison him would be clearly indicated, and – his wife's symptoms had resembled his own – let Hannah get out of the web he was spinning if she could. As for the letter she had threatened him with, let her produce it; it could only recoil upon herself. Fifty letters could not save her from the doom he was preparing for her. It was her life or his, and he would show no mercy. For three days he doctored himself with sedulous care, watching himself anxiously the while. His nerve was going and he knew it. Before him was the strain of the discovery, the arrest, and the trial. The gruesome business of his wife's death. A long business. He would wait no longer, and he would open the proceedings with dramatic suddenness.

It was between nine and ten o'clock at night when he rang his bell, and it was not until he had rung four times that he heard the heavy steps of Hannah mounting the stairs.

'What d'you want?' she demanded, standing in the doorway.

'I'm very ill,' he said, gasping. 'Run for the doctor. Quick!'

The woman stared at him in genuine amazement. 'What, at this time o' night?' she exclaimed. 'Not likely.'

'I'm dying!' said Goddard in a broken voice.

'Not you,' she said, roughly. 'You'll be better in the morning.'

'I'm dying,' he repeated. 'Go – for – the – doctor.'

The woman hesitated. The rain beat in heavy squalls against the window, and the doctor's house was a mile distant on the lonely road. She glanced at the figure on the bed.

'I should catch my death o' cold,' she grumbled.

She stood sullenly regarding him. He certainly looked very ill, and his death would by no means benefit her. She listened, scowling, to the wind and the rain.

'All right,' she said at last, and went noisily from the room.

His face set in a mirthless smile, he heard her bustling about below. The front-door slammed violently and he was alone.

He waited for a few moments and then, getting out of bed, put on his dressing-gown and set about his preparations. With a steady hand he added a little white powder to the remains of his beef-tea and to the contents of his bottle of medicine. He stood listening a moment at some faint sound from below, and, having satisfied himself, lit a candle and made his way to Hannah's room. For a space he stood irresolute, looking about him. Then he opened one of the drawers and, placing the broken packet of powder under a pile of clothing at the back, made his way back to bed.

He was disturbed to find that he was trembling with excitement and nervousness. He longed for tobacco, but that was impossible. To reassure himself he began to rehearse his conversation with the doctor, and again he thought over every possible complication. The scene with the woman would be terrible; he would have to be too ill to take any part in it. The less he said the better. Others would do all that was necessary.

He lay for a long time listening to the sound of the wind and the rain. Inside, the house seemed unusually quiet, and with an odd sensation he suddenly realized that it was the first time he had been alone in it since his wife's death. He remembered that she would have to be disturbed. The thought was unwelcome. He did not want her to be disturbed. Let the dead sleep.

He sat up in bed and drew his watch from beneath the pillow. Hannah ought to have been back before; in any case she could not be long now. At any moment he might hear her key in the lock. He lay down again and reminded himself that things were shaping well. He had shaped them, and some of the satisfaction of the artist was his.

The silence was oppressive. The house seemed to be listening, waiting. He looked at his watch again and wondered, with a curse, what had happened to the woman. It was clear that the doctor must be out, but that was no reason for her delay. It was close on midnight, and the atmosphere of the house seemed in some strange fashion to be brooding and hostile.

In a lull in the wind he thought he heard footsteps outside, and his face cleared as he sat up listening for the sound of the key in the door below. In another moment the woman would be in the house and the fears engendered by a disordered fancy would have flown. The sound of the steps had ceased, but he could hear no sound of entrance. Until all hope had gone, he sat listening. He was certain he had heard footsteps. Whose?

Trembling and haggard he sat waiting, assailed by a crowd of murmuring fears. One whispered that he had failed and would have to pay the penalty of failing; that he had gambled with Death and lost.

By a strong effort he fought down these fancies and, closing his eyes, tried to compose himself to rest. It was evident now that the doctor was out and that Hannah was waiting to return with him in his car. He was frightening himself for nothing. At any moment he might hear the sound of their arrival.

He heard something else, and, sitting up, suddenly, tried to think what it was and what had caused it. It was a very faint sound – stealthy. Holding his breath he waited for it to be repeated. He heard it again, the mere ghost of a sound – a whisper of a sound, but significant as most whispers are.

He wiped his brow with his sleeve and told himself firmly that it was nerves, and nothing but nerves; but, against his will, he still listened. He fancied now that the sound came from his wife's room, the other side of the landing. It increased in loudness and became more insistent, but with his eyes fixed on the door of his room he still kept himself in hand, and tried to listen instead to the wind and the rain.

For a time he heard nothing but that. Then there came a scraping, scurrying noise from his wife's room, and a sudden, terrific crash.

With a loud scream his nerve broke, and springing from the bed he sped downstairs and, flinging open the front-door, dashed into the night. The door, caught by the wind, slammed behind him.

With his hand holding the garden gate open ready for further flight, he stood sobbing for breath. His bare feet were bruised and the rain was very cold, but he took no heed. Then he ran a little way along the road and stood for some time, hoping and listening.

He came back slowly. The wind was bitter and he was soaked to the skin. The garden was black and forbidding, and unspeakable horror might be lurking in the bushes. He went up the road again, trembling with cold. Then, in desperation, he passed through the terrors of the garden to the house, only to find the door closed. The porch gave a little protection from the icy rain, but none from the wind, and, shaking in every limb, he leaned in abject misery against the door. He pulled himself together after a time and stumbled round to the back-door. Locked! And all the lower windows were shuttered. He made his way back to the porch and, crouching there in hopeless misery, waited for the woman to return.

He had a dim memory when he awoke of somebody questioning him, and then of being half-pushed, half-carried upstairs to bed. There was something wrong with his head and his chest and he was trembling violently, and very cold. Somebody was speaking.

'You must have taken leave of your senses,' said the voice of Hannah. 'I thought you were dead.'

He forced his eyes to open. 'Doctor,' he muttered, 'doctor.'

'Out on a bad case,' said Hannah. 'I waited till I was tired of waiting, and then came along. Good thing for you I did. He'll be round first thing this morning. He ought to be here now.'

She bustled about, tidying up the room, his leaded eyes following her as she collected the beef-tea and other things on a tray and carried them out.

'Nice thing I did yesterday,' she remarked, as she came back. 'Left the missus's bedroom window open. When I opened the door this morning I found that beautiful Chippendale glass of hers had blown off the table and smashed to pieces. Did you hear it?'

Goddard made no reply. In a confused fashion he was trying to think. Accident or not, the fall of the glass had served its purpose. Were there such things as accidents? Or was Life a puzzle – a puzzle into which every piece was made to fit? Fear and the wind ... no: conscience and the wind ... had saved the woman. He must get the powder back from her drawer ... before she discovered it and denounced him. The medicine ... he must remember not to take it ...

He was very ill, seriously ill. He must have taken a chill owing to that panic flight into the garden. Why didn't the doctor come? He had come ... at last ... he was doing something to his chest ... it was cold.

Again ... the doctor ... there was something he wanted to tell him.... Hannah and a powder ... what was it?

Later on he remembered, together with other things that he had hoped to forget. He lay watching an endless procession of memories, broken at times by a glance at the doctor, the nurse, and Hannah, who were all standing near the bed regarding him. They had been there a long time and they were all very quiet. The last time he looked at Hannah was the first time for months that he had looked at her without loathing and hatred. Then he knew that he was dying.

Back from the Grave

ROBERT SILVERBERG

MASSEY WOKE SLOWLY, AS if the return to awareness were almost painful to him. He had the ghastly sensation of being closed in. The air around him was warm and moist and faintly foul-tasting as it passed into his lungs, and everything was dark.

He yawned, tried to stretch. Probably the windows were closed in the bedroom, that was all. That was why everything seemed so muggy in here. All he had to do was to call his wife, have her get the maid or someone else to draw back the curtains and let some fresh air into the room ...

'Louise! Louise!'

His voice sounded oddly muffled, flat and indistinct in his own ears. It seemed to bounce back at him from the walls and ceiling of his bedroom.

'Louise? I'm calling you!'

Massey suddenly became conscious of the noxious humidity all about him. *Very well*, he thought, *if there's no one else here I'll have to open the windows myself!* He levered himself up on his elbows, tried to swing himself out of bed.

He realized that he was not in bed at all.

A pallid quiver of fear lanced through him as he discovered he did not have room to rise to a sitting position. Above him, only inches above his head, he felt the smooth sheen of satin. There was satin all about. He reached to his left in the darkness and felt satin again, barely an inch from his shoulder. It was the same to his right.

Moment after moment, the air was growing murkier and harder to breathe. And he did not have room to move. He seemed to be in a container just about the length and width of his own body.

There is only one purpose for a container of such dimensions.

Massey felt the clammy hand of panic brush his cheeks. *My God*, he thought. *They've made a mistake! They thought I was dead and they buried me! I'm not dead! I'm – I'm – buried alive!*

Massey lay quite still for several moments after the terrible truth had become apparent. He did not want to panic. He was a reasonable man; he knew that to panic now would mean certain death. He had to be calm. Think this thing out. Don't panic.

The first fact to consider was that he was in a coffin. Coffins are not built

200

with much air-space. Massey was a heavy-set man, and that meant not only that he needed a lot of air but that there could be little air in the coffin to begin with. And that air was rapidly being exhausted. He began taking shallower and less frequent breaths.

Perhaps they had not buried him yet. Maybe he was still lying in state in a funeral parlour somewhere. They had lowered the coffin lid already, but there was still the chance they had not yet placed him in the grave. In that case——

He summoned up his energy and released it in one mighty cry for help. He waited.

Nothing happened.

Massey realized that such shouting was wasteful of oxygen. Probably they could not hear him through the heavy lid of the coffin. Or – he quivered at the possibility – perhaps they had lowered him into the ground already, said the proper words over him, shovelled the soil back into the cavity.

That would mean that five feet of packed-down earth lay above his head. Not even a superman could raise a coffin lid with that kind of weight pressing down. Lying there in the darkness, Massey tried to force himself not to think of that possibility. Despite himself, the vision came – of himself, two yards beneath the ground, wasting his last strength in a desperate and ultimately futile attempt to raise a coffin lid held down by hundreds of pounds of soil. Pushing and pushing, while the moist air around him gradually gave up its life-saving oxygen and became unfit to breathe, until finally he clutched at his purpling throat in agony, unable even to double up because of the dimensions of the coffin.

No, he thought. *I won't think of it!*

The only situation he would allow his numbed mind to consider was a more hopeful one, that he was still above the surface of the ground. Otherwise there would be no hope, and he might as well lie back and die. But...

How could such a thing happen to me?

He had heard cases of premature burial before. Most of them were apocryphal, of course – tales out of Poe, placed in real life by glib-tongued liars. But this was no lie, nor was it a story by Poe. Here he was: James Ronald Massey, forty-four years old, assets better than five hundred thousand dollars, holding responsible positions in no less than seven important corporations – here he was, lying in a coffin hardly bigger than his own body, while his life flickered like a dying candle.

It was like a dream – a nightmare. But it was real.

Massey allowed himself the luxury of a deep breath and raised his arms until his hands pressed against the satin-lined lid of the coffin. Tensing his body, he pushed upwards until his wrists ached. Nothing happened; not even the smallest upwards motion of the coffin lid was apparent.

He let his hands drop.

Droplets of sweat broke out all over his body. His clothes itched; he was wearing, not one of his own costly suits, but some cheap outfit supplied by the undertaker, and the coarse fabric felt rough and unfamiliar against his skin.

He wondered how much more time he had, before the air would be totally vitiated. Ten minutes? An hour? A day, perhaps?

He wondered how he could possibly have been buried alive at all.

As he lay there, gathering his strength for another attempt to raise the lid, his thoughts drifted back – back over an entire lifetime, really, but centring on only the last three years, the years of his marriage to Louise. Massey had been past forty when he married her; she had been only twenty-three.

He had never had time to marry when he was young. He was always too busy, involved in complex corporate schemes, pyramiding his investments, building up his money to provide himself with a luxurious middle age. Despite himself he smiled ironically, lying in the coffin, as he recalled his frantic planning, the long hours of pacing the floor at night to devise yet another investment plan.

For what? Here at the age of forty-four he lay trapped alive in his coffin – with his life ticking away with every beat of his heart. Unless he freed himself through a miracle, there would be no old age for him.

And he would not have Louise any more.

The thoughts of Louise made the fear return. He had met her at a summer resort, one of his rare vacations; she was with her parents, and they had danced a few times, and before the two weeks were over Massey had astonished himself by proposing marriage to her. She had astonished him even more by accepting.

They had been married a month later. It was a small ceremony though he did send announcements to all of his business associates, and they honeymooned for a month in South America. Massey could not spare more than a month away from his desk. Louise didn't seem to object to his devotion to his work, especially when he explained his financial status to her and their children after he was gone.

Those early married months had been the happiest of his life, Massey thought. To watch Louise moving around the big mansion was a delight; she seemed to bring a glowing radiance wherever she went.

I have to get out of here! The thought took on new urgency as he pictured Louise in his mind, tall, slim, so graceful she seemed to float instead of to walk, with her hair a golden halo round her head. So lovely, so warm, so loving.

Massey's breath came in panicky harsh gasps now, even though he fought for control over his rebellious lungs. There still was plenty of time, he told himself. Just get in the right position and lift. How much can a coffin-lid weigh, anyway?

Plenty, came the answer, *if there's a ton of dirt holding it down.*

'No! It isn't so!' Massey shouted, and the booming sound ricocheted mockingly from the walls of his coffin. 'I'm not underground yet! I can still get out!'

He squirmed around on one hip after a good deal of wriggling, and put his shoulder to the coffin lid. He took a deep breath.

Now – lift!

He pushed upward, anchoring himself with his left hand and pressing up with his right shoulder, until it seemed that his left arm would buckle under the strain. Bands of pain coursed through his body, across his chest, down his back.

The lid would not budge.

Massey's calmness began to desert him. The air was so close it stank now, stank with musty graveyard odours and with his own perspiration and with the killing dankness of the carbon dioxide that was rapidly replacing its oxygen. He began to laugh hysterically, suddenly, without warning. He threw his head back and laughed, not seeming to care that by so laughing he was consuming more of his precious remnant of breathable air.

It was all so funny! He remembered his last day of consciousness. Remembered Louise – in Henry Marshall's arms!

Henry Marshall had arrived on the scene in the first year of Massey's marriage to Louise. She had told Massey, one night, in that casual way of hers, 'I'm having a guest for dinner.'

'Oh? Anyone I know?'

'A boy named Henry Marshall. An old playmate of mine; I haven't seen him for years.'

Massey had smiled indulgently. Above all else, he wanted Louise to be happy, and never to fear that because she had married a husband nearly twice her age she was condemned to a life of solemn loneliness.

Henry Marshall arrived at the dot of six that night. He was a boy of about twenty-five, tall and handsome, with wavy blond hair and an easy, likeable manner about him. Something in his very charm made Massey dislike him almost on sight. He was too casual, took things too much for granted. Massey noticed that Henry Marshall was dressed rather shabbily, too.

It was not a pleasant evening. Louise and Henry Marshall reminisced together, chuckled over old times that meant nothing to Massey, told stories of friends long since unseen. Henry Marshall stayed late, past eleven, and when he finally left and Massey held Louise tightly in the quiet of her bedroom he sensed a certain remoteness about her that he had never felt before. It was as if she were making love mechanically, not really caring.

Massey brooded about that in the days that followed, though he never spoke a word to Louise. And Henry Marshall became a frequent visitor at the Masseys, coming sometimes for dinner, occasionally remaining as a house guest for two or three days. Massey resented the younger man's presence, but, as always, he remained silent out of deference to his wife's happiness.

He had almost come to accept Marshall's regular visits, even though they were occurring more frequently now, twice a month where they had been only once a month. But, thought Massey as he lay in the clammy darkness of the coffin where he had been interred alive, this final visit – only a few days ago, was it, or had years gone by? – this final visit had been too much.

Young Marshall had arrived on Friday night in time for dinner, as usual. By now he was well known among the servants, and they gave him his usual room in the north wing of the building. He was gay and amusing at dinner and afterwards.

Massey retired early that night, pleading a headache. But he lay awake, tossing restlessly in his bed, perturbed half by the problems involved in a large steel manoeuvre coming up on Monday, half by the presence of this flippant youngster under his own roof.

Half the sleepless night went by, and visions danced before him: Louise, lovely, tempting, belonging to him. A current of excitement rose in Massey. He left his bed, donned a housecoat, and made his way down the hallway to his wife's bedroom. The great clock in the corridor told him that the time was past three in the morning, and the big house was quiet.

Louise had left the 'do not disturb' sign on her bedroom door. Massey opened the door gently, silently, thinking that if she were asleep he would not awaken her, but hoping that perhaps she, too, had tossed and turned this evening, and would welcome him into her bed, into her arms.

He tiptoed towards the canopied bed.

Louise was not asleep. She was looking up at him, eyes bright with fear (or was it defiance?).

Louise was not alone.

Henry Marshall lay beside her, an arm thrown negligently over her bare shoulders.

In one stunned instant of understanding, Massey saw confirmed what he had barely dared to suspect, these past years when Henry Marshall had visited them so many times. Louise was deceiving him!

A hot ribbon of pain coursed across the front of his body, centering like a cauterizing knife just behind his ribs. He gasped in agony and confusion.

'Louise – I didn't know——'

They were sitting up in bed, both of them, smiling at him. They were unafraid.

'Well, now you *do* know,' Henry Marshall said. 'And it's been going on for years. What are you going to do about it old boy?'

Massey's heart thundered agonizingly. He staggered, nearly fell, grabbed a bedpost to support himself. His arms and legs felt cold with a deadly chill.

Louise said quietly, 'You were bound to find out about us sooner or later. Henry and I have been in love for years ever since we were nineteen. But we couldn't afford to marry – and he agreed to wait a few years, when I met you. Only a few years; that's what your doctor told me, privately. He didn't want you to know.'

Massey put his hands to the fiery ball of palpitating hell that his heart had abruptly become. He could almost feel the blood circulating through his body, pounding at his brain.

Louise said, 'Dr Robinson said you had a serious heart defect – any shock was likely to carry you off. But he didn't want you to know about it; he said your days were numbered anyway, so you might as well live them out in peace. But *I* knew – and Henry knew! And now we'll inherit your money, James. We're both still young, and we'll have each other for years to come!'

Massey took two uncertain steps towards the couple in the bed. Red flashes of light were interfering with his vision, and his legs were numb.

'Louise – it isn't so, Louise – this is all a dream, isn't it?'

'You're wide awake! It's actually happening! Why don't you die, you old fool? Die! Die!'

And then he had started to fall, toppling into the thick wine-red carpet of Louise's bedroom, lying there with his hands dug deep into the high pile rug, while eddies of pain ripped through him, and above him sounded their mocking laughter and Louise's repeated cry of 'Die, you old fool! Die! Die.'

So that was the way it had been. Massey recalled everything, now, and he understood. The shock of finding Louise and Henry Marshall that way had touched off the heart attack that had been inevitable for so long. He had lain on the floor in Louise's bedroom, unconscious, in a coma, perhaps, and somehow – somehow – the doctors had decided he was dead.

It was incredible. Had life indeed been flickering so feebly in him that the high-priced medicos had failed to realize he still lived? Or – the thought chilled Massey there in the darkness – had Louise and her lover found some complacent doctor who, for a fee, would certify death when death had not really come? What if Louise had known he was still alive, though unconscious, and had knowingly placed him in this coffin and sent him to the darkness of the grave?

A terrible passion came to life in Massey. He *would* get out! He had won before, in corporation matters, in proxy fights, in struggles of every kind.

He was a mild-mannered man on the surface, but his will was

all-consuming once it was aroused.

He would free himself.

Somehow.

Massey vowed to escape from his grave, whether he lay under a ton of soil or not. He would return to life, come back from the grave. Punish Louise for her crime, make her atone for her mocking infidelity.

I'll get out, he swore to himself. *I won't die here like a trapped rat.*

The word 'rat' brought a new and even more ghastly thought to mind. He had heard legends of the graveyard rats, great slug-shaped creatures with blazing red eyes and tails like scaled serpents, who tunnelled under the graveyards and gnawed their way into the new graves to devour the flesh of recent corpses.

Suppose they came for him? Suppose, even now as he lay here, the graveyard beasts squatted in their unmentionable tunnels below his coffin, nibbling at the wood with yellowed teeth, gnawing, biting, scratching, boring ominously inward.

How the rats would rejoice when they found a living man within the coffin!

Massey had always had a vivid imagination. Now, with darkness settled like a cloak about him, he found himself unable to make that imagination cease functioning. Sharply in the eye of his mind he saw the gleeful cascade of rats pouring through the breach in the coffin wall, saw dozens of the foul beasts launching themselves on him with more burrowing greedily in from all sides. He pictured the rats madly joyous at the discovery of a live being, of fresh meat.

He saw their bristly snouts nuzzling at the soft pink flesh of his throat. He would picture their razor-keen teeth meeting beneath his chin, while his outraged blood spurted out over them. He could feel the animals quarrelling with each other for the right to devour the tender morsels that were his eyes.

'What was that? That sound?'

A fitful champing and chewing sound, was it? As of hundreds of rats patiently gnawing at the sleek fresh wood of his coffin?

No, he thought. More imagination. There was no sound. Everything was utterly silent. It was, he thought, the silence of – the grave.

Then he wondered how he could still retain a sense of humour. How for that matter, he could still retain any shred of his sanity, trapped like this.

He could no longer preserve the fiction that he was still lying in state in some undertaker's parlour. Coffins do not normally have locks; the only reason why he had been unable to lift the lid was that he was already in the ground. No doubt Louise and her lover had rushed him into the ground as fast as they could.

They would be in for a surprise, Massey thought with calmness that surprised himself. Calmness was what he needed now. In the same way as he had piloted so many complicated financial manoeuvres, James Ronald Massey now set to work to think of a way to escape from the living grave to which he had been condemned.

Pushing at the lid was futile. He had already tried that a dozen unsuccessful times. But perhaps he would break the lid, claw his way upward through the dirt till he reached the surface.

He felt in the darkness for the satin lining of the coffin. The air hung like a moist cloth around him now. He realized he had no more than a few minutes' air left, and then the hideous slow death of strangulation would start.

Better than that the rats, he told himself. I don't want to be alive if the rats break into the coffin. I'd rather choke to death than be eaten alive. Yes. Much better to choke.

His hands clawed at the satin and ripped it away, shredding the expensive cloth. Now he could feel the smooth, cool pine boards from which his coffin had been made. The wood had been planed and sanded to a perfect finish. He laughed, a little wildly, Probably Louise had bought him the most expensive coffin that could be found. 'Nothing but the best for my poor dead darling husband,' she must have told the undertaker.

He began to pound at the wood, hoping he would hear it splinter. But the wood held. He gasped for breath, knowing just a bit of fresh air remained, that now the torture would begin. He could barely fill his lungs. He drew in a deep breath and nearly retched at the nauseous taste of the stale air.

Weirdly he wondered if perhaps they had laid him in his grave upsidedown. Perhaps he did not face the sky, and perhaps he was really digging at the bottom of his coffin instead of the top. In that case, even if he did succeed in breaking through the solid wood he would be far from free.

Impossible, he thought. *A joke of my tired mind.* He had to keep trying. Couldn't give up now. Not now, when the air would be gone in minutes, and the rats lay waiting for him.

His hands, which had never done any kind of manual labour, now clawed and scraped desperately at the unyielding wood of the coffin lid. His nails raked the mocking pine boards again and again, as if he thought to dig his way through the wood splinter by splinter. His nails ripped away one by one and blood streamed down his fingers, and he felt the bright hotness of the terrible pain, but still he clawed.

And screamed.

'Help me! Can't you hear me? I'm buried alive in here! Alive! I'll give ten thousand dollars to any man who gets me out! Twelve thousand! Fifty thousand! Do you hear me, fifty thousand dollars!'

He might just as well have offered the moon and the stars. No one heard his call; no one answered him. The funeral was probably long since over, the mourners dispersed. At this moment perhaps Louise and Henry Marshall were making love and laughing to each other about the fortune that was now theirs.

'Help me! Help me!'

His broken fingers clawed futilely at the wooden barrier above him, clawed until his nerves were numbed by constant agony and he could feel no more pain. The air was all but gone, now.

Part of his mind was still clear. Part was still engaged in formulating plans. Break a hole in the coffin lid, he thought. Widen it. Claw through the dirt to the surface. The soil will still be loose and soft. You can push it to one side if you can only get out of his coffin. Get your head above air, breath the fresh air again, call for help.

Then settle with Louise and Henry.

It was all so simple – all but the first step. He could not get a purchase on the wood. The air was a vile moist thing now, and he could feel the cold hand of asphyxiation tightening steadily round his throat. The staleness of the air was making thought more difficult; he could barely think clearly any more. And he seemed to hear the rats again, chewing tirelessly at the wood, as if they knew that a living being lay in the wooden box, as if they yearned to get to Massey while the warm blood still pulsed in his veins.

And his heart, the heart whose sudden failure had been mistaken for death – his heart now pounded wildly from his exertions, and the pain that shot through him was ten times the torment he had experienced that night in Louise's bedroom. He wondered how long he could stand the combined assault.

The rats ... the rats coming to get me ... and the air almost gone ... the darkness ... my heart, my heart! ... I'll need a miracle to get out of here now ... my heart! The pain!

The pain!

Suddenly tranquillity stole over Massey. He smiled, and realized that the pain had diminished. He felt calm and assured now.

How foolish he had been to work so hard to get out of his coffin! There was much as easier way to do it!

All he had to do was drift. He drifted upwards, passed lightly through the sturdy wood he had failed to break, drifted up through five feet of dark earth, and stood once more on the surface of the green land.

Free!

It was mid-afternoon. The sun glinted brightly, the sun Massey had thought never to see again. Fifty feet away, a group of people were gathered round a marble headstone, placing a wreath. Massey shouted to them.

'I'm free! They buried me, but I escaped from the grave! Get the sexton! Tell him there's been a mistake, please!'

Curiously, they ignored him. They did not even turn round to see who called. Massey repeated the words, to no avail.

He took a deep breath -- and discovered for the first time that he could not taste the spring-like freshness of the air. He felt no cool fragrance on his nostrils.

Massey looked down. Then, suddenly, it was as if the ground parted beneath him, and he could see clearly the coffin lying deep in the earth, and he could see into the coffin, where the dead body of a middle-aged man lay – his fingers torn and bloodied, his face mottled with the discolouration of asphyxiation and the redness of a sudden and fatal heart attack.

The Derelict

WILLIAM HOPE HODGSON

'IT'S THE *MATERIAL*,' SAID the old ship's doctor.... 'The *Material*, plus the conditions; and, maybe,' he added slowly, 'a third factor – yes, a third factor; but there, there....' He broke off his half-meditative sentence, and began to charge his pipe.

'Go on, Doctor,' we said encouragingly, and with more than a little expectancy. We were in the smoke-room of the *Sand-a-lea*, running across the North Atlantic; and the doctor was a character. He concluded the charging of his pipe, and lit it; then settled himself, and began to express himself more fully:

'The *Material*,' he said, with conviction, 'is inevitably the medium of expression of the Life-Force – the fulcrum, as it were; lacking which, it is unable to exert itself, or, indeed, to express itself in any form or fashion that would be intelligible or evident to us.

'So potent is the share of the *Material* in the production of that thing which we name Life, and so eager the Life-Force to express itself, that I am convinced it would, if given the right conditions, make itself manifest even through so hopeless-seeming a medium as a simple block of sawn wood; for I tell you, gentlemen, the Life-Force is both as fiercely urgent and as indiscriminate as Fire the Destructor; yet which some are now growing to consider the very essence of Life rampant.... There is a quaint-seeming paradox there,' he concluded, nodding his old grey head.

'Yes, Doctor,' I said. 'In brief, your argument is that Life is a thing, state, fact, or element, call-it-what-you-like, which requires the *Material* through which to manifest itself, and that given the *Material*, plus the conditions, the result is Life. In other words, that Life is an evolved product, manifested through Matter and bred of conditions – eh?'

'As we understand the word,' said the old doctor. 'Though mind you, there *may* be a third factor. But, in my heart, I believe that it is a matter of chemistry; conditions and a suitable medium; but given the conditions, the Brute is so almighty that it will seize upon anything through which to manifest itself. It is a force generated by conditions; but nevertheless this does not bring us one iota nearer to its *explanation*, any more than to the explanation of electricity or fire. They are, all three, of the Outer Forces – Monsters of the Void. Nothing we can do will *create* any one of them; our

210

power is merely to be able, by providing the conditions, to make each one of them manifest to our physical senses. Am I clear?'

'Yes, Doctor in a way you are,' I said. 'But I don't agree with you; though I think I understand you. Electricity and fire are both what I might call natural things; but life is an abstract something – a kind of all-permeating wakefulness. Oh I can't explain it; who could? But it's spiritual; not just a thing bred out of a condition, like fire, as you say, or electricity. It's a horrible thought of yours. Life's a kind of spiritual mystery. . . .'

'Easy, my boy!' said the old doctor, laughing gently to himself; 'or else I may be asking you to demonstrate the spiritual mystery of life of the limpet, or the crab, shall we say?'

He grinned at me, with ineffable perverseness. 'Anyway,' he continued, 'as I suppose you've all guessed, I've a yarn to tell you in support of my impression that life is no more a mystery or a miracle than fire or electricity. But, please to remember, gentlemen, that because we've succeeded in naming and making good use of these two forces, they're just as much mysteries, fundamentally, as ever. And, anyway, the thing I'm going to tell you, won't explain the mystery of life; but only give you one of my pegs on which I hang my feeling that life is, as I have said, a force made manifest through conditions (that is to say, natural chemistry), and that it can take for its purpose and need, the most incredible and unlikely matter; for without matter, it cannot come into existence – it cannot become manifest – .'

'I don't agree with you, Doctor,' I interrupted. 'Your theory would destroy all belief in life after death. It would – '

'Hush, sonny,' said the old man, with a quiet little smile of comprehension. 'Hark to what I've to say first; and, anyway, what objection have you to material life, after death; and if you object to a material framework, I would still have you remember that I am speaking of life, as we understand the word in this our life. Now do be quiet lad, or I'll never be done:

'It was when I was a young man, and that is a good many years ago, gentlemen. I had passed my examination; but was so run down with overwork, that it was decided that I had better take a trip to sea. I was by no means well off, and very glad, in the end, to secure a nominal post as doctor in a sailing passenger-clipper, running out to China.

'The name of the ship was the *Bheotpte*, and soon after I had got all my gear aboard, she cast off, and we dropped down the Thames, and next day were well away out in the Channel.

'The captain's name was Gannington, a very decent man; though quite illiterate. The first mate, Mr Berlies, was a quiet, sternish, reserved man, very well read. The second mate, Mr Selvern, was, perhaps, by birth and upbringing, the most socially cultured of the three; but he lacked the stamina and indomitable pluck of the two others. He was more of a sensitive; and emotionally and even mentally, the most alert man of the three.

'On our way out, we called at Madagascar, where we landed some of our passengers; then we ran eastward, meaning to call at North-West Cape; but about a hundred degrees east, we encountered very dreadful weather, which carried away all our sails and sprung the jibboom and fore t'gallant mast.

'The storm carried us northward for several hundred miles, and when it dropped us finally, we found ourselves in a very bad state. The ship had been strained, and had taken some three feet of water through her seams; the main topmast had been sprung, in addition to the jibboom and fore t'gallant mast; two of our boats had gone, as also one of the pigsties (with three fine pigs), this latter having been washed overboard but some half-hour before the wind began to ease, which it did quickly; though a very ugly sea ran for some hours after.

'The wind left us just before dark, and when morning came, it brought splendid weather; a calm, mildly undulating sea, and a brilliant sun, with no wind. It showed us also that we were not alone; for about two miles away to the westward was another vessel, which Mr Selvern, the second mate, pointed out to me.

' "That's a pretty rum-looking packet, Doctor," he said, and handed me his glass. I looked through it, at the other vessel, and saw what he meant; at least, I thought I did.

' "Yes, Mr Selvern," I said, "she's got a pretty oldfashioned look about her."

'He laughed at me, in his pleasant way.

' "It's easy to see you're not a sailor, Doctor," he remarked. "There's a dozen rum things about her. She's a derelict, and has been floating round, by the look of her, for many a score of years. Look at the shape of her counter, and the bows and cut-water. She's as old as the hills, as you might say, and ought to have gone down to Davy Jones a long time ago. Look at the growths on her, and the thickness of her standing rigging; that's all salt encrustations, I fancy, if you notice the white colour. She's been a small barque; but don't you see she's not a yard left aloft. They've all dropped out of the slings; everything rotted away; wonder the standing rigging hasn't gone too. I wish the Old Man would let us take the boat, and have a look at her; she'd be well worth it."

'There seemed little chance, however, of this; for all hands were turned-to and kept hard at it all day long, repairing the damage to the masts and gear, and this took a long while, as you may think. Part of the time I gave a hand, heaving on one of the deck-capstans; for the exercise was good for my liver. Old Captain Gannington approved, and I persuaded him to come along and try some of the same medicine, which he did; and we grew very chummy over the job.

212

'We got talking about the derelict, and he remarked how lucky we were not to have run full tilt on to her, in the darkness; for she lay right away to leeward of us, according to the way that we had been drifting in the storm. He also was of the opinion that she had a strange look about her, and that she was pretty old but on this latter point, he plainly had far less knowledge than the second mate; for he was, as I have said, an illiterate man, and he knew nothing of sea-craft beyond what experience had taught him. He lacked the book knowledge, which the second mate had, of vessels previous to his day, which it appeared the derelict was.

' "She's an old'un, Doctor," was the extent of his observations in this direction.

'Yet, when I mentioned to him that it would be interesting to go aboard, and give her a bit of an overhaul, he nodded his head, as if the idea had been already in his mind, and accorded with his own inclinations.

' "When the work's over, Doctor," he said. "Can't spare the men now, ye know. Got to get all shipshape an' ready as smart as we can. But we'll take my gig, an' go off in the second dog watch. The glass is steady, an' it'll be a bit of jam for us."

'That evening, after tea, the captain gave orders to clear the gig and get overboard. The second mate was to come with us, and the skipper gave him word to see that two or three lamps were put into the boat, as it would soon fall dark. A little later, we were pulling across the calmness of the sea with a crew of six at the oars, and making very good speed of it.

'Now, gentlemen, I have detailed to you with great exactness, all the facts, both big and little, so that you can follow step by step each incident in this extraordinary affair; and I want you now to pay the closest attention.

'I was sitting in the stern-sheets, with the second mate and the captain, who was steering; and as we drew nearer and nearer to the stranger, I studied her with an ever-growing attention, as, indeed, did Captain Gannington and the second mate. She was, as you know, to the westward of us, and the sunset was making a great flame of red light to the back of her, so that she showed a little blurred and indistinct, by reason of the halation of the light, which almost defeated the eye in any attempt to see her rotting spars and standing rigging, submerged as they were in the fiery glory of the sunset.

'It was because of this effect of the sunset, that we had come quite close, comparatively, to the derelict before we saw that she was surrounded by a sort of curious scum, the colour of which was difficult to decide upon, by reason of the red light that was in the atmosphere; but which afterwards we discovered to be brown. This scum spread all about the old vessel for many hundreds of yards, in a huge, irregular patch, a great stretch of which reached out to the eastward, upon our starboard side, some score, or so, fathoms away.

' "Queer stuff," said Captain Gannington, leaning to the side, and looking over. "Something in the cargo as 'as gone rotten an' worked out through 'er seams."

' "Look at her bows and stern, " said the second mate; "just look at the growth of her."

'There were, as he said, great clumpings of strange-looking sea-fungi under the bows and the short counter astern. From the stump of her jibboom and her cutwater, great beards of rime and marine growths hung downward into the scum that held her in. Her blank starboard side was presented to us, all a dead, dirtyish white, streaked and mottled vaguely with dull masses of heavier colour.

' "There's a steam or haze rising off her,' said the second mate, speaking again; "you can see it against the light. It keeps coming and going. Look!"

'I saw then what he meant – a faint haze or steam, either suspended above the old vessel, or rising from her; and Captain Gannington saw it also:

' "Spontaneous combustion!" he exclaimed. "We'll 'ave to watch w'en we lift the 'atches; 'nless it's some poor devil that got aboard of her; but that ain't likely."

'We were now within a couple of hundred yards of the old derelict, and had entered into the brown scum. As it poured off the lifted oars, I heard one of the men mutter to himself – 'dam treacle!' and indeed, it was something like it. As the boat continued to forge nearer and nearer to the old ship, the scum grew thicker and thicker; so that, at last, it perceptibly slowed us.

' "Give way, lads! Put some beef to it!" sung out Captain Gannington; and thereafter there was no sound, except the panting of the men, and the faint, reiterated suck, suck, of the sullen brown scum upon the oars, as the boat was forced ahead. As we went, I was conscious of a peculiar smell in the evening air, and whilst I had no doubt that the puddling of the scum, by the oars, made it rise, I felt that in some way, it was vaguely familiar; yet I could give it no name.

'We were now very close to the old vessel, and presently she was high above us, against the dying light. The captain called out then to – "in with the bow oars, and stand-by with the boat-hook," which was done.

' "Aboard there! Ahoy! Aboard there! Ahoy!" shouted Captain Gannington, but there came no answer, only the flat sound of his voice going lost into the open sea, each time he sang out.

' "Ahoy! Aboard there! Ahoy!" he shouted, time after time; but there was only the weary silence of the old hulk that answered us; and, somehow as he shouted, the while that I stared up half expectantly at her, a queer little sense of oppression, that amounted almost to nervousness, came upon me. It passed, but I remember how I was suddenly aware that it was

214

growing dark. Darkness comes fairly rapidly in the tropics, though not so quickly as many fiction-writers seem to think; but it was not that the coming dusk had perceptibly deepened in that brief time, of only a few moments, but rather that my nerves had made me suddenly a little hyper-sensitive. I mention my state particularly; for I am not a nervy man, normally; and my abrupt touch of nerves is significant, in the light of what happened.

' "There's no one aboard there!" said Captain Gannington. "Give way, men!" For the boat's crew had instinctively rested on their oars, as the captain hailed the old craft. The men gave way again; and then the second mate called out excitedly – "Why, look there, there's our pigsty! See, it's got *Bheotpte* painted on the end. It's drifted down here, and the scum's caught it. What a blessed wonder!"

'It was, as he had said, our pigsty that had been washed over-board in the storm, and most extraordinary to come across it there.

' "We'll tow it off with us, when we go," remarked the captain, and shouted to the crew to get down to their oars; for they were hardly moving the boat, because the scum was so thick, close in around the old ship, that it literally clogged the boat from going ahead. I remember that it struck me, in a half-conscious sort of way, as curious that the pigsty, containing our three dead pigs, had managed to drift in so far, unaided, whilst we could scarcely manage to *force* the boat in now that we had come right into the scum. But the thought passed from my mind; for so many things happened within the next few minutes.

'The men managed to bring the boat in alongside, within a couple of feet of the derelict, and the man with the boat-hook hooked on.

' " 'Ave you got 'old there, forrard?" asked Captain Gannington.

' "Yessir!" said the bow man; and as he spoke there came a queer noise of tearing.

' "What's that?" asked the Captain.

' "It's tore, sir. Tore clean away!" said the man; and his tone showed that he had received something of a shock.

' "Get a hold again then!" said Captain Gannington, irritably. "You don't s'pose this packet was built yesterday! Shove the hook into the main chains." The man did so gingerly, as you might say; for it seemed to me, in the growing dusk, that he put no strain on to the hook, though of course, there was no need; you see, the boat could not go very far, of herself, in the stuff in which it was embedded. I remember thinking this, also, as I looked up at the bulging side of the old vessel. Then I heard Captain Gannington's voice:

' "Lord! but she's old! An' what a colour, Doctor! She don't half want paint, do she! ... Now then somebody – one of them oars."

'An oar was passed to him, and he leant it up against the ancient, bulging side, then he paused, and called to the second mate to light a couple of the lamps, and stand by to pass them up; for darkness had settled down now upon the sea.

'The second mate lit two of the lamps, and told one of the men to light a third, and keep it handy in the boat; then he stepped across, with a lamp in each hand, to where Captain Gannington stood by the oar against the side of the ship.

' "Now, my lad," said the captain, to the man who had pulled stroke, "up with you, an' we'll pass ye up the lamps."

'The man jumped to obey; caught the oar, and put his weight upon it, and as he did so, something seemed to give a little.

' "Look!" cried out the second mate, and pointed, lamp in hand ... "It's sunk in!"

'This was true. The oar had made quite an indentation into the bulging, somewhat slimy side of the old vessel.

' "Mould, I reckon," said Captain Gannington, bending towards the derelict, to look. Then to the man:

' "Up you go, my lad, and be smart ... Don't stand there waitin'!"

'At that, the man, who had paused a moment as he felt the oar give beneath his weight, began to shin up, and in a few seconds he was aboard, and leant out over the rail for the lamps. These were passed up to him, and the captain called to him to steady the oar. Then Captain Gannington went, calling to me to follow, and after me the second mate.

'As the captain put his face over the rail, he gave a cry of astonishment:

' "Mould, by gum! Mould ... Tons of it! ... Good Lord!"

'As I heard him shout that, I scrambled the more eagerly after him, and in a moment or two, I was able to see what he meant – everywhere that the light from the two lamps struck, there was nothing but smooth great masses and surfaces of a dirty-white mould.

'I climbed over the rail, with the second mate close behind, and stood upon the mould-covered decks. There might have been no planking beneath the mould, for all that our feet could feel. It gave under our tread, with a spongy, puddingy feel. It covered the deck-furniture of the old ship, so that the shape of each article and fitment was often no more than suggested through it.

'Captain Gannington snatched a lamp from the other man, and the second mate reached for the other. They held the lamps high, and we all stared. It was most extraordinary, and, somehow, most abominable. I can think of no other word, gentlemen, that so much describes the predominant feeling that affected me at the moment.

' "Good Lord!" said Captain Gannington, several times. "Good Lord!" But neither the second mate nor the man said anything, and for my part I just stared, and at the same time began to smell a little at the air, for there was again a vague odour of something half familiar, that somehow brought to me a sense of half-known fright.

'I turned this way and that, staring, as I have said. Here and there, the mould was so heavy as to entirely disguise what lay beneath, converting the deck-fittings into indistinguishable mounds of mould, all dirty-white, and blotched and veined with irregular, dull purplish markings.

'There was a strange thing about the mould, which Captain Gannington drew attention to – it was that our feet did not crush into it and break the surface, as might have been expected but merely indented it.

'"Never seen nothin' like it before! ...Never!" said the Captain, after having stooped with his lamp to examine the mould under our feet. He stamped with his heel, and the stuff gave out a dull, puddingy sound. He stooped again, with a quick movement, and stared, holding the lamp close to the deck. "Blest if it ain't a reg'lar skin to it!" he said.

'The second mate and the man and I all stooped, and looked at it. The second mate progged it with his forefinger, and I remember I rapped it several times with my knuckles, listening to the dead sound it gave out, and noticing the close, firm texture of the mould.

'"Dough!" said the second mate. "It's just like blessed dough! ... Pouf!" He stood up with a quick movement. "I could fancy it stinks a bit," he said.

'As he said this, I knew suddenly what the familiar thing was in the vague odour that hung about us – it was that the smell had something animal-like in it; something of the same smell only *heavier*, that you will smell in any place that is infested with mice. I began to look about with a sudden very real uneasiness ... There might be vast numbers of hungry rats aboard.... They might prove exceedingly dangerous, if in a starving condition, yet, as you will understand, somehow I hesitated to put forward my idea as a reason for caution, it was too fanciful.

'Captain Gannington had begun to go aft, along the mould-covered main-deck, with the second mate; each of them holding his lamp high up, so as to cast a good light about the vessel. I turned quickly and followed them, the man with me keeping close to my heels, and plainly uneasy. As we went, I became aware that there was a feeling of moisture in the air, and I remembered the slight mist, or smoke, above the hulk, which had made Captain Gannington suggest spontaneous combustion in explanation.

'And always, as we went, there was that vague animal smell; and suddenly I found myself wishing we were well away from the old vessel.

'Abruptly, after a few paces, the captain stopped and pointed at a row of mould-hidden shapes on either side of the main-deck.

'"Guns," he said. "Been a privateer in the old days, I guess; maybe worse! We'll 'ave a look below, Doctor; there may be something worth touchin'. She's older than I thought. Mr Selvern thinks she's about three hundred years old; but I scarce think it."

'We continued our way aft, and I remember that I found myself walking as lightly and gingerly as possible; as if I were subconsciously afraid of treading through the rotten, mould-hid decks. I think the others had a touch of the same feeling, from the way that they walked. Occasionally the soft mould would grip our heels, releasing them with a little, sullen suck.

'The Captain forged somewhat ahead of the second mate, and I know that the suggestion he had made himself, that perhaps there might be something below, worth the carrying away, had stimulated his imagination. The second mate was, however, beginning to feel somewhat the same way that I did; at least, I have that impression. I think if it had not been for what I might truly describe as Captain Gannington's sturdy courage, we should all of us have gone back over the side very soon; for there was most certainly an unwholesome feeling aboard, that made one feel queerly lacking in pluck, and you will soon perceive that this feeling was justified.

'Just as the Captain reached the few, mould-covered steps, leading up on to the short half-poop, I was suddenly aware that the feeling of moisture in the air had grown very much more definite. It was perceptible now, intermittently, as a sort of thin, moist, fog-like vapour, that came and went oddly, and seemed to make the decks a little indistinct to the view, this time and that. Once, an odd puff of it beat up suddenly from somewhere, and caught me in the face, carrying a queer, sickly, heavy odour with it, that somehow frightened me strangely, with a suggestion of a waiting and half-comprehended danger.

'We had followed Captain Gannington up the three mould-covered steps, and now went slowly aft along the raised after-deck.

'By the mizzen-mast, Captain Gannington paused, and held his lantern near to it. . . .

' "My word, Mister," he said to the second mate, "it's fair thickened up with the mould; why, I'll g'antee it's close on four foot thick." He shone the light down to where it met the deck. "Good Lord!" he said, "look at the sea-lice on it!" I stepped up; and it was as he had said; the sea-lice were thick upon it, some of them huge, not less than the size of large beetles, and all a clear, colourless shade, like water, except where there were little spots of grey in them, evidently their internal organisms.

' "I've never seen the like of them, 'cept on a live cod!" said Captain Gannington, in an extremely puzzled voice. "My word! but they're whoppers!" Then he passed on, but a few paces farther aft, he stopped again, and held his lamp near to the mould-hidden deck.

' "Lord bless me, Doctor!" he called out, in a low voice, "did ye ever see the like of that? Why, it's a foot long, if it's a hinch!"

'I stooped over his shoulder, and saw what he meant; it was a clear colourless creature, about a foot long, and about eight inches high, with a curved back that was extraordinarily narrow. As we stared, all in a group, it gave a queer little flick, and was gone.

218

' "Jumped!" said the captain. "Well, if that ain't a giant of all the sea-lice that ever I've seen! I guess it jumped twenty-foot clear." He straightened his back, and scratched his head a moment, swinging the lantern this way and that with the other hand, and staring about us. "Wot are *they* doin' aboard 'ere!" he said. "You'll see 'em (little things) on fat cod, an' such like. . . . I'm blowed, Doctor, if I understand."

'He held his lamp towards a big mound of the mould, that occupied part of the after portion of the low poop-deck, a little foreside of where there came a two-foot high "break" to a kind of second and loftier poop, that ran away aft to the taffrail. The mound was pretty big, several feet across, and more than a yard high. Captain Gannington walked up to it:

' "I reckon this 's the scuttle," he remarked, and gave it a heavy kick. The only result was a deep indentation into the huge, whitish hump of mould, as if he had driven his foot into a mass of some doughy substance. Yet, I am not altogether correct in saying that this was the only result; for a certain other thing happened – from a place made by the captain's foot, there came a little gush of a purplish fluid, accompanied by a peculiar smell, that was, and was not, half familiar. Some of the mould-like substance had stuck to the toe of the captain's boot, and from this, likewise, there issued a sweat, as it were, of the same colour.

' "Well!" said Captain Gannington, in surprise, and drew back his foot to make another kick at the hump of mould; but he paused, at an exclamation from the second mate:

' "Don't, sir!" said the second mate.

'I glanced at him, and the light from Captain Gannington's lamp showed me that his face had a bewildered, half-frightened look, as if it were suddenly and unexpectedly half afraid of something, and as if his tongue had given way to his sudden fright, without any intention on his part to speak.

'The captain also turned and stared at him.

' "Why, Mister?" he asked, in a somewhat puzzled voice, through which there sounded the vaguest hint of annoyance. "We've got to shift this muck, if we're to get below."

'I looked at the second mate, and it seemed to me that, curiously enough, he was listening less to the captain, than to some other sound.

Suddenly, he said in a queer voice – "Listen, everybody!"

'Yet we heard nothing, beyond the faint murmur of the men talking together in the boat alongside.

' "I don't hear nothin'," said Captain Gannington, after a short pause. "Do you, Doctor?"

' "No," I said.

' "Wot was it you thought you heard?" asked the captain, turning again to the second mate. But the second mate shook his head, in a curious, almost irritable way; as if the captain's question interrupted his listening.

Captain Gannington stared a moment at him, then held his lantern up, and glanced about him, almost uneasily. I know I felt a queer sense of strain. But the light showed nothing, beyond the greyish-dirty-white of the mould in all directions.

' "Mister Selvern," said the captain at last, looking at him, "don't get fancying things. Get hold of your bloomin' self. Ye know ye heard nothin'?"

' "I'm quite sure I heard something sir!" said the second mate. "I seemed to hear – " He broke off sharply, and appeared to listen, with an almost painful intensity.

' "What did it sound like?" I asked.

' "It's all right, Doctor," said Captain Gannington, laughing gently. "Ye can give him a tonic when we get back. I'm goin' to shift this stuff."

'He drew back, and kicked for the second time at the ugly mass, which he took to hide the companion-way. The result of his kick was startling; for the whole thing wobbled sloppily, like a mound of unhealthy-looking jelly.

'He drew his foot out of it quickly, and took a step backwards, staring, and holding his lamp towards it:

' "By gum!" he said, and it was plain that he was genuinely startled, "the blessed thing's gone soft!"

'The man had run back several steps from the suddenly flaccid mound, and looked horribly frightened. Though, of what, I am sure he had not the least idea. The second mate stood where he was, and stared. For my part, I know I had a most hideous uneasiness upon me. The captain continued to hold his light towards the wobbling mound, and stare.

' "It's gone squashy all through!" he said. "There's no scuttle there. There's no bally woodwork inside that lot! Phoo! what a rum smell!"

'He walked round to the after-side of the strange mound, to see whether there might be some signs of an opening into the hull at the back of the great heap of mould-stuff. And then:

' "*Listen!*" said the second mate, again, and in the strangest sort of voice.

'Captain Gannington straightened himself upright, and there succeeded a pause of the most intense quietness, in which there was not even the hum of talk from the men alongside in the boat. We all heard it – a kind of dull, soft Thud! Thud! Thud! Thud! somewhere in the hull under us, yet so vague that I might have been half doubtful I heard it, only that the others did so, too.

'Captain Gannington turned suddenly to where the man stood:

' "Tell them – " he began. But the fellow cried out something, and pointed. There had come a strange intensity into his somewhat un-emotional face; so that the captain's glance followed his action instantly. I stared, also, as you may think. It was the great mound, at which the man was pointing. I saw what he meant.

'From the two gaps made in the mould-like stuff by Captain

Gannington's boot, the purple fluid was jetting out in a queerly regular fashion, almost as if it were being forced out by a pump. My word! but I stared. And even as I stared, a larger jet squirted out, and splashed as far as the man, spattering his boots and trouser-legs.

'The fellow had been pretty nervous before, in a stolid, ignorant sort of way, and his funk had been growing steadily; but, at this, he simply let out a yell, and turned about to run. He paused an instant, as if a sudden fear of the darkness that held the decks between him and the boat had taken him. He snatched at the second mate's lantern, tore it out of his hand, and plunged heavily away over the vile stretch of mould.

'Mr Selvern, the second mate, said not a word; he was just standing, staring at the strange-smelling twin streams of dull purple, that were jetting out from the wobbling mound. Captain Gannington, however, roared an order to the man to come back; but the man plunged on and on across the mould, his feet seeming to be clogged by the stuff, as if it had grown suddenly soft. He zigzagged as he ran, the lantern swaying in wild circles as he wrenched his feet free, with a constant plop, plop; and I could hear his frightened gasps, even from where I stood.

' "Come back with that lamp!" roared the captain again; but still the man took no notice, and Captain Gannington was silent an instant, his lips working in a queer, inarticulate fashion; as if he were stunned momentarily by the very violence of his anger at the man's insubordination. And in the silence, I heard the sounds again: – Thud! Thud! Thud! Thud! Quite distinctly now, beating, it seemed suddenly to me, right down under my feet, but deep.

'I stared down at the mould on which I was standing, with a quick, disgusting sense of the terrible all about me; then I looked at the captain, and tried to say something, without appearing frightened. I saw that he had turned again to the mound, and all the anger had gone out of his face. He had his lamp out towards the mound, and was listening. There was a further moment of absolute silence; at least, I know that I was not conscious of any sound at all, in all the world, except that extraordinary Thud! Thud! Thud! Thud! down somewhere in the huge bulk under us.

'The captain shifted his feet, with a sudden, nervous movement; and as he lifted them, the mould went plop! plop! He looked quickly at me, trying to smile, as if he were not thinking anything very much about it: "What do you make of it, Doctor?" he said.

' "I think – " I began. But the second mate interrupted with a single word; his voice pitched a little high, in a tone that made both stare instantly at him:

' "Look!" he said, and pointed at the mound. The thing was all of a slow quiver. A strange ripple ran outward from it, along the deck, like you will see a ripple run inshore out of a calm sea. It reached a mound a little fore-side of us, which I had supposed to be the cabin-skylight; and in a moment the second mound sank nearly level with the surrounding decks, quivering floppily in a most extraordinary fashion. A sudden quick tremor took the mound right under the second mate, and he gave out a hoarse little cry, and held his arms out on each side of him, to keep his balance. The tremor in the mound spread, and Captain Gannington swayed, and spread his feet with a sudden curse of fright. The second mate jumped across to him, and caught him by the wrist:

' "The boat, sir!" he said, saying the very thing that I had lacked the pluck to say. "For God's sake – "

'But he never finished; for a tremendous hoarse scream cut off his words. They hove themselves round, and looked. I could see without turning. The man who had run from us was standing in the waist of the ship, about a fathom from the starboard bulwarks. He was swaying from side to side and screaming in a dreadful fashion. He appeared to be trying to lift his feet, and the light from his swaying latern showed an almost incredible sight. All about him the mould was in active movement. His feet had sunk out of sight. The stuff appeared to be *lapping* at his legs; and abruptly his bare flesh showed. The hideous stuff had rent his trouser-legs away as if they were paper. He gave out a simply sickening scream, and, with a vast effort, wrenched one leg free. It was partly destroyed. The next instant he pitched face downwards, and the stuff heaped itself upon him, as if it were actually alive, with a dreadful savage life. It was simply infernal. The man had gone from sight. Where he had fallen was now a writhing, elongated mound, in constant and horrible increase, as the mould appeared to move towards it in strange ripples from all sides.

'Captain Gannington and the second mate were stone silent, in amazed and incredulous horror; but I had begun to reach towards a grotesque and terrific conclusion, both helped and hindered by my professional training.

'From the men in the boat alongside, there was a loud shouting, and I saw two of their faces appear suddenly above the rail. They showed clearly a moment in the light from the lamp which the man had snatched from Mr Selvern; for strangely enough, this lamp was standing upright and unharmed on the deck, a little way fore-side of that dreadful, elongated, growing mound, that still swayed and writhed with an incredible horror. The lamp rose and fell on the passing ripples of the mould just – for all the world – as you will see a boat rise and fall on little swells. It is of some interest to me now, psychologically, to remember how that rising and falling lantern brought home to me, more than anything, the incomprehensible, dreadful strangeness of it all.

'The men's faces disappeared, with sudden yells, as if they had slipped or been suddenly hurt; and there was a fresh uproar of shouting from the boat. The men were calling to us to come away; to come away. In the same instant, I felt my left boot drawn suddenly and forcibly downwards, with a horrible painful grip. I wrenched it free, with a yell of angry fear. Forrard of us, I saw that the vile surface was all a-move, and abruptly I found myself shouting in a queer frightened voice:

' "The boat, Captain! The boat, Captain!"

'Captain Gannington stared round at me, over his right shoulder, in a peculiar, dull way, that told me he was utterly dazed with bewilderment and the incomprehensibleness of it all. I took a quick, clogged, nervous step towards him, and gripped his arm and shook it fiercely.

' "The boat!" I shouted at him. "The boat! For God's sake, tell the men to bring the boat aft!"

'Then the mould must have drawn his feet down; for, abruptly, he bellowed fiercely with terror, his momentary apathy giving place to furious energy. His thick-set, vastly muscular body doubled and 'writhed with his enormous effort, and he struck out madly, dropping the lantern. He tore his feet free, something ripped as he did so. The *reality* and necessity of the situation had come upon him, brutishly real, and he was roaring to the men in the boat:

' "Bring the boat aft! Bring 'er aft! Bring 'er aft!"

'The second mate and I were shouting the same thing, madly.

' "For God's sake be smart, lads!" roared the captain, and stooped quickly for his lamp, which still burned. His feet were gripped again, and he hove them out, blaspheming breathlessly, and leaping a yard high with his effort. Then he made a run for the side, wrenching his feet free at each step. In the same instant, the second mate cried out something, and grabbed at the captain:

' "It's got hold of my feet! It's got hold of my feet!" he screamed. His feet had disappeared up to his boot-tops, and Captain Gannington caught him round the waist with his powerful left arm, gave a mighty heave, and the next instant had him free; but both his boot-soles had almost gone.

'For my part, I jumped madly from foot to foot, to avoid the plucking of the mould; and suddenly I made a run for the ship's side. But before I got there, a queer gap came in the mould, between us and the side, at least a couple of feet wide, and how deep I don't know. It closed up in an instant, and all the mould, where the gap had been, went into a sort of flurry of horrible ripplings, so that I ran back from it; for I did not dare to put my foot upon it. Then the captain was shouting at me: ﹅

' "Aft, Doctor! Aft, Doctor! This way, Doctor! Run!" I saw then that he had passed me, and was up on the after raised portion of the poop. He had the second mate thrown like a sack, all loose and quiet, over his left shoulder; for Mr Selvern had fainted, and his long legs flopped, limp and helpless, against the captain's massive knees as the captain ran. I saw, with a queer unconscious noting of minor details, how the torn soles of the second mate's boots flapped and jigged, as the captain staggered aft.

' "Boat ahoy! Boat ahoy! Boat ahoy!" shouted the captain; and then I was beside him shouting also. The men were answering with loud yells of

223

encouragement, and it was plain they were working desperately to force the boat aft, through the thick scum about the ship.

'We reached the ancient, mould-hid taffrail, and slewed about, breathlessly, in the half darkness, to see what was happening. Captain Gannington had left his lantern by the big mound, when he picked up the second mate; and as we stood gasping, we discovered suddenly that all the mould between us and the light was full of movement. Yet, the part on which we stood, for about six or eight feet forrard of us, was still firm.

'Every couple of seconds, we shouted to the men to hasten, and they kept on calling to us they would be with us in an instant. And all the time, we watched the deck of that dreadful hulk, feeling, for my part, literally sick with mad suspense, and ready to jump overboard into that filthy scum all about us.

'Down somewhere in the huge bulk of the ship, there was all the time that extraordinary, dull, ponderous Thud! Thud! Thud! Thud! growing ever louder. I seemed to feel the whole of the derelict beginning to quiver and thrill with each dull beat. And to me, with the grotesque and monstrous suspicion of what made that noise, it was, at once, the most dreadful and incredible sound I have ever heard.

'As we waited desperately for the boat, I scanned incessantly so much of the grey-white bulk as the lamp showed. The whole of the decks seemed to be in strange movement. Forrard of the lamp I could see, indistinctly, the moundings of the mould swaying and nodding hideously, beyond the circle of the brightest rays. Nearer, and full in the glow of the lamp, the mound which should have indicated the skylight, was swelling steadily. There were ugly purple veinings on it, and as it swelled, it seemed to me that the veinings and mottling on it were becoming plainer – rising, as though embossed upon it, like you will see the veins stand out on the body of a powerful full-blooded horse. It was most extraordinary. The mound that we had supposed to cover the companion-way had sunk flat with the surrounding mould and I could not see that it jetted out any more of the purplish fluid.

'A quaking movement of the mould began, away forrard of the lamp, and came flurrying away aft towards us; and at the sight of that, I climbed up on to the spongy-feeling taffrail, and yelled afresh for the boat. The men answered with a shout, which told me they were nearer, but the beastly scum was so thick that it was evidently a fight to move the boat at all. Beside me, Captain Gannington was shaking the second mate furiously, and the man stirred and began to moan. The captain shook him awake.

'"Wake up! Wake up, Mister!" he shouted.

'The second mate staggered out of the captain's arms, and collapsed suddenly shrieking: "My feet! Oh, God! My feet!" The captain and I lugged him off the mould, and got him into a sitting postion upon the taffrail, where he kept up a continual moaning.

' "Hold 'im Doctor," said the captain, and whilst I did so, he ran forrard a few yards, and peered down over the starboard quarter rail. "For God's sake, be smart, lads! Be smart! Be smart!" he shouted down to the men; and they answered him, breathless, from close at hand; yet still too far away for the boat to be any use to us on the instant.

'I was holding the moaning, half-unconscious officer, and staring forrard along the poop decks. The flurrying of the mould was coming aft, slowly and noiselessly. And then, suddenly, I saw something closer:

' "Look out, Captain!" I shouted, and even as I shouted, the mould near to him gave a sudden peculiar slobber. I had seen a ripple stealing towards him through the horrible stuff. He gave an enormous, clumsy leap, and landed near to us on the sound part of the mould, but the movement followed him. He turned and faced it, swearing fiercely. All about his feet came abruptly little gapings, which made horrid sucking noises.

' "Come *back*, Captain!" I yelled. "Come back, *quick!*"

'As I shouted, a ripple came at his feet -- lipping at them; and he stamped insanely at it, and leaped back, his boot torn half off his foot. He swore madly with pain and anger, and jumped swiftly for the taffrail.

' "Come on, Doctor! Over we go!" he called. Then he remembered the filthy scum, and hesitated, roaring out desperately to the men to hurry. I stared down, also.

' "The second mate?" I said.

' "I'll take charge, Doctor," said Captain Gannington, and caught hold of Mr Selvern. As he spoke, I thought I saw something beneath us, outlined against the scum. I leaned out over the stern, and peered. There was something under the port quarter.

' "There's something down there, Captain!" I called, and pointed in the darkness.

'He stooped far over, and stared.

' "A boat, by gum! *A boat!*" he yelled, and began to wriggle swiftly along the taffrail, dragging the second mate after him. I followed.

' "A boat it is, sure!" he exclaimed, a few moments later, and, picking up the second mate clear of the rail, he hove him down into the boat, where he fell with a crash into the bottom.

' "Over ye go, Doctor!" he yelled at me, and pulled me bodily off the rail, and dropped me after the officer. As he did so, I felt the whole of the ancient, spongy rail give a peculiar sickening quiver, and began to wobble. I fell on to the second mate, and the captain came after, almost in the same instant; but fortunately he landed clear of us, on to the fore-thwart, which broke under his weight, with a loud crack and splintering of wood.

' "Thank God!" I heard him mutter. "Thank God! . . . I guess that was a mighty near thing to goin' to hell."

'He struck a match, just as I got to my feet, and between us we got the second mate straightened out on one of the after-thwarts. We shouted to the men in the boat, telling them where we were, and saw the light of their lantern shining round the starboard counter of the derelict. They called back to us, to tell us they were doing their best, and then, while we waited, Captain Gannington struck another match, and began to overhaul the boat we had dropped into. She was a modern, two-oared boat, and on the stern there was painted *Cyclone Glasgow*. She was in pretty fair condition, and had evidently drifted into the scum and been held by it.

'Captain Gannington struck several matches, and went forrard towards the derelict. Suddenly he called to me, and I jumped over the thwarts to him.

' "Look Doctor," he said; and I saw what he meant – a mass of bones, up in the bows of the boat. I stooped over them and looked. They were bones of at least three people, all mixed together, in an extraordinary fashion, and quite clean and dry. I had a sudden thought concerning the bones; but I said nothing; for my thought was vague, in some ways, and concerned the grotesque and incredible suggestion that had come to me, as to the cause of that ponderous, dull Thud! Thud! Thud! Thud! that beat on so infernally within the hull, and was plain to hear even now that we had got off the vessel herself. And all the while, you know, I had a sick, horrible, mental picture of that frightful wriggling mound aboard the hulk.

'As Captain Gannington struck a final match I saw something that sickened me, and the captain saw it in the same instant. The match went out, and he fumbled clumsily for another, and struck it. We saw the thing again. We had not been mistaken.... A great lip of grey-white was protruding in over the edge of the boat – a great lappet of the mould was coming stealthily towards us; a live mass of *the very hull itself*. And suddenly Captain Gannington yelled out, in so many words, the grotesque and incredible thing I was thinking:

' "*She's alive!*"

'I never heard such a sound of *comprehension* and terror in a man's voice. The very horrified assurance of it made actual to me the thing that, before, had only lurked in my subconscious mind. I knew he was right; I knew that the explanation my reason and my training both repelled and reached towards was the true one.... I wonder whether anyone can possibly understand our feelings in that moment.... The unmitigable horror of it, and the *incredibleness*.

'As the light of the match burned up fully, I saw that the mass of living matter, coming towards us, was streaked and veined with purple, the veins standing out, enormously distended. The whole thing quivered continuously to each ponderous Thud! Thud! Thud! Thud! of that gargantuan organ that pulsed within the huge grey-white bulk. The flame of the match reached the captain's fingers, and there came to me a little sickly whiff of burned flesh; but he seemed unconscious of any pain. Then the flame went out, in a brief sizzle, yet at the last moment I had seen an extraordinary raw look become visible upon the end of that monstrous, protruding lappet. It had become dewed with a hideous, purplish sweat. And with the darkness, there came a sudden charnel-like stench.

'I heard the match-box split in Captain Gannington's hands, as he wrenched it open. Then he swore, in a queer frightened voice; for he had come to the end of his matches. He turned clumsily in the darkness, and tumbled over the nearest thwart, in his eagerness to get to the stern of the boat, and I after him; for he knew that thing was coming towards us through the darkness, reaching over that piteous mingled heap of human bones, all jumbled together in the bows. We shouted madly to the men, and for answer saw the bows of the boat emerge dimly into view, round the starboard counter of the derelict.

' "Thank God!" I gasped out; but Captain Gannington yelled to them to show a light. Yet this they could not do, for the lamp had just been stepped on, in their desperate efforts to force the boat round to us.

' "Quick! Quick!" I shouted.

' "For God's sake be smart, men!" roared the captain; and both of us faced the darkness under the port counter, out of which we knew (but could not see) the thing was coming towards us.

' "An oar! Smart now; pass me an oar!" shouted the captain; and reached out his hands through the gloom towards the oncoming boat. I saw a figure stand up in the bows, and hold something out to us, across the intervening yards of scum. Captain Gannington swept his hands through the darkness, and encountered it.

' "I've got it. Let go there!" he said, in a quick, tense voice.

'In the same instant, the boat we were in, was pressed over suddenly to starboard by some tremendous weight. Then I heard the captain shout: "Duck y'r head, Doctor," and directly afterwards he swung the heavy fourteen-foot ash oar round his head, and struck into the darkness. There came a sudden squelch, and he struck again, with a savage grunt of fierce energy. At the second blow, the boat righted, with a slow movement, and directly afterwards the other boat bumped gently into ours.

'Captain Gannington dropped the oar, and springing across to the second mate, hove him up off the thwart and pitched him with knee and arms clear in over the bows among the men; then he shouted to me to follow, which I did, and he came after me, bringing the oar with him. We carried the second mate aft, and the captain shouted to the men to back the boat a little; then they got her bows clear of the boat we had just left, and so headed out through the scum for the open sea.

' "Where's Tom 'Arrison?" gasped one of the men, in the midst of his exertions. He happened to be Tom Harrison's particular chum; And captain Gannington answered him briefly enough:

' "Dead! Pull! Don't talk!"

'Now, difficult as it had been to force the boat through the scum to our rescue, the difficulty to get clear seemed tenfold. After some five minutes' pulling, the boat seemed hardly to have moved a fathom, if so much; and a quite dreadful fear took me afresh; which one of the panting men put suddenly into words:

' "It's got us!" he gasped out; "same as poor Tom!" It was the man who had inquired where Harrison was.

' "Shut y'r mouth an' *pull!*" roared the captain. And so another few minutes passed. Abruptly, it seemed to me that the dull, ponderous Thud! Thud! Thud! Thud! came more plainly through the dark, and I stared intently over the stern. I sickened a little; for I could almost swear that the dark mass of the monster was actually *nearer* . . . that it was coming nearer to us through the darkness. Captain Gannington must have had the same thought; for after a brief look into the darkness, he made one jump to the stroke-oar, and began to double-bank it.

' "Get forrid under the thwarts, Doctor!" he said to me, rather breathlessly. Get in the bows, an' see if you can't free the stuff a bit round the bows."

'I did as he told me, and a minute later I was in the bows of the boat, puddling the scum from side to side with the boat-hook, and trying to break up the viscid, clinging muck. A heavy, almost animal-like odour rose off it, and all the air seemed full of the deadening smell. I shall never find words to tell any one the whole horror of it all – the threat that seemed to hang in the very air around us; and, but a little astern, that incredible thing, coming, as I firmly believe, nearer, and the scum holding us like half-melted glue.

'The minutes passed in a deadly, eternal fashion, and I kept staring back astern into the darkness; but never ceased to puddle that filthy scum, striking at it and switching it from side to side, until I sweated.

'Abruptly, Captain Gannington sang out:

' "We're gaining, lads. Pull!" And I felt the boat forge ahead perceptibly, as they gave way, with renewed hope and energy. There was soon no doubt of it; for presently that hideous Thud! Thud! Thud! Thud! had grown quite dim and vague somewhat astern, and I could no longer see the derelict! for the night had come down tremendously dark, and all the sky was thick overset with heavy clouds. As we drew nearer and nearer to the edge of the scum, the boat moved more and more freely, until suddenly we emerged with a clean, sweet, fresh sound into the open sea.

' "Thank God!" I said aloud, and drew in the boat-hook, and made my way aft again to where Captain Gannington now sat once more at the tiller. I saw him looking anxiously up at the sky, and across to where the lights of our vessel burned, and again he would seem to listen intently; so that I found myself listening also.

' "What's that, Captain?" I said sharply; for it seemed to me that I heard a sound far astern, something between a queer whine and a low whistling. "What's that?"

'"It's wind, Doctor," he said, in a low voice. "I wish to God we were aboard."

'Then, to the men: "Pull! put y'r backs into it, or ye'll never put y'r teeth through good bread again!"

'The men obeyed nobly, and we reached the vessel safely, and had the boat safely stowed, before the storm came, which it did in a furious white smother out of the west. I could see it for some minutes beforehand, tearing the sea, in the gloom, into a wall of phosphorescent foam; and as it came nearer, that peculiar whining, piping sound grew louder and louder, until it was like a vast steam-whistle, rushing towards us across the sea.

'And when it did come, we got it very heavy indeed; so that the morning showed us nothing but a welter of white seas; and that grim derelict was many a score of miles away in the smother, lost as utterly as our hearts could wish to lose her.

When I came to examine the second mate's feet, I found them in a very extraordinary condition. The soles of them had the appearance of having been partly digested. I know of no other word that so exactly describes their condition; and the agony the man suffered must have been dreadful.

'Now,' concluded the doctor, 'that is what I call a case in point. If we could know exactly what that old vessel had originally been loaded with, and the juxtaposition of the various articles of her cargo, plus the heat and time she had endured, plus one or two other only guessable quantities, we should have solved the chemistry of the Life-Force, gentlemen. Not necessarily the *Origin*, mind you; but, at least, we should have taken a big step on the way. I've often regretted that gale, you know – in a way, that is, in a way! It was a most amazing discovery; but, at the time, I had nothing but thankfulness to be rid of it. ... A most amazing chance. I often think of the way the monster woke out of its torpor. And that scum.... The dead pigs caught in it.... I fancy that was a grim kind of net, gentlemen.... It caught many things.... It ...'

The old doctor sighed and nodded.

'If I could have had her bill of lading,' he said, his eyes full of regret. 'If ... It might have told me something to help. But, anyway ...' He began to fill his pipe again.... 'I suppose,' he ended, looking round at us gravely, 'I s'pose we humans are an ungrateful lot of beggars, at the best! ... But ... but what a chance! What a chance – eh?'

Vendetta

GUY DE MAUPASSANT

PALO SAVERINI'S WIDOW dwelt alone with her son in a small, mean house on the ramparts of Bonifacio. Built on a spur of the mountain and in places actually overhanging the sea, the town looks across the rock-strewn Straits to the low-lying coast of Sardinia. On the other side, girdling it almost completely, there is a fissure in the cliff, like an immense corridor, which serves as a port, and down this long channel, as far as the first houses, sail the small Italian and Sardinian fishing-boats, and once a fortnight the broken-winded old steamer from Ajaccio. Clustered together on the white hillside, the houses form a patch of even more dazzling whiteness. Clinging to the rock, gazing down upon those deadly Straits where scarcely a ship ventures, they look like the nests of birds of prey. The sea and the barren coast, stripped of all but a scanty covering of grass, are forever harassed by a restless wind, which sweeps along the narrow funnel, ravaging the banks on either side. In all directions the black points of innumerable rocks jut out from the water, with trails of white foam streaming from them, like torn shreds of cloth, floating and quivering on the surface of the waves.

The widow Saverini's house was planted on the very edge of the cliff, and its three windows opened upon this wild and dreary prospect. She lived there with her son Antoine and their dog Sémillante, a great gaunt brute of the sheep-dog variety, with a long, rough coat, whom the young man took with him when he went out shooting.

One evening, Antoine Saverini was treacherously stabbed in a quarrel by Nicolas Ravolati, who escaped that same night to Sardinia.

At the sight of the body, which was brought home by passers-by, the old mother shed no tears, but she gazed long and silently at her dead son. Then, laying her wrinkled hand upon the corpse, she promised him the Vendetta. She would not allow anyone to remain with her, and shut herself up with the dead body. The dog Sémillante, who remained with her, stood at the foot of the bed and howled, with her head turned towards her master and her tail between her legs. Neither of them stirred, neither the dog nor the old mother, who was now leaning over the body, gazing at it fixedly, and silently shedding great tears. Still wearing his rough jacket, which was pierced and torn at the breast, the boy lay on his back as if asleep, but there was blood all about him, on his shirt, which had been stripped off in order to expose the wound, on his waistcoat, trousers, face and hands. His beard and hair were matted with clots of blood.

The old mother began to talk to him, and at the sound of her voice the dog stopped howling.

'Never fear, never fear, you shall be avenged, my son, my little son, my poor child. You may sleep in peace. You shall be avenged, I tell you. You have your mother's word, and you know she never breaks it.'

Slowly she bent down and pressed her cold lips to the dead lips of her son.

Sémillante resumed her howling, uttering a monotonous, long-drawn wail, heart-rending and terrible. And thus the two remained, the woman and the dog, till morning.

The next day Antoine Saverini was buried, and soon his name ceased to be mentioned in Bonifacio.

He had no brother, nor any near male relation. There was no man in the family who could take up the vendetta. Only his mother, his old mother, brooded over it.

From morning till night she could see, just across the Straits, a white speck upon the coast. This was the little Sardinian village of Longosardo, where the Corsican bandits took refuge whenever the hunt for them grew too hot. They formed almost the entire population of the hamlet. In full view of their native shores they waited for a chance to return home and regain the bush. She knew that Nicolas Ravolati had sought shelter in that village.

All day long she sat alone at her window gazing at the opposite coast and thinking of her revenge, but what was she to do with no one to help her, and she herself so feeble and near her end? But she had promised, she had sworn by the dead body of her son, she could not forget, and she dared not delay. What was she to do? She could not sleep at night, she knew not a moment of rest or peace, but racked her brains unceasingly. Sémillante asleep at her feet, would now and then raise her head and emit a piercing howl. Since her master had disappeared, this had become a habit, it was as if she were calling him, as if she, too, were inconsolable and preserved in her canine soul an ineffaceable memory of the dead.

One night, when Sémillante began to whine, the old mother had an inspiration of savage, vindictive ferocity. She thought about it till morning. At daybreak she rose and betook herself to church. Prostrate on the stone floor, humbling herself before God, she besought Him to aid and support her, to lend to her poor, worn-out body the strength she needed to avenge her son.

Then she returned home. In the yard stood an old barrel with one end knocked in, in which was caught the rain-water from the eaves. She turned it over, emptied it, and fixed it to the ground with stakes and stones. Then she chained up Sémillante to this kennel and went into the house.

With her eyes fixed on the Sardinian coast, she walked restlessly up and down her room. He was over there, the murderer.

The dog howled all day and all night. The next morning the old woman brought her a bowl of water, but no food, neither soup nor bread. Another day passed. Sémillante was worn out and slept. The next morning her eyes were gleaming, and her coat standing, and she tugged frantically at her chain. And again the old woman gave her nothing to eat. Maddened with hunger, Sémillante barked hoarsely. Another night went by.

At daybreak, the widow went to a neighbour and begged for two trusses of straw. She took some old clothes that had belonged to her husband, stuffed them with straw to represent a human figure, and made a head out of a bundle of old rags. Then, in front of Sémillante's kennel, she fixed a stake in the ground and fastened the dummy to it in an upright position.

The dog looked at the straw figure in surprise and, although she was famished, stopped howling.

The old woman went to the pork butcher and bought a long piece of black pudding. When she came home she lighted a wood fire in the yard, close to the kennel, and fried the black pudding. Sémillante bounded up and down in a frenzy, foaming at the mouth, her eyes fixed on the gridiron with its maddening smell of meat.

Her mistress took the steaming pudding and wound it like a tie round the dummy's neck. She fastened it on tightly with string as if to force it inwards. When she had finished she unchained the dog.

With one ferocious leap, Sémillante flew at the dummy's throat and with her paws on its shoulders began to tear it. She fell back with a portion of her prey between her jaws, sprang at it again, slashing the string with her fangs, tore away some scraps of food, dropped for a moment, and hurled herself at it in renewed fury. She tore away the whole face with savage rendings and reduced the neck to shreds.

Motionless and silent, with burning eyes, the old woman looked on. Presently she chained the dog up again. She starved her another two days, and then put her through the same strange performance. For three months she accustomed her to this method of attack, and to tear her meals away with her fangs. She was no longer kept on the chain. At the sign from her mistress, the dog would fly at the dummy's throat.

She learned to tear it to pieces even when no food was concealed about its throat. Afterwards as a reward she was always given the black pudding her mistress had cooked for her.

As soon as she caught sight of the dummy, Sémillante quivered with excitement and looked at her mistress, who would raise her finger and cry in a shrill voice, 'Tear him.'

One Sunday morning when she thought the time had come, the widow

Saverini went to Confession and Communion, in an ecstasy of devotion. Then she disguised herself like a tattered old beggar man, and struck a bargain with a Sardinian fisherman, who took her and her dog across to the opposite shore.

She carried a large piece of black pudding wrapped in a cloth bag. Sémillante had been starved for two days and her mistress kept exciting her by letting her smell the savoury food.

The pair entered the village of Longosardo. The old woman hobbled along to a baker and asked for the house of Nicolas Ravolati. He had resumed his former occupation, which was that of a joiner, and he was working alone in the back of his shop.

The old woman threw open the door and cried:

'Nicolas! Nicolas!'

He turned round. Slipping the dog's lead, she cried:

'Tear him! Tear him!'

The maddened dog flew at his throat. The man flung out his arms, grappled with the brute and they rolled on the ground together. For some moments he struggled, kicking the floor with his feet. Then lay still, while Sémillante tore his throat to shreds.

Two neighbours seated at their doors, remembered to have seen an old beggar man emerge from the house and, at his heels, a lean black dog, which was eating as it went along, some brown substance that its master was giving it.

By evening the old woman had reached home again.

That night she slept well.

Edifice Complex
ROBERT BLOCH

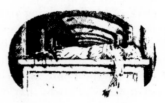

WAYNE LOOKED AT NORA AND laughed.

'You're a good kid,' he said.

Nora's smile was bleary. Even though the ship was in grav, she had difficulty standing because she was bashed to the gills.

'You keep saying that, but you never do nothing. I thought this was a pleasure trip,' she giggled.

'Wait until we land,' Wayne reassured her. 'I told you last night when I brought you aboard, we can't do anything in freefall. Besides, you've got your pay.'

Nora staggered over and put her plump hand on his shoulder as he bent over the scanner. Her voice was soft. 'I was hoping you wouldn't say that,' she murmured. 'I know what you think, picking me up in a stinking dive like that, but when I said yes, it wasn't just the money. I kind of went for you, hon, you know? And when you sweet-talked me into this I was thinking it would be, well, romantic like. Running off on your ship to a secret hideaway – '

She paused, blinking down into the scanner. They were cruising just a few thousand feet above the cloudless surface at a slow speed, circling over gentle, rolling sandy slopes with broad flat areas between. There was no water, no vegetation, no sign of life.

'Where are we, anyhow?' she asked.

'Vergis IV,' Wayne told her.

'Don't look like much of a place for a weekend,' Nora said. 'Lonely.'

Wayne grinned and pulled her close. 'That's just why I picked it out,' he muttered. There'll be nobody around to bother you – except me.'

The plump, voluptuous brunette ran her hand along his spine. 'When you plan to start bothering, hon?' she whispered.

'Soon. Let me put us down first. I'm looking for a spot.'

Nora put her head close to his and stared into the scanner. 'Who told you about this place?' she asked.

'Friend of mine – a space-rat. Luke, they call him.'

The full-figured brunette giggled. 'Old Luke? The guy who hit Port City last week for a big bash-out? The one with all them diamonds?'

'That's right,' Wayne answered. 'Diamonds.'

234

'He sure was tossing 'em around. Dorine, she's my girlfriend, she was out with him night before last. He was real bashed, and Dorine tried to find out where he got the loot. But he wasn't talking.'

'He told me,' Wayne said. 'The diamonds came from here.'

Nora dug her nails into his arm.

'Is that why you picked this place, on account of the diamonds?' Her breath quickened, and Wayne could smell the sickly-sweet odour of bash. 'You gonna get me some diamonds, hon?'

Wayne smiled down on her. 'I said you were a good kid, didn't I? If there are any diamonds here, you'll get them.'

'Oh, hon – '

'Hold it,' Wayne told her, disengaging her arms. 'We land first, remember? Meanwhile, how are you fixed for bash? I've got some prime stuff here in the pouch.'

'Sure, hon. Give me a pop. The more I bash, the better I am – you'll see – '

Wayne pulled the pouch from his pocket and poured a minute mound of the grayish seeds into her palm. She raised it to her nostrils and sniffed, inhaling with a deep sigh that ended in a sneeze.

'Now I'm cruising,' she said. The whites of her eyes turned yellow as the pupils contracted. 'Come on, hon – '

'Let me set us down,' Wayne urged. He squinted through the scanner. 'Right over there,' he told her.

'What's that big brown thing?' Nora asked, trying to focus her gaze. 'Looks like a snake.'

Wayne studied the brown, irregular oblong. 'It does at that, from this height,' he agreed. 'But it's really a hut. Luke told me to find a hut if I wanted to get hold of the natives. Besides, we'll need a place to stay.'

'How about right here on the ship?' Nora suggested. 'Right here on the ship, and right now – ' She was beginning to breathe heavily.

'Don't forget the diamonds,' Wayne reminded.

'Diamonds.' Nora's voice trailed off as the bash took hold. She fell back upon the bunk. 'Hon, I'm dizzy. Don't leave me, hon.'

'I wouldn't think of it,' Wayne assured her. 'You're a good kid, remember?'

He grinned and bent over the controls. Slowly, the ship glided in for a landing on a sandy plain only a few hundred yards from the brown oblong. As Nora murmured incoherently, Wayne put out the landing platform and packed a small kit-bag which he slung over his shoulder. Then he stepped over to Nora and shook her.

'Wake up,' he said. 'We're going out.'

Eyes closed, Nora tried to pull him down on the bunk, 'Wait, hon,' she whispered. 'Let's not go now.'

'We've got to,' he told her. 'The way I figure it, there's less than an hour of daylight left. I want to look around.'

'You promised – '

'First let's see about the diamonds. If there's anybody in that hut they'll spot us.'

He raised the girl to her feet. She had to hang on to him as they walked down the ramp, and her legs went rubbery as she waded through the sand.

'Take your shoes off,' he suggested.

She kicked them aside. 'Hot,' Nora murmured, eyes closed against the sun's glare. 'Too hot.'

'Cooler in the hut,' he replied. 'Come on.'

They trudged over to the oblong. It was perhaps thirty feet in length, seven or eight feet high, and nine feet wide. Seen at close range it no longer resembled a serpent, except to Nora's bash-distorted vision.

'Looks creepy,' she whispered. 'What's it made of, anyway?'

'Some kind of hide, I guess. See how it's stretched? Wonder how they pieced it together – '

Wayne broke off as Nora stumbled against him. The girl was bashed, all right. Maybe he shouldn't have given her that last pop. But she was a good kid, he had to remember that.

And now, where were the natives?

He approached the dark doorway of the hut and tried to peer into the dimness beyond. There didn't seem to be any door at all, and no windows. The interior flooring slanted down away from the opening and he couldn't see very far within.

'Place must be deserted, all right,' he said. 'Let's take a peek inside.'

Nora tugged at his arm. 'I don't want to go in there. It's too dark.'

'Here's a light.' Wayne produced a small tube from his pack. 'Got a stunner attachment, too, following the beam. We're ready for anything.' He pulled her toward the doorway.

'It smells so,' the girl whimpered. 'Like snakes. And I think someone's looking at us.'

Wayne glanced behind him, scanning the desert horizon, then shook his head. 'You're just bash-happy.'

'I'm scared, that's all.'

He shrugged and moved forward. She had no choice but to follow. They walked down the slanting floor into the hut.

It did smell in here, Wayne realized. The odour was atrocious. No wonder the place was deserted. He swept the beam up and over the rough, unfinished walls. There was no furnishing, no sign of occupancy.

They stood in the outer chamber and gazed forward, noting that the interior of the hut was divided into several sections. Ahead of them was a narrow passageway leading to a second chamber. As Wayne moved forward the odour grew stronger and the girl held back.

'Let's go outside,' she urged. 'I'm choking, hon.' Wayne shook his head and advanced to the head of the passageway. He stood there and played his beam on the empty chamber beyond. The stench was almost intolerable, and it seemed to be coming from the floor, which was inches deep in stagnant muck. Maybe the natives used this hut as a cesspool. Maybe this is where they disposed of the –

'Look!' Nora had crept close behind him, and now she was cowering against him and pointing. 'See, in that slime in the corner? There's bones, and a skull!'

Wayne swept the beam around, away from the opening. 'You're imagining things,' he told her.

But he'd seen them too, and now he knew everything was all right.

'Want to go back outside?' he asked.

'Yes. Oh, please, hurry – I think I'm going to be sick.'

He half-supported Nora as she staggered back up the slanting slope leading to the doorway. The sky had darkened over the desert beyond, and the air was suddenly chill.

'Take a deep breath,' he commanded. 'You'll feel better.'

'Not until we get back to the ship,' the girl whispered. 'I can't stand being near this place. There's something awful about it. It isn't just a house, it's – ' Abruptly she paused and stared back at the oblong bulk of the hut. 'We're being watched,' she said. 'I know it.'

'Nonsense. You can see for yourself there's nobody around.'

'Then where are the natives?'

'Hunting, perhaps.'

'Are there animals around, too?'

'No.'

'Then what do they hunt?'

'Each other.'

'You mean they're – '

'Cannibals.' Wayne nodded. 'It's a dying world. No real civilization. No wonder they give diamonds as gifts. They're so grateful when anyone brings them a present.'

'Is that how Luke got his loot?' Nora asked. 'What kind of present did he give them?'

Wayne grinned at her. 'His partner, Brady.'

Nora's mouth twitched. 'You're joking. Or – he was lying to you – '

'Dying men don't lie,' Wayne said, softly. 'I picked old Luke up in an alley, two nights ago, bashed to the lungs and coughing his guts out. Dragged him into my place, and ten minutes later he was dead. But he talked, first. I thought he was delirious, until I saw the diamonds. Then I knew he was telling the truth.

'It had all been an accident, really. He and Brady were scavengers, operating a little wildcat freighter. They were on their way back from Cybele when Luke got sick. Brady must have figured it was better to find a place to stop, and he put down here. Luke was unconscious at the time.

'When he came to, he was alone on the freighter. Apparently Brady had decided to step out and take a look around. It was night, but the moon was up and Luke could see out – he was in desert country, like this. And there was nobody around. Off in the distance was one of these huts, and Luke wondered if Brady had gone to investigate. He felt pretty weak, but he just about made up his mind to follow his partner when the natives came.

'Luke didn't let them get aboard, of course. But he stood in the airlock and gestured at them. I guess they caught on to his sign language in a hurry. Anyway, they nodded at him and pantomimed. The way it looked, they'd found Brady wandering outside and jumped him.

'Luke said there were a dozen or more of them, all carrying long spears. He couldn't possibly handle them all, so he did the next best thing – smiled, looked friendly, and tried to find out what they'd done with Brady.

'So he made stabbing gestures and cutting gestures, but they just shook their heads and kept gesturing over at the hut in the distance. Then some of them bowed down facing it, and the rest bowed down facing the ship. And the biggest one, whom Luke took to be the chief, pulled out the sack of diamonds. He set it down and bowed again. Then he pointed at the hut once more and started to rub his belly. That's when Luke guessed the rest. You see, he thought Luke was some kind of god who had brought them Brady as an offering. And they were repaying him in diamonds.'

The moon was rising redly over the black bulk of the hut, and Wayne could see Nora's face flaming in the light. Her eyes were glazed.

'The natives left, then, and after a while Luke opened the lock and picked up the diamonds. He wanted to go to the hut and find Brady, but he was afraid. Instead, he took off. That's why he went on the bash when he hit port. He knew he'd been a coward.'

'I don't believe it,' Nora murmured. 'He was out of his head.'

'I saw the diamonds,' Wayne reminded her.

'But it doesn't make sense. Maybe he and Brady found diamonds here and they quarreled. So he killed his partner and took the loot for himself. That crazy yarn about the natives eating each other – '

'You saw the bones in the hut,' Wayne muttered. 'And in a little while, you'll see the natives, too.'

Nora stepped back. 'I don't want to see them,' she wailed. 'I want to go back to the ship. Why did you bring me here in the first place? Why – '

'Because you're a good kid,' Wayne said, and hit her across the face with his flash.

She fell forward heavily and he put his knee in her back, pressing her down as he got the rope out of his pack. The bash had weakened her and she couldn't put up much of a struggle. He tied her wrists expertly and then dragged her along the sand by her ankles. She moaned a little, but didn't come around until he'd propped her up on a small rise a few hundred feet from the entrance to the hut.

'There we are,' he told her. 'All wrapped and ready. Like I said, you're a good kid. But I suppose you don't know what I mean, do you?'

'Hon, let me go – '

'A kid is a baby goat. Once upon a time, back on Terra, in a place called India, there were other animals called tigers. Some of them man-eaters. When the natives wanted to attract a man-eater, they staked a kid out.

'So when I heard Luke's story, I knew what to do. I started looking for bait for a man-eater, and I found you.'

'You can't – '

'I can.' Wayne stared down at her soberly. 'Nobody saw us together last night. Nobody knows you sneaked off with me on an unauthorized flight. The Port is filled with tramps like you – they come and go. Even if somebody notices your disappearance, I'll never be involved.'

'But why me?' she was sobbing now, wheezing in panic.

Wayne reached forward and started ripping away her garments, slowly and deliberately.

'This is why,' he murmured. 'Because you're white and soft. Because you're plump and rounded and tender. Because you're a good kid.'

'Stop! let me go!'

Wayne stood up, nodding. 'That's right,' he said. 'Go ahead and scream. If they don't see that body of yours in the moonlight, at least they'll hear your voice. When the kid bleats, the man-eater comes.'

'No – don't leave me -- come back – I'll do anything you want, anything!'

'You'll get me the diamonds,' Wayne told her. 'I'll be waiting, never fear.'

He walked over to the dark shadow of the oblong hut and crouched just inside the doorway. The charnel stench was strong on the night air, but he wanted to keep out of sight. After they came, that was the psychological moment. With the weapon in his hand, he had nothing to fear. They'd treated old Luke like a god, and he'd get the same consideration.

Nora was crying softly in the distance. Her nude body was radiant in the moonlight. If there were any natives around, they'd be here soon.

For a moment he wondered if Nora had been right. Could the old scavenger have made up the whole yarn just as she said? Maybe there were no natives after all. The whole idea of cannibals with spears seemed a bit naïve and ridiculous. Brady could have wandered off, found some diamonds, then brought them back with him. Maybe he'd tried to hide them from his partner, only to have Luke discover them and kill him in a quarrel over the loot. That made a lot more sense.

Yes, the old space-rat had probably been lying. And who could blame him under the circumstances? Wayne hadn't told Nora the whole story – what he'd gotten out of Luke at the end wasn't a voluntary confession. Sure, he'd picked the old man up in the alley and dragged him inside, but only after he'd gone through the dying man's pockets and found the diamonds. That's why he put him on his bed, and started choking him;

choking him until the story came out in bits and pieces, like the bits and pieces of lung he coughed up in the final dying spasm.

Wayne frowned at himself. He'd been a little too rough; otherwise he'd have gotten more of the details. He'd have found out how to separate fact from fancy. As it was, all he really knew was that Luke had found the diamonds here on Vergis IV.

If there was nothing to the yarn about the cannibal natives, then Wayne was wasting his time. He'd have to dispose of the girl himself and then go diamond-hunting.

On the other hand, he reminded himself, there were the huts, just like Luke described them. Someone must have built them. And now he remembered the bones. The bones and the stench. There had to be man-eaters around. There had to be –

A whiff of carrion odour caused him to wrinkle his noise in revulsion. He wished there was another place of concealment available. Nora had been right; something about this hut made him feel uneasy. What kind of creatures could have built it? Where did they get the hides? Maybe they used their own skins – that is, the skins of their victims. Wayne tried to imagine a completely cannibalistic civilization. Had there ever been any on Terra?

Wayne tried to think about that for a moment, but there was something else that disturbed him, something he couldn't quite account for.

Maybe it was the red moon. It gave him the feeling Nora had complained about in the hut, the feeling of being watched. It was too much like an accusing eye.

Maybe it was remembering how he'd choked the story out of that bash-crazed old man; maybe it was seeing that naked, moaning girl up there on the rise.

He stared at her silhouette as it writhed on the horizon and wondered when something was going to happen. He hoped it would be soon, because he had to get out of here, the smell was getting worse –

Suddenly Wayne stiffened and crouched back in the doorway.

Something was coming over the rim of the hill.

The bait was luring the man-eater.

Wayne squinted into the wastes, trying to distinguish individual forms in the black blur that moved across the hilltop. Why, there must be an army of them, moving packed together in a solid mass!

Nora saw the movement too, because she was screaming, now. And there was another sound – a soft, slow rumbling. The black bulk was flowing forward. It wasn't black, really; more of a reddish brown. The same colour as the hut.

Then Wayne realized why he couldn't make out individual figures. There were no figures – just the solid mass. The thing crawling sluggishly over the hillside was a single great form. A brown oblong form, moving slowly but surely.

As Wayne recognized the object, another realization came to him. Now he knew what had eluded his mind. It was something about this hut. With no wind to disturb the sand, why hadn't he noticed the footprints of the natives leading to and from the doorway?

He had the answer, now. There were no natives – at least, no humanoid cannibals. Nora's guess had been correct. Brady found the diamonds and Luke killed him, then made up the story about natives dragging him into their hut. Brady hadn't been dragged to a hut – *the hut had come to him.*

And it was coming to Nora, now, out there on the hillside, its brown bulk inching toward her, towering over her, the black doorway gaping to engulf her like a ravenous mouth.

But it is a mouth, Wayne told himself, and suddenly there was a shock of final recognition as he remembered the hide-like covering that was hide, and the second inner compartment with the stagnant stench bubbling over the bones.

The huts were man-eaters, and he had to get out of here! He moved up the slanting slope leading to the doorway, eyes intent on the spectacle before him. Nora was screaming, the maw was closing over her – and then the vision was blotted out.

The maw was closing over him.

The doorway ahead of him disappeared, and the slanting slope moved beneath his feet. It contracted in a series of ripples, convulsing like a throat in the act of swallowing. Wayne gasped, the stench suddenly stronger in his nostrils. He clawed out at the walls, dropping his weapon as the slope tilted, pushing him back. And now a wave of nauseous liquid gushed out from the floor, and Wayne felt himself forced back, thinking idiotically, *salivation, that's what it is,* and wondering why there were no teeth in the house.

The odour was overpowering, and he felt the slimy waves wash over him as he retreated, forcing his way along the narrow passage toward the second chamber.

It squeezed him clammily, and all too late he realized that this must be the esophagus.

Snakes. Nora had said. The thing smelled like a snake, it looked like a snake, it was a snake. A snake that devours its victims whole and alive. And then digests them in its stomach.

Wayne clawed the constricting walls of the narrow passage, trying to hold himself back. But the creature was moving and shuddering all around him, and then it gave a great gulp and swallowed. Wayne fell into the second compartment, and the bubbling liquid surged and seared ...

When daylight came, the hut was sluggish and quiescent. The dark doorway opened once more, but there was no other sign of movement.

The hut belched once, then settled back to wait.

The Red Lodge

H. RUSSELL WAKEFIELD

I AM WRITING THIS FROM AN imperative sense of duty, for I consider the Red Lodge is a foul death-trap and utterly unfit to be a human habitation – it has its own proper denizens – and because I know its owner to be an unspeakable blackguard to allow it so to be used for his financial advantage. He knows the perils of the place perfectly well; I wrote him of our experiences, and he didn't even acknowledge the letter, and two days ago I saw the ghastly pest-house advertised in *Country Life*. So anyone who rents the Red Lodge in future will receive a copy of this document as well as some uncomfortable words from Sir William, and that scoundrel Wilkes can take what action he pleases.

I certainly didn't carry any prejudice against the place down to it with me: I had been too busy to look over it myself, but my wife reported extremely favourably – I take her word for most things – and I could tell by the photographs that it was a magnificent specimen of the medium-sized Queen Anne house, just the ideal thing for me. Mary said the garden was perfect, and there was the river for Tim at the bottom of it. I had been longing for a holiday, and was in the highest spirits as I travelled down. I have not been in the highest spirits since.

My first vague, faint uncertainty came to me so soon as I had crossed the threshold. I am a painter by profession, and therefore sharply responsive to colour tone. Well, it was a brilliantly fine day, the hall of the Red Lodge was fully lighted, yet it seemed a shade off the key, as it were, as though I were regarding it through a pair of slightly darkened glasses. Only a painter would have noticed it, I fancy.

When Mary came out to greet me, she was not looking as well as I had hoped, or as well as a week in the country should have made her look.

'Everything all right?' I asked.

'Oh, yes,' she replied, but I thought she found it difficult to say so, and then my eye detected a curious little spot of green on the maroon rug in front of the fire-place. I picked it up – it seemed like a patch of river slime.

'I suppose Tim brings those in,' said Mary. 'I've found several; of course, he promises he doesn't.' And then for a moment we were silent, and a very unusual sense of constraint seemed to set a barrier between us. I went out into the garden to smoke a cigarette before lunch, and sat myself

242

down under a very fine mulberry tree.

I wondered if, after all, I had been wise to have left it all to Mary. There was nothing wrong with the house, of course, but I am a bit psychic, and I always know the mood or character of a house. One welcomes you with the tail-writhing enthusiasm of a really nice dog, makes you at home, and at your ease at once. Others are sullen, watchful, hostile, with things to hide. They make you feel that you have obtruded yourself into some curious affairs which are none of your business. I had never encountered so hostile, aloof, and secretive a living place as the Red Lodge seemed when I first entered it. Well, it couldn't be helped, though it was disappointing; and there was Tim coming back from his walk, and the luncheon-gong. My son seemed a little subdued and thoughtful, though he looked pretty well, and soon we were all chattering away with those quick changes of key which occur when the respective ages of the conversationalists are 40, 33, and $6\frac{1}{2}$, and after half a bottle of Meursault and a glass of port I began to think I had been a morbid ass. I was still so thinking when I began my holiday in the best possible way by going to sleep in an exquisitely comfortable chair under the mulberry tree. But I have slept better. I dozed off, but I had a silly impression of being watched, so that I kept waking up in case there might be someone with his eye on me. I was lying back, and could just see a window on the second floor framed by a gap in the leaves, and on one occasion, when I woke rather sharply from one of these dozes, I thought I saw for a moment a face peering down at me, and this face seemed curiously flattened against the pane – just a 'carry over' from a dream, I concluded. However, I didn't feel like sleeping any more, and began to explore the garden. It was completely walled in, I found, except at the far end, where there was a door leading through to a path which, running parallel to the right-hand wall, led to the river a few yards away. I noticed on this door several of those patches of green slime for which Tim was supposedly responsible. It was a dark little corner cut off from the rest of the garden by two rowan trees, a cool, silent little place I thought it. And then it was time for Tim's cricket lesson, which was interrupted by the arrival of some infernal callers. But they were pleasant people, as a matter of fact, the Local Knuts, I gathered, who owned the Manor House: Sir William Prowse and his lady and his daughter. I went for a walk with him after tea.

'Who had this house before us?' I asked.

'People called Hawker,' he replied. 'That was two years ago.'

'I wonder the owner doesn't live in it,' I said. 'It isn't an expensive place to keep up.'

Sir William paused as if considering his reply.

'I think he dislikes being so near the river. I'm not sorry, for I detest the fellow. By the way, how long have you taken it for?'

'Three months,' I replied, 'till the end of October.'

'Well, if I can do anything for you I shall be delighted. If you are in any trouble, come straight to me.' He slightly emphasized the last sentence.

I rather wondered what sort of trouble Sir William envisaged for me. Probably he shared the general opinion that artists were quite mad at times, and that when I had one of my lapses I should destroy the peace in some manner. However, I was duly grateful.

I was sorry to find Tim didn't seem to like the river; he appeared nervous of it, and I determined to help him to overcome this, for the fewer terrors one carries through life with one the better, and they can often be laid by delicate treatment in childhood. Curiously enough, the year before at Frinton he seemed to have no fear of the sea.

The rest of the day passed uneventfully – at least I think I can say so. After dinner I strolled down to the end of the garden, meaning to go through the door and have a look at the river. Just as I got my hand on the latch there came a very sharp, furtive whistle. I turned round quickly, but seeing no one, concluded it had come from someone in the lane outside. However, I didn't investigate further, but went back to the house.

I woke up the next morning feeling a shade depressed. My dressing-room smelled stale and bitter, and I flung its windows open. As I did so I felt my right foot slip on something. It was one of those small, slimy, green patches. Now Tim would never come into my dressing-room. An annoying little puzzle. How on earth had that patch –? Which question kept forcing its way into my mind as I dressed. How could a patch of green slime . . . ? How could a patch of green slime . . . ? Dropped from something? From what? I am very fond of my wife – she slaved for me when I was poor, and always kept me happy, comfortable, and faithful, and she gave me my small son Timothy. I must stand between her and patches of green slime! What in hell's name was I talking about? And it was a flamingly fine day. Yet all during breakfast my mind was trying to find some sufficient reason for these funny little patches of green slime, and not finding it.

After breakfast I told Tim I would take him out in a boat on the river.

'Must I, Daddy?' he asked, looking anxiously at me.

'No, of course not,' I replied, a trifle irritably, 'but I believe you'll enjoy it.'

'Should I be a funk if I didn't come?'

'No, Tim, but I think you should try it once, anyway.'

'All right,' he said.

He's a plucky little chap, and did his very best to pretend to be enjoying himself, but I saw it was a failure from the start.

Perplexed and upset, I asked his nurse if she knew of any reason for this sudden fear of water.

'No, sir,' she said. 'The first day he ran down to the river just as he used to run down to the sea, but all of a sudden he started crying and ran back to the house. It seemed to me he'd seen something in the water which frightened him.'

We spent the afternoon motoring round the neighbourhood, and already I found a faint distaste at the idea of returning to the house, and again I had the impression that we were intruding, and that something had been going on during our absence which our return had interrupted.

Mary, pleading a headache, went to bed soon after dinner, and I went to the study to read.

Directly I had shut the door I had again that very unpleasant sensation of being watched. It made the reading of Sidgwick's *The Use of Words in Reasoning* – an old favourite of mine, which requires concentration – a difficult business. Time after time I found myself peeping into dark corners and shifting my position. And there were little sharp sounds; just the oak-panelling cracking, I supposed. After a time I became more absorbed in the book, and less fidgety, and then I heard a very soft cough just behind me. I felt little icy rays pour down and through me, but I would *not* look round, and I *would* go on reading. I had just reached the following passage: 'However many things may be said about Socrates, or about any fact observed, there remains still more that might be said if the need arose; the need is the determining factor. Hence the distinction between complete and incomplete description, though perfectly sharp and clear in the abstract, can only have a meaning – can only be applied to actual cases – if it be taken as equivalent to *sufficient* description, the sufficiency being relative to some purpose. Evidently the description of Socrates as a man, scanty though it is, may be fully sufficient for the purpose of the modest inquiry whether he is *mortal* or not' – when my eye caught by a green patch which suddenly appeared on the floor beside me, and then another and another, following a straight line towards the door. I picked up the nearest one, and it was a bit of soaking slime. I called on all my will-power, for I feared something worse to come, and it should *not* materialize – and then no more patches appeared. I got up and walked deliberately, slowly, to the door, turned on the light in the middle of the room, and then came back and turned out the reading-lamp and went to my dressing-room. I sat down and thought things over. There was something very wrong with this house. I had passed the stage of pretending otherwise, and my inclination was to take my family away from it the next day. But that meant sacrificing £168, and we had nowhere else to go. It was conceivable that these phenomena were perceptible only to me, being half a Highlander. I might be able to stick it out if I were careful and kept my tail up, for apparitions of this sort are partially subjective – one brings something of oneself to their materialization. This is a hard saying, but I believe it to be true. If Mary and Tim and the servants were immune it was up to me to face and fight this nastiness. As I undressed, I came to the decision that I would decide nothing then and there, and that I would see what happened. I made this decision against my better judgement, I think.

In bed I tried to thrust all this away from me by a conscious effort to 'change the subject,' as it were. The easiest subject for me to switch over to is the myriad-sided, useless, consistently abused business of creating things, stories out of pens and ink and paper, representations of things and moods out of paint, brushes and canvas, and our own miseries, perhaps, out of wine, women and song. With a considerable effort, therefore, and with the edges of my brain anxious to be busy with bits of green slime, I recalled an article I had read that day on a glorious word 'Jugendbewegung,' the 'Youth Movement,' that pregnant or merely wind-swollen Teutonism! How ponderously it attempted to canonize with its polysyllabic sonority that inverted Boy-Scoutishness of the said youths and maidens. 'One bad, mad deed – sonnet – scribble of some kind – lousy daub – a day.' Bunk without spunk, sauce without force, Futurism without a past, merely a *Transition* from one yelping pose to another. And then I suddenly found myself at the end of the garden, attempting desperately to hide myself behind a rowan tree, while my eyes were held relentlessly to face the door. And then it began slowly to open, and something which was horridly unlike anything I had seen before began passing through it, and *I* knew It knew I was there, and then my head seemed burst and flamed asunder, splintered and destroyed, and I awoke trembling to feel that something in the darkness was poised an inch or two above me, and then drip, drip, something began falling on my face. Mary was in the bed next to mine, and I *would not* scream, but flung the clothes over my head, my eyes streaming with the tears of terror. And so I remained cowering till I heard the clock strike five, and dawn, the ally I longed for, came, and the birds began to sing, and then I slept.

I awoke a wreck, and after breakfast, feeling the need to be alone, I pretended I wanted to sketch, and went out into the garden. Suddenly I recalled Sir William's remark about coming to see him if there was any trouble. Not much difficulty in guessing what he had meant. I'd go and see him about it at once. I wished I knew whether Mary was troubled too. I hesitated to ask her, for, if she were not, she was certain to become suspicious and uneasy if I questioned her. And then I discovered that, while my brain had been busy with its thoughts, my hand had also not been idle, but had been occupied in drawing a very singular design on the sketching-block. I watched it as it went automatically on. Was it a design or a figure of some sort? When had I seen something like it before? My God, in my dream last night! I tore it to pieces, and got up in agitation and made my way to the Manor House along a path through tall, bowing, stippled grasses hissing lightly in the breeze. My inclination was to run to the station and take the next train to anywhere; pure undiluted panic – an insufficiently analysed word – that which causes men to trample on women and children when Death is making his choice. Of course, I had Mary and Tim and the servants to keep me from it, but supposing they had no claim on me, should I desert them? No, I should not. Why? Such things aren't done by respectable inhabitants of Great Britain – a people despised and respected by all other tribes. Despised as Philistines, but it took the jawbone of an ass to subdue that hardy race! Respected for what? Birkenhead stuff. No, not the noble Lord, for there were no glittering prizes for those who went down to the bottom of the sea in ships. My mind deliberately restricting itself to such highly debatable jingoism, I reached the Manor House, to be told that Sir William was up in London for the day, but would return that evening. Would he ring me up on his return? 'Yes, sir.' And then, with lagging steps, back to the Red Lodge.

I took Mary for a drive in the car after lunch. Anything to get out of the beastly place. Tim didn't come, as he preferred to play in the garden. In the light of what happened I shall be criticized for leaving him alone, with a nurse, but at that time I held the theory that these appearances were in no way malignant, and that it was more than possible that even if Tim did see anything he wouldn't be frightened, not realizing it was out of the ordinary in any way. After all, nothing that I had seen or heard, at any rate during the daytime, would strike him as unusual.

Mary was silent, and I was beginning to feel sure, from a certain depression and oppression in her manner and appearance, that my trouble was hers. It was on the tip of my tongue to say something, but I resolved to wait until I had heard what Sir William had to say. It was a dark, sombre, and brooding afternoon, and my spirits fell as we turned for home. What a home!

We got back at six, and I had just stopped the engine and helped Mary out when I heard a scream from the garden. I rushed round, to see Tim, his hands to his eyes, staggering across the lawn, the nurse running behind him. And then he screamed again and fell. I carried him into the house and laid him down on a sofa in the drawing-room, and Mary went to him. I took the nurse by the arm and out of the room; she was panting and crying down a face of chalk.

'What happened? What happened?' I asked.

'I don't know what it was, sir, but we had been walking in the lane, and had left the door open. Master Tim was a bit ahead of me, and went through the door first, and then he screamed like that.'

'Did you see anything that could have frightened him?'

'No, sir, nothing.'

I went back to them. It was no good questioning Tim, and there was nothing coherent to be learnt from his hysterical sobbing. He grew calmer presently, and was taken up to bed. Suddenly he turned to Mary, and looked at her with eyes of terror.

'The green monkey won't get me, will it, Mummy?'

'No, no, it's all right now,' said Mary, and soon after he went to sleep, and then she and I went down to the drawing-room. She was on the border of hysteria herself.

'Oh, Tom, what is the matter with this awful house? I'm *terrified*. Ever since I've been here I've been terrified. Do you see things?'

'Yes,' I replied.

'Oh, I wish I'd known. I didn't want to worry you if you hadn't. Let me tell you what it's been like. On the day we arrived I saw a man pass ahead of me into my bedroom. Of course, I only *thought* I had. And then I've heard beastly whisperings and every time I pass that turn in the corridor I *know* there's someone just round the corner. And then the day before you arrived I woke suddenly, and something seemed to force me to go to the window, and I crawled there on hands and knees and peeped through the blind. It was just light enough to see. And suddenly I saw someone running down the lawn, his or her hands outstretched, and there was something ghastly just beside him, and they disappeared behind the trees at the end. I'm terrified every minute.'

'What about the servants?'

'Nurse hasn't seen anything, but the others have, I'm certain. And then there are those slimy patches, I think they're the vilest of all. I don't think Tim has been troubled till now, but I'm sure he's been puzzled and uncertain several times.'

'Well,' I said, 'it's pretty obvious we must clear out. I'm seeing Sir William about it tomorrow, I hope, and I'm certain enough of what he'll advise. Meanwhile we must think over where to go. It was a nasty jar, though; I don't mean merely the money, though that's bad enough, but the fuss – just when I hoped we were going to be so happy and settled. However, it's got to be done. We should be mad after a week of this filth-drenched hole.'

Just then the telephone-bell rang. It was a message to say Sir William would be pleased to see me at half-past ten tomorrow.

With the dusk came that sense of being watched, waited for, followed about, plotted against, an atmosphere of quiet, hunting malignancy. A thick mist came up from the river, and as I was changing for dinner I noticed the lights from the window seemed to project a series of swiftly changing pictures on its grey, crawling screen. The one opposite my window, for example, was unpleasantly suggestive of three figures staring in and seeming to grow nearer and larger. The effect must have been slightly hypnotic, for suddenly I started back, for it was as if they were about to close on me. I pulled down the blind and hurried downstairs. During dinner we decided that unless Sir William had something very reassuring to say we would go back to London two days later and stay at a hotel till we could find somewhere to spend the next six weeks. Just before going to bed we went up to the night nursery to see if Tim was all right. This room was at the top of a short flight of stairs. As these stairs were covered with green slime, and there was a pool of the muck just outside the door, we took him down to sleep with us.

The Permanent Occupants of the Red Lodge waited till the light was out, but then I felt them come thronging, slipping in one by one, their weapon fear. It seemed to me they were massed for the attack. A yard away my wife was lying with my son in her arms, so I must fight. I lay back, gripped the sides of the bed and strove with all my might to hold my assailants back. As the hours went by I felt myself beginning to get the upper hand, and a sense of exaltation came to me. But an hour before dawn they made their greatest effort. I knew that they were willing me to creep on my hands and knees to the window and peep through the blind, and that if I did so we were doomed. As I set my teeth and tightened my grip till I felt racked with agony, the sweat poured from me. I felt them come crowding round the bed and thrusting their faces into mine, and a voice in my head kept saying insistently, 'You must crawl to the window and look through the blind.' In my mind's eyes I could see myself crawling stealthily across the floor and pulling the blind aside, but who would be staring back at me? Just when I felt my resistance breaking I heard a sweet, sleepy twitter from a tree outside, and saw the blind touched by a faint suggestion of light, and at once those with whom I had been struggling left me and went their way, and, utterly exhausted, I slept.

In the morning I found, somewhat ironically, that Mary had slept better than on any night since she came down.

Half-past ten found me entering the Manor House, a delightful nondescript old place, which started wagging its tail as soon as I entered it. Sir William was waiting me in the library. 'I expected this would happen,' he said gravely, 'and now tell me.'

I gave him a short outline of our experiences.

'Yes,' he said, 'it's always much the same story. Every time that horrible place has been let I have felt a sense of personal responsibility, and yet I cannot give a proper warning, for the letting of haunted houses is not yet a criminal offence – though it ought to be – and I couldn't afford a libel action, and, as a matter of fact, one old couple had the house for fifteen years and were perfectly delighted with it, being troubled in no way. But now let me tell you what I know of the Red Lodge. I have studied it for forty years, and I regard it as my personal enemy.

'The local tradition is that the second owner, early in the eighteenth century, wished to get rid of his wife, and bribed his servants to frighten her to death – just the sort of ancestor I can imagine that blackguard Wilkes being descended from.

'What devilries they perpetrated I don't know, but she is supposed to have rushed from the house just before dawn one day and drowned herself. Whereupon her husband installed a small harem in the house; but it was a failure, for each of these charmers one by one rushed down to the river just before dawn, and finally the husband himself did the same. Of the period between then and forty years ago I have no record, but the local tradition has it that it was the scene of tragedy after tragedy, and then was shut up for a long time. When I first began to study it, it was occupied by two bachelor brothers. One shot himself in the room which I imagine you use as your bedroom, and the other drowned himself in the usual way. I may tell you that the worst room in the house, the one the unfortunate lady is supposed to have occupied, is locked up, you know, the one on the second floor. I imagine Wilkes mentioned it to you.'

'Yes, he did,' I replied. 'Said he kept important papers there.'

'Yes; well, he was forced in self-defence to do so ten years ago, and since then the death rate has been lower, but in those forty years twenty people have taken their lives in the house or in the river, six children have been drowned accidentally. The last case was Lord Passover's butler in 1924. He was seen to run down to the river and leap in. He was pulled out, but had died of shock.

The people who took the house two years ago left in a week, and threatened to bring an action against Wilkes, but they were warned they had no legal case. And I strongly advise you, more than that, *implore* you, to follow their example, though I can imagine the financial loss and great inconvenience, for that house is a death-trap.'

'I will,' I replied. 'I forgot to mention one thing; when my little boy was so badly frightened he said something about "a green monkey." '

'He did!' said Sir William sharply. 'Well then, it is absolutely imperative that you should leave at once. You remember I mentioned the death of certain children. Well, in each case they had been found drowned in the reeds just at the end of that lane, and the people about here have a firm belief that "The Green Thing," or "The Green Death" – it is sometimes referred to as the first and sometimes as the other – is connected with danger to children.'

Have you ever seen anything yourself?' I asked.

'I go to the infernal place as little as possible,' replied Sir William, 'but when I called on your predecessors I most distinctly saw someone leave the drawing-room as we entered it, otherwise all I have noted is a certain dream which recurs with curious regularity. I find myself standing at the end of the land and watching the river – always in a sort of brassy half-light. And presently something comes floating down the stream. I can see it jerking up and down, and I always feel passionately anxious to see what it may be. At first I think that it is a log, but when it gets exactly opposite me it changes its course and comes towards me, and then I see that it is a dead body, very decomposed. And when it reaches the bank it begins to climb up towards me, and then I am thankful to say I always awake. Sometimes I have thought that one day I shall not wake just then, and that on this occasion something will happen to me, but that is probably merely the silly fancy of an old gentleman who has concerned himself with these singular events rather more than is good for his nerves.'

'That is obviously the explanation,' I said, 'and I am extremely grateful to you. We will leave to-morrow. But don't you think we should attempt to devise some means by which other people may be spared this sort of thing, and this brute Wilkes be prevented from letting the house again?'

'I certainly do so, and we will discuss it further on some other occasion. And now go and pack!'

A very great and charming gentleman, Sir William, I reflected, as I walked back to the Red Lodge.

Tim seemed to have recovered excellently well, but I thought it wise to keep him out of the house as much as possible, so while Mary and the maids packed after lunch I went with him for a walk through the fields. We took our time, and it was only when the sky grew black and there was a distant rumble of thunder and a menacing little breeze came from the west that we turned to come back. We had to hurry, and as we reached the meadow next to the house there came a ripping flash and the storm broke. We started to run for the door into the garden when I tripped over my bootlace, which had come undone, and fell. Tim ran on. I had just tied the lace and was on my feet again when I saw something slip through the door. It was green, thin, tall. It seemed to glance back at me, and what should have been its face was a patch of soused slime. At that moment Tim saw it, screamed, and ran for the river. The figure turned and followed him, and before I could reach him hovered over him. Tim screamed again and flung himself in. A moment later I passed through a green and stenching film and dived after him. I found him writhing in the reeds and brought him to the bank. I ran with him in my arms to the house, and I shall not forget Mary's face as she saw us from the bedroom window.

By nine o'clock we were all in a hotel in London, and the Red Lodge an evil, fading memory. I shut the front door when I had packed them all into the car. As I took hold of the knob I felt a quick and powerful pressure from the other side, and it shut with a crash. The Permanent Occupants of the Red Lodge were in sole possession once more.

Mary Postgate

RUDYARD KIPLING

OF MISS MARY POSTGATE, Lady McCausland wrote that she was 'thoroughly conscientious, tidy, companionable, and ladylike. I am very sorry to part with her, and shall always be interested in her welfare.'

Miss Fowler engaged her on this recommendation, and to her surprise, for she had had experience of companions, found that it was true. Miss Fowler was nearer sixty than fifty at the time, but though she needed care she did not exhaust her attendant's vitality. On the contrary, she gave out, stimulatingly and with reminiscences. Her father had been a minor Court official in the days when the Great Exhibition of 1851 had just set its seal on Civilisation made perfect. Some of Miss Fowler's tales, none the less, were not always for the young. Mary was not young, and though her speech was as colourless as her eyes or her hair, she was never shocked. She listened unflinchingly to every one; said at the end, 'How interesting!' or 'How shocking!' as the case might be, and never again referred to it, for she prided herself on a trained mind, which 'did not dwell on these things.' She was, too, a treasure at domestic accounts, for which the village tradesmen, with their weekly books, loved her not. Otherwise she had no enemies; provoked no jealousy even among the plainest; neither gossip nor slander had ever been traced to her; she supplied the odd place at the Rector's or the Doctor's table at half an hour's notice; she was a sort of public aunt to very many small children of the village street, whose parents, while accepting everything, would have been swift to resent what they called 'patronage'; she served on the Village Nursing Committee as Miss Fowler's nominee when Miss Fowler was crippled by rheumatoid arthritis, and came out of six months' fortnightly meetings equally respected by all the cliques.

And when Fate threw Miss Fowler's nephew, an unlovely orphan of eleven, on Miss Fowler's hands, Mary Postgate stood to her share of the business of education as practised in private and public schools. She checked printed clothes-lists, and unitemised bills of extras; wrote to Head and House masters, matrons, nurses and doctors, and grieved or rejoiced over half-term reports. Young Wyndham Fowler repaid her in his holidays by calling her 'Gatepost,' 'Postey,' or 'Packthread,' by thumping her between her narrow shoulders, or by chasing her bleating, round the garden, her large mouth open, her large nose high in air, at a stiff-necked shamble very like a camel's. Later on he filled the house with clamour, argument, and harangues as to his personal needs, likes and dislikes, and the limitations of 'you women,' reducing Mary to tears of physical fatigue, or, when he chose to be humorous, of helpless laughter. At crises, which multiplied as he grew older, she was his ambassadress and his interpretress to Miss Fowler, who had no large sympathy with the young; a vote in his interest at the councils on his future; his sewing-woman, strictly accountable for mislaid boots and garments; always his butt and his slave.

And when he decided to become a solicitor, and had entered an office in London; when his greeting had changed from 'Hullo, Postey, you old beast,' to 'Mornin', Packthread,' there came a war which, unlike all wars that Mary could remember, did not stay decently outside England and in the newspapers, but intruded on the lives of people whom she knew. As she said to Miss Fowler, it was 'most vexatious.' It took the Rector's son who was going into business with his elder brother; it took the Colonel's nephew on the eve of fruit-farming in Canada; it took Mrs Grant's son who, his mother said, was devoted to the ministry; and, very early indeed, it took Wynn Fowler, who announced on a postcard that he had joined the Flying Corps and wanted a cardigan waistcoat.

'He must go, and he must have the waistcoat,' said Miss Fowler. So Mary got the proper-sized needles and wool, while Miss Fowler told the men of her establishment – two gardeners and an odd man, aged sixty – that those who could join the Army had better do so. The gardeners left. Cheape, the odd man, stayed on, and was promoted to the gardener's cottage. The cook, scorning to be limited in luxuries, also left, after a spirited scene with Miss Fowler, and took the housemaid with her. Miss Fowler gazetted Nellie, Cheape's seventeen-year-old daughter, to the vacant post; Mrs Cheape to the rank of cook, with occasional cleaning bouts; and the reduced establishment moved forward smoothly.

Wynn demanded an increase in his allowance. Miss Fowler, who always looked facts in the face, said, 'He must have it. The chances are he won't live long to draw it, and if three hundred makes him happy——'

Wynn was grateful, and came over, in his tight-buttoned uniform, to say so. His training centre was not thirty miles away, and his talk was so technical that it had to be explained by charts of the various types of machines. He gave Mary such a chart.

'And you'd better study it, Postey,' he said. 'You'll be seeing a lot of 'em soon.' So Mary studied the chart, but when Wynn next arrived to swell and exalt himself before his womenfolk, she failed badly in cross-examination, and he rated her as in the old days.

'You *look* more or less like a human being,' he said in his new Service voice. 'You *must* have had a brain at some time in your past. What have you done with it? Where d'you keep it? A sheep would know more than you do, Postey. You're lamentable. You are less use than an empty tin can, you dowey old cassowary.'

'I suppose that's how your superior officer talks to *you*?' said Miss Fowler from her chair.

'But Postey doesn't mind,' Wynn replied. 'Do you, Packthread?'

'Why? Was Wynn saying anything? I shall get this right next time you come,' she muttered, and knitted her pale brows again over the diagrams of Taubes, Farmans, and Zeppelins.

In a few weeks the mere land and sea battles which she read to Miss Fowler after breakfast passed her like idle breath. Her heart and her interest were high in the air with Wynn, who had finished 'rolling' (whatever that might be) and had gone on from a 'taxi' to a machine more or less his own. One morning it circled over their very chimneys, alighted on Vegg's Heath, almost outside the garden gate, and Wynn came in, blue with cold, shouting for food. He and she drew Miss Fowler's bath-chair, as they had often done, along the Heath foot-path to look at the biplane. Mary observed that 'it smelt very badly.'

'Postey, I believe you think with your nose,' said Wynn. 'I know you don't with your mind. Now, what type's that?'

'I'll go and get the chart,' said Mary.

'You're hopeless! You haven't the mental capacity of a white mouse,' he cried, and explained the dials and the sockets for bomb-dropping till it was time to mount and ride the wet clouds once more.

'Ah!' said Mary, as the stinking thing flared upward. 'Wait till our Flying Corps gets to work! Wynn says it's much safer than in the trenches.'

'I wonder,' said Miss Fowler. 'Tell Cheape to come and tow me home again.'

'It's all downhill. I can do it,' said Mary, 'if you put the brake on.' She laid her lean self against the pushing-bar and home they trundled.

'Now, be careful you aren't heated and catch a chill,' said overdressed Miss Fowler.

'Nothing makes me perspire,' said Mary. As she bumped the chair under the porch she straightened her long back. The exertion had given her a colour, and the wind had loosened a wisp of hair across her forehead. Miss Fowler glanced at her.

'What do you ever think of, Mary?' she demanded suddenly.

'Oh, Wynn says he wants another three pairs of stockings – as thick as we can make them.'

'Yes. But I mean the things that women think about. Here you are, more than forty——'

'Forty-four,' said truthful Mary.

'Well?'

'Well?' Mary offered Miss Fowler her shoulder as usual.

'And you've been with me ten years now.'

'Let's see,' said Mary. 'Wynn was eleven when he came. He's twenty now, and I came two years before that. It must be eleven.'

'Eleven! And you've never told me anything that matters in all that while. Looking back, it seems to me that I've done all the talking.'

'I'm afraid I'm not much of a conversationalist. As Wynn says, I haven't the mind. Let me take your hat.'

Miss Fowler, moving stiffly from the hip, stamped her rubber-tipped stick on the tiled-hall floor. 'Mary, aren't you *anything* except a companion? Would you *ever* have been anything except a companion?'

Mary hung up the garden hat on its proper peg. 'No,' she said after consideration. 'I don't imagine I ever should. But I've no imagination, I'm afraid.'

She fetched Miss Fowler her eleven-o'clock glass of Contrexeville.

That was the wet December when it rained six inches to the month, and the women went abroad as little as might be. Wynn's flying chariot visited them several times, and for two mornings (he had warned her by postcard) Mary heard the thresh of his propellers at dawn. The second time she ran to the window, and stared at the whitening sky. A little blur passed overhead. She lifted her lean arms towards it.

That evening at six o'clock there came an announcement in an official envelope that Second Lieutenant W. Fowler had been killed during a trial flight. Death was instantaneous. She read it and carried it to Miss Fowler.

'I never expected anything else,' said Miss Fowler; 'but I'm sorry it happened before he had done anything.'

The room was whirling round Mary Postgate, but she found herself quite steady in the midst of it.

'Yes,' she said. 'It's a great pity he didn't die in action after he had killed somebody.'

'He was killed instantly. That's one comfort,' Miss Fowler went on.

'But Wynn says the shock of a fall kills a man at once – whatever happens to the tanks,' quoted Mary.

The room was coming to rest now. She heard Miss Fowler say impatiently, 'But why can't we cry, Mary?' and herself replying, 'There's nothing to cry for. He has done his duty as much as Mrs Grant's son did.'

'And when he died, *she* came and cried all the morning,' said Miss Fowler. 'This only makes me feel tired – terribly tired. Will you help me to bed, please, Mary? – And I think I'd like the hot-water bottle.'

So Mary helped her and sat beside, talking of Wynn in his riotous youth.

'I believe,' said Miss Fowler suddenly, 'that old people and young people slip from under a stroke like this. The middle-aged feel it most.'

'I expect that's true,' said Mary, rising. 'I'm going to put away the things in his room now. Shall we wear mourning?'

'Certainly not,' said Miss Fowler. 'Except, of course, at the funeral. I can't go. You will. I want you to arrange about his being buried here.

255

What a blessing it didn't happen at Salisbury!'

Every one, from the Authorities of the Flying Corps to the Rector, was most kind and sympathetic. Mary found herself for the moment in a world where bodies were in the habit of being despatched by all sorts of conveyances to all sorts of places. And at the funeral two young men in buttoned-up uniforms stood beside the grave and spoke to her afterwards.

'You're Miss Postgate, aren't you?' said one. 'Fowler told me about you. He was a good chap – a first-class fellow – a great loss.'

'Great loss!' growled his companion. 'We're all awfully sorry.'

'How high did he fall from?' Mary whispered.

'Pretty nearly four thousand feet, I should think, didn't he? You were up that day, Monkey?'

'All of that,' the other child replied. 'My bar made three thousand, and I wasn't as high as him by a lot.'

'Then *that's* all right,' said Mary. 'Thank you very much.'

They moved away as Mrs Grant flung herself weeping on Mary's flat chest, under the lych-gate and cried, '*I* know how it feels! *I* know how it feels!'

'But both his parents are dead,' Mary returned, and she fended her off. 'Perhaps they've all met by now,' she added vaguely as she escaped towards the coach.

'I've thought of that too,' wailed Mrs Grant; 'but then he'll be practically a stranger to them. Quite embarrassing!'

Mary faithfully reported every detail of the ceremony to Miss Fowler, who, when she described Mrs Grant's outburst, laughed aloud.

'Oh, how Wynn would have enjoyed it! He was always utterly unreliable at funerals. D'you remember——' And they talked of him again, each piecing out the other's gaps. 'And now,' said Miss Fowler, 'we'll pull up the blinds and we'll have a general tidy. That always does us good. Have you seen to Wynn's things?'

'Everything – since he first came,' said Mary. 'He was never destructive – even with his toys.'

They faced that neat room.

'It can't be natural not to cry,' Mary said at last. 'I'm *so* afraid you'll have a reaction.'

'As I told you, we old people slip from under the stroke. It's you I'm afraid for. Have you cried yet?'

'I can't. It only makes me angry with the Germans.'

'That's sheer waste of vitality,' said Miss Fowler. 'We must live till the war's finished.' She opened a full wardrobe. 'Now, I've been thinking things over. This is my plan. All his civilian clothes can be given away – Belgian refugees, and so on.'

Mary nodded. 'Boots, collars, and gloves?'

'Yes. We don't need to keep anything except his cap and belt.'

'They came back yesterday with his Flying Corps clothes' - Mary pointed to a roll on the little iron bed.

'Ah, but keep his Service things. Someone may be glad of them later. Do you remember his sizes?'

'Five feet eight and a half; thirty-six inches round the chest. But he told me he's just put on an inch and a half. I'll mark it on a label and tie it on his sleeping-bag.'

'So that disposes of *that*,' said Miss Fowler, tapping the palm of one hand with the ringed third finger of the other. 'What waste it all is! We'll get his old school trunk tomorrow and pack his civilian clothes.'

'And the rest?' said Mary. 'His books and pictures and the games and the toys - and - and the rest?'

'My plan is to burn every single thing,' said Miss Fowler. 'Then we shall know where they are and no one can handle them afterwards. What do you think?' 'I think that would be much the best,' said Mary. 'But there's such a lot of them.'

'We'll burn them in the destructor,' said Miss Fowler.

This was an open-air furnace for the consumption of refuse; a little circular four-foot tower of pierced brick over an iron grating. Miss Fowler had noticed the design in a gardening journal years ago, and had had it built at the bottom of the garden. It suited her tidy soul, for it saved unsightly rubbish-heaps, and the ashes lightened the stiff clay soil.

Mary considered for a moment, saw her way clear, and nodded again. They spent the evening putting away well-remembered civilian suits, underclothes that Mary had marked, and the regiments of very gaudy socks and ties. A second trunk was needed, and, after that, a little packing-case, and it was late next day when Cheape and the local carrier lifted them to the cart. The Rector luckily knew of a friend's son, about five feet eight and a half inches high, to whom a complete Flying Corps outfit would be most acceptable, and sent his gardener's son down with a barrow to take delivery of it. The cap was hung up in Miss Fowler's bedroom, the belt in Miss Postgate's; for, as Miss Fowler said, they had no desire to make tea-party talk of them.

'That disposes of *that*,' said Miss Fowler. 'I'll leave the rest to you, Mary. I can't run up and down the garden. You'd better take the big clothes-basket and get Nellie to help you.'

'I shall take the wheel-barrow and do it myself,' said Mary, and for once in her life closed her mouth.

Miss Fowler, in moments of irritation, had called Mary deadly methodical. She put on her oldest waterproof and gardening-hat and her ever-slipping goloshes, for the weather was on the edge of more rain. She gathered fire-lighters from the kitchen, a half-scuttle of coals, and a faggot of brushwood. These she wheeled in the barrow down the mossed paths to the dank little laurel shrubbery where the destructor stood under the drip of three oaks. She climbed the wire fence into the Rector's glebe just behind, and from his tenant's rick pulled two large armfuls of good hay, which she spread neatly on the fire-bars. Next, journey by journey, passing Miss Fowler's white face at the morning-room window each time, she brought down in the towel-covered clothes-basket, on the wheelbarrow, thumbed and used Hentys, Marryats, Levers, Stevensons, Baroness Orczys, Garvices, schoolbooks, and atlases, unrelated piles of the *Motor Cyclist*, the *Light Car*, and catalogues of Olympia Exhibitions; the remnants of a fleet of sailing-ships from ninepenny cutters to a three-guinea yacht; a prep.-school dressing-gown; bats from three-and-sixpence to twenty-four shillings; cricket and tennis balls; disintegrated steam and clockwork locomotives with their twisted rails; a grey and red tin model of a submarine; a dumb gramophone and cracked records; golf-clubs that had to be broken across the knee, like his walking-sticks, and an assegai; photographs of private and public school cricket and football elevens, and his OTC on the line of march; kodaks, and film-rolls; some pewters, and one real silver cup, for boxing competitions and Junior Hurdles; sheaves of school photographs; Miss Fowler's photograph; her own which he had borne off in fun and (good care she took not to ask!) had never returned; a playbox with a secret drawer; a load of flannels, belts, and jerseys, and a pair of spiked shoes unearthed in the attic; a packet of all the letters that Miss Fowler and she had ever written to him, kept for some absurd reason through all these years; a five-day attempt at a diary; framed pictures of racing motors in full Brooklands career, and load upon load of undistinguishable wreckage of tool-boxes, rabbit-hutches, electric batteries, tin soldiers, fret-saw outfits, and jig-saw puzzles.

Miss Fowler at the window watched her come and go, and said to herself, 'Mary's an old woman. I never realised it before.'

After lunch she recommended her to rest.

'I'm not in the least tired,' said Mary. 'I've got it all arranged. I'm going to the village at two o'clock for some paraffin. Nellie hasn't enough, and the walk will do me good.'

She made one last quest round the house before she started, and found that she had overlooked nothing. It began to mist as soon as she had skirted Vegg's Heath, where Wynn used to descend – it seemed to her that she could almost hear the beat of his propellers overhead, but there was nothing to see. She hoisted her umbrella and lunged into the blind wet till she had reached the shelter of the empty village. As she came out of Mr Kidd's shop with a bottle full of paraffin in her string shopping-bag, she met Nurse Eden, the village nurse, and fell into talk with her, as usual, about the village children. They were just parting opposite the 'Royal Oak,' when a gun, they fancied, was fired immediately behind the house. It was followed by a child's shriek dying into a wail.

'Accident!' said Nurse Eden promptly, and dashed through the empty bar, followed by Mary. They found Mrs Gerritt, the publican's wife, who could only gasp and point to the yard, where a little cart-lodge was sliding sideways amid a clatter of tiles. Nurse Eden snatched up a sheet drying before the fire, ran out, lifted something from the ground, and flung the sheet round it. The sheet turned scarlet and half her uniform too, as she bore the load into the kitchen. It was little Edna Gerritt, aged nine, whom Mary had known since her perambulator days.

'Am I hurted bad?' Edna asked, and died between Nurse Eden's dripping hands. The sheet fell aside and for an instant, before she could shut her eyes, Mary saw the ripped and shredded body.

'It's a wonder she spoke at all,' said Nurse Eden. 'What in God's name was it?'

'A bomb,' said Mary.

'One o' the Zeppelins?'

'No. An aeroplane. I thought I heard it on the Heath, but I fancied it was one of ours. It must have shut off its engines as it came down. That's why we didn't notice it.'

'The filthy pigs!' said Nurse Eden, all white and shaken. 'See the pickle I'm in! Go and tell Dr Hennis, Miss Postgate.' Nurse looked at the mother, who had dropped face down on the floor. 'She's only in a fit. Turn her over.'

Mary heaved Mrs Gerritt right side up, and hurried off for the doctor. When she told her tale, he asked her to sit down in the surgery till he got her something.

'But I don't need it, I assure you,' said she. 'I don't think it would be wise to tell Miss Fowler about it, do you? Her heart is so irritable in this weather.'

Dr Hennis looked at her admiringly as he packed up his bag.

'No. Don't tell anybody till we're sure,' he said, and hastened to the 'Royal Oak,' while Mary went on with the paraffin. The village behind her was as quiet as usual, for the news had not yet spread. She frowned a little to herself, her large nostrils expanded uglily, and from time to time she muttered a phrase which Wynn, who never restrained himself before his women-folk, had applied to the enemy. 'Bloody pagans! They *are* bloody pagans. But,' she continued, falling back on the teaching that had made her what she was, 'one mustn't let one's mind dwell on these things.'

Before she reached the house Dr Hennis, who was also a special constable, overtook her in his car.

'Oh, Miss Postgate,' he said, 'I wanted to tell you that that accident at the "Royal Oak" was due to Gerritt's stable tumbling down. It's been dangerous for a long time. It ought to have been condemned.'

'I thought I heard an explosion too,' said Mary.

'You might have been misled by the beams snapping. I've been looking at 'em. They were dry-rotted through and through. Of course, as they broke, they would make a noise just like a gun.'

'Yes?' said Mary politely.

'Poor little Edna was playing underneath it,' he went on, still holding her with his eyes, 'and that and the tiles cut her to pieces, you see?'

'I saw it,' said Mary, shaking her head. 'I heard it too.'

'Well, we cannot be sure.' Dr Hennis changed his tone completely. 'I know both you and Nurse Eden (I've been speaking to her) are perfectly trustworthy, and I can relay on you not to say anything – yet at least. It is no good to stir up people unless———'

'Oh, I never do – anyhow,' said Mary, and Dr Hennis went on to the county town.

After all, she told herself, it might, just possibly, have been the collapse of the old stable that had done all those things to poor little Edna. She was sorry she had even hinted at other things, but Nurse Eden was discretion itself. By the time she reached home the affair seemed increasingly remote by its very monstrosity. As she came in, Miss Fowler told her that a couple of aeroplanes had passed half an hour ago.

'I thought I heard them,' she replied, 'I'm going down to the garden now. I've got the paraffin.'

'Yes, but – what *have* you got on your boots? They're soaking wet. Change them at once.'

Not only did Mary obey but she wrapped the boots in a newspaper, and put them into the string bag with the bottle. So, armed with the longest kitchen poker, she left.

'It's raining again,' was Miss Fowler's last word, 'but – I know you won't be happy till that's disposed of.'

'It won't take long. I've got everything down there, and I've put the lid on the destructor to keep the wet out.'

The shrubbery was filling with twilight by the time she had completed her arrangements and sprinkled the sacrificial oil. As she lit the match that would burn her heart to ashes, she heard a groan or a grunt behind the dense Portugal laurels.

'Cheape?' she called impatiently, but Cheape, with his ancient lumbago, in his comfortable cottage would be the last man to profane the sanctuary. 'Sheep,' she concluded, and threw in the fusee. The pyre went up in a roar, and the immediate flame hastened night around her.

'How Wynn would have loved this!' she thought, stepping back from the blaze.

By its light she saw, half hidden behind a laurel not five paces away, a bareheaded man sitting very stiffly at the foot of one of the oaks. A broken branch lay across his lap – one booted leg protruding from beneath it. His head moved ceaselessly from side to side, but his body was as still as the tree's trunk. He was dressed – she moved sideways to look more closely – in a uniform something like Wynn's, with a flap buttoned across the chest.

For an instant, she had some idea that it might be one of the young flying men she had met at the funeral. But their heads were dark and glossy. This man's was as pale as a baby's, and so closely cropped that she could see the disgusting pinky skin beneath. His lips moved.

'What do you say?' Mary moved towards him and stopped.

'Laty! Laty! Laty!' he muttered, while his hands picked at the dead wet leaves. There was no doubt as to his nationality. It made her so angry that she strode back to the destructor, though it was still too hot to use the poker there. Wynn's books seemed to be catching well. She looked up at the oak behind the man; several of the light upper and two or three rotten lower branches had broken and scattered their rubbish on the shrubbery path. On the lowest fork a helmet with dependent strings, showed like a bird's-nest in the light of a long-tongued flame. Evidently this person had fallen through the tree. Wynn had told her that it was quite possible for people to fall out of aeroplanes. Wynn told her too, that trees were useful things to break an aviator's fall, but in this case the aviator must have been broken or he would have moved from his queer position. He seemed helpless except for his horrible rolling head. On the other hand, she could see a pistol case at his belt – and Mary loathed pistols. Months ago, after reading certain Belgian reports together, she and Miss Fowler had had dealings with one – a huge revolver with flat-nosed bullets, which latter, Wynn said, were forbidden by the rules of war to be used against civilized enemies. 'They're good enough for us,' Miss Fowler had replied. 'Show Mary how it works.' And Wynn, laughing at the mere possibility of any such need, had led the craven winking Mary into the Rector's disused quarry, and had shown her how to fire the terrible machine. It lay now in the top-left-hand drawer of her toilet-table – a memento not included in the burning. Wynn would be pleased to see how she was not afraid.

She slipped up to the house to get it. When she came through the rain, the eyes in the head were alive with expectation. The mouth even tried to smile. But at the sight of the revolver its corners went down just like Edna Gerritt's. A tear trickled from one eye, and the head rolled from shoulder to shoulder as though trying to point out something.

'Cassée. Tout cassée,' it whimpered.

'What do you say?' said Mary disgustedly, keeping well to one side, though only the head moved.

'Cassée,' it repeated. 'Che me rends. Le médicin! Toctor!'

'Nein!' said she, bringing all her small German to bear with the big pistol. 'Ich haben der todt Kinder gesehn.'

The head was still. Mary's hand dropped. She had been careful to keep her finger off the trigger for fear of accidents. After a few moments' waiting, she returned to the destructor, where the flames were falling, and churned up Wynn's charring books with the poker. Again the head groaned for the doctor.

'Stop that!' said Mary, and stamped her foot. 'Stop that, you bloody pagan!'

The words came quite smoothly and naturally. They were Wynn's own words, and Wynn was a gentleman who for no consideration on earth would have torn little Edna into those vividly coloured strips and strings. But this thing hunched under the oak-tree had done that thing. It was no question of reading horrors out of newspapers to Miss Fowler. Mary had seen it with her own eyes on the 'Royal Oak' kitchen table. She must not allow her mind to dwell upon it. Now Wynn was dead, and everything connected with him was lumping and rustling and tinkling under her busy poker into red black dust and grey leaves of ash. The thing beneath the oak would die too. Mary had seen death more than once. She came of a family that had a knack of dying under, as she told Miss Fowler, 'most distressing circumstances.' She would stay where she was till she was entirely satisfied that It was dead – dead as dear papa in the late 'eighties; aunt Mary in 'eighty-nine; mamma in 'ninety-one; cousin Dick in 'ninety-five; Lady McCausland's housemaid in 'ninety-nine; Lady McCausland's sister in nineteen hundred and one; Wynn buried five days ago; and Edna Gerritt still waiting for decent earth to hide her. As she thought – her underlip caught up by one faded canine, brows knit and nostrils wide – she wielded the poker with lunges that jarred the grating at the bottom, and careful scrapes round the brick-work above. She looked at her wrist-watch. It was getting on to half-past four, and the rain was coming down in earnest. Tea would be at five. If It did not die before that time, she would be soaked and would have to change. Meantime, and this occupied her, Wynn's things were burning well in spite of the hissing wet, though now and again a book-back with a quite distinguishable title would be heaved up out of the mass. The exercise of stoking had given her a glow which seemed to reach to the marrow of her bones. She hummed – Mary never had a voice – to herself. She had never believed in all those advanced views – though Miss Fowler herself leaned a little that way – of woman's work in the world; but now she saw there was much to be said for them. This, for instance, was *her* work – work which no man, least of all Dr Hennis, would ever have done. A man, at such a crisis, would be what Wynn called a 'sportsman'; would leave everything to fetch help, and would certainly bring It into the house. Now a woman's business was to make a happy home for – for a husband and children. Failing these – it was not a thing one should allow one's mind to dwell upon – but——

'Stop it!' Mary cried once more across the shadows. 'Nein, I tell you! Ich haben der todt Kinder gesehn.'

But it was a fact. A woman who had missed these things could still be useful – more useful than a man in certain respects. She thumped like a pavior through the settling ashes at the secret thrill of it. The rain was damping the fire, but she could feel – it was too dark to see – that her work was done. There was a dull red glow at the bottom of the destructor, not enough to char the wooden lid if she slipped it half over against the driving wet. This arranged, she leaned on the poker and waited, while an increasing rapture laid hold on her. She ceased to think. She gave herself up to feel. Her long pleasure was broken by a sound that she had waited for in agony several times in her life. She leaned forward and listened, smiling. There could be no mistake. She closed her eyes and drank it in. Once it ceased abruptly.

'Go on,' she murmured, half aloud. 'That isn't the end.'

Then the end came very distinctly in a lull between two rain-gusts. Mary Postgate drew her breath short between her teeth and shivered from head to foot. '*That's* all right,' said she contentedly, and went up to the house, where she scandalized the whole routine by taking a luxurious hot bath before tea, and came down looking, as Miss Fowler said when she saw her lying all relaxed on the other sofa, 'quite handsome!'

The Cradle Demon
R. CHETWYND-HAYES

THEY BROUGHT HIM BACK from the christening, placed him with all the reverence that is due to the first-born in the blue-lined cot, then looked down upon him with moist, fond eyes.

'Isn't he sweet!' exclaimed the young mother, whose carefully prepared plans for no family before thirty had somehow gone awry. 'Isn't he perfect?'

'He's all right,' said the young father complacently. 'I've seen worse.'

The young mother slapped her spouse with playful coyness.

'Listen to you! Who was up all last night because he sneezed once? A teeny-weasy little sneeze.'

'I was afraid he might keep me awake.'

The young mother bent down and tucked the blue blanket more firmly round Adam Paul Tom O'Malley Jones's minute body, then caressed his near bald head.

'Look at his eyes! I ask you, have you *ever* seen the like? He looks so intelligent, one could swear he knows what I'm talking about. Yes, he does. Ickle didums-didums knows what Mummy is talking about. Yes, he does.'

'Very unlikely,' his father remarked with irritating commonsense. 'After all, he's only six weeks old.'

'That's what you think, know-all. Anyone that's not blind can see he's very exceptional.'

The young father put his head on to one side and surveyed his son and heir with thoughtful interest.

'Perhaps you're right,' he agreed. 'He does rather favour me.'

Adam Paul Tom O'Malley Jones – for It had accepted the name which the creatures had bestowed upon It – gazed up at his adopted parents, but did not bother to probe their brains. He had already done so. Whatever knowledge they contained had been his since the second day after the birth of his flesh and blood vessel. He recognized that both the female and the male were important to his well-being during the formative years, but later he would be able to absorb them and discard their husks. In the meanwhile he must listen, watch, add to his growing fund of knowledge, and most important, adapt the flesh and blood vessel to his particular needs.

He had already begun work on the tiny brain. Under the pressure of his will, every minute cell was emerging into pulsating life and was in turn sending its stream of commands along every nerve link in the body. In a few weeks the vocal cords would be fully active, the eyes capable of long and short sight, the ears attuned to hear over large distances.

Others of his kind had drifted up from the lower planes and taken over flesh and blood vessels, but they had always been fully mature ones. In consequence, the brains had broken down under the sudden influx of power, or the hearts had not been able to cope with the changing body patterns, and the result had been disaster. But he was in on the ground floor. Soon he would be able to enjoy all fleshy appetites to the full.

Eating ... drinking ... and ...

Mavis Thurlow was seventeen, healthy of body, pretty of face, and simple of mind. She lived in a world made up of circles and squares. The Jones's for example were square, otherwise why would they have green wallpaper and a collection of Bing Crosby records? She felt rather sorry for them. Mavis, of course, was distinctly round. She liked ugly boys, off-beat music, not wearing a bra, chamber-pots with plants in them, and work which required the smallest possible effort for the largest return. Baby-sitting seemed to fit under that category.

She was seated in the Jones's most comfortable armchair, aimlessly watching their colour television (with the sound turned off) and sipping from a cup of their tea, while a plate of their ham sandwiches sat on a conveniently nearby table awaiting her pleasure and inclination. The baby – the sole object of Mavis's comfortable sitting – was in its cot, which had been brought down to the lounge so that she would not be forced to ascend the stairs.

It was without doubt a round baby. It did not howl, demand a napkin change, insist on being rocked, cuddled or any other failing that square babies are heir to. On the other hand, it did not crow, gurgle, kick its legs up and down or toss its rattle on the floor, and therefore merited the added appellation of Weird-baby.

When Mavis had eaten the Jones's sandwiches, she decided that it might be as well if she at least took a brief look at her charge. She got up, ambled across the room and peered into the cot. As babies went, it did seem to be a reasonable enough looking specimen. Mavis was at an age when she appreciated the sowing, without being particularly enamoured over the harvest. It was lying flat on its back with wide open eyes, and not a muscle twitched or a finger moved. For a moment Mavis wondered if it were dead.

'Hey!' she prodded the flat little stomach gingerly. 'Are you all right?'

The head jerked round, a pair of dark and strangely intense eyes stared at her, then the lips parted and baby grinned. It could not under any circumstances be classified as a smile. It was a horrible, leering grin that bared a row of pink gums, from which sprouted one or two minute teeth. Neither could the accompanying expression be dismissed as an infantile beam of goodwill. Mavis had seen it only too often before. Only then it had been on the faces of middle-aged gentlemen with young ideas. She said, 'Oh, my Gawd!' and retreated to her armchair with all the speed of a Red Riding Hood who has spotted a particularly well-toothed wolf.

After a while she gathered together her meagre stock of reasoning power and came to the conclusion she had been a 'nit'. After all, the little weirdie wasn't more than eighteen months old, and even if it were rounder than a blood-orange, it couldn't possibly be on the rampage at that age. After one or two anxious glances at the cot, she fumbled in her large and with-it bag and produced a copy of *Sex and How to Enjoy It* which entertained and instructed her for the next ten minutes.

Then she yawned, stretched and was about to get up and switch the television over to another channel, when her bored glance alighted to the cot. Baby was sitting up and staring at her.

True, he no longer grinned. But there was a cold, calculating scrutiny; the dark little eyes glittered like chips of ice in yellow moonlight and the tiny pink-tipped hands opened and closed as they clawed at the rumpled bed-clothes. Mavis made a funny little noise when the small figure swung its pudgy legs over the cot edge, then slid easily to the floor. It came trotting to her. Not crawling, not lurching from one leg to another, neither did it actually run – but came forward with an awful little jogging trot.

It reached her legs, which she kicked outwards in an automatic effort to push it away, and this made a kind of ramp for the diminutive arms to grasp, the legs to straddle; and up it came – gripping, wriggling, the face set in a frown of concentrated effort, the tiny throat contorting like an overworked concertina and sending out little, rasping cries.

Presently Baby was on Mavis's lap where, having reached this elevated platform, it immediately began a programme of investigation. One dimpled paw ripped her green shirt, and red-glass buttons flew across the room and landed on the carpet like a shower of blood-tinted hailstones. A petrified Mavis withdrew her allegiance to the Women's Liberation Movement when the shirt was pulled open and Baby took note of what lay therein. It was not until her limp hand was seized and her little finger pushed back by a grip of steel, that movement returned to her paralysed body.

She screamed very loudly, and flung the – once again – grinning infant from her. It seemed to bounce on the carpet, rolled over, then with one liquid movement, came up onto its feet. The round face was now a mask of naked, burning hate, and the rosebud mouth opened as a harsh, almost croaking voice said, 'You bloody bitch! I'll make you sing.'

It was then that Mavis remembered that legs could be useful as well as decorative, for she sprang up from her chair and ran for the door with even greater speed than on the memorable occasion when her mother's lodger had made known his intentions in the front parlour. Of course there was trouble with the door handle and she lost a few feet of essential lead, but the sound of a little croak of triumph soon enabled her to go all out for a record sprint once the door condescended to open. The rapid patter of pursuing feet was within a hand's length of her nylon-clad legs when she saw the open dining-room door, and such are the brain-alerting results of terror, she was inside the room and had the door slammed before the infant hunter had time to change its direction.

There was no key in the lock but Mavis made good use of two chairs, reinforced by a heavy bookcase that normally she would not have been able to move.

The sounds that came from beyond the barricaded door were not at all reassuring. Kicking, pounding, scratching, interposed with shrieks of baffled rage, were answered by Mavis's terrified whimpers, and she might well have done something so square as to faint if the sound of the key being inserted in the front door had not come as a reprieve. Instantly Baby ceased its door pounding activities and a wonderful blessed silence temporarily descended on to the house. Mavis sank down on to the floor and had a good cry.

The united efforts of the young parents finally broke through the barricade, and voices that carried a tone of both anger and alarm brought Mavis to the stage of explanation.

'The baby!' she exclaimed. 'It can walk – and talk.'

'There,' the young mother said, 'didn't I say he was exceptional? Fifteen months, three weeks, two days, and five hours old, and he can walk and talk.'

'He certainly shows promise,' the young father admitted. 'But that doesn't explain why our son was left all alone, while this stupid girl shuts herself up in the dining-room.'

'Indeed it doesn't.' The mother glared at the weeping Mavis. 'We are waiting for an explanation.'

'He got out of his cot ... did awful things to me ... swore at me ... then chased me along the passage ... and I did not dare come out.' She raised an appealing face to the young father, who was not unmindful of her gaping shirt-front. 'I am sure he meant to do something absolutely dreadful.'

For a while shocked silence prevailed, then the young mother expressed an opinion.

'Drugs! She's been taking some awful stuff. I really think it's too bad. I blame you, David, for not making more searching enquiries into her background.'

The young father assumed an expression of hurt dignity.

'Now really, Doris, that is going too far. How was I to know the girl was on the hard stuff? She looked all right.'

Anger was driving fear into temporary retirement and Mavis loudly proclaimed her innocence.

'Who are you calling a druggie? I've never touched the stuff and I'll have my dad on you if you say I did. I tell you that kid attacked me. It can belt along like a bloody greyhound. It's a monster.'

The young mother became as an outraged manufacturer whose product had been slandered. 'How dare you! My child is the sweetest, the most most wonderful baby that's ever been. Don't stand there, David – say something.'

The young father decided to be reasonable. He prided himself on this ability. 'Now, Mavis, I'll tell you what we're going to do. You are coming with me – with us – into the lounge, and you're going to take a long look at our son ...'

'Not on your nelly ...'

'Look at our son and then ask yourself if he could possibly be – what you said he was. Okay?'

Mavis gave the matter some little thought.

'You will stand between me and him?'

'If you insist – yes.'

Mavis nodded and wiped away the last lingering tear.

'All right. Then you'll see – and hear – for yourself.'

They went into the lounge and approached the cot. Fond parents looked down at that which they had produced. Mavis addressed her would-be ravisher. 'Now, you little basket – did you, or did you not, chase me into the dining-room?'

Baby looked up at her with his innocent blue-eyed, smiled a sweet, angelic smile and gave utterance.

'Glug ... glug ... glug ...'

'Oh, he can talk!' simpered the young mother.

'He's coming along,' admitted the young father.

Baby decided to give them a bonus.

'Mum ... ma. Mum ... ma.'

For a moment it seemed as if the young mother might be due for a severe attack of convulsions. She clasped her hands, wriggled her hips, gasped, all but choked, then managed to transform joy into a few words. 'David, did you hear? He called me ... mumma!'

'It certainly sounded like it,' the young father agreed.

'Now what have you to say for yourself?' the young mother asked Mavis.

'He's having you on. He's evil, I tell you. When he grows up, he'll be a sex murderer – or something.'

The baby said, 'Glug ... glug ...', in a most agreeable manner.

'I wouldn't be at all surprised,' Mavis went on, ignoring the young mother's shriek of rage, 'if he doesn't take people over and make them do terrible things, like in the film *The Horror From Down Below.*'

The baby's chortles grew into a croon of delight.

All this was too much for the young mother, for she broke down and had to be led over to a sofa by her husband, who did his best to console her by comforting words and rye whisky. Mavis, who dimly realized that square minds are not good receptacles for round truths, was about to explain what she meant and how she should have said it, when her attention was attracted by the baby. He raised his little head and whispered in a low, but perfectly audible croak: 'You wait until I'm a little bigger. I'll come looking for you, and then...'

The sentences lapsed into a horrible gurgling chuckle, that excited an already overheated imagination, and created the suspicion that Baby was not a maker of empty promises. Without waiting to finish her scream, Mavis sped for the door and did not stop running until she was safely at home, explaining her adventures to an extremely incredulous mother.

The young parents did not speak for some time after Mavis's abrupt departure, until the young father said: 'I think you're right, dear. Dope without a doubt.'

'You can't deceive a mother,' his wife commented complacently. 'But never again must we trust our precious to a stranger.'

'I suppose not,' said the young father reflectively. 'Pity, we have to go out sometime.'

Suddenly the young mother sat up and assumed the expression of a Newton who has just remembered why the apple fell. 'My young niece! Educated in a convent, never been out with a boy in her life, and hasn't taken so much as an aspirin. Let's invite her over. She can spend the summer with us.'

Her husband tried to show enthusiasm. 'Yes, it's an idea. Pretty enough. Certainly willing. Loves children. But she doesn't move very fast.'

'She can't help that, darling,' the young mother protested. 'The psychiatrist explained she has a mental block that won't allow her to run.'

'But she'd lose out even if a snail was chasing her.'

'Never mind, all she will have to do is sit next to Baby and keep an eye on him.'

The young father surrendered. He always did. He got up and moved towards the telephone. 'I'll give her mother a ring.'

In the cot Baby's eyes glittered like hot coals as he crushed his rattle between the thumb and forefinger of his left hand.

The Horror of Abbot's Grange

FREDERICK COWLES

IT WAS JOAN WHO FELL IN LOVE with Abbot's Grange. I must confess that, from the first, I thought the place had a brooding and sinister air about it.

For three months we had been house-hunting, and then a chance visit to Ritton had led to the discovery of the Grange. As far as country houses go it was perfect. It had been erected in the fifteenth century by the Cistercian monks of Ritton Abbey, and a tiny detached chapel was a relic of the monastic days. Yet, in spite of the fact that Joan was mad about it, I did not like the place.

The next day we sought out the estate agent, and he willingly agreed to conduct us over the house. It turned out to be the property of Lord Salton, and it was his desire to let the place furnished. That suited us as, being birds of passage, we had no furniture of our own.

It was not a large house, but the rooms were spacious. The entrance hall was really quite palatial and hung with paintings of the dead and gone Saltons. I examined the portraits whilst the agent was revealing the charms of the Grange to Joan.

They were not a very imposing lot, those Saltons of the past. One was a bishop, looking very uncomfortable in his robes; another a general, mounted on a weird-looking charger. Not one of them really interested me until I came upon a dingy painting hung in a dark corner near the stairs.

It represented a tall, sallow-featured man, dressed in sombre garments of early sixteenth-century style. His face was thin and brooding and strangely pale, but the lips were intensely red and were drawn back to show white, fang-like teeth. The whole expression was one of diabolical cruelty, and I shuddered involuntarily as I looked at it.

An inscription in the right-hand corner of the painting caught my eye. The writing was rather faded, but I was just able to make out the words: 'William Salton, pxt. 1572', and below, in rather brighter colours, was a small cross and the sentence: 'Seeking whom he may devour. God frustrate him always.'

Joan and the agent returned just then, and I called their attention to the portrait. It may have been my imagination, but I thought a shade of fear passed over the man's face. I asked him who the sinister gentleman was, and, with some slight show of reluctance, he answered: 'That is a picture of the first Lord Salton. He is said to have been a monk at Ritton Abbey, but they turned him out. At the dissolution he revenged himself upon the community by giving evidence against them. Many of the monks were executed, and as a reward William Salton was made Lord Salton, and this house was given to him.'

'How exciting,' exclaimed Joan. 'He looks just the sort of person to do a thing like that. We really must have this house, Michael. It is just what we have been looking for.'

When Joan makes up her mind there is no gainsaying her. Within an hour I had paid a deposit, signed the lease, and received the keys of Abbot's Grange.

As he handed the keys over to me the agent pointed out an exceptionally large one, and said: 'This, sir, is the key of the chapel. It has been closed for nearly three hundred years, and Lord Salton particularly requests that you will not enter the place. If you should feel you want to visit it go in the daytime, and be sure to lock the door when you leave. *On no account allow the door to be unlocked between dusk and daybreak.*'

'But,' I exclaimed, 'that is a curious condition. What is the reason for it?'

The agent's face was blank as he answered: 'I do not know, sir. Those are Lord Salton's instructions to me.' With that I had to be content, although I felt that the man could have told more if he had cared to.

Three weeks later, with a staff engaged by Joan and my sister, we took up residence at Abbot's Grange.

Of course Joan had to have a house-warming party. By making up extra beds on sofas and floors we managed to invite about twenty people down. Then there were a few local residents, such as the vicar and the doctor, who were asked to dinner.

Before the meal I was standing in front of the fire in the hall. The others were all dressing, and there was only a dim light burning on the staircase. I was thinking how impressive the place looked when, quite suddenly, somebody switched on all the lights. It was the butler taking some glasses to the dining-room.

'Good lord, man,' I shouted, 'why on earth did you switch all those lights on like that?'

He looked rather confused, and then he blurted out: 'I always do it, sir. None of us will come into the hall after dark unless the lights are full on.'

'What on earth is there to be frightened of here?' I stormed. 'You must be like a lot of children afraid of the dark.'

The man's voice was apologetic as he replied: 'It isn't that, sir. It's that painting under the stairs. His eyes seem to follow you about.'

I glanced over at the portrait of the first Lord Salton, and, whether it was a trick of the artist or a trick of the light, the eyes certainly did seem to glare out of the canvas. They almost seemed to be illuminated by an uncanny glow.

The butler stood expecting a further reprimand when the vicar was announced. The clergyman turned out to be quite an affable little man, the usual type of country parson, but endowed with more brains than most. We discussed the weather, the political situation, and a few other minor things. Then I asked him if he knew anything about the first Lord Salton.

'Quite enough to make me detest him,' he replied. 'He was a hateful type. A man who became a Cistercian monk, and then gave information against the abbot and brethren.'

'Wasn't he turned out of the Abbey long before the suppression?' I inquired.

'Yes. He was accused of practising black magic and they expelled him from the Order. I think the details are given in a manuscript that used to be in the library. If you like we will look and see if it is still there.'

I readily agreed, and we were just moving off when the gong went and the guests began to come down for dinner. So we had to postpone our visit to the library.

The meal was quite a jolly function. As usual, Joan had managed to assemble quite a distinguished and interesting company. There was Vincent Dunn, the actor; Rita Young, the film star; Edmund Morton, the novelist; Malcolm Dale, the explorer; and a host of other celebrities of one sort or another. And they were all quite human, which says a lot for Joan's taste. It was Morton who asked about the chapel, and I had to tell them all about the conditions relating to it.

'And have you been inside yet?' asked Dale.

'Not I,' I replied. 'I put the key in the Chinese vase in the hall and there it stays until my lease is up.'

They all seemed to think it very jolly to have a private chapel, and the possibility of it being haunted was freely discussed. Then the talk drifted round to plays and films, and the chapel was forgotten – at least I thought it was.

There was dancing in the hall afterwards, and as soon as we could reasonably do so, the vicar and I slipped off to the library.

He found the book without any trouble. It was a musty, calf-bound volume filled with crabbed handwriting. It seemed to be a catalogue of the pictures in the hall, with some biographical notes, and the first person mentioned was William Salton. The following is the extract relating to him:

William Salton born 1501. Entered the Abbey of Our Lady of

Ritton 1522. Accused of practising witchcraft, sorcery and black magic, and expelled from the monastery in 1530. In 1539 gave evidence before the commissioners against the abbot and community, which resulted in the abbot and six of the brethren being condemned to death. Evidence afterwards proved to be false, but Salton was made Lord Salton and received the Abbey Grange. Lived the life of a recluse, and commonly believed to have been a wizard and a vampire. Died in 1597, and buried in the private chapel of Abbot's Grange. No priest would perform the burial-rites, and he was interred without prayer or ceremony.

Then, in another hand, followed a later entry:

On the 16th day of May 1640 the tomb of William Lord Salton was sealed by me, John Rogers, clerk in holy orders. Let none loose the chapel door between sunset and sunrise lest, perchance, he come abroad again seeking whom he may devour. God frustrate him always.

'What does that mean?' I asked.

'Well,' answered the parson, 'I should say that the first Lord Salton could not rest in his grave, and John Rogers was called in to lay his unquiet spirit.'

An argument on ghosts seemed to be impending when Malcolm Dale burst into the room. I have never seen a man looking so utterly terrified. He sank into a chair, asked for a drink, and gulped down the brandy I handed to him. It was some time before he could speak coherently, but, at last, he managed to blurt out his story.

It appeared that the mention of the chapel had fired his curiosity, and that, when the dancing was well on the go, he had taken the key from the vase and had gone out to investigate. He took an electric flash-light with him, but had some difficulty in unlocking the door. The keyhole, he declared, was filled with rubbish, and he had to scrape it clean with his pocket-knife. As last he got the key in, and then it wouldn't turn. So he went over to the garage and got a spanner. With this he managed to twist the key in the lock. The rest of the story shall be told in his own words.

'When I got into the place I noticed at once how intensely cold it was, even colder than most old churches. My light was just enough for me to see that there were no seats in the building, and precious little else. I had almost decided to go out again when I noticed a sort of table tomb near the east end, and so went up to examine it. Suddenly, without any warning, it seemed to crack, and out of it sprang the figure of a man with a deadly white face and long, sharp teeth. He glared at me for a moment, and I saw the beam of my light reflect redly in his eyes. Then I turned tail and fled, but, all the way back, I felt that he was after me.'

His voice rose to a scream as he came to the end of his tale, and I could see that he was all in.

'Then you left the chapel door open?' asked the vicar.

Dale nodded dumbly as if he dared not trust himself to speak.

'God frustrate him,' the parson murmured, and then, springing to his feet, he said to me: 'Come. There is not a moment to be lost. We must go over and lock the door.'

I seized the torch which Dale still held, and within a few minutes we had reached the chapel. It looked quiet and desolate enough, but the vicar insisted on entering and seeing the tomb. It was quite an ordinary table tomb of white marble, but the top of it was cracked right across, and it was easy to see that *the crack was newly made.*

The parson crossed himself, and together we left the building, swung the ponderous door shut and locked it. We did not speak as we returned to the house.

We got Dale to bed without letting any other members of the party suspect that anything was wrong. He was in a blue funk, and I was nearly as bad. When the vicar suggested that I should give him a shake-down in my room and let him stay the night I almost embraced him.

Well, dancing went on until about half-past one, and by two o'clock everybody had gone to bed. The vicar (whose name, by the way, was Parker) went round the house with me, and we saw that all windows and doors were secured. Wolf, the Alsatian, we brought into the hall, and left him comfortably settled in front of the fire. Then we went upstairs, and, in spite of the excitement, I, for one, was soon asleep.

It must have been about three o'clock when I was suddenly awakened by the howling of the dog. Parker was already astir. 'Did you hear that?' he whispered.

Again it came – not an ordinary howl, but a howl of sheer terror. It was a sound that seemed to freeze the blood in my veins, and made my hair literally stand on end. Then came a shriek of horrible laughter that was even more nerve-racking.

'Come along,' said Parker, 'we must see what is wrong,' and he made for the door.

I slipped into a dressing-gown and followed him, although, I must confess, I would have preferred to have stayed in my room with the door locked.

The landing was dark, except for the pale light of the moon filtering through the leaded windows, and the electric-light switch was at the head of the stairs. Before we could reach it Parker suddenly gripped my arm and whispered: 'Look! Just beyond that suit of armour.' I looked to the spot he indicated. At first only a shadow was visible, and then, gradually appearing out of the darkness, I made out a white, grinning face – the features of the first Lord Salton. Even as I looked the figure moved and glided away down the staircase.

I was badly shaken, but Parker, who seemed to possess nerves of steel, bounded over to the switch and flooded the staircase with light. There was nothing to be seen, but, in a wave, a deadly, sickening smell came up the stairs to us. It was the fetid odour of corruption, a nauseating, vile stink that made me feel ill.

Parker led the way down the staircase, and at once turned all the lights on in the hall. I noticed that his lips were moving in prayer, and beads of perspiration stood on his brow. The place was empty and it was some minutes before we saw the dog. Poor Wolf was lying near the door, and he was quite dead. Somehow the body seemed shrunken, although, when we examined it, the only marks we could find were two tiny wounds in the throat.

'Doesn't he look to you as if he has shrunk?' I asked Parker.

'Yes,' he replied. 'Every drop of blood has been drained from his body.'

At that moment a voice came from the top of the stairs. 'Is anything wrong, sir?' It was the butler, and he was shaking with fright.

'Come down, man,' I called, and then turned back to the dog.

'We are up against a——' began Parker, and then he was interrupted by a terrified scream. We jumped up at once and there was the butler, gibbering like a maniac, at the foot of the stairs.

'Be quiet,' hissed. Parker, crossing the hall.

'Look! Look!' wailed the man. His quivering finger pointed towards the picture of the first Lord Salton, but there was no picture in the frame. The canvas was blank.

It is difficult to write of those three hours before daybreak. We sat together in the library, and prayed for the dawn. It found us wild-eyed, and white-faced.

When it was quite light, Parker said: 'I must see that picture again.'

We followed him out into the hall, and there was the portrait of William Lord Salton leering at us from its frame. It was only a painting (we touched it to see), but the eyes glowed with a hellish fire, and the cruel lips seemed twisted in a triumphant smile.

Back in the library we sat down to discuss our plan of action. The butler, his name was Clarke, took things quite well, and Parker included him in the discussion.

'It all seems too terrible to be true,' I said. 'What can we do?'

'Well,' replied Parker, 'I am going to make a suggestion. I have a friend, a Benedictine monk at Fairly Abbey. He happens to be an expert on occult matters, and has often been brought up against queer things. I wonder if you would allow me to invite him over?'

Naturally I agreed at once, and Parker telephoned to the Abbey, which was only about five miles from Ritton. He gave no particulars over the line, but I heard him assuring the priest that it was 'something of vital and terrible importance'.

'Good,' he said, as he laid the receiver down. 'Father Vincent will be over about ten o'clock.'

After that we went upstairs to dress and freshen ourselves up. Clarke saw to the removal of the body of the dog before any of the guests came down, and breakfast was almost a jolly meal. Most of the visitors left soon after nine, but Dale and Morton were staying on until the week-end.

Punctually at ten o'clock Father Vincent was announced and joined the vicar and myself in the library. He was a quiet little man, with twinkling brown eyes shining behind thick spectacles. Anyone less like a ghost-hunter it would be difficult to imagine.

Parker told him all that had happened since Dale had unlocked the chapel, and Clarke was called in to confirm the part about the portrait. The monk asked a few questions, and then he said: 'I may as well tell you that you are up against a most hellish thing – a man who should have died over three hundred years ago, and yet, by devilish arts, has kept his evil mind alive within the tomb.'

He went on to suggest that Joan, Dale, and Morton be taken into our confidence, and asked to help if necessary. I was a little doubtful about frightening Joan, but Father Vincent soon convinced me that it would be unwise to leave her in ignorance. So we asked the three of them to come down to the library.

Dale, with his experience of the previous night fresh in his mind, was easily convinced; Morton and Joan were frankly incredulous but, I could see, our seriousness impressed them.

It was finally decided that the Benedictine should return to his abbey for some things he required, and then stay the night with us.

'If it is what I suspect I shall have to ask you to get in touch with Lord Salton,' he said. 'But we can leave that until tomorrow.'

'A wonderful man,' remarked Parker, when the monk had gone. 'These Roman priests are the only chaps who understand anything about occult phenomena. I take off my hat to them when it comes to a real tussle with the Devil.'

Lunch was a quiet meal, and, afterwards, Morton and Joan played tennis, and Dale, Parker, and I went over to the chapel. The key turned quite easily in the lock, and the interior did not look at all sinister in the bright light of the afternoon sun.

It was quite an interesting little building, dating, I should say, mostly from the middle fifteenth century. Some fragments of good stained glass remained in the windows, there was a stone altar, a few benches, and the marble table tomb.

Whilst we were looking round Father Vincent joined us.

'I have just arrived,' he exclaimed, 'and they told me you were here, so I thought I would stroll down and look over the place.'

We showed him the crack in the tomb, and he agreed that it was certainly new. He also pointed out a number of dark stains on the flat top of the monument, and it was not long before he discovered similar stains on the stone slab of the altar.

'What do you make of them?' asked Parker.

'They look to me like bloodstains,' answered the priest. 'It is a horrible thought but, if they are, something has been killed on this altar. You notice how the stain runs down the side, just as if the blood of a victim has dropped from the slab to the floor.'

Clarke met us, as we were returning to the house, with the news that one of the parlour-maids had been found in the hall in a dead faint. On recovering she had declared that she was going upstairs when a man dressed in black, with a deathly white face, had pounced out at her.

We interviewed the girl and she not only stuck to her story, but also avowed that she could still feel the grip of his cold fingers on her wrist.

At dinner we were a very dull company in spite of the little priest's efforts to keep us amused. Afterwards we all went along to the library, and Joan, Parker, Morton, and Dale made up a four for bridge, whilst Father Vincent and I settled down to talk and smoke. I never knew that a monk could be such good company. He seemed to have travelled all over the world, and had a fund of excellent stories about all manner of places and all sorts of people.

The time passed pleasantly enough until about eleven o'clock when Clarke came in with the whisky. I remember that he was just squirting the soda into Parker's drink when, eerie and shrill, a burst of wicked laughter echoed through the house.

For a moment or so none moved, then the priest sprang to his feet and rushed out into the hall. We were not slow to follow him. Instinctively our first glance was towards the portrait of William Salton. Only a blank canvas filled the frame: the figure had gone.

'I don't think the servants will come to any harm,' said the priest later on. 'He will hardly go into the new wing of the house.'

We had sent Joan off to bed, and Father Vincent had carefully fastened a crucifix to the door of her room, and sprinkled the threshold with holy water. The rest of us, including Clarke the butler, had agreed to keep watch in the hall.

The monk had made us sit in a semi-circle round the fire. All around he had sprinkled his holy water, and on the mantelpiece he had lighted two blessed candles. He himself took up a position near the fireplace.

'It is as well for you to know what you are up against,' he went on. 'This William Salton, however melodramatic it may sound, undoubtedly sold his soul to the Devil. Unholy sacrifices were offered by him in the chapel, and, after death, there was no rest for him in the grave. He became what we call a vampire. Evidently the portrait is connected with him in some very intimate way, and he can, by some fell means, animate the painted figure for his own ends.

'Around you I have sprinkled holy water, blessed with the rites of Holy Church, and I want no one to pass beyond that circle until the portrait is back in its frame.'

'You think it will return, then?' asked Morton.

'It must return,' was the reply. 'You', the monk went on, turning to me, 'must watch the frame very carefully and let us know if you see anything out of the ordinary. I want Mr Parker to keep an eye on the staircase, Mr Dale to watch the door, and Mr Morton to keep the passage to the kitchens under observation.'

We sat there smoking in silence. The priest had his Breviary and was reading his Office, and Parker idly turned the pages of a magazine. Then, without any warning, the place seemed to go very cold, and again came that rotten odour of decay.

Father Vincent motioned us to remain still, and I could see that his lips were moving rapidly in prayer. Suddenly the candle-flames flickered, and changed to a peculiar shade of blue.

It was getting too much for us. Our nerves were all keyed up to breaking-pitch, and I was not surprised to hear Dale move his chair, and notice him throw his head back in a queer way he had. What followed is too horrible to think about. There came a sickening sucking sound, poor Dale screamed, and I had a vague vision of two fang-like teeth at his throat.

It was all over in a moment. We jumped up, and, as we did so, there came that peal of wicked laughter again. We looked towards the picture: the figure was there once more.

Dale was unconscious, and the others carried him up to his room whilst I telephoned for the doctor.

'Better not say too much to the medico,' said Parker. 'He wouldn't understand.'

'I wonder exactly what did happen,' remarked Morton.

'I think poor Dale pushed his chair back and got his head beyond the circle of holy water,' answered Father Vincent.

We waited up in Dale's room for the doctor to come, and, as soon as we heard the sound of his car in the drive, Clarke went to let him in. He was a fussy little man, and cleared us all out of the room whilst he made his

THE HORROR OF ABBOT'S GRANGE

examination.

He was soon out again. His brow was crinkled in a puzzled frown, and he inquired at once how it had happened.

'We were sitting in the hall,' I replied, 'and he suddenly went off – just a gasp, and then he was unconscious.'

'Just so! Just so!' he went on. 'Weak heart. Seems to me that the trouble is long-standing. Has he been in the tropics at all?'

'He is an explorer,' I answered, 'and has been in all parts of the world. In fact, he has only just come back from the East.'

'That accounts for it. So many of these people get heart trouble and never bother about it. One thing puzzles me, and that is two tiny, festering punctures in the throat. Looks as if he may have scraped a couple of pimples whilst shaving.'

We made no comment, but I saw Parker start forward as if to say something and then thought better of it.

'Don't worry about him. He will be all right as soon as he recovers consciousness,' the doctor assured us.

But he was wrong. Poor Dale never recovered consciousness, and by eight o'clock he was dead.

Father Vincent put a telephone call through to Lord Salton, and was fortunate enough to find him at home. He promised to leave London at once, and, true to his word, he was at Abbot's Grange soon after lunch. He turned out to be quite a young man, and greeted both Parker and Father Vincent as old friends.

We gathered in the library, and Father Vincent gave him the facts of the case. I could see that the boy was very much upset, particularly when we had to tell him of the death of Dale.

'I will most willingly tell you all I know,' he said. 'William Salton has always been the skeleton in our cupboard. Each heir to the title, at his coming of age, is told the story of the first Lord, and warned never to leave the chapel door open between dusk and sunrise. I have never taken the matter very seriously, and, I am afraid, I ought not to have left the key with the agent.

'As you already know, my ancestor was once a Cistercian monk, but he was turned out of the monastery for practising witchcraft and the black art. Really he was a greater villain than even the monks suspected.

'At the dissolution he gave evidence against the abbot and brethren of Ritton, and, for his services, was made Lord Salton, and given this house.

'Under his rule Abbot's Grange became a temple of Satan. He is said to have celebrated the Black Mass in the chapel, and to have sacrificed living children on the altar. The picture in the hall is a self-portrait, and tradition says that the canvas is really the skin of one of his victims coated over with human blood.

'Even after his death he terrorized the district. For over half a century there were tales of children stolen from their cradles in the dead of night by a man with a strangely white face. Then, in 1640, the Lord Salton of the time went into the chapel and found the altar dripping with fresh blood. He called in a parson named John Rogers, who carried out some religious ceremony there, and, since then, the chapel has not been opened after sunset until this week.'

With a word of apology he got up and went over to one of the oak bookcases. Sliding a concealed panel at the end, he took out, from the cavity behind, two small vellum-bound books. Laying these on the table, he went on:

'These books are diaries kept by William Salton. I have never read them through, but I know of two passages which may interest you.' He opened one of the books and read from it.

'At last I have completed the portrait in the manner laid down by the master Setharius. Now, even if my body decays, I have that which will give me the semblance of life.'

'The other note,' he continued, 'was made in the second volume by John Rogers. Ah! Here it is.

'Terrible is the power of the evil one. He that is dead yet wanders abroad seeking whom he may devour. I have watched and prayed, and it seems that he may only be free of the grave for three days at a time. Then for three days he must rest within the tomb. I have sealed him there, but should he ever break free again let it be remembered that on the third day he will return to the grave.'

'That will be tomorrow,' interpolated Father Vincent. 'God grant that nothing happens tonight.'

'You must see that it doesn't,' answered Salton.

'If I am able to keep him within the picture for tonight have I your permission to do whatever I think fit in the morning?' asked the priest.

'You can do whatever you like,' was the reply. 'I am only too anxious that such a heritage of evil shall not be handed on to my successors.'

Salton asked if I could put him up for the night, and we were all very glad to have him to stay. With Dale dead upstairs and the horror of the unknown hanging over us, we were not a very lively party.

The priest made his preparations early in the evening. A semi-circle of salt was made round the picture, this was sprinkled with holy water, and, in the centre, he placed a crucifix.

Just before midnight we began our watch. We hadn't long to wait.

About twenty minutes past the hour the figure in the frame began to move. It jumped to life with curious, jerky, mechanical movements. Then it tried to step down, but was evidently prevented by the arrangements the monk had made.

A look of diabolical hate passed over its features, and then it laughed. As the laughter died it began to intone a kind of weird chant. I could not understand the words, but I knew it for some incantation to the devil.

Suddenly Morton screamed, and pointed to the stairs. We all looked up, and there, moving slowly down, was the figure of Malcolm Dale, the man whose dead body lay upstairs.

Morton screamed again, and then fainted. I saw the monk step forward with crucifix in one hand and Breviary in the other. In a clear voice he began to read the office of exorcism, and all the time that terrible incantation went on. Louder and louder rose the infernal chant, and clearer rang the voice of the priest. It seemed that the forces of good were waging a battle with the powers of evil. The perspiration ran in great drops down the monk's face, and I found myself praying the words of the 'Our Father' – the only prayer I knew.

Gradually the hellish chant got quieter, whilst Father Vincent's voice grew stronger in volume. Then a strange thing happened. A beautiful smile came over the face of the thing that looked like Malcolm Dale, and, still smiling, it slowly faded away.

From the picture came a most unearthly shriek and, for a few moments, the figure in the frame seemed to writhe in agony. Then it became still. It was only a painting once again.

'We have won the first round of the fight, my friends,' said the little priest.

It was three o'clock in the afternoon of the following day.

'If John Rogers' calculations are correct,' said Father Vincent, 'the monster should be back in his grave by now.'

Armed with crowbars we were making our way to the chapel. The priest carried a small Spanish dagger with a cross handle.

Salton unlocked the door and we went inside. The place was rather gloomy, for it was a dull day, but nothing seemed to have been disturbed.

'Now we come to the worst part of this horrible business,' said the priest.

Taking a crowbar from Morton he went up to the tomb, and inserted the implement under the slab. I put mine under the other side, and together we levered until the top swung up. It was an easy matter to lift it off. Inside was a brass-bound coffin, and all over it were dark-brown stains.

We lifted the coffin out of the tomb, and laid it before the altar.

'If any of you feel at all nervous you may go outside,' said Father Vincent. Morton took him at his word, but Salton, Parker, and I stayed on.

It did not take long to remove the lid, and inside was no crumbling skeleton, but the body of William, Lord Salton, looking just as he must have looked in life. His eyes gleamed at us with a malevolent stare; his lips were unnaturally red; and his white, fang-like teeth protruded over his bottom lip.

'Stand back!' cried the monk.

He raised his dagger aloft, and then, praying in Latin, brought it down into the creature's heart. The red mouth opened in a piercing shriek, the body writhed as if in agony, and then it slowly crumbled to dust before our eyes.

We sealed the coffin and placed it back in the tomb. The slab was returned to its position, and Salton promised to see that it was cemented down.

One more task remained. We took down the portrait of William Salton, carried it into the grounds, soaked it in petrol, and set fire to it. As the flames licked that white face it seemed to leer at us again, and I fancied the lips parted in a snarl.

Salton was very good about the lease for, naturally, neither Joan nor I felt that we could remain on at Abbot's Grange after what had happened. I took her away to the south of France, where the sunshine and gaiety helped her to forget the nightmare of that tragic week.

But I saw Malcolm Dale die, the picture come to life, Dale's ghost walk at the bidding of the monster, and the corpse of William Salton living after over three hundred years in the tomb. It will be many years before I can forget the horror of Abbot's Grange.

Sredni Vashtar

SAKI

CONRADIN WAS TEN YEARS OLD, and the doctor had pronounced his professional opinion that the boy would not live another five years. The doctor was silky and effete, and counted for little, but his opinion was endorsed by Mrs Dr Ropp, who counted for nearly everything. Mrs De Ropp was Conradin's cousin and guardian, and in his eyes she represented those three-fifths of the world that are necessary and disagreeable and real; the other two-fifths, in perpetual antagonism to the foregoing, were summed up in himself and his imagination. One of these days Conradin supposed he would succumb to the mastering pressure of wearisome necessary things – such as illnesses and coddling restrictions and drawn out dullness. Without his imagination, which was rampant under the spur of loneliness, he would have succumbed long ago.

Mrs De Ropp would never, in her honestest moments, have confessed to herself that she disliked Conradin, though she might have been dimly aware that thwarting him 'for his good' was a duty which she did not find particularly irksome. Conradin hated her with a desperate sincerity which he was perfectly able to mask. Such few pleasures as he could contrive for himself gained an added relish from the likelihood that they would be displeasing to his guardian, and from the realm of his imagination she was locked out – an unclean thing, which should find no entrance.

In the dull, cheerless garden, overlooked by so many windows that were ready to open with a message not to do this or that, or a reminder that medicines were due, he found little attraction. The few fruit trees that it contained were set jealously apart from his plucking, as though they were rare specimens of their kind blooming in an arid waste; it would probably have been difficult to find a market-gardener who would have offered ten shillings for their entire yearly produce. In a forgotten corner, however, almost hidden behind a dismal shrubbery, was a disused tool-shed of respectable proportions, and within its walls Conradin found a haven, something that took on the varying aspects of a playroom and a cathedral. He had peopled it with a legion of familiar phantoms, evoked partly from fragments of history and partly from his own brain, but it also boasted two inmates of flesh and blood. In one corner lived a ragged-plumaged Houdan hen, on which the boy lavished an affection that had scarcely another outlet. Farther back in the gloom stood a large hutch, divided into two compartments, one of which was fronted with close iron bars. This was the abode of a large polecat-ferret, which a friendly butcher-boy had once smuggled, cage and all, into its present quarters, in exchange for a long-secreted hoard of small silver. Conradin was dreadfully afraid of the lithe, sharp-fanged beast, but it was his most treasured possession. Its very presence in the tool-shed was a secret and fearful joy, to be kept scrupulously from the knowledge of the Woman, as he privately dubbed his cousin. And one day, out of Heaven knows what material, he spun the beast a wonderful name, and from that moment it grew into a god and a religion. The Woman indulged in religion once a week at a church near by, and took Conradin with her, but to him the church service was an alien rite in the House of Rimmon. Every Thursday, in the dim and musty silence of the tool-shed, he worshipped with mystic and elaborate ceremonial before the wooden hutch where dwelt Sredni Vashtar, the great ferret. Red flowers in their season and scarlet berries in the winter-time were offered at his shrine, for he was a god who laid some special stress on the fierce impatient side of things, as opposed to the Woman's religion, which, as far as Conradin could observe, went to great lengths in the contrary direction. And on great festivals powdered nutmeg was strewn in front of his hutch, an important feature of the offering being that the nutmeg had to be stolen. These festivals were of irregular occurrence, and were chiefly appointed to celebrate some passing event. On one occasion, when Mrs De Ropp suffered from acute toothache for three days, Conradin kept up the festival during the entire three days, and almost succeeded in persuading himself that Sredni Vashtar was personally responsible for the toothache. If the malady had lasted for another day the supply of nutmeg would have given out.

The Houdan hen was never drawn into the cult of Sredni Vashtar. Conradin had long ago settled that she was Anabaptist. He did not pretend to have the remotest knowledge as to what an Anabaptist was, but he privately hoped that it was dashing and not very respectable. Mrs De Ropp was the ground plan on which he based and detested all respectability.

After a while Conradin's absorption in the tool-shed began to attract the notice of his guardian. 'It is not good for him to be pottering down there in all weathers,' she promptly decided, and at breakfast one morning she announced that the Houdan hen had been sold and taken away overnight. With her short-sighted eyes she peered at Conradin, waiting for an outbreak of rage and sorrow, which she was ready to rebuke with a flow of excellent precepts and reasoning. But Conradin said nothing; there was nothing to be said. Something perhaps in his white set face gave her a momentary qualm, for at tea that afternoon there was toast on the table, a delicacy which she usually banned on the ground that it was bad for him;

also because the making of it 'gave trouble,' a deadly offence in the middle-class feminine eye.

'I thought you liked toast,' she exclaimed, with an injured air, observing that he did not touch it.

'Sometimes,' said Conradin.

In the shed that evening there was an innovation in the worship of the hutch-god. Conradin had been wont to chant his praises; tonight he asked a boon.

'Do one thing for me, Sredni Vashtar.'

The thing was not specified. As Sredni Vashtar was a god he must be supposed to know. And choking back a sob as he looked at that other empty corner, Conradin went back to the world he so hated.

And every night, in the welcome darkness of his bedroom, and every evening in the dusk of the tool-shed, Conradin's bitter litany went up: 'Do one thing for me, Sredni Vashtar.'

Mrs De Ropp noticed that the visits to the shed did not cease, and one day she made a further journey of inspection.

'What are you keeping in that locked hutch?' she asked. 'I believe it's guinea-pigs. I'll have them all cleared away.'

Conradin shut his lips tight, but the Woman ransacked his bedroom till she found the carefully hidden key, and forthwith marched down to the shed to complete her discovery. It was a cold afternoon, and Conradin had been bidden to keep to the house. From the farthest window of the dining-room the door of the shed could just be seen beyond the corner of the shrubbery, and there Conradin stationed himself. He saw the Woman enter, and then he imagined her opening the door of the sacred hutch and peering down with her short-sighted eyes into the thick straw bed where his god lay hidden. Perhaps she would prod at the straw in her clumsy impatience. And Conradin fervently breathed his prayer for the last time. But he knew as he prayed that he did not believe. He knew that the Woman would come out presently with that pursed smile he loathed so well on her face, and that in an hour or two the gardener would carry away his wonderful god, a god no longer, but a simple brown ferret in a hutch. And he knew that the Woman would triumph always as she triumphed now, and that he would grow ever more sickly under her pestering and domineering and superior wisdom, till one day nothing would matter much more with him, and the doctor would be proved right. And in the sting and misery of his defeat, he began to chant loudly and defiantly the hymn of his threatened idol:

> *Sredni Vashtar went forth,*
> *His thoughts were red thoughts and his teeth were white.*
> *His enemies called for peace, but he brought them death.*
> *Sredni Vashtar the Beautiful.*

And then of a sudden he stopped his chanting and drew closer to the window-pane. The door of the shed still stood ajar as it had been left, and the minutes were slipping by. They were long minutes, but they slipped by nervertheless. He watched the starlings running and flying in little parties across the lawn; he counted them over and over again, with one eye always on that swinging door. A sour-faced maid came in to lay the table for tea, and still Conradin stood and waited and watched. Hope had crept by inches into his heart, and now a look of triumph began to blaze in his eyes that had only known the wistful patience of defeat. Under his breath, with a furtive exultation, he began once again the paean of victory and devastation. And presently his eyes were rewarded: out through that doorway came a long, low, yellow-and-brown beast, with eyes a-blink at the waning daylight, and dark wet stains around the fur of jaws and throat. Conradin dropped on his knees. The great polecat-ferret made its way down to a small brook at the foot of the garden, drank for a moment, then crossed a little plank bridge and was lost to sight in the bushes. Such was the passing of Sredni Vashtar.

'Tea is ready,' said the sour-faced maid; 'where is the mistress?'

'She went down to the shed some time ago,' said Conradin.

And while the maid went to summon her mistress to tea, Conradin fished a toasting-fork out of the sideboard drawer and proceeded to toast himself a piece of bread. And during the toasting of it and the buttering of it with much butter and the slow enjoyment of eating it, Conradin listened to the noises and silences which fell in quick spasms beyond the dining-room door. The loud, foolish screaming of the maid, the answering chorus of wondering ejaculations from the kitchen region, the scuttering footsteps and hurried embassies for outside help, and then, after a lull, the scared sobbings and the shuffling tread of those who bore a heavy burden into the house.

'Whoever will break it to the poor child? I couldn't for the life of me!' exclaimed a shrill voice. And while they debated the matter among themselves, Conradin made himself another piece of toast.

The Wall

ROBERT HAINING

HOW ABSURD IT SEEMED IN those first few minutes! I awoke, got dressed, had breakfast, picked up my coat and as I opened the door to leave I found that during the night someone had come and bricked up the doorway. Where once I could see the passageway in the block of flats where I lived, now all I could see was a crudely made brick wall. The jagged edges of the concrete showed it to have been a hastily built thing; tongues of cement, now solidified, hung down from between the rows of neatly ordered bricks.

I felt no immediate reaction in those early seconds. I was amazed, bewildered, confused – all these feelings, but, I was not afraid. Fear of such a strange imprisonment had not yet affected me – the period I am describing came even before I had time to be afraid. I looked at the wall, I touched it. I pushed it. It was a solid brick wall and for all its crudity, it did not yield to my weight. I stood back from it, uncertain of what to do.

I suppose that initially I was somewhat amused by the turn of events, for a number of ludicrous explanations occurred to me. The first such explanation was that the whole thing was a practical joke. Some of my fellow workers at the bank had devised this at my expense – just imagine:

Chief Clerk: You were late for work on Thursday.
I: Yes, sir.
Chief Clerk: Can you explain this?
I: I could not leave my apartment, sir, someone had built a brick wall across the doorway.

No, I should have to make up another explanation. I could say that I felt a little ill – I could say I drank some bad milk. At least that way I could avoid the humiliation of offering an absurd and unacceptable explanation for my lateness.

Such an easy escape from the predicament, suggested that perhaps this was not a practical joke. After all, why go to the trouble of buying bricks and cement, dragging them up twenty floors and then not have any reward for the trick? In any case, how would they have explained what they were doing if the apartment manager had caught them. It is not easy to bring over a hundred bricks and fresh cement into an apartment block without being noticed. Surely they would have been seen and the police notified. No, it did not seem likely that this wall was the result of a practical joke. That left the possibility that the apartment owners were responsible. True, I had not paid last month's rent and had received a warning notice only yesterday. But I considered it unlikely that they should take such drastic action as to brick up one of their tenants for non-payment of rent. After all, they were responsible for the upkeep of the building and they would have to go to the expense of knocking the wall down. I recalled a story by Poe, *The Cask of Amontillado*, and wondered whether the apartment owners had a similar savage turn of mind. Perhaps even now there was a plaque outside my sarcophagus *Let this be a warning to those who do not pay their rent*. No, that too was an unlikely explanation.

Perhaps, then, it was a practical joke that had succeeded against the odds. Perhaps they had come in the dead of the night, when the night watchman dozes by his little electric fire, and carried out their plan with such haste and silence that no one had been disturbed.

No explanation convinced me. I sat down in one of my armchairs and looked at the wall. I could hardly tell whether I was asleep or awake. In the end I had to conclude that I was awake and that, though fully prepared to leave for work, I had been prevented from so doing by the overnight appearance of a brick wall where once I had had a door.

Though I sat for a while, I was slowly being filled with a mixture of frustration and perhaps the first hint of fear. I jumped up and started to push firmly, but with as yet no great conviction, against the wall. For a wall with no foundations it withstood my pressure remarkably well. Indeed it did not yield in any sense. I pushed harder, my mind filling now with a greater sense of anger and frustration. I wanted to leave and I could not. For whatever reason, some damn fool had come along and maliciously bricked up my door. I no longer cared if it was a trick with friendly or evil intentions, the fact was I could not get out and the injustice and absurdity of the situation were becoming stronger to me with every second.

After pushing for only a short while I found myself perspiring. I had not yet taken off my coat and, as I paused to remove it, I realized how stupidly I was behaving. If I can see the brick wall, I reasoned, so can the people in the passageway. I listed everyone who went to work at this time and realized that there would be at least ten to fifteen people passing through the hallway at about this time. They, for the most part, knew me and would presumably not go past simply observing, 'Oh, he's had his door bricked up.' They would enquire at the manager's office and surely any time now there would be a voice outside telling me to be calm and that they would immediately get some workmen in to smash down the wall. No doubt they would also add that in view of the inconvenience the little matter of last month's rent could be considered forgotten. Perhaps after all there would be some chance to profit from this experience.

I listened at the wall to hear if people were moving about. It was strange, for I heard nothing. Normally the paper-thin walls carry the sound of every footstep from the uncarpeted hallway. Moreover, since my room is at the end of the hallway by the stairs, I normally hear the odd hardly soul plodding down the twenty flights. This morning I could hear nothing – it was as if . . . My mind ran on and I stopped myself.

'This is absurd,' I muttered, ' "as if" nothing.'

Nonetheless it was odd that there should be no noise, and I went to the window. Down in the street I could see people moving about – a large number were leaving the apartment block, getting into their cars and driving off to their day's work. What a strange distant world that was becoming. All about me, a normal Thursday was starting up for millions of people but for me the absurd had happened.

Perhaps, I reasoned, if there is no sound on this floor it means that the whole floor has been sealed off. But why? If it was a malicious attempt to scare the people how long could they expect to keep it up? Friends and relatives would start to ask questions, and then the whole wretched business would be exposed. At worst it was some bloody bunch of psychologists doing an experiment.

Then I realized that I was not cut off from help – the building had an internal telephone service. Retaining my composure I walked to the telephone – but then paused. What should I say? I could not tell the manager that I was unable to leave because my door was bricked up – what if this were an hallucination, I'd get myself certified. I decided to ask him to come up and take a look at my plumbing. I could say it had broken down and needed his immediate attention.

I picked up the telephone and listened to the low distant purring sound. I waited expectantly for a reply and grew impatient as the seconds ticked interminably on. There was no reply – and quite suddenly there came a crackling, sharp jarring noise and the purr turned to the rapid pips of the engaged signal. I replaced the receiver.

I was now a good deal more shaken. I was truly isolated and it was no comfort to feel that probably all the other people on this floor were in a similar position. I decided to test this theory by trying to communicate on the one wall I had which adjoined a neighbour's flat. I took a large spoon and rapped a few times on the wall but got no response. The people next door, a married couple, did not get up for work till after me, but by now they should have realized that they were trapped. I rapped loudly but there was no response and once again the thought swept over me that it was I, and I alone, who was the victim of this game. I took a tumbler from the cabinet in the kitchen and placing it against the wall listened for any trace of sound. There was none. Nor was there any sound from the hall or the stair-well. I was enveloped by the most frightening of silences and as I sat on the bed the first fear gripped me that perhaps no one would come up here to free me. After all it was now fully an hour since I had discovered my imprisonment, fully an hour since at least ten people would have seen the wall, fully an hour since the apartment manager should have been informed of my problem, and still no one had come. I had heard nothing, there had been no attempt to communicate, and downstairs in the street people were going about their daily business on a normal Thursday morning. I tried the telephone again, but all I heard now was the repeating sound of the engaged signal. As I listened I felt comforted to know that somewhere there was a noise.

For the next few hours I sat and waited. At first I tried banging on the wall and shouting for help. Though I kept this up for fully fifteen minutes on one occasion I could never tell if there was anyone who could hear me and certainly no one made a returning sound. From time to time I would push and heave at the wall, I would try waving and shouting to people in the street – neither was to any avail. The wall remained solid and firm, the people in the street never looked up. Nor was there any indication that outside people were trying to break in; for all I could tell, if there were people outside they might be adding to the wall, not trying to knock it down.

As the midday warmth turned to the chill of a November afternoon, I closed the window of the apartment. Now even the faint sounds of the street were cut off and I began to regret that I had never bought a television or radio, or even a gramophone. The only contact I preserved with the outside world was through the engaged signal on the telephone.

I had to preserve the feeling that, whatever had happened, there were people somewhere working on my behalf to get me out. I, for my part, had to stay calm and wait. I likened my position to a coalminer trapped underground by a sudden collapse. At least I had all the comforts of home and could see the sun and feel the wind and rain, and I decided the best plan was to make myself something to eat. The thought of doing something raised my spirits and for a while I busied myself frying eggs and bacon. But when I had eaten, and was sitting back in my chair, once again contemplating the stark reality of the clumsy but stubborn wall, the earlier fears and despondency slowly took over like a prickly cancer working outwards from the pit of my stomach. I shivered though the room was warm. It had been eight hours, the sun was setting, people were returning from work. No one had missed me, no one had come to get me out, for all I knew I had disappeared from the face of the earth and the world had treated my departure with indifference. As these thoughts gave way to a new panic, they were almost instantly dispelled – there was still Rachel. We had a date for dinner this evening. She was due at my apartment at half past six and here at least was the chance I needed. She would come, of that I felt certain, and then she at least would be able to deal with the situation. Providing ... As despair had given way to hope, now hope was itself dashed by a new despair. What if the outside of the wall was like the normal front of my apartment? She, like everyone else would knock, receive no answer and go away. Indeed that must be why no one had come looking for me. From the outside everything looked normal. How long before Rachel, the bank manager, my friends came looking for me? How long before they broke down the door? (If only that damned telephone would work!) In a panic I picked up the telephone and paced the carpet listening to the sound of the rapid pips. I dropped my arm and the telephone fell from my grip. The monotonous staccato continued as I fell back into a chair. I sat watching the receiver until, quite suddenly, the regular beat was interrupted by a mechanical grinding. There was now no sound and I lunged at the receiver. As I listened my worst fears were confirmed. The telephone was dead.

Half past six came and went. I stood close to the wall anxious to detect the slightest hint that Rachel had come. I heard nothing. I had prepared myself with a large metal ladle to beat on the wall at the first sound, but I heard nothing and after a while I let the ladle slip to the floor and I walked slowly to the armchair and slumped down. The emotional tension was too much – I flung the empty dinner plate across the room where it smashed against the wall, littering the carpet with pottery fragments and leaving a greasy smear on the wall.

I slumped into a state of despondency and self-pity for nearly an hour, staring blankly at the wall. Outside it was dark and when I arose and walked to the window the only light came from the headlights of distant cars and the regular patchwork of street lamps that were scattered like fairy lights over the black urban sprawl. There was at least one escape, indeed two not counting throwing myself from the window (and as yet I had not reached that stage). I still had half a bottle of scotch and a full bottle of sherry. The night was young; by the time it was old, the scotch was empty, half the sherry was gone and I was asleep.

I was sick in the night and the next morning the smell of vomit was overwhelming. I got up slowly, dragged my aching body to the bathroom and washed my mouth. The new day had brought with it a child-like innocence of the events of the preceding day, but as I hung my head limply over the basin events were recalled in rapid succession and I moved quickly to the door. A wave of nausea caught me as the realization was made plain again. I was a prisoner and there was to be no easy escape. Again I beat violently against the walls of my flat in a vain hope that, unlike the day before, this time someone would hear me and return my cries. But there was no reply, only the silence that had become a familiar part of my life since the whole stupid and absurd affair had begun.

In a vain attempt to cut out the reality of the wall I closed the door so that I could not see it and stumbled back into my bedroom. I fell asleep again and awoke with the worst of headaches and once again stumbled into the bathroom for relief.

I had only partly undressed from the night before and as I was about to pull on my shirt I laughed quietly. Social convention hardly seemed relevant now.

I took my usual cure for a hangover followed by a bowl of cereal. The long day stretched before me and none of yesterday's glimmerings of hope. The best I could imagine was that after two or three days someone might make inquiries. But how long before they beat down the wall? Outside it was a grey, misty day. The drizzle fell in a murky half light and car headlights reflected from the lacquered streets. Red, amber, green, amber, red, amber, green ... I watched mesmerized as the traffic lights flashed their mechanical instructions and the little toy cars shuffled past the crossroads. People scurried along beneath umbrellas, some running from awning to awning trying to avoid the chilly rain. I felt almost glad to be out of such a miserable existence. In every direction I could see the low grey clouds heralding a day of unrelieved gloom, whilst in my own miserable apartment the greasy wall and shattered pottery reminded me of my own despair and of the day that stretched before me.

I felt ashamed at how soon I had become demoralised. I decided that the stench from the bedroom was at least in part to blame. I took the sheet from the bed – but what to do now? Here perhaps was a chance to communicate. I took a pen from my case and wrote in big letters 'Help I am trapped in room 2002'. I took the sheet to the window, rolled it into a ball and, waiting till I thought it would attract attention, threw it down. I watched it fall, rapidly at first, but then opening like a parachute to drift down more slowly, eventually coming to rest some fifty yards away in the middle of the plaza. And there it lay getting some attention from curious passersby, but receiving only the full attention of the caretaker who rolled it up and stuffed it into his waste bin.

The phone was still dead, and my attempts at communication had failed. The day offered no prospect of relief and my mind was tormented with the thoughts of when I might be relieved and then, more depressingly, whether indeed anyone would free me. These thoughts dominated my moods and my actions for many hours. Never raising my spirits much beyond the level of despondency, I occasionally fell into the most morbid of states, imagining my death long before any possible help could come. At these times I would jump up and start scraping at the wall with any blunt instrument I could find. Occasionally, if I thought I had heard the noise of some passerby in the hall, I would start banging on the wall and shouting for help. I tried stripping the walls of the apartment in an attempt to escape that way. All my many tactics were useless and soon I had reduced my room to the most dejected state. The wallpaper was scarred and ripped, the floor covered with pieces of plaster, strips of paper and the fragments and debris of the implements I had used to try and free myself. It was all too futile.

My activities at these times alternated between the most frenzied rushing about accompanied by wild slashings at the walls and shrieks if I thought someone was in the passageway, and the most abject inertia. I would sit for a while staring blankly at the floor or the wall. I had long since given up reasoning about the situation, my only thought was to get out. Nor could I attract attention from the street. I threw all my plates down on to the plaza where they crashed and splintered. The people ran for cover and when I was finished and had thrown all the plates I saw the caretaker walk out slowly, wave his fist up at me, and slowly sweep up the debris. The people drifted out from the shops and life on the plaza resumed its normal course. And still there was no sound outside my door.

I cannot remember how long I was in this state. Perhaps for three days, for I remember the alternating of light and dark outside, but I slept in snatches and cannot remember clearly. It was at least three days, and by now my movements about the apartment were slow and leaden. And so it was that this time passed and nothing happened to alter my predicament. I remained a prisoner for cause unknown. It was some time later that there was a change.

I had by now ceased trying to escape from the room and was content – such as I had any self-control to plan my actions – merely to try and conserve my small supply of food in the event that help was coming. I no longer seriously expected help and what exactly it was that kept me going is also a mystery. I was sleeping a lot, mainly from boredom and lack of food, and it was on one occasion after a lengthy sleep that I awoke to discover the first change in my situation. I awoke in almost complete darkness. I stumbled to my feet, feeling cold and sick. I went to the light switch and flicked it on and then off. There was no light. No light and no heat! But that was not the only reason for my darkness and coldness. For as my eyes cleared and I looked about me I saw that the window of my bedroom had also been bricked up. In a panic I rushed at the new wall and found it as solid as the one covering the door. Not a chink of light passed through its solid construction, not an inch did it yield as I pushed fiercely against it. My tormentors had laid on yet another act in this absurd and frightening game. Yet there was more – of the two windows in the living-room one of these had also been bricked up. I had only one window left to look out on to the world – one to that grey miserable world below me that harboured only mindless ants running frantically about in their own individual states of madness.

And so it was that I entered upon a new stage of my captivity. A single solitary shaft of light pierced the gloom of my squalid apartment now littered with the filth and debris that bespoke the hopelessness of my position. The new turn of events briefly awakened my sensitivities and I responded with a stronger awareness to the world that I could still perceive through my solitary window. Now the question became even more inexplicable. Who could have built these two new walls? No one

293

from the outside could have done so. Did anyone come in whilst I was asleep? But as I checked the old wall it seemed that nothing had been disturbed. Gone was any vestige of a rational explanation, or a reasonable hope of release. This was no ordinary game – no malicious trick by a normal opponent.

By day I lay on the floor, frightened to sleep in case the final window to the world was denied me whilst I slept. Frightened to grope my way into the kitchen to eat, though there was really nothing left. Frightened to wash. I slumped into the most squalid dejection. I no longer fought for my release, I saw now that my final destruction was only hours away.

I was too frightened to leave the solitary square of light cast by the open window. I watched the grey clouds tumbling over the sky, whilst in the streets the same monotonous patterns repeated themselves in the movements of the tiny mindless dots that littered the streets. The sun began to sink and I found myself gripping the window ledge watching the sky darken and the tiny pinpricks of light, that were such an inadequate substitute, appear. I felt the darkness overwhelm me like the shroud of death itself and I lay on the floor shivering and praying only for release from this torment.

That night was a turning point. Afraid to sleep for fear that there would be no morning, yet plagued every second by the despair that told me there was to be no escape. My mind raced uncontrollably over the events of the days. I relived every second searching for a clue. At other times my memory is a blank for I must have relapsed into a coma. I would break from my stupor and rush to the window anxious in case my last exit had been sealed. But no, there was no sealing up of this exit and as dawn came again the rays of the new sun lit up – oh how ironically – the wall that was the first cause of my suffering.

There could not be another night such as the last. The red shafts of light of the dawn that can be so beautiful from the crest of a lonely hill or a cliff top, merely heralded for me the start of yet another torment. I struggled to the window ledge – a final gesture to the crowd, my mutilated body on the plaza. (Then, by God, they will know!) I poised on the ledge, the cold wind blowing me out over the parapet. I looked down and swayed. Not a soul was looking for me. And as I felt the urge to die sweep still more strongly over me, I felt a faint tug at my jacket. I passed out, though I remember falling.

I awoke much later. My world was in total darkness. I was alive but there was no light. I stood up uncertainly and stretching out before me I felt an armchair and table. My feet slithered in filth. I knew that I was back in my room and that the final horror had been realized. My last window was sealed and I was in total gloom. In my attempt to die I had fallen backwards and had returned to the arms of my tormentor.

Then, as I lay on the floor, there appeared a single beam of light, from what source I do not know. It caught in its rays a crudely made noose, and beneath the noose was a chair. There was perfect silence and gone too was the evil odour that had hung in the air. There was no light save for this solitary beam.

The torments of the night returned, and my senses were revolted by the prospect of any more pain and suffering. Now, too, all hope had gone. Whoever or whatever had played with me these last few days had tired of the game and the pieces had to be put away. Should I ever see this tormentor?

'Who are you? For God's sake let me see who you are.'

I listened for any response but there was none. In despair I searched for a meaning, some sense to be made from this absurd game that seemingly had no point except my destruction. Was there no point except the certainty of avoiding fresh torment?

Silence invaded the room like an unseen ether, its delicate fingers curling about me. A cold clammy fog that wrapped itself around me, moving slowly about my neck and stretching upwards over my lips and nose. It was as if a new and stronger presence had invaded the room, a silence so profound that any sound would have served only to emphasize that silence as it reverberated over the emptiness. Here was a despair that had no meaning and no prospect of an end. Above me the noose swayed slowly as if swept by the gentlest of breezes. So it was that I climbed the chair and placed the rope about my neck and kicked the chair away.

I remember the searing pain and the rope burning my flesh. The coarse matted fibre dug deeply into my flesh and my nose was again haunted by the odour from the filth littering the floor. My eyes saw only darkness. *If these were or are my senses, tell me how it is that I am now speaking to you? Who are you? My senses are no longer revolted by the degradation around me, so tell me what has happened.*

My companion remained silent and motionless, but when I asked him if it was he who had been playing this game with me he shook his head. He did not speak but instead rose slowly, massively before me, his cowled head rising into the darkness that stretched endlessly above and before me. I saw his arm reach out towards me and long crooked fingers open outwards as if preparing to grasp me. As I looked up he slowly raised his head so that a single beam of light moved upwards across his face. I saw reflected in his eyes a figure slumped motionless across a bed, I saw a wall where fresh cement hung in slender tongues over neatly ordered bricks, I saw upturned faces from a distant plaza, I saw clouds scudding over a silent world. The clouds became thicker, darker and the shadows lengthened over a desolate land. My companion leant forward and embraced me, recalling the time when as a child I had first perceived my morality in a timeless world. Now he was speaking to me again, indeed it was as if he had always been speaking to me, as I to him. He whispered softly,

'I am the scream.'

An Account of Some Strange Disturbances in Aungier Street

J. SHERIDAN LE FANU

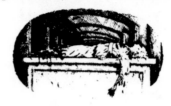

IT IS NOT WORTH TELLING, this story of mine – at least, not worth writing. Told indeed, as I have sometimes been called upon to tell it, to a circle of intelligent and eager faces, lighted up by a good after-dinner fire on a winter's evening, with a cold wind rising and wailing outside, all snug and cosy within, it has gone off – though I say it, who should not – indifferent well. But it is a venture to do as you would have me. Pen, ink, and paper are cold vehicles for the marvellous, and a 'reader' decidedly a more critical animal than a 'listener'. If, however, you can induce your friends to read it after nightfall, and when the fireside talk has run for a while on shapeless terror; in short, if you will secure me the *mollia tempora fandi*, I will go to my work, and say my say, with better heart. Well, then, these conditions presupposed, I shall waste no more words, but tell you simply how it happened.

My cousin (Tom Ludlow) and I studied medicine together. I think he would have succeeded, had he stuck to the profession; but he preferred the Church, poor fellow, and died early, a sacrifice to contagion, contracted in the noble discharge of his duties. For my present purpose, I say enough of his character when I mention that he was of a sedate but frank and cheerful nature; very exact in his observance of truth, and not by any means like myself – of an excitable or nervous temperament.

My uncle Ludlow – Tom's father – while we were attending lectures, purchased three of four old houses in Aungier Street, one of which was occupied. *He* resided in the country, and Tom proposed that we should take up our abode in the untenanted house, so long as it should continue unlet; a move which would accomplish the double end of settling us nearer alike to our lecture-rooms and to our amusements, and of relieving us from the weekly charge of rent for our lodgings.

Our furniture was very scant – our whole equipage remarkably modest and primitive; and, in short, our arrangements pretty nearly as simple as those of a bivouac. Our new plan was, therefore, executed almost as soon as conceived. The front drawing-room was our sitting-room. I had the bedroom over it, and Tom the back bedroom on the same floor, which nothing could have induced me to occupy.

The house, to begin with, was a very old one. It had been, I believe, newly fronted about fifty years before; but with this exception, it had nothing modern about it. The agent who bought it and looked into the titles for my uncle, told me that it was sold, along with much other forfeited property, at Chichester House, I think, in 1702; and had belonged to Sir Thomas Hacket, who was Lord Mayor of Dublin in James II's time. How old it was *then*, I can't say; but, at all events, it had seen years and changes enough to have contracted all that mysterious and saddened air, at once exciting and depressing, which belongs to most old mansions.

There had been very little done in the way of modernizing details; and, perhaps, it was better so; for there was something queer and by-gone in the very walls and ceilings – in shape of doors and windows – in the odd diagonal site of the chimney-pieces – in the beams and ponderous cornices – not to mention the singular solidity of all the woodwork, from the banisters to the window-frames, which hopelessly defied disguise, and would have emphatically proclaimed their antiquity through any conceivable amount of modern finery and varnish.

An effort had, indeed, been made, to the extent of papering the drawing-rooms; but somehow the paper looked raw and out of keeping; and the old woman, who kept a little dirt-pie of a shop in the lane, and whose daughter – a girl of two and fifty – was our solitary handmaid, coming in at sunrise, and chastely receding again as soon as she had made all ready for tea in our state apartment; – this woman, I say, remembered it, when old Judge Horrocks (who, having earned the reputation of a particularly 'hanging judge', ended by hanging himself, as the coroner's jury found, under an impulse of 'temporary insanity', with a child's skipping-rope, over the massive old banisters) resided there, entertaining good company, with fine venison and rare old port. In those halcyon days, the drawing-rooms were hung with gilded leather, and, I dare say, cut a good figure, for they were really spacious rooms.

The bedrooms were wainscoted, but the front one was not gloomy; and in it the cosiness of antiquity quite overcame its sombre associations. But the back bedroom, with its two queerly-placed melancholy windows, staring vacantly at the foot of the bed, and with the shadowy recess to be found in most old houses in Dublin, like a large ghostly closet, which, from congeniality of temperament, had amalgamated with the bedchamber, and dissolved the partition. At night-time, this 'alcove' – as our 'maid' was wont to call it – had, in my eyes, a specially sinister and suggestive character. Tom's distant and solitary candle glimmered vainly into its darkness. *There* it was always overlooking him – always itself impenetrable. But this was only part of the effect. The whole room was, I can't tell how, repulsive to me. There was, I suppose, in its proportions and features, a latent discord – a certain mysterious and indescribable relation, which jarred indistinctly upon some secret sense of fitting and the safe, and raised indefinable suspicions and apprehensions of the imagination. On the whole, as I began by saying, nothing could have induced me to pass a night alone in it.

I had never pretended to conceal from poor Tom my superstitious weakness; and he, on the other hand, most unaffectedly ridiculed my tremors. The sceptic was, however, destined to receive a lesson, as you shall hear.

We had not been very long in occupation of our respective dormitories, when I began to complain of uneasy nights and disturbed sleep. I was, I suppose, the more impatient under this annoyance, as I was usually a sound sleeper, and by no means prone to nightmares. It was now, however, my destiny, instead of enjoying my customary repose, every night to 'sup full of horrors'. After a preliminary course of disagreeable and frightful dreams, my troubles took a definite form, and the same vision, without an appreciable variation in a single detail, visited me at least (on an average) every second night in the week.

Now, this dream, nightmare, or infernal illusion – which you please – of which I was the miserable sport, was on this wise:

I saw, or thought I saw, with the most abominable distinctness, although at the time in profound darkness, every article of furniture and accidental arrangement of the chamber in which I lay. This, as you know, is incidental to ordinary nightmare. Well, while in this clairvoyant condition, which seemed but the lighting up on the theatre in which was to be exhibited the monotonous tableau of horror, which made my nights insupportable, my attention invariably became, I know not why, fixed upon the windows opposite the foot of my bed; and uniformly with the same effect, a sense of dreadful anticipation always took slow but sure possession of me. I became somehow conscious of a sort of horrid but undefined preparation going forward in some unknown quarter, and by some unknown agency, for my torment; and after an interval, which always seemed to me of the same length, a picture suddenly flew up to the window, where, it remained fixed, as if by an electrical attraction, and my discipline of horror then commenced, to last perhaps for hours. The picture thus mysteriously glued to the window-panes, was the portrait of an old man, in a crimson flowered silk dressing-gown, the folds of which I could now describe, with a countenance embodying a strange mixture of intellect, sensuality, and power, but withal sinister and full of malignant omen. His nose was hooked, like the beak of a vulture; his eyes large, grey, and prominent, and lighted up with a more than mortal cruelty coldness. These features were surmounted by a crimson velvet cap, the hair that peeped from under which was white with age, while the eyebrows retained their original blackness. Well I remember every line, hue, and shadow of that stony countenance, and well I may! The gaze of this hellish visage was fixed upon me, and mine returned it with the inexplicable fascination of nightmare, for what appeared to me to be hours of agony. At last –

The cock he crew, away then flew

the fiend who had enslaved me through the awful watches of the night; and, harassed and nervous, I rose to the duties of the day.

I had – I can't say exactly why, but it may have been from the exquisite anguish and profound impressions of unearthly horror, with which this strange phantasmagoria was associated – an insurmountable antipathy to describing the exact nature of my nightly troubles to my friend and comrade. Generally, however, I told him that I was haunted by abominable dreams; and true to the imputed materialism of medicine, we put our heads together to dispel my horrors, not by exorcism, but by a tonic.

I will do this tonic justice, and frankly admit that the accursed portrait began to intermit its visits under its influence. What of that? Was this singular apparition – as full of character as of terror – therefore the creature of my fancy, or the invention of my poor stomach? Was it, in short, *subjective* (to borrow the technical slang of the day) and not the palpable aggression and intrusion of an external agent? That good friend, as we will both admit, by no means follows. The evil spirit, who enthralled my senses in the shape of that portrait, may have been just as near me, just as energetic, just as malignant, though I saw him not. What means the whole moral code of revealed religion regarding the due keeping of our bodies, soberness, temperance, etc.? Here is an obvious connection between the material and the invisible; the healthy tone of the system, and its unimpaired energy, may, for aught we can tell, guard us against influences which would otherwise render life itself terrific. The mesmerist and the electro-biologist will fail upon an average with nine patients out of ten – so may the evil spirit. Special conditions of the corporeal system are indispensable to the production of certain spiritual phenomena. The operation succeeds sometimes – sometimes fails – that is all.

I found afterwards that my would-be sceptical companion had his troubles too. But of these I knew nothing yet. One night, for a wonder, I was sleeping soundly, when I was roused by a step on the lobby outside my room, followed by a loud clang of what turned out to be a large brass candlestick, flung with all his force by poor Tom Ludlow over the banisters, and rattling with a rebound down the second flight of stairs; and almost concurrently with this, Tom burst open my door, and bounced into my room backwards, in a state of extraordinary agitation.

I had jumped out of bed and clutched him by the arm before I had any distinct idea of my own whereabouts. There we were – in our shirts – standing before the opened door – staring through the great old banister opposite, at the lobby window, through which the sickly light of a clouded moon was gleaming.

'What's the matter, Tom? what's the matter with you? What the devil's the matter with you, Tom?' I demanded, shaking him with nervous impatience.

He took a long breath before he answered me, and then it was not very coherently.

'It's nothing, nothing at all – did I speak? – what did I say? – where's the candle, Richard? It's dark; I – I had a candle!'

'Yes, dark enough,' I said; 'but what's the matter? – what *is* it? – why don't you speak, Tom? – have you lost your wits? – what is the matter?'

'The matter? – oh, it is all over. It must have been a dream – nothing at all but a dream – don't you think so? It could not be anything more than a dream.'

'Of *course*,' said I, feeling uncommonly nervous, 'it *was* a dream.'

'I thought,' he said, 'there was a man in my room, and – and I jumped out of bed; and – and – where's the candle?'

'In your room, most likely,' I said, 'shall I go and bring it?'

'No; stay here – don't go; it's no matter – don't, I tell you; it was all a dream. Bolt the door, Dick; I'll stay here with you – I feel nervous. So, Dick like a good fellow, light your candle and open the window – I am in a *shocking state*.'

I did as he asked me, and robing himself like Granuaile in one of my blankets, he seated himself close beside my bed.

Everybody knows how contagious is fear of all sorts, but more especially that particular kind of fear under which poor Tom was at that moment labouring. I would not have heard, nor I believe would he have recapitulated, just at that moment, for half the world, the details of the hideous vision which had so unmanned him.

'Don't mind telling me anything about your nonsensical dream, Tom,' said I, affecting contempt, really in a panic; 'let us talk about something else; but it is quite plain that this dirty old house disagrees with us both, and hang me if I stay here any longer, to be pestered with indigestion and – and – bad nights, so we may as well look out for lodgings – don't you think so? – at once.'

Tom agreed, and, after an interval said –

'I have been thinking, Richard, that it is a long time since I saw my father, and I have made up my mind to go down tomorrow and return in a day or two, and you can take rooms for us in the meantime.'

I fancied that this resolution, obviously the result of the vision which had so profoundly scared him, would probably vanish next morning with the damps and shadows of night. But I was mistaken. Off went Tom at peep of day to the country, having agreed that so soon as I had secured suitable lodgings, I was to recall him by letter from his visit to my Uncle Ludlow.

Now, anxious as I was to change my quarter, it so happened, owing to a series of petty procrastinations and accidents, that nearly a week elapsed before my bargain was made and my letter of recall on the wing to Tom; and, in the meantime, a trifling adventure or two had occurred to your humble servant, which, absurd as they now appear, diminished by distance, did certainly at the time serve to whet my appetite for change considerably.

A night or two after the departure of my comrade, I was sitting by my bedroom fire, the door locked, and the ingredients of a tumbler of hot whisky-punch upon the crazy spider-table; for, as the best mode of keeping the

> Black spirits and white,
> Blue spirits and grey,

with which I was environed, at bay, I had adopted the practice recommended by the wisdom of my ancestors, and 'kept my spirits up by pouring spirits down'. I had thrown aside my volume of Anatomy, and was treating myself by way of a tonic, preparatory to my punch and bed, to half-a-dozen pages of the *Spectator*, when I heard a step on the flight of stairs descending from the attics. It was two o'clock, and the streets were as silent as a churchyard – the sounds were, therefore, perfectly distinct. There was a slow, heavy tread, characterized by the emphasis and deliberation of age, descending by the narrow staircase from above; and, what made the sound more singular, it was plain that the feet which produced it were perfectly bare, measuring the descent with something between a pound and a flop, very ugly to hear.

I knew quite well that my attendant had gone away many hours before, and that nobody but myself had any business in the house. It was quite plain also that the person had no intention whatever of concealing his movements; but, on the contrary appeared disposed to make even more noise, and proceed more deliberately, than was at all necessary. When the step reached the foot of the stairs outside my room, it seemed to stop; and I expected every moment to see my door open spontaneously, and give admission to the original of my detested portrait. I was, however, relieved in a few seconds by hearing the descent renewed, just in the same manner, upon the staircase leading down to the drawing-rooms, and thence, after another pause, down the next flight, and so on to the hall, whence I heard no more.

Now, by the time the sound had ceased, I was wound up, as they say, to a very unpleasant pitch of excitement. I listened, but there was not a stir. I screwed up my courage to a decisive experiment – opened my door, and in a stentorian voice bawled over the banisters, 'Who's there?' There was no answer, but the ringing of my own voice through the empty old house, – no renewal of the movement; nothing, in short, to give my unpleasant sensations a definite direction. There is, I think, something most disagreeably disenchanting in the sound of one's own voice under such circumstances, exerted in solitude and in vain. It redoubled my sense of isolation, and my misgivings increased on perceiving that the door, which I certainly thought I had left open, was closed behind me; in a vague alarm, lest my retreat should be cut off, I got again into my room as quickly as I could, where I remained in a state of imaginary blockade, and very uncomfortable indeed, till morning.

Next night brought no return of my barefooted fellow-lodger; but the night following, being in my bed, and in the dark – somewhere, I suppose, about the same hour as before, I distinctly heard the old fellow again descending from the garrets.

This time I had had my punch, and the *morale* of the garrison was consequently excellent. I jumped out of bed, clutched the poker as I passed the expiring fire, and in a moment was upon the lobby. The sound had ceased by this time – the dark and chill were discouraging; and, guess my horror, when I saw, or thought I saw, a black monster, whether in the shape of a man or a bear I could not say, standing, with its back to the wall, on the lobby, facing me, with a pair of great greenish eyes shining dimly out. Now, I must be frank, and confess that the cupboard which displayed our plates and cups stood just there, though at the moment I did not recollect it. At the same time I must honestly say, that making every allowance for an excited imagination, I never could satisfy myself that I was made the dupe of my own fancy in this matter; for this apparition, after one or two shiftings of shape, as if in the act of incipient transformation, began, as it seemed on second thoughts, to advance upon me in its original form. From an instant of terror rather than courage, I hurled the poker, with all my force, at its head; and to the music of a horrid crash made my way into my room, and double-locked the door. Then in a minute more, I heard the horrid bare feet walk down the stairs, till the sound ceased in the hall, as on the former occasion.

If the apparition of the night before was an ocular delusion of my fancy sporting with the dark outlines of our cupboard, and if its horrid eyes were nothing but a pair of teacups, I had, at all events, the satisfaction of having launched the poker with admirable effect, and in true 'fancy' phrase, 'knocked its two daylights into one', as the commingled fragments of my tea-service testified. I did my best to gather comfort and courage from these evidences; but it would not do. And then what could I say of those horrid bare feet, and the regular tramp, tramp, tramp, which measured the distance of the entire staircase through the solitude of my haunted dwelling, and at an hour when no good influence was stirring? Confound it! – the whole affair was abominable. I was out of spirits, and dreaded the approach of night.

It came, ushered ominously in with a thunder-storm and dull torrents of depressing rain. Earlier than usual the streets grew silent; and by twelve o'clock nothing but the comfortless pattering of the rain was to be heard.

I made myself as snug as I could. I lighted *two* candles instead of one. I foreswore bed, and held myself in readiness for a sally, candle in hand; for, *coute qui coute*, I was resolved to *see* the being, if visible at all, who troubled the nightly stillness of my mansion. I was fidgety and nervous, and tried in vain to interest myself with my books. I walked up and down my room, whistling in turn martial and hilarious music, and listening ever and anon for dreaded noise. I sat down and stared at the square label on the solemn and reserved-looking black bottle, until 'FLANAGAN & CO.'s BEST OLD MALT WHISKY' grew into a sort of subdued accompaniment to all the fantastic and horrible speculations which chased one another through my brain.

Silence, meanwhile, grew more silent, and darkness darker. I listened in vain for the rumble of a vehicle, or the dull clamour of a distant row. There was nothing but the sound of a rising wind, which had succeeded the thunder-storm that had travelled over the Dublin mountains quite out of hearing. In the middle of this great city I began to feel myself alone with nature, and Heaven knows what beside. My courage was ebbing. Punch, however, which makes beasts of so many, made a man of me again – just in time to hear with tolerable nerve and firmness the lumpy, flabby, naked feet deliberately descending the stairs again.

I took a candle, not without a tremor. As I crossed the floor I tried to extemporize a prayer, but stopped short to listen, and never finished it. The steps continued. I confess I hesitated for some seconds at the door before I took heart of grace and opened it. When I peeped out the lobby was perfectly empty – there was no monster standing on the staircase; and as the detested sound ceased, I was reassured enough to venture forward nearly to the banisters. Horror of horrors! within a stair of two beneath the spot where I stood the unearthy tread smote the floor. My eye caught something in motion; it was about the size of Goliath's foot – it was grey, heavy, and flapped with a dead weight from one step to another. As I am alive, it was the most monstrous grey rat I have beheld or imagined.

Shakespeare says – 'Some men there are cannot abide a gaping pig, and some that are mad if they behold a cat.' I went well-nigh out of my wits when I beheld this *rat*; for, laugh at at me as you may, it fixed upon me, I thought, a perfectly human expression of malice; and, as it shuffled about and looked up into my face almost from between my feet, I saw, I could swear it – I felt it then, and know it now, the infernal gaze and the accursed countenance of my old friend in the portrait, transfused into the visage of the bloated vermin before me.

I bounced into my room with a feeling of loathing and horror I cannot describe, and locked and bolted my door as if a lion had been at the other side. D – n him or *it;* curse the portrait and its original! I felt in my soul that the rat – yes, yes, the *rat*, the RAT I had just seen, was that evil being in masquerade, and rambling through the house upon some infernal night lark.

Next morning I was early trudging through the miry streets; and, among other transactions, posted a peremptory note recalling Tom. On my return, however, I found a note from my absent 'chum', announcing his intended return the next day. I was doubly rejoiced at this, because I had succeeded in getting rooms; and because the change of scene and return of my comrade were rendered specially pleasant by the last night's ridiculous half horrible adventure.

I slept extemporaneously in my new quarters in Digges' Street that night, and next morning returned for breakfast to the haunted mansion, where I was certain Tom would call immediately on his arrival.

I was quite right – he came; and almost his first question referred to the primary object of our change of residence.

'Thank God,' he said with genuine fervour, on hearing that all was arranged. 'On *your* account I am delighted. As to myself, I assure you that no earthly consideration could have induced me ever again to pass a night in this disastrous old house.'

'Confound the house!' I ejaculated, with a genuine mixture of fear and detestation, 'we have not had a pleasant hour since we came to live here'; and so I went on, and related incidentally my adventure with the plethoric old rat.

'Well, if that were *all*,' said my cousin, affecting to make light of the matter, 'I don't think I should have minded it very much.'

'Ay, but its eye – its countenance, my dear Tom,' urged I; 'if you had seen *that*, you would have felt it might be *anything* but what is seemed.'

'I am inclined to think the best conjurer in such a case would be an able-bodied cat,' he said, with a provoking chuckle.

'But let us hear your own adventure,' I said tartly

At this challenge he looked uneasily round him. I had poked up a very unpleasant recollection.

'You shall hear it, Dick; I'll tell it to you,' he said. 'Begad, sir, I should feel quite queer, though, telling it *here,* though we are too strong a body for ghosts to meddle with just now.'

Though he spoke this like a joke, I think it was serious calculation. Our Hebe was in a corner of a room, packing our cracked delft tea and dinner-services in a basket. She soon suspended operations, and with mouth and eyes wide open became an absorbed listener. Tom's experiences were told nearly in these words: –

'I saw it three times, Dick – three distinct times; and I am perfectly certain it meant me some infernal harm. I was, I say, in danger – in *extreme* danger; for, if nothing else had happened, my reason would most certainly have failed me, unless I had escaped so soon. Thank God, I *did* escape.

'The first night of this hateful disturbance, I was lying in the attitude of sleep, in that lumbering old bed. I hate to think of it. I was really wide awake, though I had put out my candle, and was lying quietly as if I had been asleep; and although accidentally restless, my thoughts were running in a cheerful and agreeable channel.

'I think it must have been two o'clock at least when I thought I heard a sound in that – that odious dark recess at the far end of the bedroom. It was as if someone was drawing a piece of cord slowly along the floor, lifting it up, and dropping it softly down again in coils. I sat up once or twice in my bed, but could see nothing, so I concluded it must be mice in the wainscot. I felt no emotion graver than curiosity, and after a few minutes ceased to observe it.

'While lying in this state, strange to say; without at first a suspicion of anything supernatural, on a sudden I saw an old man, rather stout and square, in a sort of roan-red dressing-gown, and with a black cap on his head, moving stiffly and slowly in a diagonal direction, from the recess, across the floor of the bedroom, passing my bed at the foot, and entering the lumber-closet at the left. He had something under his arm; his head hung a little at one side; and merciful God! when I saw his face.'

Tom stopped for a while, and then said

'That awful countenance, which living or dying I never can forget, disclosed what he was. Without turning to the right or left, he passed beside me, and entered the closet by the bed's head.

'While this fearful and indescribable type of death and guilt was passing, I felt that I had no more power to speak or stir than if I had been myself a corpse. For hours after it had disappeared, I was too terrified and weak to move. As soon as daylight came, I took courage, and examined the room, and especially the course which the frightful intruder had seemed to take, but there was not a vestige to indicate anybody's having passed there; no sign of any disturbing agency visible among the lumber that strewed the floor of the closet.

'I now began to recover a little. I was fagged and exhausted, and at last, overpowered by a feverish sleep. I came down late; and finding you out of spirits, on account of your dreams about the portrait, whose *original* I am now certain disclosed himself to me, I did not care to talk about the infernal vision. In fact, I was trying to persuade myself that the whole thing was an illusion, and I did not like to revive in their intensity the hated impressions of the past night – or, to risk the constancy of my scepticism, by recounting the tale of my sufferings.

'It required some nerve, I can tell you, to go to my haunted chamber next night, and lie down quietly in the same bed,' continued Tom. 'I did so with a degree of trepidation, which, I am not ashamed to say, a very little matter would have sufficed to stimulate to downright panic. This night, however, passed off quietly enough, as also the next; and so too did two or three more. I grew more confident, and began to fancy that I believed in the theories of spectral illusions, with which I had at first vainly tried to impose upon my convictions.

'The apparition had been, indeed, altogether anomalous. It had crossed the room without any recognition of my presence: I had not disturbed *it*, and *it* had no mission to *me*. What, then, was the imaginable use of its crossing the room in a visible shape at all? Of course it might have *been* in the closet instead of *going* there, as easily as it introduced itself into the recess without entering the chamber in a shape discernible by the senses. Besides, how the deuce *had* I seen it? It was a dark night; I had no candle; there was no fire; and yet I saw it as distinctly, in colouring and outline, as ever I beheld human form! A cataleptic dream would explain it all; and I was determined that a dream it should be.

'One of the most remarkable phenomena connected with the practice of mendacity is the vast number of deliberate lies we tell ourselves, whom, of all persons, we can least expect to deceive. In all this, I need hardly tell you, Dick, I was simply lying to myself, and did not believe one word of the wretched humbug. Yet I went on, as men will do, like preserving charlatans and imposters, who tire people into credulity by the mere force of reiteration; so I hoped to win myself over at last to a comfortable scepticism about the ghost.

'He had not appeared a second time – that certainly was a comfort; and what, after all, did I care for him, and his queer old toggery and strange looks? Not a fig! I was nothing the worse for having seen him, and a good story the better. So I tumbled into bed, put out my candle, and cheered by a loud drunken quarrel in the back lane, went fast asleep.

'From this deep slumber I awoke with a start. I knew I had had a horrible dream; but what it was I could not remember. My heart was thumping furiously; I felt bewildered and feverish; I sat up in the bed and looked about the room. A broad flood of moonlight came through the curtainless window; everything was as I had last seen it; and though the domestic squabble in the back lane was, unhappily for me, allayed, I yet could hear a pleasant fellow singing, on his way home, the then popular comic ditty called, "Murphy Delany". Taking advantage of this diversion I lay down again, with my face towards the fireplace, and closing my eyes, did my best to think of nothing else but the song, which was every moment growing fainter in the distance:

'Twas Murphy Delany, so funny and frisky
Stept into a shebeen shop to get his skin full;

He reeled out again pretty well lined with whiskey,
As fresh as a shamrock, as blind as a bull.

'The singer, whose condition I dare say resembled that of his hero, was
soon too far off to regale my ears any more; and as his music died away. I
myself sank into a doze, neither sound nor refreshing. Somehow the song
had got into my head, and I went meandering on through the adventures
of my respectable fellow-countryman, who, on emerging from the
"shebeen shop", fell into a river, from which he was fished up to be "sat
upon" by a coroner's jury, who having learned from a "horse-doctor" that
he was "dead as a door-nail, so there was an end", returned their verdict
accordingly, just as he returned to his senses, when an angry altercation
and a pitched battle between the body and the coroner winds up the lay
with due spirit and pleasantry.

'Through this ballad I continued with a weary monotony to plod, down
to the very last line, and then *da capo*, and so on, in my uncomfortable half-
sleep, for how long, I can't conjecture. I found myself at last, however,
muttering, "*dead* as a door-nail, so there was an end"; and something like
another voice within me, seemed to say, very faintly, but sharply, "dead!
dead! *dead!* and may the Lord have mercy on your soul!" and instanta-
neously I was wide awake, and staring right before me from the pillow.

'Now – will you believe it, Dick? – I saw the same accursed figure
standing full front, and gazing at me with its stony and fiendish
countenance, not two yards from my bedside.'

Tom stopped here, and wiped the perspiration from his face. I felt very
queer. The girl was as pale as Tom; and assembled as we were in the very
scene of these adventures, we were all, I dare say, equally grateful for the
clear daylight and the resuming bustle out of doors.

'For about three seconds I saw it plainly; then it grew indistinct; but, for
a long time, there was something like a column of dark vapour where it
had been standing between me and the wall; and I felt sure that he was still
there. After a good while, this appearance went too. I took my clothes
downstairs to the hall, and dressed there, with the door half open; then
went out into the street, and walked about the town till morning, when I
came back, in a miserable state of nervousness and exhaustion. I was such
a fool, Dick to be ashamed to tell you how I came to be so upset. I thought
you would laugh at me; especially as I had always talked philosophy, and
treated *your* ghosts with contempt. I concluded you would give me no
quarter; and so kept the tale of horror to myself.

'Now, Dick, you will hardly believe me, when I assure you, that for
many nights after this last experience, I did not go to my room at all. I used
to sit up for a while in the drawing-room after you had gone up to your
bed; and then steal down softly to the hall-door, let myself out, and sit in
the "Robin Hood" tavern until the last guest went off; and then I got

through the night like a sentry, pacing the streets till morning.

'For more than a week I never slept in bed. I sometimes had a snooze on a form in the "Robin Hood", and sometimes a nap in a chair during the day; but regular sleep I had absolutely none.

'I was quite resolved that we should get into another house; but I could not bring myself to tell you the reason, and I somehow put it off from day to day, although my life was, during every hour of this procrastination, rendered as miserable as that of a felon with the constables on his track. I was growing absolutely ill from this wretched mode of life.

'One afternoon I determined to enjoy an hour's sleep upon your bed. I hated mine; so that I had never, except in a stealthy visit every day to unmake it, lest Martha should discover the secret of my nightly absence, entered the ill-omened chamber.

'As ill-luck would have it, you had locked your bedroom, and taken away the key. I went into my own to unsettle the bedclothes, as usual, and give the bed the appearance of having been slept in. Now, a variety of circumstances concurred to bring about the dreadful scene through which I was that night to pass. In the first place, I was literally overpowered with fatigue, and longing for sleep; in the next place, the effect of this extreme exhaustion upon my nerves resembled that of a narcotic, and rendered me less susceptible than, perhaps, I should in any other condition have been, of the exciting fears which had become habitual to me. Then again, a little bit of the window was open, a pleasant freshness pervaded the room, and, to crown all, the cheerful sun of day was making the room quite quite pleasant. What was to prevent my enjoying an hour's nap *here?* The whole air was resonant with the cheerful hum of life, and the broad matter-of-fact light of day filled every corner of the room.

'I yielded – stifling my qualms – to the almost overpowering temptation; and merely throwing off my coat, and loosening my cravat, I lay down, limiting myself to *half*-an-hour's doze in the unwonted enjoyment of a feather bed, a coverlet, and a bolster.

'It was horribly insidious; and the demon, no doubt, marked my infatuated preparation. Dolt that I was, I fancied, with mind and body worn out for want of sleep, and an arrear of a full week's rest to my credit, that such measure as *half-* an hour's sleep, in such a situation, was possible. My sleep was death-like, long and dreamless.

'Without a start or fearful sensation of any kind, I waked gently, but completely. It was, as you have good reason to remember, long past midnight – I believe, about two o'clock. When sleep has been deep and long enough to satisfy nature thoroughly, one often wakens in this way, suddenly, tranquilly, and completely.

'There was a figure seated in that lumbering, old sofa-chair, near the fireplace. Its back was rather towards me, but I could not be mistaken; it turned slowly round, and, merciful heavens! there was the stony face, with its infernal lineaments of malignity and despair, gloating on me. There was now no doubt as to its consciousness of my presence, and the hellish malice with which it was animated, for it arose, and drew close to the bedside. There was a rope about its neck, and the other end, coiled up, it held stiffly in its hand.

'My good angel nerved me for this horrible crisis. I remained for some seconds transfixed by the gaze of this tremendous phantom. He came close to the bed, and appeared on the point of mounting upon it. The next instant I was upon the floor at the far side, and in a moment more was, I don't know how, upon the lobby.

'But the spell was not yet broken; the valley of the shadow of death was not yet traversed. The abhorred phantom was before me there; it was standing near the banisters, stooping a little, and with one end of the rope round its own neck, was poising a noose at the other, as if to throw over mine; and while engaged in this baleful pantomime, it wore a smile so sensual, so unspeakably dreadful, that my senses were nearly overpowered. I saw and remember nothing more, until I found myself in your room.

'I had a wonderful escape, Dick – there is no diputing *that* -- an escape for which, while I live, I shall bless the mercy of heaven. No one can conceive or imagine what it is for flesh and blood to stand in the presence of such a thing, but one who has had the terrific experience. Dick, Dick, a shadow has passed over me – a chill has crossed my blood and marrow, and I will never be the same again - never, Dick – never!'

Our handmaid, a mature girl of two-and-fifty, as I have said, stayed her hand, as Tom's story proceeded, and by little and little drew near to us, with open mouth, and her brows contracted over her little, beady black eyes, till stealing a glance over her shoulder now and then, she established herself close behind us. During the relation, she had made various earnest comments, in an undertone; but these and her ejaculations, for the sake of brevity and simplicity, I have omitted in my narration.

'It's often I heard tell of it,' she now said 'but I never believed it rightly till now – though, indeed, why should not I? Does not my mother, down there in the lane, know quare stories, God bless us, beyond telling about it? But you ought not to have slept in the back bedroom. She was loath to let me be going in and out of that room even in the day time, let alone for any Christian to spend the night in it; for sure she says it was his own bedroom.'

'*Whose* own bedroom?' we asked, in a breath.

'Why, *his* – the ould Judge's – Judge Horrock's, to be sure God rest his sowl'; and she looked fearfully round.

'Amen!' I muttered. 'But did he die there?'

'Die there! No, not quite *there*,' she said. 'Shure, was not it over the banisters he hung himself, the ould sinner, God be merciful to us all? and was not it in the alcove they found the handles of the skipping-rope cut off, and the knife where he was settling the cord, God bless us, to hang himself with? It was his housekeeper's daughter owned the rope, my mother often told me, and the child never throve after, and used to be starting up out of her sleep, and screeching in the night time, wid dhrames and frights that cum an her; and they said how it was the speerit of the ould Judge that was tormentin' her; and she used to be roaring and yelling out to hould back the big old fellow with the crooked neck; and then she'd screech "Oh, the master! the master! he's stampin' at me, and beckoning to me! Mother, darling, don't let me go!" And so the poor crathure died at last, and the docthers said it was wather on the brain, for it was all they could say.'

'How long ago was all this?' I asked.

'Oh, then, how would I know?' she answered. 'But it must be a wondherful long time ago, for the housekeeper was an ould woman, with a pipe in her mouth, and not a tooth left, and better nor eighty years ould when my mother was first married; and they said she was a rale buxom, fine-dressed woman when the ould Judge come to his end; an', indeed, my mother's not far from eighty years ould herself to this day; and what made it worse for the unnatural ould villain, God rest his soul, to frighten the little girl out of the world the way did, was what was mostly thought and believed by everyone. My mother says now the poor crathure was his own child; for he was by all accounts an ould villain every way, an' the hangin'est judge that ever was known in Ireland's ground.'

'From what you said about the danger of sleeping in that bedroom,' said I, 'I suppose there were stories about ghost having appeared there to others.'

'Well, there *was* things said – quare things, surely,' she answered, as it seemed, with some reluctance. 'And why would not there? Sure was it not up in that same room he slept for more than twenty years? and was it not in the *alcove* he got the rope ready that done his own business at last, the way he done many a betther man's in his life time? – and was not the body lying in the same bed after death, and put in the coffin there, too, and carried out to his grave from it in Pether's churchyard, after the coroner was done? But there was quare stories – my mother has them all – about how one Nicholas Spaight got into trouble on the head of it.'

'And what did they say of this Nicholas Spaight?' I asked.

'Oh, for that matther, it's soon told,' she answered.

And she certainly did relate a very strange story, which so piqued my curiosity, that I took occasion to visit the ancient lady, her mother, from whom I learned many very curious particulars. Indeed, I am tempted to tell the tale, but my fingers are weary, and I must defer it. But if you wish to hear it another time, I shall do my best.

When we heard the strange tale I have *not* yet told you, we put one or two further questions to her about the alleged spectral visitations, to which the house had, ever since the death of the wicked old Judge, been subjected.

'No one ever had luck in it,' she told us. 'There was always cross accidents, sudden deaths, and short times in it. The first that tuck it was a family – I forget their name – but at any rate there was two young ladies and their papa. He was about sixty, and a stout healthy gentleman as you'd wish to see at that age. Well, he slept in that unlucky back bedroom; and, God between us an' harm! sure enough he was found dead one morning, half out of the bed, with his head as black as a sloe, and swelled like a puddin', hanging down near the floor. It was a fit, they said. He was as dead as a mackerel, and so *he* could not say what it was; but the ould people was all sure that it was nothing at all but the ould Judge, God bless us! that frightened him out of his senses and his life together.

'Some time after there was a rich old maiden lady took the house. I don't know which room *she* slept in, but she lived alone; and at any rate, one morning, the servants going down early to their work, found her sitting on the passage-stairs, shivering and talkin' to herself, quite mad; and never a word more could any of *them* or her friends get from her ever afterwards but, "Don't ask me to go, for I promised to wait for him." They never made out from her who it was she meant by *him*, but of course those that knew the ould house were at no loss for the meaning of all that happened to her.

'Then afterwards, when the house was let out in lodgings, there was Micky Byrne that took the same room, with his wife and three little children; and sure I heard Mrs Byrne myself telling how the children used to be lifted up in the bed at night, she could not see by what mains; and how they were starting and screeching every hour, just all as one as the housekeeper's little girl died, till at last one night poor Micky had a dhrop in him, the way he used now and again; and what do you think in the middle of the night he thought he heard a noise on the stairs, and being in liquor, nothing less id do him but out he must go himself to see what was wrong. Well, after that, all she ever heard him say was "Oh, God!" and a tumble that shook the very house; and there, sure enough, he was lying on the lower stairs, under the lobby, with his neck smashed double under him, where he was flung over the banisters.'

Then the handmaiden added –

'I'll go down the lane, and send up Joe Gavvey to pack up the rest of the taythings, and bring them across to your new lodgings.'

And so we all sallied out together, each of us breathing more freely, I have no doubt, as we crossed that ill-omened threshold for the last time.

Now, I may add thus much, in compliance with the immemorial usage of the realm of fiction, which sees the hero not only through his adventures, but fairly out of the world. You must have perceived that what flesh, blood, and bone hero of romance proper is to the regular compounder of fiction, this old house of brick, wood, and mortar is to the humble recorder of this true tale. I, therefore, relate, as in duty bound, the catastrophe which ultimately befell it, which was simply this – that about two years subsequently to my story it was taken by a quack doctor who called himself Baron Duhlstoerf, and filled the parlour windows with bottles of indescribable horrors preserved in brandy, and the newspapers with the usual grandiloquent and mendacious advertisements. This gentleman among his virtues did not reckon sobriety, and one night, being overcome with much wine, he set fire to his bed curtains, partially burned himself, and totally consumed the house. It was afterwards rebuilt, and for a time an undertaker established himself in the premises.

I have now told you my own and Tom's adventures, together with some valuable collateral particulars; and having acquitted myself of my engagement, I wish you a very good night, and pleasant dreams.

The Whining

RAMSEY CAMPBELL

WHEN BENTINCK FIRST SAW THE DOG he thought it was a patch of mud. He was staring from his window into Princes Park, watching the snow heap itself against folds of earth and slip softly from branches. Against the black trees on the far side of the park, flakes shimmered like light within the eyelids. Bentinck gazed, trying to calm himself, and his eye was caught by a brown heap on the gradual slope of the green.

It lanced his mood. He sighed and began to gather his coffee-cup, smashed in a momentary rage. At least he hadn't allowed his fury to touch the Radio Merseyside tape-recorder, which contained its source. He opened the French windows and hurried around the corner of the house to his bin, almost tripping over the half-buried handle of an axe. As he returned he saw that the brown heap was shaking snow from its plastered fur and staring at him. It freed its legs from the snow and struggled towards him, half-engulfed at each weak leap.

Bentinck hesitated, then he shrugged flakes from his shoulders and closed the windows. After mopping the carpet he played back the tape. He'd worked at Radio Merseyside only a month, and already here he was, allowing a councillor to feed him answers which begged specific questions, those the councillor was prepared to answer. And off the tape Bentinck was absolutely and articulately opposed to capital punishment, in fact to any violence: that was what infuriated him. Well, he might as well be calm; the incident was beyond resolution. He might as well enjoy his free afternoon. He bundled his coat about him and emerged into the park.

Small cold flakes licked his cheeks. He crossed to the lake, his footsteps squeaking. Ducks creaked throatily across the silver sky, and a flurry of gulls detached themselves from the white with rusty squawks. Behind him Bentinck heard a wet slithering. He turned and saw the dog.

As soon as he met its eyes the dog changed direction. It began to sidle around him, a few feet away, curving its body into a shape like a ballerina's expression of shame. It circled him crabwise, pointing its nose towards him. It was several shades of mud, with trailing ears like scraps of floorcloth, and large eyes. Its legs were short and bent like roots, and its tail wavered vaguely. 'All right, boy,' Bentinck said. 'Whose are you?'

He stepped towards it. At once it leapt clumsily backwards, rather as an

313

insect might, he thought. 'All right,' he said, slapping his shin. It skidded to its feet and shook off a dandruff of snow. As it did so he saw that its skin was corrugated with ribs. 'Food,' he said, remembering a bone he'd intended to use for soup. But the dog stayed where it was, tail quivering. 'Food, boy,' he said, and began to tramp back to his flat.

Then the dog commenced whining like a gate in a high wind, a reiterated glissando rising across a third. 'Food! Food!' shouted Bentinck, almost at the windows, and the couple in the first-floor flat peered out warily. I've been a fool once today, Bentinck thought, and then glared up at them; their hi-fi seemed to need a good deal less sleep than he, and while he wouldn't complain unless it became intolerable he was damned if he would whisper for them. 'Here, boy!' he shouted, and hurried to the refrigerator. Over the slight squeal of the door he heard the incessant cry from the park.

He tore a piece of meat from the bone and hurled it towards the dog. The animal made a gulping leap and began to claw up an explosion of snow where the meat had landed. Leaving the bone inside the window, Bentinck found a towel in his laundry-bag. In the living-room he halted, surprised. The dog was sitting in front of the gas fire, gnawing the bone. It snarled.

'Do sit down,' Bentinck said. 'You don't mind if I close the windows?' Out of the corner of its eye the dog watched him do so. 'I don't suppose you'd consider lying on this towel. No, I thought not,' he said. 'Just so long as we can both have the fire.' The dog grumbled as he sat down, but continued chewing. Bentinck gazed at it. Its back legs curled around and its tail followed them, as if to form a pleasing contrast to the sharp straight bone. Somehow, Bentinck thought, the contrast expressed the dog.

Gradually its jaws wound down. Bentinck had been lulled by the sight of its satiety; only the appearance of a pool seeping from beneath the animal startled him alert. Bending closer, he realized that it wasn't the thawing of the dog. 'Now wait a minute,' he said, springing up. The dog winced back from him, leaving the bone; it began to cringe, and its tongue and tail quivered. 'All right, you poor sod, it's not your fault,' he said. 'I hope you don't object to the *Echo*.'

But when he returned with the newspaper, the dog was scraping at the carpet and worrying the tape-recorder's lead. 'I'm tempted to offer you the tape, but on balance I think you've been enough of a good deed for one day,' he said. Wrapping his hand in the towel, he fished the bone out of the pool and threw it into the park. With a bark that combined a whoop with its whine, the dog followed.

Later, at Radio Merseyside, he edited the tape and had an unpleasant slow-motion conversation with his producer. As he returned to his flat he thought he saw the dog lapping at the lake, at its encroaching margin of mud and waste paper. 'I'm afraid I didn't quite manage to pin him down,' 'Well, you can't be expected to learn everything at once.' 'That's true.' 'But you'll have to work on mastering interviews.' 'Yes, I will.' 'Won't you.' 'Yes, of course.' God, thought Bentinck savagely. He filled a soup-bowl with water and set it outside the windows. Under the sill the snow was flecked with blood, and there were claw-marks on the frame.

He was awakened by dull thumps overhead, which his heart continued. He dragged the alarm clock into view and saw it was four o'clock. Then he became aware of the whining, the cause of the protests resounding through the floor above. Wearily he groped his way to the French windows. As he opened them snowballs hailed down from the first floor, and the dog yelped. Indignant, Bentinck spread newspapers on the carpet and coaxed the dog inside. It slithered through the windows like a timid snake and lay down panting. 'That's it, boy,' Bentinck said. 'Bedtime, what's left of it.'

Three hours later the whining prodded him awake. 'No, no, boy, shut up,' he mumbled – but almost at once the dog clawed open his bedroom door and crawled towards him as if under fire, leaving a snail's trail of melted snow. He stroked its back as it came within reach, and the dog attempted to writhe itself through the carpet. Leaning over to follow his hand, Bentinck saw that the animal had an erection. It peered at him from the corner of its eye, slyly. 'You go back to your own bed,' Bentinck said and retreated under the blankets.

But the whining prised him forth. He opened the French windows and the dog galloped towards them, halting at his side. 'I know, you're scared to go out alone,' he said. 'I take it I've had my sleep.' He shaved, washed and dressed, trying to hush the dog. 'A walk will do me the world of good,' he said, opening the windows. 'Jesus wept.'

His feet crunched through the glazed snow and plunged into the mire of the paths. Ducks swam through a grey coating of snow. The dog ran ahead, casting itself in a curve, struggling to its feet and running back towards him. He found a dripping stick and threw it, but it only sank into banked snow with a thud. By the time they'd circled the lake his feet were soaking. He hurried inside, closing out the dog, picked up the telephone and dialled. 'Didn't you use that tape? Good,' he said. 'I'd like to try him again.' He changed his boots and left by the front door.

But the councillor had gone to Majorca for a week. When Bentinck neared home that evening, still composing questions, he hesitated at the park gates. He could go round to the front door and avoid the dog. However, he intented to take advantage of the park while its litter and mud were draped. Nothing moved on the dimming slopes. He reached his windows and unlocked them. As he did so the dog scrambled around the corner of the house and shot into his flat.

'Well, I know what *I'm* having for dinner,' Bentinck said, cutting open cellophane. The dog lay on the kitchen tiles and watched him; its tail strained to rise and fell back. 'You see what that says?' Bentinck said, flourishing the packet. 'Dinner for one.' But as he ate, his left hand secretly passed scraps of meat beneath the table, where wet teeth snapped them away.

'It's usual for guests to leave when the host shows signs of collapse,' Bentinck said, tying his pyjama cord. He changed the newspapers by the windows and shivering, unlocked them. 'The Gents' is outside,' he said. But the dog lay down, tearing the top layer of paper. Bentinck closed the windows and his bedroom door. He set the alarm, and the whining started.

'No,' he said, opening the door. 'No,' when the dog refused the invitation of the windows. '*No*,' as it began to gaze sidelong at him. Upstairs he could hear the first rumbles of displeasure. He picked up a newspaper. He'd read that a rolled-up newspaper was the kindest instrument with which to chastise a pup. He rolled the *Echo* and struck the dog's rump with the face of the year's Miss Unilever.

The dog yelped and rolled over. Then it began to fawn, curling itself about the carpet as if all its bones were broken. It stood up in a dislocated way, its hindquarters belatedly regaining an even keel, and came towards him, licking its lips and whining. 'Be quiet,' he said and struck it again, harder. It spun over, almost somersaulting, and sidled back to him. Its tongue flopped out, dripping; it rubbed against his legs, swinging its tail in a great arc, and whined. 'Oh, get out,' he said, disgusted. 'Come on. Out now.' It climbed up his leg, pressing its crotch against him. 'Out!' he shouted and opening the windows, picked up the struggling dog and hurled it into the snow. Then he buried himself in bed. Above him the hi-fi began to howl and thump.

For the next week he kept the windows closed. He avoided the couple on the first floor but was ready with an argument should he meet them. Each night he heard the whining and the scrape of claws on wood. On the Sunday afternoon he saw the dog ploughing through the lake in pursuit of a stick thrown by three children, which had lodged beneath a bench overturned into the lake. He watched the animal as it tried to lift the bench on its shoulders, to force itself beneath the seat, and for a moment admired the dog and envied the children. Then his mind shifted, and he wondered whether they would be able to resist the creature's temptation to sadism. He rolled up a newspaper and struck himself on the arm. He was surprised by how much it hurt.

That night the dog attacked the window while he was still reading. Bentinck rolled the paper and flourished it. The dog redoubled its efforts. One of the lower panes was scribbled with crimson, and the animal's left front paw was darker tonight. Bentinck frowned and went to bed, and in the morning called the RSPCA.

When they arrived, two men in a snarling van, the dog had vanished. Bentinck had gone to the edge of the park to entice the dog into the flat, and almost didn't hear their knocking. "Clever dog you've got there," one said, stamping the snow of the search from his boots. 'Better tie him up before you ring next time.' 'It isn't mine,' Bentinck said, but it wasn't important, and besides they were already driving away. He collected together his equipment to interview the councillor. He opened the windows, and the dog hurtled out from beneath his bed into the park.

That evening the dog wasn't waiting when he returned. He inched his way through the windows and locked them. Then, controlling himself, he made coffee. At last his hand crept forward and switched on the tape. 'I'm not concerned with punishing specific criminals. I'm concerned that violence is becoming an everyday fact of life.' 'Now this is complete nonsense, isn't it?' he heard himself saying angrily, and switched off before his fury surfaced completely. Then the French windows began to shudder.

He stared at them. The dog was hurling itself against them, clawing at the frame. Bentinck leapt to his feet and gestured it away, but it swung its tail and began to dig at the sill. He wrenched open the windows to shove the dog away, but it had already squeezed into the room. 'Come on,' he said. 'I don't want you.' At that moment someone knocked at the door of the flat: a man with a thin frowning face and long grey hair tucked inside a car-coat. Of course, the landlord.

'I'll get my cheque-book,' Bentinck said, wondering why the man was frowning.

'The people upstairs have been complaining about your dog.'

'It's not my dog,' Bentinck said, dropping his cheque-book. 'And in any case I'm surprised they can hear it at all over their hi-fi, which they play till all hours.'

'Really? It's odd you haven't complained before. Whose dog is it if it isn't yours?'

'God knows. All I know is I'd like to see the last of it.'

'Do you know, I've gone through life convinced that the man's the master of the dog. What is this dog, a hypnotist?'

'No,' Bentinck snarled, 'a bloody pest.'

'Well, I'll tell you what to do with pests, just between us. You get some meat and cook it up with poison. Simple as that. I'll even let you dig in the garden if you do it quietly. There's your rent book. I'll see myself out.'

The landlord left, leaving the door ajar. I've tried the RSPCA, Bentinck said furiously, you try them if you're so bothered. I might give them a ring about you. The dog was fawning at his feet. 'Stop that,' he shouted, stamping, and stood up to close the door.

Behind him there came a thud. The dog was chewing the tape-recorder lead and had pulled the machine to the floor. 'Haven't I made myself clear?' Bentinck shouted. He opened the windows and stamped at the dog, herding it towards them. It crawled around the room, cringing back from furniture, trying to climb his leg, and he grasped it by the scruff of its neck and dragged it yelping towards the windows. Still holding the dog, he closed the windows behind him.

'Now go. Just go,' he said, kicking slush at it. It ran splashing towards the bins, its tail wagging limply, but when he turned to the windows it began to sidle back. 'Go, will you!' he shouted, running at the dog and tripping. He pushed himself to his feet, his hands gloved in ice, as the dog leapt at him and smeared his mouth with its tongue. 'Go!' he shouted and fumbling behind him for what he'd tripped over, threw it.

He heard the axe strike. The dog screamed and then began to whine, its cry rising and rising. 'Oh Christ,' Bentinck said. There was no light from the first floor, and he couldn't see what he'd done, only make out the dog dragging itself by its front paws through the crackling slush towards the park. He couldn't do anything. He couldn't bear to touch the dog. He stumbled towards it and saw the axe cleaving the snow. Closing his eyes, he picked up the axe and killed the dog.

Afterwards he found a spade standing against the house. He had to hold the dog together while he wrapped it in polythene. Shovelling and kicking, he disguised the discoloured snow. Then he dug a hole at the edge of the park, filled it in and tried to scatter snow over the disturbed earth. For hours he lay in bed shaking.

Next morning a corner of polythene was protruding from the ground. Bentinck trod it out of sight, shuddering, feeling the ground yield beneath his heel. When he came home, having successfully edited the tape, he found a whole edge of polythene billowing from a scraped hollow. Several dogs were chasing in the park. He dug the ground over, watching for a face at the first-floor window, as the first flakes of a new snow drifted down.

He awoke to the memory of a whining. He sat up, hurling the blanket to the floor. For minutes he listened, then he padded to the French windows. The garden was calm and softened by unbroken snow. A full moon floated in the clear sky, coaxing illumination from the landscape. He returned to his bedroom. Thick darkness lay beneath the bed.

The councillor blustered. Bentinck shrugged him off and turned his back. Before him, dawning from the shadows, lay a dog or a young girl. Bentinck held scissors, a red-hot poker, an axe, a saw. He awoke writhing, soaked in sweat, an eager whining in his ears. His whole body was pounding. He let his breathing ease, and groped for the clock. Before he could reach it, a tongue licked his hand.

The couple on the first floor were awakened by shouts. Groaning, they turned over and sought sleep. At eight o'clock they were eating breakfast when they saw Bentinck staggering about the park. 'He's drunk. That explains a lot,' the woman said. But something in his manner made them go to his assistance. When they drew near they saw that his trouser legs were covered with dried blood. Around him in the snow the prints of dogs' paws formed wildly fragmented patterns. 'Listen,' he said desperately. 'You realize it's impossible to exorcise an animal? They don't understand English, never mind Latin.' They took his arms and began to guide him back to his flat. But they hadn't reached the house when he looked down and started to brush at his shins, and kick, and scream.

318

Berenice

EDGAR ALLAN POE

Dicebant mihi sodales, si sepulchrum amicae visitarem, curas meas aliquar tulum fore levatas.

Ebn Zaiat

MISERY IS MANIFOLD. The wretchedness of earth is multiform. Overreaching the wide horizon as the rainbow, its hues are as various as the hues of that arch – as distinct too, yet as intimately blended. Overreaching the wide horizon as the rainbow! How is it that from beauty I have derived a type of unloveliness? – from the covenant of peace, a simile of sorrow? But, as in ethics, evil is a consequence of good, so, in fact, out of joy is sorrow born. Either the memory of past bliss is the anguish of today, or the agonies which *are*, have their origin in the ecstasies which *might have been*.

My baptismal name is Egaeus; that of my family I will not mention. Yet there are no towers in the land more time-honoured than my gloomy, grey, hereditary halls. Our line has been called a race of visionaries; and in many striking particulars – in the character of the family mansion – in the frescos of the chief saloon – in the tapestries of the dormitories – in the chiselling of some buttresses in the armoury – but more especially in the gallery of antique paintings – in the fashion of the library chamber – and, lastly, in the very peculiar nature of the library's contents – there is more than sufficient evidence to warrant the belief.

The recollections of my earliest years are connected with that chamber, and with its volumes – of which latter I will say no more. Here died my mother. Herein was I born. But it is mere idleness to say that I had not lived before – that the soul has no previous existence. You deny it? – let us not argue the matter. Convinced myself, I seek not to convince. There is, however, a remembrance of aërial forms – of spiritual and meaning eyes – of sounds, musical yet sad; a remembrance which will not be excluded; a memory like a shadow – vague, variable, indefinite, unsteady; and like a shadow, too, in the impossibility of my getting rid of it while the sunlight of my reason shall exist.

In that chamber was I born. Thus awakening from the long night of what seemed, but was not, nonentity, at once into the very regions of fairy land – into a palace of imagination – into the wild dominions of monastic thought and erudition – it is not singular that I gazed around me with a startled and ardent eye – that I loitered away my boyhood in books, and dissipated my youth in revery; but it *is* singular, that as years rolled away, and the noon of manhood found me still in the mansion of my fathers – it *is* wonderful what a stagnation there fell upon the springs of my life – wonderful how total an inversion took place in the character of my commonest thought. The realities of the world affected me as visions, and as visions only, while the wild ideas of the land of dreams became, in turn, not the material of my every-day existence, but in very deed that existence utterly and solely in itself.

Berenice and I were cousins, and we grew up together in my paternal halls. Yet differently we grew – I, ill of health, and buried in gloom – she, agile, graceful, and overflowing with energy; hers the ramble on the hillside – mine, the studies of the cloister; I, living within my own heart, and addicted, body and soul, to the most intense and painful meditation – she, roaming carelessly through life, with no thought of the shadows in her path, or the silent flight of the raven-winged hours. Berenice! – I call upon her name – Berenice! – and from the grey ruins of memory a thousand tumultuous recollections are startled at the sound! Ah, vividly is her image before me now, as in the early days of her light-heartedness and joy! Oh, gorgeous yet fantastic beauty! Oh, sylph amid the shrubberies of Arnheim! Oh, Naiad among its fountains! And then – then all is mystery and terror, and a tale which should not be told. Disease – a fatal disease, fell like the simoon upon her frame; and even, while I gazed upon her, the spirit of change swept over her, pervading her mind, her habits, and her character, and, in a manner the most subtle and terrible, disturbing even the identity of her person! Alas! the destroyer came and went! – and the victim – where is she? I knew her not – or knew her no longer as Berenice!

Among the numerous train of maladies superinduced by that fatal and primary one which effected a revolution of so horrible a kind in the moral and physical being of my cousin, may be mentioned as the most distressing and obstinate in its nature, a species of epilepsy not unfrequently terminating in *trance* itself – trance very nearly resembling positive dissolution, and from which her manner of recovery was, in most instances, startingly abrupt. In the meantime, my own disease – for I have been told that I should call it by no other appellation – my own disease, then, grew rapidly upon me, and assumed finally a monomaniac character of a novel and extraordinary form – hourly and momently gaining vigour – and at length obtaining over me the most incomprehensible ascendency. This monomania, if I must so term it, consisted in a morbid irritability of those properties of the mind in metaphysical science termed the *attentive*. It is more than probable that I am not understood; but I fear, indeed, that it is in no manner possible to convey to the mind of the merely general reader, an adequate idea of that nervous *intensity of interest* with which, in my case, the powers of meditation (not to speak technically) busied and buried themselves, in the contemplation of even the most ordinary objects of the universe.

To muse for long unwearied hours, with my attention riveted to some frivolous device on the margin or in the typography of a book; to become absorbed, for the better part of a summer's day, in a quaint shadow falling aslant upon the tapestry or upon the floor; to lose myself, for an entire night, in watching the steady flame of a lamp, or the embers of a fire; to dream away whole days over the perfume of a flower; to repeat, monotonously, some common word, until the sound, by dint of frequent repetition, ceased to convey any idea whatever to the mind; to lose all sense of motion or physical existence, by means of absolute bodily quiescence long and obstinately persevered in: such were a few of the most common and least pernicious vagaries induced by a condition of the mental faculties, not, indeed, altogether unparalleled, but certainly bidding defiance to any thing like analysis or explanation.

Yet let me not be misapprehended. The undue, earnest, and morbid attention thus excited by objects in their own nature frivolous, must not be confounded in character with that ruminating propensity common to all mankind, and more especially indulged in by persons of ardent imagination. It was not even, as might be at first supposed, an extreme condition, or exaggeration of such propensity, but primarily and essentially distinct and different. In the one instance, the dreamer, or enthusiast, being interested by an object usually *not* frivolous, imperceptibly loses sight of this object in a wilderness of deductions and suggestions issuing therefrom, until, at the conclusion of a day-dream *often replete with luxury*, he finds the *incitamentum*, or first cause of his musings, entirely vanished and forgotten. In my case, the primary object was *invariably frivolous*, although assuming, through the medium of my distempered vision, a refracted and unreal importance. Few deductions, if any, were made; and those few pertinaciously returning in upon the original object as a centre. The meditations were *never* pleasurable; and at the termination of the revery, the first cause, so far from being out of sight, had attained that supernaturally exaggerated interest which was the prevailing feature of the disease. In a word, the powers of mind more particularly exercised were, with me, as I have said before, the *attentive*, and are, with the day-dreamer, the *speculative*.

My books, at this epoch, if they did not actually serve to irritate the disorder, partook, it will be perceived, largely, in their imaginative and inconsequential nature, of the characteristic qualities of the disorder itself. I well remember, among others, the treatise of the noble Italian, Coelius Secundus Curio, '*De Amplitudine Beati Regni Dei*'; St Austin's great work, 'The City of God'; and Tertullian's '*De Carne Christi*', in which the paradoxical sentence, '*Mortuus est Dei Filius; credibile est quia ineptum est; et sepultus resurrexit; certum est quia impossible est,*' occupied my undivided time, for many weeks of laborious and fruitless investigation.

Thus it will appear that, shaken from its balance only by trivial things, my reason bore resemblance to that ocean-crag spoken of by Ptolemy Hephestion, which steadily resisting the attacks of human violence, and the fiercer fury of the waters and the winds, trembled only to the touch of the flower called Asphodel. And although, to a careless thinker, it might appear a matter beyond doubt, that the alteration produced by her unhappy malady, in the *moral* condition of Berenice, would afford me many objects for the exercise of that intense and abnormal meditation whose nature I have been at some trouble in explaining, yet such was not in any degree the case. In the lucid intervals of my infirmity, her calamity, indeed, gave me pain, and, taking deeply to heart that total wreck of her fair and gentle life, I did not fail to ponder, frequently and bitterly, upon the wonder-working means by which so strange a revolution had been so suddenly brought to pass. But these reflections partook not of the idiosyncrasy of my disease, and were such as would have occurred, under similar circumstances, to the ordinary mass of mankind. True to its own character, my disorder revelled in the less important but more startling changes wrought in the *physical* frame of Berenice – in the singular and most appalling distortion of her personal identity.

During the brightest days of her unparalleled beauty, most surely I had never loved her. In the strange anomaly of my existence, feelings with me, *had never been* of the heart, and my passions *always were* of the mind. Through the grey of the early morning – among the trellised shadows of the forest at noonday – and in the silence of my library at night – she had flitted by my eyes, and I had seen her – not as the living and breathing Berenice, but as the Berenice of a dream; not as a being of the earth, earthy, but as the abstraction of such a being; not as a thing to admire, but to analyze; not as an object of love, but as the theme of the most abstruse although desultory speculation. And *now* – now I shuddered in her presence, and grew pale at her approach; yet, bitterly lamenting her fallen and desolate condition, I called to mind that she had loved me long, and, in an evil moment, I spoke to her of marriage.

And at length the period of our nuptials was approaching, when, upon an afternoon in the winter of the year – one of those unseasonably warm, calm, and misty days which are the nurse of the beautiful Halcyon,[1] – I sat (and sat, as I thought, alone) in the inner apartment of the library. But, uplifting my eyes, I saw that Berenice stood before me.

Was it my own excited imagination – or the misty influence of the atmosphere – or the uncertain twilight of the chamber – or the grey

[1]For as Jove, during the winter season, gives twice seven days of warmth, men have called this clement and temperate time the nurse of the beautiful Halcyon. – *Simonides.*

draperies which fell around her figure – that caused in it so vacillating and indistinct an outline? I could not tell. She spoke no word; and I – not for worlds could I have uttered a syllable. An icy chill ran through my frame; a sense of insufferable anxiety oppressed me; a consuming curiosity pervaded my soul; and, sinking back upon the chair, I remained for some time breathless and motionless, with my eyes riveted upon her person. Alas! its emaciation was excessive, and not one vestige of the former being lurked in any single line of the contour. My burning glances at length fell upon the face.

The forehead was high, and very pale, and singularly placid; and the once jetty hair fell partially over it, and overshadowed the hollow temples with innumerable ringlets, now of a vivid yellow, and jarring discordantly, in their fantastic character, with the reigning melancholy of the countenance. The eyes were lifeless, and lustreless, and seemingly pupilless, and I shrank involuntarily from their glassy stare to the contemplation of the thin and shrunken lips. They parted; and in a smile of peculiar meaning, *the teeth* of the changed Berenice disclosed themselves slowly to my view. Would to God that I had never beheld them, or that, having done so, I had died!

The shutting of a door disturbed me, and looking up, I found that my cousin had departed from the chamber. But from the disordered chamber of my brain, had not, alas! departed, and would not be driven away, the white ghastly *spectrum* of the teeth. Not a speck on their surface – not a shade on their enamel – not an indenture in their edges – but what that brief period of her smile had sufficed to brand in upon my memory. I saw them *now* even more unequivocally than I beheld them *then*. The teeth! – the teeth! – they were here, and there, and everywhere, and visibly and palpably before me; long, narrow, and excessively white, with the pale lips writhing about them, as in the very moment of their first terrible development. Then came the full fury of my *monomania*, and I struggled in vain against its strange and irresistible influence. In the multiplied objects of the external world I had no thoughts but for the teeth. For these I longed with a frenzied desire. All other matters and all different interests became absorbed in their single contemplation. They – they alone were present to the mental eye, and they, in their sole individuality, became the essence of my mental life. I held them in every light. I turned them in every attitude. I surveyed their characteristics. I dwelt upon their peculiarities. I pondered upon their conformation. I mused upon the alteration in their nature. I shuddered as I assigned to them, in imagination, a sensitive and sentient power, and, even when unassisted by the lips, a capability of moral expression. Of Mademoiselle Salle it has been well said: '*Que tous ses pas étaient des sentiments,*' and of Berenice I more seriously believed *que tous ses dents étaient des idées. Des idées!* – ah, here was the idiotic thought that destroyed me! *Des idées!* – ah, *therefore* it was that I covered them so madly! I felt that their possession could alone ever restore me to peace, in giving me back to reason.

And the evening closed in upon me thus – and then the darkness came, and tarried, and went – and the day again dawned – and the mists of a second night were now gathering around – and still I sat motionless in that solitary room – and still I sat buried in meditation – and still the *phantasma* of the teeth maintained its terrible ascendancy, as, with the most vivid and hideous distinctness, it floated about amid the changing lights and shadows of the chamber. At length there broke in upon my dreams a cry as of horror and dismay; and thereunto, after a pause, succeeded the sound of troubled voices, intermingled with many low moanings of sorrow or of pain. I arose from my seat, and throwing open one of the doors of the library, saw standing out in the antechamber a servant maiden, all in tears, who told me that Berenice was – no more! She had been seized with epilepsy in the early morning, and now, at the closing in of the night, the grave was ready for its tenant, and all the preparations for the burial were completed.

I found myself sitting in the library, and again sitting there alone. It seemed to me that I had newly awakened from a confused and exciting dream. I knew that it was now midnight, and I was well aware, that since the setting of the sun, Berenice had been interred. But of that dreary period which intervened I had no positive, at least no definite, comprehension. Yet its memory was replete with horror – horror more horrible from being vague, and terror more terrible from ambiguity. It was a fearful page in the record of my existence, written all over with dim, and hideous, and unintelligible recollections. I strived to decipher them, but in vain; while ever and anon, like the spirit of a departed sound, the shrill and piercing shriek of a female voice seemed to be ringing in my ears. I had done a deed – what was it? I asked myself the question aloud, and the whispering echoes of the chamber answered me – *'What was it?'*

On the table beside me burned a lamp, and near it lay a little box. It was of no remarkable character, and I had seen it frequently before, for it was the property of the family physician; but how came it *there*, upon my table, and why did I shudder in regarding it? These things were in no manner to be accounted for, and my eyes at length dropped to the open pages of a book, and to a sentence underscored therein. The words were the singular but simple ones of the poet Ebn Zaiat: – *'Dicebant mihi sodales si sepulchrum amicae visitarem, curas meas aliquantulum fore levatas.'* Why, then, as I perused them, did the hairs of my head erect themselves on end, and the blood of my body become congealed within my veins?

There came a light tap at the library door – and, pale as the tenant of a tomb, a menial entered upon tiptoe. His looks were wild with terror, and he spoke to me in a voice tremulous, husky, and very low. What said he? – some broken sentences I heard. He told of a wild cry disturbing the silence of the night – of the gathering together of the household – of a search in the direction of the sound; and then his tones grew thrillingly distinct as he whispered me of a violated grave – of a disfigured body enshrouded, yet still breathing – still palpitating – *still alive!*

He pointed to my garments; they were muddy and clotted with gore. I spoke not, and he took me gently by the hand: it was indented with the impress of human nails. He directed my attention to some object against the wall. I looked at it for some minutes: it was a spade. With a shriek I bounded to the table, and grasped the box that lay upon it. But I could not force it open; and, in my tremor, it slipped from my hands, and fell heavily, and burst into pieces; and from it, with a rattling sound, there rolled out some instruments of dental surgery, intermingled with thirty-two small, white, and ivory-looking substances that were scattered to and fro about the floor.

The Finless Death

R. E. VERNEDE

DON MIGUEL, PROPRIETOR OF the inn grown about with orange-trees, yellow and green, that grew juicily in the warm airs of the gulf, was flustered.

It could not be the heat that flustered him, for it was still before dawn; and, though at any moment the sun might come blazing out, he was not thinking of it.

'Señores!' he said, appealingly.

The two Englishmen stopped.

'What does the fat fool want?' asked Flackman, impatiently.

'Don't know,' said Kender. 'I'll ask him' – and he put the question fluently in Spanish.

'If I might be permitted,' said the innkeeper, extending the palms of his hands in emphasis, 'I would advise the Señores.'

'The advice of Don Miguel is more precious than pearls,' said Kender, courteously, resting the butt-end of his heavy rod on the ground, 'and, without doubt, the oyster does not contain more. But in what does the advice consist?'

Don Miguel bowed to the compliment, and made answer:

'It is that the Señores should not go fishing today.'

'For what reason?'

Don Miguel had many reasons, apparently.

'The day is warm, yet on land, in the 'arbour, very cool. How pleasant to sit there and sip aguardiente. Also, Rietta will sing to the Señores. She had this morning the voice of a nightingale.'

'She has the voice of six nightingales invariably,' said Kender. 'Also, aguardiente is good. But we came to fish.'

'Consider, Señor, how easily the sun goes to the head of the unaccustomed.'

'True,' said Kender. 'But the heads of both of us are thick as the rinds of pumpkins, and are protected by sombreros.'

'The heads of the Señores are of an excellent proportion' said Don Miguel, hastily. 'And yet – there might be a hurricane.'

'I see no sign of it,' Kender maintained.

The innkeeper became yet more earnest.

'Señor,' he said, 'you will laugh, I know it, or maybe frown, for it is Don

326

Flackman that laughs always, thinking these things but superstitions, and of no account.'

'But what things?'

Don Miguel looked about him anxiously as if he feared the presence of some supernatural agency, and crossed himself, before he answered in a low voice.

'Things that are said – in fear – the Mexicans say them. Without doubt these half-breeds are mad compared to your excellencies, and yet I, who live here and know, who am of the blood of Castile, I also am afraid. Señor, I ask you, where are the German Señores that went fishing yesterday? Them also I warned and' – again he crossed – 'they have not returned.'

'Warned them of what?' said Kender, eager to get to the point.

The innkeeper dropped his voice still lower.

'Of the Finless Death,' he said.

Kender looked at him curiously. The man was evidently earnest in his warnings, for the sweat stood out in his face, and he wrung his fat hands as if in dread of some impending evil. Kender himself, a scientist, a little man, but firm-lipped, unemotional, and with a chin that betokened incredulity, was the last person to take a superstition literally, or to be moved by it. Nevertheless, he hesitated a moment. It seemed to him as if something – some danger perhaps – might underlie this manifest fear.

'Aren't you coming?' said Flackman, impatiently.

He had not understood the conversation, and was longing to reach the fishing-grounds.

'In a minute,' said Kender, and he turned to the innkeeper. 'What is the Finless Death?' he said, tapping him on the arm.

Don Miguel turned up the whites of his eyes.

'Señor, how should I know? Only this I have heard – that at the full moon the Finless Death moves on the lagoons, and makes men stark with fear. Last night it was almost full.'

'True,' said Kender, 'it was undeniably almost full.'

'And twice Pedro, that, as the Señor knows, is an unerring watchdog, bayed violently.'

'At what?'

'At nothing.'

'And therefore at this devil?' said Kender, smiling.

The innkeeper evaded insisting on this sequence.

'The German Señores have not returned,' he repeated significantly.

'Nor paid their bill?' asked Kender.

'That is nothing,' said Don Miguel, with dignity. 'I have warned the Señores.' He turned away hurt.

'And truly I am most grateful,' said Kender; 'but my friend, as you perceive, is not to be persuaded and therefore we go to fish. Maybe we shall catch the finless thing itself.'

The innkeeper threw up his hands in an ecstasy of horror as Kender
followed Flackman through the orange-groves that led down to the creek
where José, the half-breed, was getting ready the boat. Flackman was
highly amused to hear of the innkeeper's alarm.

'You refuse to be warned?'

'Don't you?'

'My dear man,' said Kender, 'I never take warnings – at least in so far as
they frighten a man away from what he does know by what he does not
know. It's my business to learn, just as it's my business to jest. I only told
you because – well – you know you've got an imagination – it might get on
your nerves.'

'Nonsense!' said Flackman, and added inconsequently: 'Miguel is a fat
man, and all fat men are fools.'

'I incline to think there's something in it.'

'Some Mexican, full of aguardiente, saw a cuttle-fish at the full moon
once.'

'Perhaps – but it's descriptive – their name for the terror?'

'Oh, that I grant you,' said Flackman, laughing. 'They make a good
case for their demons by giving them a sounding title, but they've got too
many of 'em – only they seem to have impressed you, Kender?'

'Not much,' said Kender, 'I'm interested, I admit; I take it to be some
water-devil – something connected with fish.'

'But finless.'

'An eel, perhaps – it's quite easy to imagine an eel without fins – or some
sort of water-snake.'

'Sea-serpent,' Flackman suggested. He was much amused to see Kender
– usually so sceptical – interesting himself in Don Miguel's supernatural
absurdity. For his own part, he could think of nothing but the desire to
hear his reel run again, and to hold up a fighting fish by his own skilful
handling till it should be drawn to the boat-side and the gaff, splashing
faintly a hundredweight of tired silver. And it was a day of days for fishing
– the sky already full of suppressed brightness, as if the sun were just
behind it, and the morning unwontedly fresh. Ahead of them, Flackman
could see the creek (solitary, since it was before the time when tarpon-
fishing had become a fashionable amusement), and the boat and the
Mexican boatman lolling beside it. He was almost annoyed with Kender
that with such a view before him he would go on discussing his ridiculous
subject, quite gravely too.

'But it might be some kind of sea-serpent,' he was saying, 'or merely a
delusion, as you seem to think; for it doesn't take anything tangible to give
these fellows a belief in some new devil. But I should like to know. After all,
it is strange that the civilized people should be so incurious about fish,
which are the ugliest things in earth or sea. Think how they were detested
in bygone times! The ancients considered them not only uneatable, but

unclean abominations – a part of the devilish things that lived in the sea, that was always the devil!'

'Poor old bats!' said Flackman. 'They never knew what it was to fly fish. And here's José, alive and as energetic as usual. I almost expected to find he'd been swallowed by a whale!'

José's energy was not conspicuous. He began by suggesting that it was not a good day for bites. Asked why, he said because the night before the moon was full. Flackman began to lose his temper.

'It's some trick,' he said, 'that the scamp has got up with Miguel. He wants to slack.'

'It is a possibility,' Kender admitted, thoughtfully, 'but, at the same time. . . .'

'I don't believe you want to go either.'

'Never wanted to fish more,' Kender said.

'It doesn't look like it.'

'And if we could catch this finless beast, I should be happy for days.'

'Oh! confound it!' said Flackman.

His spirits were mercurial, and this reiteration of an unpleasant topic was getting on his nerves. Doubtless, the whole thing was absurd; but it was unpleasant. Flackman himself thought nothing of it. He kept on assuring himself of that; but, at the same time, he was one of those who, not altogether self-reliant, liked to have their opinion corroborated by their company. And here was Kender frowning over this suggestion of peril as if he were assured there were some bottom in it, if one only knew. He wanted to fish, not to face a mystery. If he had known what they were going to encounter, he might have hung back. But he did not know, and Kender was remorseless in the pursuit of science.

'Hurry up, José,' said Flackman, pettishly.

It was very sullenly that the Mexican pulled seaward, and Flackman was reduced to whistling to keep his own spirits up. The sea ran from creek to creek, lagoon-like reaches, and spaces of the bluest calm, locked in from the gulf by reefs only to be passed at certain tides and points where the rollers had forced an inlet, as sheep force their way through a hedge, by incessant pressing. They had made a good many futile casts in the open, and Flackman's spirits were at zero, before, at Kender's suggestion, they made for one of these lagoons for a last throw. Kender had relieved the Mexican at the oars, and had his back turned to the bows, so that as they shot into that reach of still water, slack and shining, except where it was criss-crossed by dull patches that looked like stains on polished walnut, it was the younger man who saw and sprang to his feet pointing to something ahead: 'What's that?' he cried.

Out in the middle water, immobile, a boat floated, as though anchored in a pond. A single oar, broken at the blade, was caught in the left rollock and suspended.

As Kender stood up, he observed that there were two men in the stern, who seemed to be standing in stiff attitudes.

'H'm,' he said, and he sat himself down again to row for the boat, unconcernedly enough, but with a little extra speed. Flackman remained standing: his eyes moved uneasily.

'Ship your oars,' he said excitedly, as they came bow to bow with the other boat.

Kender shipped his oars, and sat steadying the boat in the expectation that Flackman would step across to it, if it were only for curiosity. But Flackman had no curiosity and he had gone very pale.

'Hadn't you better – hadn't we better be getting back?' he said.

Kender carefully refrained from expressing anything, but he picked up his rod which lay in the way, and stepped across past the shrinking Mexican into the other boat. Flackman was flushing now with shame at his own poltroonery.

'What's the matter with them?' he sang out, for the swing of Kender stepping across had sent the two boats apart.

The little man had rammed his rod methodically under the bow-seat, the line overboard to prevent a tangle, and was contemplating the two figures. He saw at once they were the Germans of whom Don Miguel had spoken.

'What's the matter?' cried Flackman again.

He was in an agony of uneasiness, and in the merest pretence began making casts. Again he appealed to Kender:

'You might say what's the matter with them.'

'Death!' said Kender, curtly.

'Why do they look like that?'

'I don't know.'

Kender sat on the thwarts and considered them. Never had he seen such dead men – in attitude exaggeratedly alive, rigid as waxworks, and hideous in their mimic intensity! One, a great bearded man, with spectacles, had his hand on the dragging oar and half knelt to it, as if he had been caught by a blinding cramp in the act of pulling; the other, of a slighter build, was bent forward standing, a gaff in his hand, menacing, as it seemed, the empty space in the middle of the boat – at least it should have been empty, but there was a slime over it, as if a great snail had crawled there. The faces of the two were indescribably afraid.

'Now, how did that slime get there?' said Kender to himself.

Almost as if in answer, Flackman gave a shout.

'I've hooked something!' he said. 'By gad! and a heavy one!' he went on, as the thick rod bent nearly double under the weight.

'You'd better cut your line,' said Kender, gruffly. 'It's hardly time to fish.'

'Right,' said Flackman. But he didn't.

Mechanically he had struck, and equally mechanically he began to reel up. He had a semi-conscious idea of saving as much of his line as possible before he cut loose, and as he saw far down the loom of a great white fish, the zeal of sport carried him away. He reeled steadily, the rod seemed strained with a dead weight, but there was no rush or plunging. Quite suddenly, the white mass was on the surface, and as Flackman tightened his hold and yelled for the gaff, it seemed to fly up into the boat. It fell, facing the bows, where the Mexican was sitting, the hook in its mouth, the line broken.

Flackman stared. From its size the fish could not have weighed less than a hundred pounds, yet it had come up without a struggle, and had been landed ungaffed. Now it lay there heaving equably – a white-bellied, shapeless thing, rotund and flabby, with the detestable lidless fish eyes.

'It's a remarkable fish,' said Flackman, curiously.

'Very,' said Kender.

'Did you see how it came up?'

'Yes. What are you going to do with it?'

'Chuck it over, if possible.'

'I should.'

They seemed unanimous in thinking it would be a good riddance.

'Hi, José! give me a hand. Hullo! what's wrong?' Flackman saw that some strange malady had seized the Mexican. He seemed to be stiffening as he crouched in the bows; his arms were stretched out fixedly, like the arms of a sign-post. Kender started.

'What's he pointing at?' he shouted.

'The fish. Ugh! it's oozing slime!'

'Slime!'

'A sort of snail slime.'

Flackman drew back from the fish, disgusted. 'It's too filthy to touch,' he went on. It's – by gad – Kender – it's got no fins!' His voice rose nervously. 'What is it? What's it doing, and to José.'

He began to stammer, frightened at he knew not what. The Mexican was growing most rigid.

'José!' shouted Kender, imperiously.

There was no answer but Flackman's.

'He's – he's being poisoned, I think.'

'Go and shake him!'

'I daren't.'

The two Englishmen eyed each other from the boats. Then Flackman, seized with a spasm of shame or horror, snatched up the gaff and stabbed the fish through the grey-skinned back. A white ichor spurted up and took him on the arm. Kender saw him drop the gaff, clutch at his elbow, and begin to mumble wildly. It was then that a fear began to take hold of him also; he could do nothing where he sat, for there were no oars to the boat.

331

'Flackman!' he said, sharply.

'No fins, no fins!' muttered the other.

'Come here!' commanded Kender.

Flackman looked up in a dazed manner, and took a step towards the oars. Then, as his eye caught the white-bellied fish lying there, he shrank back, crying out:

'No fins, no fins!'

Even while he cried another spurt of the fluid came from the cut in the creature's back, and dribbled over his arm. He cried out, and unsheathed his knife. Before Kender could say anything, he had stuck it into his arm and stabbed again and again. Kender watched the blood stream helplessly, for he could do nothing unless Flackman would bring the boats together. He longed for an oar, longed to be able to swim. Again he shouted sharply:

'Bring her up!'

'No, no, Kender,' the young man spoke in a strange voice. 'I mustn't do that – I mustn't do that.'

'Why not?'

'Because . . .' Flackman paused, and looked out of the corner of his eyes slyly. 'You understand, Kender, don't you?'

'I tell you to come here,' said Kender, firmly.

'It's – no – it's impossible.'

It seemed to be, for Flackman was like a child in his obstinacy. Kender changed his tactics accordingly.

'The fish will have you then,' he called.

The effect was magical. Flackman sprang up, looked at the fish, shuddered, and, diving into the sea began to swim to the other boat. Kender watched. Surely it was the most peaceful scene in the world, a man swimming silently in a sea still to the horizon, scattering bubbles like diamonds before him, and leaving behind him the clear curve of his wake – a blue sky, unbeaten by any storm, a swimmer, and two pleasure-boats. And yet Kender was beginning to feel afraid. He tried to argue the fear away, but it would not go. It crept over him jointless, inexplicable, binding as a nightmare. He laughed at himself in sheer bravado, and the laugh stuck in his throat and became a shrill giggling that seemed to carry his reason with it high up above his reach. He clutched after it, to recall it and could not. For he knew that the man that was swimming towards him had a face distorted with terror; that the boat in which he sat and giggled held two men grotesquely dead: that the blue, calm sea was vacant of human help. And in the other boat lay that monstrous fish without fins, staring the life out of the Mexican. It was with a struggle that he drew himself together, shivering, and pulled his friend on board.

Flackman fell in the bottom of the boat exhausted. He muttered continually, and was plainly delirious, for through his multifarious imaginings there ran always the vague thread of terror that haunts delirious men.

'No fins, no fins,' he would moan, and clutch at the arm Kender had bound up.

It was impossible to relieve him. Kender wished for his own sake that anything could be done, for in this feeling of impotence was evil, and he was aware that his own hysteria was growing. Must they wait, then, for ever on that hateful sea? He tried the broken oar, but it would not move the heavy boat an inch. They must lie there, it seemed, and grow to knowledge of what fear could be. He sat and stared before him, and then, without warning, the last horror came. The bows of the other boat lifted suddenly, so that the Mexican rolled over and was seen to sink, while almost imperceptibly the boat itself began to glide towards them, the fish on board. As it came near, throwing no ripples before it, Kender bit his lips in agony.

There was no help – none! The boat was gliding with so swift a motion that it seemed upon them, and yet he could see still far down in the water the corpse of the Mexican, all huddled up and stiff – still twirling head over heels, round and round, deeper and deeper, to the bottom ooze. Not ten yards separated them now from the horror that blinked there in the other boat and heaved its hideous whiteness – not eight – and it was death – the death without fins – not five!

Kender shrieked aloud and ran about the boat, so that it rocked violently. For a moment it seemed an added terror, and then he saw the reason. The rod – his rod – clinched in the bows as he stepped on board, had hooked something with its dangling bait – something that went with jerks and rushes, darting ahead, towing the boat after it – some huge tarpon. It made for the opening by which they had passed into the lagoon and for the open sea. Behind, always quickening, the other boat came, drawn on by its own mysterious power. With tense eyes, Kender watched this strange race, in which he and his friend stood for both prize and spoil. Without reasoning the matter, he somehow knew (so he said afterwards) that that which reached the open sea would win away. The line taken zigzagged for the outlet. Kender dared not stir, but he prayed to reach it, and the boat seemed to go quick with his longing.

The water flew under them – surely the outlet could not be far off – the other boat was gaining – no – yes – ah, but the outlet was before them. Their boat was through it. With a rasping noise, the ghastly boat behind drove on a sunken reef to the left. Kender, as his senses went from him in a swoon, fancied that he saw leap from it, like a great curl of smoke, the great white fish that turned in mid-air and plunged noiselessly into the sea. . . .

It was towards dusk, and some seven miles off shore, that the yacht *Swallow* came on a drifting boat, noticeable for a rod bent in its bows like a bowsprit and snapped off as if by the jerk of some fish that had been hooked and had escaped. Besides this, there were on board two dead men, half standing in constrained positions, and two alive, a young man obviously raving, and another man – older – who might have been sane, except that his lips twitched continuously, and he told this story.

And the Dead Spake—

E. F. BENSON

THERE IS NOT IN ALL LONDON a quieter spot, or one, apparently, more withdrawn from the heat and bustle of life than Newsome Terrace. It is a cul-de-sac, for at the upper end the roadway between its two lines of square, compact little residences is brought to an end by a high brick wall, while at the lower end, the only access to it is through Newsome Square, that small discreet oblong of Georgian houses, a relic of the time when Kensington was a suburban village sundered from the metropolis by a stretch of pastures stretching to the river. Both square and terrace are most inconveniently situated for those whose ideal environment includes a rank of taxicabs immediately opposite their door, a spate of buses roaring down the street, and a procession of underground trains, accessible by a station a few yards away, shaking and rattling the cutlery and silver on their dining tables. In consequence Newsome Terrace had come, two years ago, to be inhabited by leisurely and retired folk or by those who wished to pursue their work in quiet and tranquillity. Children with hoops and scooters are phenomena rarely encountered in the Terrace and dogs are equally uncommon.

In front of each of the couple of dozen houses of which the Terrace is composed lies a little square of railinged garden, in which you may often see the middle-aged or elderly mistress of the residence horticulturally employed. By five o'clock of a winter's evening the pavements will generally be empty of all passengers except the policeman, who with felted step, at intervals throughout the night, peers with his bull's-eyes into these small front gardens, and never finds anything more suspicious there than an early crocus or an aconite. For by the time it is dark the inhabitants of the Terrace have got themselves home, where behind drawn curtains and bolted shutters they will pass a domestic and uninterrupted evening. No funeral (up to the time I speak of) had I ever seen leave the Terrace, no marriage party had strewed its pavements with confetti, and perambulators were unknown. It and its inhabitants seemed to be quietly mellowing like bottles of sound wine. No doubt there was stored within them the sunshine and summer of youth long past, and now, dozing in a cool place, they waited for the turn of the key in the cellar door, and the entry of one who would draw them forth and see what they were worth.

Yet, after the time of which I shall now speak, I have never passed down its pavement without wondering whether each house, so seemingly tranquil, is not, like some dynamo, softly and smoothly bringing into being vast and terrible forces, such as those I once saw at work in the last house at the upper end of the Terrace, the quietest, you would have said, of all the row. Had you observed it with continuous scrutiny, for all the length of a summer day, it is quite possible that you might have only seen issue from it in the morning an elderly woman whom you would have rightly conjectured to be the housekeeper, with her basket for marketing on her arm, who returned an hour later. Except for her the entire day might often pass without there being either ingress or egress from the door. Occasionally a middle-aged man, lean and wiry, came swiftly down the pavement, but his exit was by no means a daily occurrence, and indeed when he did emerge, he broke the almost universal usage of the Terrace, for his appearances took place, when such there were, between nine and ten in the evening. At that hour sometimes he would come round to my house in Newsome Square to see if I was at home and inclined for a talk a little later on. For the sake of air and exercise he would then have an hour's tramp through the lit and noisy streets, and return about ten, still pale and unflushed, for one of those talks which grew to have an absorbing fascination for me. More rarely through the telephone I proposed that I should drop in on him: this I did not often do, since I found that if he did not come out himself, it implied that he was busy with some investigation, and though he made me welcome, I could easily see that he burned for my departure, so that he might get busy with his batteries and pieces of tissue, hot on the track of discoveries that never yet had presented themselves to the mind of man as coming within the horizon of possibility.

My last sentence may have led the reader to guess that I am indeed speaking of none other than that recluse and mysterious physicist Sir James Horton, with whose death a hundred half-hewn avenues into the dark forest from which life comes must wait completion till another pioneer as bold as he takes up the axe which hitherto none but himself has been able to wield. Probably there was never a man to whom humanity owed more, and of whom humanity knew less. He seemed utterly independent of the race to whom (though indeed with no service of love) he devoted himself: for years he lived aloof and apart in his house at the end of the Terrace. Men and women were to him like fossils to the geologist, things to be tapped and hammered and dissected and studied with a view not only to the reconstruction of past ages, but to construction in the future. It is known, for instance, that he made an artificial being formed of the tissue, still living, of animals lately killed, with the brain of an ape and the heart of a bullock, and a sheep's thyroid, and so forth. Of that I can give no first-hand account; Horton, it is true, told me something about it, and in his will directed that certain memoranda on the subject

336

should on his death be sent to me. But on the bulky envelope there is the direction, 'Not to be opened till January, 1925.' He spoke with some reserve and, so I think, with slight horror at the strange things which had happened on the completion of this creature. It evidently made him uncomfortable to talk about it, and for that reason I fancy he put what was then a rather remote date to the day when his record should reach my eye. Finally, in these preliminaries, for the last five years before the war, he had scarcely entered, for the sake of companionship, any house other than his own and mine. Ours was a friendship dating from school-days, which he had never suffered to drop entirely, but I doubt if in those years he spoke except on matters of business to half a dozen other people. He had already retired from surgical practice in which his skill was unapproached, and most completely now did he avoid the slightest intercourse with his colleagues, whom he regarded as ignorant pedants without courage or the rudiments of knowledge. Now and then he would write an epoch-making little monograph, which he flung to them like a bone to a starving dog, but for the most part, utterly absorbed in his own investigations, he left them to grope along unaided. He frankly told me that he enjoyed talking to me about such subjects, since I was utterly unacquainted with them. It clarified his mind to be obliged to put his theories and guesses and confirmations with such simplicity that anyone could understand them.

I well remember his coming in to see me on the evening of the 4th of August, 1914.

'So the war has broken out,' he said, 'and the streets are impassable with excited crowds. Odd, isn't it? Just as if each of us already was not a far more murderous battlefield than any which can be conceived between warring nations.'

'How's that?' said I.

'Let me try to put it plainly, though it isn't that I want to talk about. Your blood is one eternal battlefield. It is full of armies eternally marching and counter-marching. As long as the armies friendly to you are in a superior position, you remain in good health; if a detachment of microbes that, if suffered to establish themselves, would give you a cold in the head, entrench themselves in your mucous membrane, the commander-in-chief sends a regiment down and drives them out. He doesn't give his orders from your brain, mind you – those aren't his headquarters, for your brain knows nothing about the landing of the enemy till they have made good their position and given you a cold.'

He paused a moment.

'There isn't one headquarters inside you,' he said, 'there are many. For instance, I killed a frog this morning; at least most people would say I killed it. But had I killed it, though its head lay in one place and its severed body in another? Not a bit: I had only killed a piece of it. For I opened the body afterwards and took out the heart, which I put in a sterilized

337

chamber of suitable temperature, so that it wouldn't get cold or be infected by any microbe. That was about twelve o'clock today. And when I came out just now, the heart was beating still. It was alive, in fact. That's full of suggestions, you know. Come and see it.'

The Terrace had been stirred into volcanic activity by the news of war: the vendor of some late edition had penetrated into its quietude, and there were half a dozen parlourmaids fluttering about like black and white moths. But once inside Horton's door isolation as of an Arctic night seemed to close round me. He had forgotten his latch-key, but his housekeeper, then newly come to him, who became so regular and familiar a figure in the Terrace, must have heard his step, for before he rang the bell she had opened the door, and stood with his forgotten latch-key in her hand.

'Thanks, Mrs Gabriel,' said he, and without a sound the door shut behind us. Both her name and face, as reproduced in some illustrated daily paper, seemed familiar, rather terribly familiar, but before I had time to grope for the association, Horton supplied it.

'Tried for the murder of her husband six months ago,' he said. 'Odd case. The point is that she is the one and perfect housekeeper. I once had four servants, and everything was all mucky, as we used to say at school. Now I live in amazing comfort and propriety with one. She does everything. She is cook, valet, housemaid, butler, and won't have anyone to help her. No doubt she killed her husband, but she planned it so well that she could not be convicted. She told me quite frankly who she was when I engaged her.'

Of course I remembered the whole trial vividly now. Her husband, a morose, quarrelsome fellow, tipsy as often as sober, had, according to the defence cut his own throat while shaving; according to the prosecution, she had done that for him. There was the usual discrepancy of evidence as to whether the wound could have been self-inflicted, and the prosecution tried to prove that the face had been lathered after his throat had been cut. So singular an exhibition of forethought and nerve had hurt rather than helped their case, and after prolonged deliberation on the part of the jury, she had been acquitted. Yet not less singular was Horton's selection of a probable murderess, however efficient, as housekeeper.

He anticipated this reflection.

'Apart from the wonderful comfort of having a perfectly appointed and absolutely silent house,' he said, 'I regard Mrs Gabriel as a short of insurance against my being murdered. If you had been tried for your life, you would take very especial care not to find yourself in suspicious proximity to a murdered body again: no more deaths in your house, if you could help it. Come through to my laboratory, and look at my little instance of life after death.'

Certainly it was amazing to see that little piece of tissue still pulsating with what must be called life; it contracted and expanded faintly indeed but perceptibly, though for nine hours now it had been severed from the rest of the organization. All by itself it went on living, and if the heart could go on living with nothing, you would say, to feed and stimulate its energy, there must also, so reasoned Horton, reside in all the other vital organs of the body other independent focuses of life,

'Of course a severed organ like that,' he said, 'will run down quicker than if it had the co-operation of the others, and presently I shall apply a gentle electric stimulus to it. If I can keep that glass bowl under which it beats at the temperature of a frog's body, in sterilized air, I don't see why it should not go on living. Food – of course there's the question of feeding it. Do you see what that opens up in the way of surgery? Imagine a shop with glass cases containing healthy organs taken from the dead. Say a man dies of pneumonia. He should, as soon as ever the breath is out of his body, be dissected, and though they would, of course, destroy his lungs, as they will be full of pneumococci, his liver and digestive organs are probably healthy. Take them out, keep them in a sterilized atmosphere with the temperature at 98·4, and sell the liver, let us say, to another poor devil who has cancer there. Fit him with a new healthy liver, eh?'

'And insert the brain of someone who has died of heart disease into the skull of a congenital idiot?' I asked.

'Yes, perhaps; but the brain's tiresomely complicated in its connections and the joining up of the nerves, you know. Surgery will have to learn a lot before it fits new brains in. And the brain has got such a lot of functions. All thinking, all inventing seem to belong to it, though, as you have seen, the heart can get on quite well without it. But there are other functions of the brain I want to study first. I've been trying some experiments already.'

He made some little readjustment to the flame of the spirit lamp which kept at the right temperature the water that surrounded the sterilized receptacle in which the frog's heart was beating.

'Start with the more simple and mechanical uses of the brain,' he said. 'Primarily it is a sort of record office, a diary. Say that I rap your knuckles with that ruler. What happens? The nerves there send a message to the brain, of course, saying – how can I put it most simply – saying, "Somebody is hurting me." And the eye sends another, saying "I perceive a ruler hitting my knuckles," and the ear sends another, saying "I hear the rap of it." But leaving all that alone, what else happens? Why, the brain records it. It makes a note of your knuckles having been hit.'

He had been moving about the room as he spoke, taking off his coat and waistcoat and putting on in their place a thin black dressing-gown, and by now he was seated in his favourite attitude cross-legged on the hearth-rug, looking like some magician or perhaps the afrit which a magician of black arts had caused to appear. He was thinking intently now, passing through his fingers his string of amber beans, and talking more to himself than to me.

339

'And how does it make that note?' he went on. 'Why, in the manner in which phonograph records are made. There are millions of minute dots, depressions, pockmarks on your brain which certainly record what you remember, what you have enjoyed or disliked, or done or said. The surface of the brain anyhow is large enough to furnish writing-paper for the record of all these things, of all your memories. If the impression of an experience has not been acute, the dot is not sharply impressed, and the record fades: in other words, you come to forget it. But if it has been vividly impressed, the record is never obliterated. Mrs Gabriel, for instance, won't lose the impression of how she lathered her husband's face after she had cut his throat. That's to say, if she did it.'

'Now do you see what I'm driving at? Of course you do. There is stored within a man's head the complete record of all the memorable things he has done and said: there are all his thoughts there, and all his speeches, and, most well-marked of all, his habitual thoughts and the things he has often said; for habit, there is reason to believe, wears a sort of rut in the brain, so that the life-principle, whatever it is, as it gropes and steals about the brain, is continually stumbling into it. There's your record, your gramophone plate all ready. What we want, and what I'm trying to arrive at, is a needle which, as it traces its minute way over these dots, will come across words or sentences which the dead have uttered, and will reproduce them. My word, what Judgment Books! What a resurrection!'

Here in this withdrawn situation no remotest echo of the excitement which was seething through the streets penetrated; through the open window there came in only the tide of the midnight silence. But from somewhere closer at hand, through the wall surely of the laboratory, there came a low, somewhat persistent murmur.

'Perhaps our needle – unhappily not yet invented – as it passed over the record of speech in the brain, might induce even facial expression,' he said. 'Enjoyment or horror might even pass over dead features. There might be gestures and movements even, as the words were reproduced in our gramophone of the dead. Some people when they want to think intensely walk about: some, there's an instance of it audible now, talk to themselves aloud.'.

He held up his finger for silence.

'Yes, that's Mrs Gabriel,' he said. 'She talks to herself by the hour together. She's always done that, she tells me. I shouldn't wonder if she has plenty to talk about.'

It was that night when, first of all, the notion of intense activity going on below the placid house-fronts of the Terrace occurred to me. None looked more quiet than this, and yet there was seething here a volcanic activity and intensity of living, both in the man who sat cross-legged on the floor and behind that voice just audible through the partition wall. But I thought of that no more, for Horton began speaking of the brain-gramophone again. . . . Were it possible to trace those infinitesimal dots and pockmarks in the brain by some needle exquisitely fine, it might follow that by the aid of some such contrivance as translated the pock-marks on a gramophone record into sound, some audible rendering of speech might be recovered from the brain of a dead man. It was necessary, so he pointed out to me, that this strange gramophone record should be new; it must be that of one lately dead, for corruption and decay would soon obliterate these infinitesimal markings. He was not of opinion that unspoken thought could be thus recovered: the utmost he hoped for from his pioneering work was to be able to recapture actual speech, especially when such speech had habitually dwelt on one subject, and thus had worn a rut on that part of the brain known as the speech-centre.

'Let me get, for instance,' he said, 'the brain of a railway porter, newly dead, who has been accustomed for years to call out the name of a station, and I do not despair of hearing his voice through my gramophone trumpet. Or again, given that Mrs Gabriel, in all her interminable conversations with herself, talks about one subject, I might, in similar circumstances, recapture what she had been constantly saying. Of course my instrument must be of a power and delicacy still unknown, one of which the needle can trace the minutest irregularities of surface, and of which the trumpet must be of immense magnifying power, able to translate the smallest whisper into a shout. But just as a microscope will show you the details of an object invisible to the eye, so there are instruments which act in the same way on sound. Here, for instance, is one of remarkable magnifying power. Try it if you like.'

He took me over to a table on which was standing an electric battery connected with a round steel globe, out of the side of which sprang a gramophone trumpet of curious construction. He adjusted the battery, and directed me to click my fingers quite gently opposite an aperture in the globe, and the noise, ordinarily scarcely audible, resounded through the room like a thunderclap.

'Something of that sort might permit us to hear the record on a brain,' he said.

After this night my visits to Horton became far more common than they had hitherto been. Having once admitted me into the region of his strange explorations, he seemed to welcome me there. Partly, as he had said, it clarified his own thought to put it into simple language, partly, as he subsequently admitted, he was beginning to penetrate into such lonely fields of knowledge by paths so utterly untrodden, that even he, the most aloof and independent of mankind, wanted some human presence near him. Despite his utter indifference to the issues of the war – for, in his regard, issues far more crucial demanded his energies – he offered himself as surgeon to a London hospital for operations on the brain, and his services, naturally, were welcomed, for none brought knowledge or skill like his to such work. Occupied all day, he performed miracles of healing, with bold and dexterous excisions which none but he would have dared to attempt. He would operate, often successfully, for lesions that seemed certainly fatal, and all the time he was learning. He refused to accept any salary; he only asked, in cases where he had removed pieces of brain matter, to take these away, in order by further examination and dissection, to add to the knowledge and manipulative skill which he devoted to the wounded. He wrapped these morsels in sterilized lint, and took them back to the Terrace in a box, electrically heated to maintain the normal temperature of a man's blood. His fragment might then, so he reasoned, keep some sort of independent life of its own, even as the severed heart of a frog had continued to beat for hours without connection with the rest of the body. Then for half the night he would continue to work on these sundered pieces of tissue scarcely dead, which his operations during the day had given him. Simultaneously, he was busy over the needle that must be of such infinite delicacy.

One evening, fatigued with a long day's work, I had just heard with a certain tremor of uneasy anticipation the whistles of warning which heralded an air-raid, when my telephone bell rang. My servants, according to custom, had already betaken themselves to the cellar, and I went to see what the summons was, determined in any case not to go out into the streets. I recognized Horton's voice. 'I want you at once,' he said.

'But the warning whistles have gone,' said I. 'And I don't like showers of shrapnel.'

'Oh, never mind that,' said he. 'You must come. I'm so excited that I distrust the evidence of my own ears. I want a witness. Just come.'

He did not pause for my reply, for I heard the click of his receiver going back into its place. Clearly he assumed that I was coming, and that I suppose had the effect of suggestion on my mind. I told myself that I would not go, but in a couple of minutes his certainty that I was coming, coupled with the prospect of being interested in something else than air-raids, made me fidget in my chair and eventually go to the street door and look out. The moon was brilliantly bright, the square quite empty, and far away the coughings of very distant guns. Next moment, almost against my will, I was running down the deserted pavements of Newsome Terrace. My ring at his bell was answered by Horton, before Mrs Gabriel could come to the door, and he positively dragged me in.

'I shan't tell you a word of what I am doing,' he said. 'I want you to tell me what you hear. Come into the laboratory.'

The remote guns were silent again as I sat myself, as directed, in a chair close to the gramophone trumpet, but suddenly through the wall I heard the familiar mutter of Mrs Gabriel's voice. Horton, already busy with his battery, sprang to his feet.

'That won't do,' he said. 'I want absolute silence.'

He went out of the room, and I heard him calling to her. While he was gone I observed more closely what was on the table. Battery, round steel globe, and gramophone trumpet were there, and some sort of a needle on a spiral steel spring linked up with the battery and the glass vessel, in which I had seen the frog's heart beat. In it now there lay a fragment of grey matter.

Horton came back in a minute or two, and stood in the middle of the room listening.

'That's better,' he said. 'Now I want you to listen at the mouth of the trumpet. I'll answer any questions afterwards.'

With my ear turned to the trumpet, I could see nothing of what he was doing, and I listened till the silence became a rustling in my ears. Then suddenly that rustling ceased, for it was overscored by a whisper which undoubtedly came from the aperture on which my aural attention was fixed. It was no more than the faintest murmur, and though no words were audible, it had the timbre of a human voice.

'Well, do you hear anything?' asked Horton.

'Yes, something very faint, scarcely audible.'

'Describe it,' said he.

'Somebody whispering.'

'I'll try a fresh place,' said he.

The silence descended again; the mutter of the distant guns was still mute, and some slight creaking from my shirt front, as I breathed, alone broke it. And then the whispering from the gramophone trumpet began again, this time much louder than it had been before – it was as if the speaker (still whispering) had advanced a dozen yards – but still blurred and indistinct. More unmistakable, too, was it that the whisper was that of a human voice, and every now and then, whether fancifully or not, I thought I caught a word or two. For a moment it was silent altogether, and then with a sudden inkling of what I was listening to I heard something begin to sing. Though the words were still inaudible there was melody, and the tune was 'Tipperary'. From that convolvulus-shaped trumpet there came two bars of it.

'And what do you hear now?' cried Horton with a crack of exultation in his voice. 'Singing, singing! That's the tune they all sang. Fine music that from a dead man. Encore! you say? Yes, wait a second, and he'll sing it again for you. Confound it, I can't get on to the place. Ah! I've got it: listen again.'

Surely that was the strangest manner of song ever yet heard on the earth, this melody from the brain of the dead. Horror and fascination strove within me, and I suppose the first for the moment prevailed, for with a shudder I jumped up.

'Stop it!' I said. 'It's terrible.'

His face, thin and eager, gleamed in the strong ray of the lamp which he had placed close to him. His hand was on the metal rod from which depended the spiral spring and the needle, which just rested on that fragment of grey stuff which I had seen in the glass vessel.

'Yes, I'm going to stop it now,' he said, 'or the germs will be getting at my gramophone record, or the record will get cold. See, I spray it with carbolic vapour, I put it back into its nice warm bed. It will sing to us again. But terrible? What do you mean by terrible?'

Indeed, when he asked that I scarcely knew myself what I meant. I had been witness to a new marvel of science as wonderful perhaps as any that had ever astounded the beholder, and my nerves – these childish whimperers – had cried out at the darkness and the profundity. But the horror diminished, the fascination increased as he quite shortly told me the history of this phenomenon. He had attended that day and operated upon a young soldier in whose brain was embedded a piece of shrapnel. The boy was *in extremis*, but Horton had hoped for the possibility of saving him. To extract the shrapnel was the only chance, and this involved the cutting away of a piece of brain known as the speech-centre, and taking from it what was embedded there. But the hope was not realized, and two hours later the boy died. It was to this fragment of brain that, when Horton returned home, he had applied the needle of his gramophone, and had obtained the faint whisperings which had caused him to ring me up, so that he might have a witness of this wonder. Witness I had been, not to these whisperings along, but to the fragment of singing.

'And this is but the first step on the new road,' said he. 'Who knows where it may lead, or to what new temple of knowledge it may not be the avenue? Well, it is late: I shall do no more tonight. What about the raid, by the way?'

To my amazement I saw that the time was verging on midnight. Two hours had elapsed since he let me in at his door; they had passed like a couple of minutes. Next morning some neighbours spoke of the prolonged firing that had gone on, of which I had been wholly unconscious.

Week after week Horton worked on this new road of research, perfecting the sensitiveness and subtlety of the needle, and, by vastly increasing the power of his batteries, enlarging the magnifying power of his trumpet. Many and many an evening during the next year did I listen to voices that were dumb in death, and the sounds which had been blurred and unintelligible mutterings in the earlier experiments, developed, as the delicacy of his mechanical devices increased, into coherence and clear articulation. It was no longer necessary to impose silence on Mrs Gabriel when the gramophone was at work, for now the voice we listened to had risen to the pitch of ordinary human utterance, while as for the faithfulness and individuality of these records, striking testimony was given more than once by some living friend of the dead, who, without knowing what he was about to hear, recognized the tones of the speaker. More than once also, Mrs Gabriel, bringing in syphons and whisky, provided us with three glasses, for she had heard, so she told us, three different voices in talk. But for the present no fresh phenomenon occurred: Horton was but perfecting the mechanism of his previous discovery and, rather grudging the time, was scribbling at a monograph, which presently he would toss to his colleagues, concerning the results he had already obtained. And then, even while Horton was on the threshold of new wonders, which he had already foreseen and spoken of as theoretically possible, there came an evening of marvel and of swift catastrophe.

I had dined with him that day, Mrs Gabriel deftly serving the meal that she had so daintily prepared, and towards the end, as she was clearing the table for our dessert, she stumbled, I supposed, on a loose edge of carpet, quickly recovering herself. But instantly Horton checked some half-finished sentence, and turned to her.

'You're all right, Mrs Gabriel?' he asked quickly.

'Yes, sir, thank you,' said she, and went on with her serving.

'As I was saying,' began Horton again, but his attention clearly wandered, and without concluding his narrative, he relapsed into silence, till Mrs Gabriel had given us our coffee and left the room.

'I'm sadly afraid my domestic felicity may be disturbed,' he said. 'Mrs Gabriel had an epileptic fit yesterday, and she confessed when she recovered that she had been subject to them when a child, and since then had occasionally experienced them.'

'Dangerous, then?' I asked.

'In themselves not in the least,' said he. 'If she was sitting in her chair or lying in bed when one occurred, there would be nothing to trouble about. But if one occurred while she was cooking my dinner or beginning to come downstairs, she might fall into the fire or tumble down the whole flight. We'll hope no such deplorable calamity will happen. Now, if you've finished your coffee, let us go into the laboratory. Not that I've got anything very interesting in the way of new records. But I've introduced a second battery with a very strong induction coil into my apparatus. I find that if I link it up with my record, given that the record is a – a fresh one, it stimulates certain nerve centres. It's odd, isn't it, that the same forces which so encourage the dead to live would certainly encourage the living to die, if a man received the full current. One has to be careful in handling it. Yes, and what then? you ask.'

The night was very hot, and he threw the windows wide before he settled himself cross-legged on the floor.

'I'll answer your question for you,' he said, 'though I believe we've talked of it before. Supposing I had not a fragment of brain-tissue only, but a whole head, let us say, or best of all, a complete corpse, I think I could expect to produce more than mere speech through the gramophone. The dead lips themselves perhaps might utter – God! what's that?'

From close outside, at the bottom of the stairs leading from the dining room which we had just quitted to the laboratory where we now sat, there came a crash of glass followed by the fall as of something heavy which bumped from step to step, and was finally flung on the threshold against the door with the sound as of knuckles rapping at it, and demanding admittance. Horton sprang up and threw the door open, and there lay, half inside the room and half on the landing outside, the body of Mrs Gabriel. Round her were splinters of broken bottles and glasses, and from a cut in her forehead, as she lay ghastly with face upturned, the blood trickled into her thick grey hair.

Horton was on his knees beside her, dabbing his handkerchief on her forehead.

'Ah! that's not serious,' he said; 'there's neither vein nor artery cut. I'll just bind that up first.'

He tore his handkerchief into strips which he tied together, and made a dexterous bandage covering the lower part of her forehead, but leaving her eyes unobscured. They stared with a fixed meaningless steadiness, and he scrutinized them closely.

'But there's worse yet,' he said. 'There's been some severe blow on the head. Help me to carry her into the laboratory. Get round to her feet and lift underneath the knees when I am ready. There! Now put your arm right under her and carry her.'

Her head swung limply back as he lifted her shoulders, and he propped it up against his knee, where it mutely nodded and bowed, as his leg moved, as if in silent assent to what we were doing, and the mouth, at the extremity of which there had gathered a little lather, lolled open. He still supported her shoulders as I fetched a cushion on which to place her head, and presently she was lying close to the low table on which stood the gramophone of the dead. Then with light deft fingers he passed his hands over her skull, pausing as he came to the spot just above and behind her right ear. Twice and again his fingers groped and lightly pressed, while with shut eyes and concentrated attention he interpreted what his trained touch revealed.

'Her skull is broken to fragments just here,' he said. 'In the middle there is a piece completely severed from the rest, and the edges of the cracked pieces must be pressing on her brain.'

Her right arm was lying palm upwards on the floor, and with one hand he felt her wrist with finger-tips.

'Not a sign of pulse,' he said. 'She's dead in the ordinary sense of the word. But life persists in an extraordinary manner, you may remember. She can't be wholly dead: no one is wholly dead in a moment, unless every organ is blown to bits. But she soon will be dead, if we don't relieve the pressure on the brain. That's the first thing to be done. While I'm busy at that, shut the window, will you, and make up the fire. In this sort of case the vital heat, whatever that is, leaves the body very quickly. Make the room as hot as you can – fetch an oil-stove, and turn on the electric radiator, and stoke up a roaring fire. The hotter the room is the more slowly will the heat of life leave her.'

Already he had opened his cabinet of surgical instruments, and taken out of it two drawers full of bright steel which he laid on the floor beside her. I heard the grating chink of scissors severing her long grey hair, and as I busied myself with laying and lighting the fire in the hearth, and kindling the oil-stove, which I found, by Horton's directions, in the pantry, I saw that his lancet was busy on the exposed skin. He had placed some vaporizing spray, heated by a spirit lamp close to her head, and as he worked its fizzing nozzle filled the air with some clean and aromatic odour. Now and then he threw out an order.

'Bring me that electric lamp on the long cord,' he said. 'I haven't got enough light. Don't look at what I'm doing if you're squeamish, for if it makes you feel faint, I shan't be able to attend to you.'

I suppose that violent interest in what he was doing overcame any qualm that I might have had, for I looked quite unflinching over his shoulder as I moved the lamp about till it was in such a place that it threw its beam directly into a dark hole at the edge of which depended a flap of skin. Into this he put his forceps, and as he withdrew them they grasped a piece of blood-stained bone.

'That's better,' he said, 'and the room's warming up well. But there's no sign of pulse yet. Go on stoking, will you, till the thermometer on the wall there registers a hundred degrees.'

When next, on my journey from the coal-cellar, I looked, two more pieces of bone lay beside the one I had seen extracted, and presently referring to the thermometer, I saw that between the oil-stove and the roaring fire and the electric radiator, I had raised the room to the temperature he wanted. Soon, peering fixedly at the seat of his operation, he felt for her pulse again.

'Not a sign of returning vitality,' he said, 'and I've done all I can. There's nothing more possible that can be devised to restore her.'

As he spoke the zeal of the unrivalled surgeon relaxed, and with a sigh and a shrug he rose to his feet and mopped his face. Then suddenly the fire and eagerness blazed there again. 'The gramophone!' he said. 'The speech centre is close to where I've been working, and it is quite uninjured. Good heavens, what a wonderful opportunity. She served me well living, and she shall serve me dead. And I can stimulate the motor nerve-centre, too, with the second battery. We may see a new wonder tonight.'

Some qualm of horror shook me.

'No, don't!' I said. 'It's terrible: she's just dead. I shall go if you do.'

'But I've got exactly all the conditions I have long been wanting,' said he. 'And I simply can't spare you. You must be witness: I must have a witness. Why, man, there's not a surgeon or a physiologist in the kingdom who would not give an eye or an ear to be in your place now. She's dead. I pledge you my honour on that, and it's grand to be dead if you can help the living.'

Once again, in a far fiercer struggle, horror and the intensest curiosity strove together in me.

'Be quick, then,' said I.

'Ha! That's right,' exclaimed Horton. 'Help me to lift her on to the table by the gramophone. The cushion too; I can get at the place more easily with her head a little raised.'

He turned on the battery and with the movable light close beside him, brilliantly illuminating what he sought, he inserted the needle of the gramophone into the jagged aperture in her skull. For a few minutes, as he groped and explored there, there was silence, and then quite suddenly Mrs Gabriel's voice, clear and unmistakable and of the normal loudness of human speech, issued from the trumpet.

'Yes, I always said that I'd be even with him,' came the articulated syllables. 'He used to knock me about, he did, when he came home drunk, and often I was black and blue with bruises. But I'll give him a redness for the black and blue.'

The record grew blurred; instead of articulate words there came from it a gobbling noise. By degrees that cleared, and we were listening to some dreadful suppressed sort of laughter, hideous to hear. On and on it went.

'I've got into some sort of rut,' said Horton. 'She must have laughed a lot to herself.'

For a long time we got nothing more except the repetition of the words we had already heard and the sound of that suppressed laughter. Then Horton drew towards him the second battery.

'I'll try a stimulation of the motor nerve-centres,' he said. 'Watch her face.'

He propped the gramophone needle in position, and inserted into the fractured skull the two poles of the second battery, moving them about there very carefully. And as I watched her face, I saw with a freezing horror that her lips were beginning to move.

'Her mouth's moving,' I cried. 'She can't be dead.'

He peered into her face.

'Nonsense,' he said. 'That's only the stimulus from the current. She's been dead half an hour. Ah! what's coming now?'

The lips lengthened into a smile, the lower jaw dropped, and from her mouth came the laughter we had heard just now through the gramophone. And then the dead mouth spoke, with a mumble of unintelligible words, a bubbling torrent of incoherent syllables.

'I'll turn the full current on,' he said.

The head jerked and raised itself, the lips struggled for utterance, and suddenly she spoke swiftly and distinctly.

'Just when he'd got his razor out,' she said, 'I came up behind him, and put my hand over his face and bent his neck back over his chair with all my strength. And I picked up his razor and with one slit – ha, ha, that was the way to pay him out. And I didn't lose my head, but I lathered his chin well, and put the razor in his hand, and left him there, and went downstairs and cooked his dinner for him, and then an hour afterwards, as he didn't come down, up I went to see what kept him. It was a nasty cut in his neck that had kept him——'

Horton suddenly withdrew the two poles of the battery from her head, and even in the middle of her word the mouth ceased working, and lay rigid and open.

'By God!' he said. 'There's a tale for dead lips to tell. But we'll get more yet.'

Exactly what happened then I never knew. It appeared to me that as he still leaned over the table with the two poles of the battery in his hand, his foot slipped, and he fell forward across it. There came a sharp crack, and a flash of blue dazzling light, and there he lay face downwards, with arms that just stirred and quivered. With his fall the two poles that must momentarily have come into contact with his hand were jerked away again, and I lifted him and laid him on the floor. But his lips as well as those of the dead woman had spoken for the last time.

Acknowledgments

The Publishers would like to thank the following authors, publishers and others for their permission to reproduce the copyright material in this volume:

Wood by Robert Aickman. From *Tales of Love and Death* by Robert Aickman, published by Victor Gollancz Ltd. Reprinted by permission of the Publishers and the Author's agents. © Robert Aickman 1977.

A Thing About Machines by Rod Serling. Reprinted by permission of Singer Communications Inc.

A Woman Seldom Found by William Sansom. From *The Short Stories of William Sansom*, published by The Hogarth Press. Reprinted by permission of the Author's agents. © William Sansom 1963.

The Cloth of Madness by Seabury Quinn. Reprinted by permission of Kirby McCauley Ltd.

The Sea Raiders by H. G. Wells. Reprinted by permission of A. P. Watt Ltd and the Executors of the Estate of H. G. Wells.

The Dunwich Horror by H. P. Lovecraft. Reprinted by permission of the Author and the Author's agents, Scott Meredith Literary Agency, Inc., 845 Third Avenue, New York, New York 10022.

Dad by John Blackburn. Reprinted by permission of the Author and A. M. Heath & Co. Ltd.

Royal Jelly by Roald Dahl. From *Kiss, Kiss*, published by Michael Joseph Ltd, Penguin Books Ltd and Alfred A. Knopf, Inc. Reprinted by permission of the Author, the Publishers and Laurence Pollinger Ltd. Copyright © 1959 by Roald Dahl.

Earth to Earth by Robert Graves. From *The Collected Short Stories of Robert Graves*, published by Cassell Ltd. Reprinted by permission of the Author and A. P. Watt Ltd. © Robert Graves 1955.

A Warning to the Curious by M. R. James. From *The Ghost Stories of M. R. James second edition*, published by Edward Arnold (Publishers) Ltd. Reprinted by permission of the Author and the Publishers.

The Night of the Tiger by Stephen King. Reprinted by permission of Kirby McCauley Ltd. © 1979 by Mercury Productions, Inc.

The Interruption by W. W. Jacobs. Reprinted by permission of the Society of Authors as the literary representative of the Estate of W. W. Jacobs.